Anarchy in Bloom

ANARCHY

IN BLOOM

PAUL HEALY

Ink & Anarchy
Press

Anarchy In Bloom by Paul Healy

Published by:
Ink & Anarchy Press
6525 Gunpark Dr. Suite 370-149
Boulder, CO 80301
www.inkandanarchy.com

First Paperback Edition May 2018

ISBN 978-1-7321582-0-7

Cover and interior design by Paul Healy.
Cover photos by Martin Allinger and Tami Freed (123rf.com).
Cover font: ROMAN SD designed by Steve Deffeyes.
Other fonts used: McHandwriting designed by Chris McPeters;
Learning Curve designed by Blue vinyl Fonts; Homemade Apples
designed by Font Diner.

This is a work of fiction. Names, characters, businesses, places and
events are either the products of the author's imagination or used in a
fictitious manner. Any resemblance to actual persons, living or
dead—or actual events—is purely coincidental.

For my family

After all these years

Anarchy

Noun
/ˈæn-ar-kē/

1. A state of disorder due to absence or non-recognition of authority or other controlling systems.

2. Absence of government and absolute freedom of the individual, regarded as a political ideal.

Oxford English Dictionary

Prologue

"What was that?"

"What?"

Sean thought he'd heard something move by the unlocked gate behind them. With narrowed eyes he scanned the dark construction yard but didn't detect any movement.

"I didn't hear anything," Julie whispered. The silver light of the waxing half-moon gleamed in her eyes and glittered on a few wisps of blond hair her black cap could not contain.

"Over there," Sean said, matching her lowered tone as he pointed with one black-gloved hand toward the gate.

Julie did her own quick survey of the area. "You're being paranoid," she said.

Sean felt he had every right to be paranoid. Breaking and entering wasn't something he did every day. And by the time this night was over that would likely be the least offense on a long list of broken laws trailing out behind him like the tail on a ragged kite.

Two days ago he'd been out water-skiing on the glassy surface of Lake Tahoe, enjoying the late-June sun. Now—3:40 a.m. Thursday morning—he found himself crouched painfully on this cold, hard concrete helping Julie and two of her friends sabotage these not-yet-completed timeshares on the lake's South Shore. Not exactly the kind of thing you wanted to be doing on the third day back in your hometown after more than a decade away. Maybe that explained why the chorus of that old John Lennon song kept running through his head: *Nobody told me there'd be days like these.*

As Julie eased the six pipe bombs from her backpack and handed three to Sean he mumbled to himself, "Strange days indeed."

"What?"

"Nothing."

Sean was spent. They'd been here over half an hour and his raging adrenaline level had tanked ten minutes ago. Luckily they were almost done. He and Julie had drilled holes for the bombs in the bases of the six vertical support beams in the middle of this building while Derrick and Jean had done the same in the next. The idea was to take out the central buildings of the timeshare complex—the two closest to completion.

Sean had asked if the noise of them drilling into the giant wooden pillars would draw unwanted attention, but Derrick assured them the cordless drills weren't as loud as they would seem at 3 a.m. on a deserted construction site. Apparently he'd been right—unless Sean *had* actually heard something back by that gate. He glanced around once more and again saw nothing moving.

He and Julie inserted one pipe bomb in each post then strung the long fuses into the center of the six beams, lacing the ends together in a coarse braid.

"All set," Julie said from her hunched position on the floor. The fat, conjoined fuse-end rested softly in her palm, waiting only for a flame to set it alight.

Sean stood and pulled the small radio from his belt. "We're all set over here," he whispered into it. He wondered if anyone else would notice the quaver in his voice.

"Stand by," came Derrick's rock-solid reply.

Even Derrick had seemed unsure if his bombs packed the needed punch to take the structures down completely. He'd only said he expected the damage to be extensive enough that the builders would need to raze them. Sean was in no position to argue. As a software developer—and mostly law-abiding citizen—he'd had little experience with building demolition before tonight.

Julie pulled a pack of matches from her pocket, ripped one from the fold and pressed the head against the small strip of sandpaper on the back with her index finger. Then she looked up at Sean, the match a half-inch stroke away from ignition. He glanced at the next building then back at Julie, wondering for the umpteenth time in the last few hours why he'd let himself get sucked into this.

Julie's eyes remained locked with Sean's, a shimmering aura of blond hair framing her face. Her eyebrows were slightly raised, lips pursed in anticipation. A photographer's black and white study of female beauty in the pale light. He couldn't resist. He leaned down and kissed her. When he stood back her eyes were closed, a smile pulling gently at the corners of her mouth.

From the radio, Derrick's voice interrupted. "We're ready over here," he said. "Do it and go. We're lighting ours now."

Sean straightened his shoulders and spoke quietly into the radio. "Ten-four."

"You remember what to do," Julie said. A statement not a question. She struck the match as Sean marked the time on his watch—3:48:15.

The fuse caught quickly. Not the Fourth of July sparkler Sean had expected, it burned low and quiet, a glowing ember creeping forward through the night. Julie grabbed her bag, stuffed drill, matches and other assorted gear inside and stood up. Sean watched as the large spark split into six smaller ones. The offspring inched along the ground on their predetermined courses.

Well that's it, he thought. *I'm going to jail.*

As Sean looked around for anything Julie might have missed, a metallic squeal shattered the relative silence. He turned to see the gate swinging open before a spotlight breached the darkness, blinding him.

"Shit!" Julie hissed. "Come on!"

She grabbed Sean's hand and yanked him forward as she took off, away from the gate, toward the lake. Bright white blurs on his retinas clouded his vision as he stumbled along like a drunk behind her. The adrenaline he'd thought exhausted surged through his veins again.

They'd gone thirty feet before he noticed something off. "Aren't we going the wrong way?" he said.

"No time," Julie said, still dragging him along. "Let's go."

With little cover they dashed between the huge posts of the open first floor. The spotlight beam scanned the building's skeleton and swept just over their heads before they ducked behind a pile of lumber. When Julie tried to stop, her feet shot out from under her. She hit the concrete floor with a thud and Sean landed on top of her.

"This is the Police," a tinny voice boomed from a PA. "You're trespassing on private property. Come out of there with your hands up."

"How did he creep up on us like that?" Julie whispered as she wiggled out from under him. "You were supposed to be keeping a lookout?"

"I said I heard something."

"Shhh," she hissed as she snatched the radio from his hand. Into the mic she said, "Derrick, retreat, retreat. Cops on site. Repeat: Cops on site." Then she followed their pre-established protocol and shut the two-way off to avoid drawing attention if Derrick answered.

Sean looked at his watch. After taking a moment to focus through the fading spotlight image burned on his retinas he saw that a minute and a half had passed since Julie lit the five-minute-long fuses. "Three and a half minutes before this place comes down on top of us," he said.

Julie seemed too busy looking for an escape route to answer. Sean scanned the area as well. He saw no way out that wouldn't leave them in plain view. Currently they weren't visible from the gate but if they stood or ran all bets were off because the front of the building wasn't finished. Behind them, on the lake side, the one standing wall on the first floor prevented their escape in the only direction with cover.

"What the hell are we gonna do?" Sean said as the spotlight hit the beams over their heads again.

"Hush," Julie said, less harshly this time. Then she leaned into him and placed her head on his shoulder. "We wait."

"For what?"

"I don't know. A break. Now zip it."

Sean tried to relax against the pile of lumber as Julie's breath tickled the side of his neck. He didn't much like her plan but he didn't have a better one at the moment. After all, Derrick had said the blasts might not take the buildings down. The question was: Were they willing to risk their lives based on nothing more than Derrick's ignorance of what his bombs might or might not do?

And if an unfinished building crashing down on their heads didn't kill them Sean figured they could look forward to some decent jail time. For the first time in his thirty-three years he would find out what it was like to be slammed down on the hood of a patrol car and cuffed like a common criminal. But that's what he was now, wasn't he? He'd made the transition from CEO of his own software company to the lead story on "Cops" in less than a year. He thought again about why he'd let himself get talked into this.

"Shhh," Julie hushed from beside him.

Sean wasn't aware he'd made a sound. He'd add that to the lengthening list of things he'd learned tonight: just how difficult it was to keep a human body truly motionless and quiet.

Another shocker he was still digesting, despite the situation, was that Julie was a member of the Eco-Militia—a group of radical activists similar to the Earth Liberation Front. For Sean it had been a bit of a J. Geils Band "Centerfold" moment finding out his unrequited high school sweetheart liked to blow things up in her spare time—though she'd sworn to him this was the first time she'd ever been involved in anything but non-violent protests.

Julie was still as beautiful as Sean remembered from their late teens, but he wasn't sure he wanted to be dating a militant in a monkey wrench gang. He wasn't even sure he could call what they'd been doing the last eighteen hours "dating." It was more just getting to know each other again, but with a mutual romantic side that hadn't been there years before when Julie had insisted they remain "just friends."

Yet getting reacquainted had somehow led them here: hiding from the police behind a stack of freshly hewn wood not two miles from the house where Sean had grown up. What confused him most was that it wasn't all bad. With Julie's slim, muscular body huddled up close, her right breast pressing on his left arm and one of her legs looped over his, everything would have been fine if it wasn't for Dirty Harry back there with the spotlight. Sean said a silent prayer to a God he wasn't sure he believed in that something would draw the cop away with more important things to do than figure out who had cut the lock on that gate.

"All right folks, I know you're in there. Come on out with your hands up."

The voice over the PA was surreal, booming through the dark, quiet night. Sean didn't know how many patrolmen were on duty at 4 a.m. on a Thursday morning in South Lake Tahoe, but he bet none of them got to use their PA's anywhere near as much as they wanted. The spotlight again traced the outline of posts and beams that made up the project they were trying to bring down: The South Tahoe Beach Resort.

Why didn't the cop just come in and have a look around? Was he waiting for backup? It wouldn't take him long to find them if he put his mind to it, they were only a couple hundred feet from the gate. Of course, the guy didn't know about the bombs and if he wandered into the building…

"What the hell is he doing out there, putting on riot gear?" Sean whispered in Julie's ear. He looked at his watch again—3:51:07. "I think we need to make a run for it," he added with a touch of panic.

"Shhh," Julie responded.

"This place is gonna blow in two minutes."

"I don't think we'll make it out if we don't wait for cover from the explosions."

"What if the cop comes inside?"

Julie placed one hand on his thigh and nuzzled her face into the soft spot between his neck and shoulder. "Then we'll figure something out. Now hush."

Sean eyed his watch as the seconds flashed by like drops down a drain. He didn't know how much longer he could sit still.

I

Part I

One

From the other side of the crowded café a cheerful, female voice cut through the din.

"Sean?"

He looked to the counter for his breakfast order, but the call hadn't originated there.

"Sean Connors, is that you?!"

When he finally picked her out of the crowd, the speaker was already striding toward him, a beaming smile on her face. As she walked, her shoulder-length blond hair trailed slightly back from her neck. The low cut jeans and short t-shirt she wore left prominently displayed a bent, golden bar piercing her belly-button.

Arriving at his table, she said, "It is you, isn't it?" then pushed a few golden strands of hair out of her face.

Sean found himself speechless. Did he know this woman?

She crossed her arms. "If you're not Sean Connors could you let me know so I can stop making a fool of myself and go finish my coffee?"

As unaccustomed as he was to strange, attractive women approaching him in cafés he did finally manage some actual words. "Uhh, yeah. I'm Sean Connors."

When he stood to greet her his chair grated across the stone floor like a cheap fork on fine china. Conversation in the café stopped long enough for everyone in the place to look directly at him as if he'd personally slapped each one.

"Don't tell me you don't remember me?" the woman said, ignoring the café-wide response. She tilted her head to the left and raised her eyebrows as a sly grin crossed her lips.

Sean looked closer. The upward curl of the right corner of her lip; that pert, well-proportioned nose; the electric green eyes that lit up the room. This beautiful woman approaching him like a mirage across the crowded room had so surprised him he'd failed to even consider that she had the right Sean Connors. But amazingly, he knew her. Or used to anyway.

They spoke at the same time.

"Julie Thompson!"

Then she hugged him. Arms around his back, giving him a good, solid squeeze. The embrace startled Sean and he almost failed to return it.

"My God," Julie said as she stepped back. "How long has it been?"

"Awhile," Sean said. "Quite awhile."

"Sean?" another female voice called from behind him. He couldn't remember the last time he'd had so many women asking for him in a public place. This time it was just his breakfast, though.

"Why don't you join me?" Julie said after he'd retrieved his food from the counter.

She started back toward the front window and he followed, snatching the drink from his own table as he passed. Her backside swayed left to right as she crossed the room, the top of some Celtic looking tattoo peeking over the waistband of her jeans. He found himself wondering how far down the design might go and forced his attention elsewhere before his thoughts could descend any further into the gutter.

Sean couldn't believe that Julie Thompson had picked him out of the crowd in this little café. He hadn't really expected that she even lived around here anymore—though the thought had crossed his mind a few times since his return. It had been what? Thirteen years since he'd heard from her?

Julie slid into the chair across from him with an almost practiced grace as he fumbled his way into his own seat. The table was small and it took them a few moments of shuffling to make two people's meals fit on the crowded surface.

"My God, I can't believe it's you!" she spouted. "You look great! What are you doing back in town?" She took a sip of coffee. Her intent, intense eyes held Sean's steadily, waiting for a reply.

"You look good, too," Sean said. "I'm just back for a visit, I guess."

"How long are you staying?"

"I don't know. It's been a long time and I just wanted to see the place again." He swallowed a bit of his own drink before continuing. "What are you up to these days? You still live here?"

"Yeah, over on Lakeview," Julie said, pointing past Sean, out toward the silvery-blue expanse of Lake Tahoe visible through the trees. "I've got my own Yoga studio and I do massages on the side." She'd finished her coffee, but still held the empty cup in her hand.

"Your own studio? That's great. How's business?"

"Pretty good." Julie cleared her throat. "Considering I just opened last year."

Sean knew from experience that the first year could be tough when starting your own business. He took a bite of his bagel and sat thoughtfully chewing. The pause gave him time to dredge up some long buried memories of their past together.

Julie turned his question back on him. "How about you?" she asked. "What have you been up to?" She seemed to be avoiding his eyes now, keeping hers on her hands. Maybe she'd been thinking about the way things had ended between them as well.

"I'm on a bit of a sabbatical right now," Sean said, "but I've mostly been in software development since college." He left out what had happened to the company he'd help found. It was still a sore subject with him.

"Are you married? Kids?" Julie said, quietly enough that Sean barely caught the words over the noise and clatter of the café.

"No," he answered. "You?"

"No." A flicker of eye contact and Julie's attention returned to her hands.

The sudden infusion of awkwardness had them acting like two teenagers at their first dance. Julie's personality had pulled a complete one-eighty from where it was when she'd first greeted him. The fire had lapsed from her eyes as the bubbly, outgoing flirt morphed into a brooding, quiet beauty.

Reuniting with old friends usually caused some discomfort, but this encounter had turned downright odd. As Sean sat there attempting to swallow more of his bagel, he wondered why Julie had approached him at all, considering she was the one who'd blown him off when he was still a sophomore at the University of Southern California.

The more he thought about it the more the anger rose up in him at the way she'd stopped returning his letters and calls without a word as to why. He hadn't realized it still bothered him so much, but their whole relationship appeared before him now like an unfinished book, open on a table in an abandoned room. When Julie had called out his name a few minutes ago she'd kicked in that door, stirring up a bunch of old, settled dust. Sean sipped his coffee and waited to hear what she had to say for herself.

Julie fiddled with her empty cup and tucked a few stray wisps of hair behind her left ear. Her face had drawn itself into a mask of tension, jaw clenched, eyes tight. The silence between them stretched out as Sean finished his breakfast. Julie seemed to be struggling with something internal. She looked from her hands to the street and back, never focusing on anything.

Unable to keep quiet any longer, Sean finally asked, "Are you okay?"

Julie met his eyes momentarily. "Yeah," she said, nodding her head. "Yeah." She took two deep breaths, in and out, before her eyes calmed and her face relaxed. Reaching across the table, she took one of Sean's hands in both of her own. Her skin was cold, yet Sean felt himself flush as if the temperature inside the restaurant had just shot up over one hundred degrees.

"Sean, I'm sorry about how things ended between us," Julie said, her attention focused intently on his plate now. "I can't change the past. All I can do is apologize."

"Well," Sean said, withdrawing his hand from her grasp and leaning back from the table, "you could at least explain."

Julie turned abruptly in her chair, as if about to rise. "Look," she said. "I just thought we could sit and catch up on what we're both up to. I didn't want to dig up our entire history, okay?"

Sean crossed his arms. "How long did you think we could avoid it? It's been thirteen years since you dropped off the face of the earth. You didn't think I might wonder why?"

Julie's eyes met his. The anger was unmistakable, but her face showed surprise as well. Perhaps at the fact he'd dared to confront her on the issue. It was something he'd rarely done when they were younger.

She brushed off both emotions with an irritated sigh and reached under the table for her purse. "I don't really know what happened, Sean," she said. "We just kind of lost touch. My life got really complicated there for a while."

Now Sean took a deep breath of his own. "*We* didn't lose touch. *You* stopped writing and returning my calls."

Julie's attention snapped back to Sean. Her narrowed, green eyes edged toward black under a now-furrowed brow and Sean felt his face flush. It turned out he still hated having Julie Thompson mad at him, even after all these years.

"I'm talking to you now, aren't I?" She stood and threw her purse over one shoulder, then snatched her plate and cup from the table and started for the door. "Not for long, though."

"Julie, wait," Sean called to her back.

"Maybe I'll see you around," she said and dropped her dishes in the bus tray by the garbage can.

"Julie," Sean said again, standing now. "Come on."

She hesitated only slightly at the door before heaving it open and continuing out, and around the corner, without a single look back.

When the door slammed shut Sean became aware of the quiet in the room as the rest of the patrons eyed him. He searched face to face, but saw no sympathy anywhere as, one by one, they began to turn away. He'd been back in his hometown less than forty-eight hours and was already starting to feel like his old self: jilted by the girl and ostracized by everyone else.

As he sat back down his eyes fell on the empty chair opposite him. After a moment, a smile began to grow on his face. On the chair's back, Julie's pink sweater hung forgotten.

Two

"What the hell was I thinking?" Julie huffed to herself as she stormed around the corner of the café. She'd been so surprised to see Sean—to even recognize him after all these years—that the whole of their previous relationship had failed to surface in her mind until a few minutes after they arrived back at her table. It wasn't until Sean got all fidgety and quiet that Julie realized he remembered as well.

Even then she would have been content to sit and catch up on what each of them had been up to the past few years. But expecting her to explain what had happened? Right there on the spot? She couldn't do that. After not seeing him in how long? Most likely she'd never be able to explain it to his satisfaction anyway.

Now, as she trotted down Harrison Avenue toward the lake with her face still hot with anger and shame, she felt like a moron, but thoughts of Sean refused to leave her mind. He'd put a bit of weight on his previously thin frame that helped fill his face with a handsome warmth and give him a certain presence he'd never been able to muster before. Truth was, Sean was an attractive man. And that had made it easier for her to forget she was the one who'd stopped writing.

Oh look, it's Sean! He used to be my friend. No thought as to why he no longer was. *Stupid!*

The sun warmed Julie's shoulders, casting her shadow on the road in front of her as she rounded the corner onto Lakeview Ave. The morning had warmed quickly and she was comfortable without the sweater she'd forgotten at the café. She wasn't worried about it. Everyone there knew her so she figured she'd get it back eventually.

Off to the right, Tahoe was intermittently visible between trees and multi-million dollar homes. Where others saw different shades of blue, green or gray in the water, Julie saw different moods. She'd lived on the South Shore of Lake Tahoe her entire life and felt tuned in to the natural rhythms of the environment that had produced her. Left to her own devices, her feelings mirrored the different hues of the lake. On days when that wasn't true the cause was almost always related to social interactions. Today, for instance, when she had walked in the other direction on her way to breakfast, she'd been in a glorious mood and the water had been an uplifting, cheerful blue. Now the lake was still sporting the same brilliant azure, but her state of mind, thanks to Sean, had soured to black.

It's my own fault, really, she told herself as she walked past the entrance to Regan Beach, but she caught the direction of her thoughts before she could beat herself up too badly. The support group she'd been attending lately at the Women's Center emphasized the need to avoid feeling personally responsible for others' reactions to you. She reminded herself that—though she certainly wasn't blameless—Sean was the one responsible for his own reaction and response to her.

Sean wasn't like any of the other guys Julie had known growing up. He'd always been there to listen to her, to support her—not just try and get in her pants. Back then he'd been a skinny kid, all gangly limbs and long hair. Now, though, she found herself wondering if he worked out and had to cut that train of thought off before it could get any further from the station.

The way he'd jumped on her about their past was new, too. But people changed. Staying her same naïve and innocent self hadn't been an option, had it?

Lakeview Avenue petered out at the entrance to The Lake's Edge Apartments. Julie crossed the parking lot to her building, wandering through the old Subarus and beat up Toyota pickups that seemed to grow like winter snow banks around Tahoe. She'd called this place home for three years now, but didn't know how much longer that would last. The complex and—more importantly—the land it sat on had been sold eight months ago to a development company.

The Lake's Edge occupied a vanishing niche in the Tahoe real estate market: affordable housing with a view. Actually, affordable housing of any kind was increasingly hard to come by in the basin, but a place with a lake view that a single, working stiff could afford was unheard of. Julie's name had been on a waiting list for a year and half before an apartment here opened up. It was only a medium-sized studio, but it suited her needs for now. And it was right in the middle of town, making it easy to get anywhere on foot or bicycle.

Julie climbed the stairs to the second floor and noticed a flyer on her doorknob. She pulled it loose as she entered the apartment, tossed her keys and purse on the kitchen table and pushed the door shut behind her with one foot. The flyer was another announcement for the City Council meeting at 8:00 p.m. They would be addressing the Lake's Edge resident's request for emergency rent control. The new owners had been less than forthcoming about their plans for the complex, but it was apparent they were trying to force the residents out with exorbitant rent increases. The word around town was that Eagle Development wanted to build the largest timeshare resort yet to grace the South Shore.

Julie's friend Derrick had once compared timeshares to non-native weeds. The multiply-owned monstrosities spread across the Tahoe basin destroying affordable housing and pushing out locals the same way invasive plants choked out native foliage. So many of Julie's friends had been forced from the area by the rising cost of living that it was hard to believe anyone could get away with turning any more local's housing into tourist units. Unfortunately she'd witnessed greed overcome common sense too many times to have much of a positive outlook for her home.

Anyhow, nothing was known for sure and, as she tossed the flyer on the coffee table, she wondered if this meeting would be any better than the others. The last two had turned into shouting matches between people with little to no information. Until the new owners actually stated their plans for the complex, there wasn't much that could be done. Like boxing blindfolded, it was hard to know where to hit someone if you couldn't see what they were doing.

Julie pushed the button on her answering machine and was greeted by Derrick's voice discretely reminding her about the "action" he had planned for the following evening. "Don't forget about our plans tomorrow night," he said. She wondered if the outcome of tonight's meeting might affect his decision to go ahead with the sabotage. Eagle Development was not only the buyer of the Lake's Edge Apartments, but also the developer of the currently-under-construction South Tahoe Beach Resort—where you could buy a quarter-share for a cool million—and Derrick wanted to teach them a painful lesson.

Julie wasn't completely onboard with Derrick's tactics, but she did want Eagle to understand that South Shore locals didn't care for the corporation's development and business practices. She abhorred violence of any kind, but when the voice of the people was consistently drowned out by corporate clout and backroom deals someone had to find a way to create a little racket. Her friend Derrick had become a virtuoso in the art of making noise.

Derrick Masterson provided the brains and bankroll to a very loose cell of environmental radicals that covered the Sierra Nevada Mountains and the Lake Tahoe region. They claimed allegiance to the Eco-Militia, an organization with no centralized leadership of any kind. If you held the same beliefs the name espoused—"Fight to the Death for Mother Earth"—then you might as well call yourself a member. But, as a few people Julie knew had told her, you weren't a real E-M-er until you engaged in some sort of sabotage in defense of the environment. "If you want to be a pacifist, join Earth First!," one had said—showing just how far, in their estimation, that organization had moved toward the mainstream.

Julie hadn't told Derrick she would definitely help with his plan. She had done any number of peaceful protests—had even been arrested once at a tree-sit—but she'd never been involved in any form of monkey-wrenching. The thought of participating in an actual act of sabotage sent a shiver down her spine that was part fear, part excitement. She wasn't sure what to make of the feeling, but she knew if she went through with the action she would be stepping over a line that had previously been unthinkable. Once on the other side, she feared there would be no returning to the person she was before.

As Julie filled a glass with water, three quick knocks on the door jolted her from her reverie.

Three

Sean sat for less than five minutes after Julie left before coming to the conclusion that he was a complete idiot. A beautiful woman had approached him to renew his acquaintance—if not friendship—and his response had been downright pettiness about how she'd ended it with him years earlier. What the hell was wrong with him? He'd been deeply in love with Julie Thompson at one time. Hadn't he grown even slightly since the last time he'd seen her?

Sitting there, alone at his table amid the clatter and roar of the small café, Sean found that he already missed Julie's presence. He felt like he could even detect the faint floral scent of her perfume hanging in the air. Maybe it was the sweater she'd forgotten.

After fiddling with his phone for a minute or two he had what he needed. He grabbed his dishes, snagged the garment from the back of her chair and made his way to the door. A few minutes later he was headed west down Lakeview Avenue with the sweater in his hand. It was a perfect June day and he relished the scent of pines in the air as he strolled—a beautiful day for a walk.

Sean passed a huge house under construction on the right. The lot it sat on didn't seem much larger than a generous parking space, but the building itself expanded with every upward level—of which there were three. He wondered how much a beachfront parking spot on Tahoe sold for these days.

Past the house the view opened up and Sean gazed out at the blue lake, The Lake of the Sky. The peaks on the northeast shore still sported caps of white, reflected on the still water's surface. When he'd been out water skiing yesterday the boat captain said the past winter had been pretty extreme. That explained all the snow still showing in the upper elevations. Having spent his childhood on the South Shore, Sean had probably seen a few winters more brutal than the previous one. He couldn't really remember any of them specifically, though. Snow had just been a fact of life growing up, not anything to get overly excited about.

Sean's wandering thoughts eventually took him back to Julie. Things had finally seemed to be progressing with her that last spring he'd talked to her. And then, suddenly, it was as if she'd vanished. It had taken him almost a year before he really even noticed other women. He still would have come looking for her that summer if it hadn't been for his parents' accident. That had changed a lot of things in his life.

Here in the present he realized he'd really had no idea how close to the surface his feelings were until Julie called out his name in the middle of that café. Years of what should have represented some kind of emotional maturation had slipped away as if they never happened and he felt like he had whenever he picked up the phone way back then and her voice sprung unexpectedly from the receiver—flat-out, fall-down amazed that Julie Thompson wanted to talk to *him*.

◀

In the dark, Sean grapples with the bedside phone for a moment before he gets a handle on it. Putting it to his ear he says, "Hello," and tries to drag himself up the steep hill out of sleep.

"Hey, Sean, it's me."

"Julie?"

There is a rattle on the line as another phone is picked up in the house. A deep voice grumbles, "Hello."

"I've got it, Dad," Sean says. He looks at his bedside clock as the other receiver clatters back in its cradle. "Julie, it's two o'clock in the morning."

"I know. But I really wanted to talk to you."

Sean wonders what his father will have to say in the morning about the phone ringing at this hour. "Are you drunk?" he asks her.

"Maybe." One breath. In and out. "A little."

Sean settles back on his pillow with a quiet sigh. Home for Christmas break after his first semester of college he is not used to living under his parents' roof again.

"Sean, I miss you."

What a strange thing to say. Since she seems to have been avoiding him the entire time he's been home. He's due to return to school in five days, having seen her only once in the previous three weeks.

"I want to see you," Julie says. "Can you come over?"

"It's—" the clock now reads 2:06 a.m., "—late, Julie, and I really don't think my parents would appreciate me leaving the house... especially since you just woke them up."

"Maybe I could come there."

"You're drunk. You shouldn't be driving."

"You're right." Julie sighs a broken sigh that sounds as if it might dissolve into sobs. "Dillon broke up with me tonight."

Sean isn't surprised. He figured something must have gotten Julie depressed for her to call him. "I'm sorry," he says, "but wasn't he kind of a jerk?"

There is no sound at the other end of the line for over a minute. She's probably crying, holding her hand over the mouthpiece. Why does she insist on dating so many asshole pretty-boys that always dump her when they realize she won't put out? He is slowly drifting off when Julie's voice startles him awake.

"I know you didn't like him," she says between sniffles, "but how many of my boyfriends have you liked?"

There's a stupid question, Sean thinks.

Out loud he says, "There was Glenn." Eyes closed, this is beginning to feel like a dream.

"Glenn's your best friend."

"Well..." That had been true at one time. Not so much anymore.

"Sean, you know I care about you, don't you?"

Do I?

Julie begins crying in earnest, not bothering to cover the receiver this time. In this moment, Sean can't think of anything she cares about other than partying and dating other guys. But this whole conversation feels unreal, distant, and he continues to drift along silently.

When Julie gets herself under control she says, "So that's what you think? That I don't care about you?"

"I don't know," Sean says, floating in that netherworld between waking and sleep. "I've been home for three weeks and I've only seen you once. Wouldn't someone that cares about me want to see me?" The words seem to be coming from somewhere other than his own mouth.

There is silence from the earpiece before Julie quietly says, "I just said I wanted to see you."

"Would you still want to see me if you hadn't just been dumped?"

"Why are you being such a jerk?"

"What?" Sean's eyes flash open as the blood rushes to his head. *What did I just say?*

"You're being an asshole," Julie chokes out through more tears.

"I'm sorry," he says, scrambling for damage control. "I'm tired, it's late, I don't know what I'm saying."

"Yeah, right," Julie says, an undercurrent of anger beneath the tears. "You really want to know why I haven't seen you while you've been home?"

Sean's muddled mind decides the best course of action is to keep his mouth shut on the off chance his foot might find it again.

"It's too hard, okay? It's too hard to see you when I know you're just going to leave again."

"It's too hard to see a friend when you know they're leaving?" Sean says slowly. "So... what? You'd rather not see me at all? What kind of thing is that to say?"

"Sean, you're so much more than a friend to me. I think about you all the time, but it's— You're out there in left field, you know? I've got all this other stuff going on and," another sniffle from her as she pauses, "I can't take having another guy leave me."

Sean sits bolt upright in his bed, scaring away the cat he hadn't noticed sleeping at his feet. "M-more than a friend?" he stammers. "What happened to you not wanting to ruin our friendship?"

"I don't want to ruin it," Julie whines, her voice breaking apart. "That's the whole problem." She dissolves into tears again.

Sean sits in the dark, confused. Turning, he kicks off the covers and sets his feet on the floor, hoping to ground himself. He switches on the bedside lamp to convince himself this isn't a dream. The pain behind his eyes from the blinding light finally forces him to believe he is awake. Resting his head in his left hand, he gathers all of his courage and says, "So you want to date me, but won't because we're friends?" His right hand has gone numb from gripping the receiver too tightly.

"I don't know," Julie says. "Maybe… but we can't." Her voice cracks as she adds, "I can't."

Sean shakes his head slowly from side to side. "I am so lost."

"Listen." Julie says, seeming to gather herself. "I just don't think I'm ready for that."

"Ready for what?"

"For me and you, okay? I'm only eighteen. I just want to have some fun, you know? I'm not ready for a serious relationship like it would be with you."

"So a relationship with me wouldn't be any fun?" Sean's heart is pounding so hard he can hear it.

"That's not what I meant at all," she says, the whine trying to creep back into her voice. "Sean, I love you, okay? I can see myself marrying you some day. But if we go out with each other right now… it won't work. Especially with you being away at college. And then I'd just lose you, too."

Had he heard her right? Had Julie Thompson just said that she loves him and can see herself marrying him? Sean opens his eyes to the blinding light again so he can register the pain. "But you start college next year," he says. "You can come to USC… with me."

"You know I can't. My grades aren't that good."

"I could quit school then."

"Don't be stupid," Julie says. "It's just not the right time… okay?"

No! he wants to scream, *it's not okay! Nothing about this is okay!* but his mouth remains closed.

While Sean's mind is raging about hurtful injustices and cupid's poor timing, though, a warm glow is growing somewhere deep in his chest after what she's told him. He lies back on the bed and closes his eyes, not wanting to let that feeling go.

"I do want to see you," Julie says.

"What about tomorrow?"

"I'll call you in the morning."

▶

Sean distinctly remembered that Julie hadn't called the next day. It wasn't until his last night home that he'd finally seen her again. They'd spent less than an hour together and neither mentioned their late night phone conversation. Sean thought there was a good chance she didn't even remember it.

While he'd been reminiscing, his legs had carried him to the end of Lakeview Avenue. The street ended in the parking lot of an apartment complex that bore the number he'd looked up. He glanced down at the sweater in his hand then lifted it to his face, inhaling the heady scent.

He wondered if he was doing the right thing.

Four

Julie hesitated, hand on her doorknob. Outside Sean stood in the mid-morning sun looking toward the parking lot. When she'd first peered though the peephole a moment ago her heart had skipped a beat at the sight of him. Her breath was still caught somewhere between her mouth and where it was sorely needed in her lungs.

What was he doing at her door? *Probably here to point out the hundred other ways I was at fault for the crash and burn of our relationship.*

And how had he found her? Had someone at the café told him where she lived? She decided to pretend she wasn't home as she forced herself to breathe. He couldn't be sure she was here, could he? Unless he'd followed behind her the whole way.

He knocked again and called out, "Julie? I just came to return your sweater. And apologize." His voice was muffled by the closed door between them.

Through the distortion of the peephole lens his handsome face managed to pull off the look of a lost puppy almost perfectly and Julie's hesitance melted away, though not her anger. She turned the knob and jerked the door open with a *swoosh*. "Apologize, huh?" she said, then crossed her arms and leaned her shoulder against the jamb.

Sean took a step back. "Uh, yeah," he said. He held her sweater in front of him with both hands, just above the waist. "Look, I didn't mean to be a jerk. You just… You took me by surprise back at the restaurant." He looked down at the sweater, then up into her eyes as he held it out to her. "I wanted to make sure you got this back," he said.

"I'm sure they would have kept it for me," Julie said, snatching the sweater from his hands.

Sean's face visibly drooped.

Stop being such a bitch, Julie! He's apologizing and you're reaming him for it—say something nice!

"Well," Sean said, turning and starting for the stairs. "Take care."

Are you going to push him away again? Is that really what you want?

She'd been a scared and naïve little girl the first time she'd done it. What was her excuse now?

"Wait," she said and stepped out onto the deck before she could talk herself out of it. "Please? Just wait a minute."

Sean stopped, looking back at her from halfway down the stairs. Hope animated his features, but his words betrayed the expression. "Julie," he said with a shake of his head, "I don't think I can do this again."

She wasn't sure what he meant. Walk back up the stairs? "Do what again?" she asked.

"This," he said, a finger pointing back and forth from him to her. "You and me."

Time slowed to a crawl as Julie watched his hand. The air seemed to almost crystallize around her and a moment of clarity washed over her like a cold front. Then, from deep within her skull, a voice shouted, *He really loved you back then, stupid!* It wasn't just some thing he'd said—he'd really meant it.

The strength drained from her lower body and she swayed for a moment before her legs buckled under her and she sat down hard on the deck in a semi-lotus position. The sweater flopped into her lap and she stared at it, dumbfounded. Had she really been that distracted and down on herself back then that she hadn't seen what seemed so obvious now?

Then Sean was at her side, bending down, hand on her shoulder, asking if she was alright. Coming to her rescue, of course, like he almost always had years before.

"Yeah, I'm okay. I'm alright." She said then reached up, grabbed the bottom of his T-shirt and pulled. "Sit down for a minute. Please?"

"Right here?"

"Yeah. Right here."

Sean hesitated, then lowered himself to the deck, trying his best to imitate her leg position. After a few moments of pulling his ankles this way and that he gave up and leaned back against the railing, knees up and enveloped by his arms.

"Listen," she began, looking at her hands as she rubbed the

scratchy wool of her sweater between her fingers, "I'm not sure—"
She cleared her throat and turned her head to look at him. "I don't
know what my problem is, okay? But don't leave." She resisted the
urge to put a hand on his knee, remembering the way he'd reacted to
her touch at the café.

Sean breathed out slowly through clenched lips. His cheeks
puffed up as he looked her over then shook his head. "I don't know
what to say to that, Julie." His eyes moved over to a tree swaying
lightly in the June breeze.

Julie inhaled deeply, exhaled, and inhaled again. *Here we go.*

"Sean, I probably can't say I'm sorry enough times, but I'm sorry.
I really am. About today, about what happened in the past, about
everything from back then." She closed her eyes and considered the
possibility of telling him everything—kicked it around like a lead ball
for a couple of seconds—but she couldn't. There were only a few
people she'd ever told. "We're both different people than we were
then," she finished before opening her eyes.

Sean stared at the peeling paint on the boards between his feet.
"Julie, do you have any idea how much of a surprise it was to see you
today? I haven't thought about you much in probably five or six
years. But it didn't take long for all the memories to come rushing
back in at once, you know what I mean?"

"Yeah," Julie said. *Do I ever.*

"Anyway…" He met her eyes briefly before continuing. "If this
is going to be anything like before I think I need to be going."

"Why did you come over here with my sweater then?"

"I acted like a jerk and didn't want to leave it that way between
us."

"I see."

There had to be more to it than that, didn't there? Sean had
never been a good liar, couldn't maintain eye contact. Julie wasn't
very skilled at it either—unless she counted lying to herself.

"Here's the thing," she said, staring back down at the sweater in
her hands while she worked at swallowing the last of her pride. "I
didn't consider what your reaction would be to seeing me. Hell, I
didn't consider what my own reaction would be. And maybe I
shouldn't have approached you in the first place, but here we are."
She raised her head and looked at him. "I want to know what's going

on with you, Sean Connors. It's been a long time and I've changed a lot, okay? I'm sure you have, too. Can we please, please, *please* just start over?"

Sean eyed her with suspicion as he appeared to kick the idea around. "Start over from where? From what point in time?"

Julie pivoted her whole body to face him and planted an index finger on the deck between them. "From right here, right now," she said. Then, before she could second guess herself, she set the sweater aside and reached out, taking both of his hands in her own. He didn't recoil from her touch this time.

"Right here, right now?" Sean said, a smile edging slowly around the corners of his mouth. "Are we in a Jesus Jones song or something?"

A grin took root on Julie's lips as well. "I don't know, are we?" She dropped one of Sean's hands and turned to lean back against the railing next to him, keeping her right in his left as she let herself relax slightly.

Though she hadn't chosen her words intentionally, Julie knew the song Sean referenced. "Right here, right now, watching the world wake up from history," the lyrics went. Sitting here on the hard wood of the deck, a warm summer breeze blowing lightly on her face and the warmth of her old friend's hand in her own, Julie wondered if, like her, Sean was beginning to grasp the myriad possibilities in that simple line.

Five

Right here. Right now. Watching the world wake up from history.

Sean sat on the couch in Julie's studio apartment waiting for her to change clothes. He'd agreed to join her for a walk on the beach. "To catch up," she said. Since Julie was unwilling to discuss what had happened to make her cut ties with him, Sean wondered how long the conversation could last.

It was odd how appropriate those lyrics were to their situation. They had been the first thing to pop into Sean's head when Julie mentioned she wanted to start over, "Right here, right now." But he had to question if that was what they were actually doing. Were they waking up from history and getting on with it? Or just regressing? Falling back to sleep, per se?

There was no way to know. Best to relax and go with the flow. They were just old friends, right? They would spend a little time catching up and that would be that. Then he would probably never hear from Julie Thompson again.

She certainly was beautiful, though. The picture of Julie he'd had tucked away in some dark corner of his mind prior to seeing her that morning didn't do justice to the actual present-day woman. She was dynamic, frightening, bubbly and brooding. Childish and yet somehow mature at the same time.

Sean groaned, rubbed his face with his hands and scanned the coffee table in front of him for a remote control. He figured he'd check the weather while he waited for Julie to come out of the bathroom. The table only held some papers, a couple of yoga magazines and two candles. He looked over the couch and around the rest of the small apartment but didn't see a remote anywhere. The single room had the couch, a dining table and twin bed jammed into it, with the kitchen tucked away in a corner nook. The bathroom was probably tiny as well. Not too many places to look, but—

Sean did a whole-room double-take. He saw no television.

Who didn't own a television? Even in a little apartment like this there was always room for a television. What did you point all of your furniture at without a TV? Based on the direction Sean currently faced, Julie had decided on the kitchen.

Sean stood and physically perused Julie's space. The only electronic device he saw anywhere was a bedside clock. No computer, no TV, not even a digital watch. Strange in this day and age. The groaning bookshelves to the left of the bed, though, looked to be stuffed with more volumes than some small-town libraries. Julie had apparently found another passion.

Sean checked out some of the titles: *A Language Older Than Words* and *The Culture of Make Believe*, by Derrick Jensen; *When Corporations Rule the World*, by David Korten; *The Party's Over: Oil, War and the Fate of Industrial Societies*, by Richard Heinberg; five different titles by Daniel Quinn, one entitled: *Beyond Civilization*, another: *Ishmael*. A graduate student in sociology or cultural studies might do well researching their thesis here, he thought.

On the bottom shelf, near another large candle and a few dog-eared novels by a women who had the unlikely first name "Nevada", Sean found a small paperback entitled *Ecodefense: A Field Guide to Monkeywrenching*. According to the back of the book, the author was a founding member of the radical environmental group Earth First!. A noise from the bathroom startled him and he stuffed the book back in its place then quickly returned to the couch.

Julie emerged from the bathroom a minute later jean shorts and a white, button-down shirt. She'd only fastened three of the buttons and Sean could make out a shadow of what he guessed was a turquoise bikini top beneath.

"Do you want something to drink?" she asked as she rummaged through the refrigerator. "I'm bringing water. You want some?"

"Sure," Sean said, struggling to keep his eyes on her face. To avoid the problem altogether he looked down at the coffee table and noticed a flyer. "City Council Meeting Tonight - 8:00 PM - Be There," it read.

"What's this all about?" he asked, holding it up.

"It's nothing," Julie said

"Looks like a little more than nothing." He quoted from the announcement, "'Come Help Save Your Home'?"

"Well…" Julie's weight shifted from one leg to the other as she filled the water bottles at the sink. "I don't want to burden you with my problems, Sean."

"What are friends for?" he said as non-sarcastically as he could manage.

Julie looked back and sized him up with a stern face, but it softened in an instant with a smile. "A development company bought this complex a while back. We're just waiting to find out when we get evicted."

"Evicted? Why?"

"Me-thinks you've been away too long," Julie said. "The big money is in timeshares these days, not low-income housing."

"But they can't just throw you out, can they?"

"Well, maybe not just throw you out, but they can force you to leave by raising the rent to insane levels."

"Really? They can do that?"

"It's supposedly a free country, right?" Julie walked over to the kitchen table and slipped on a pair of sandals. She looked ready to go.

"Then they can just knock this place down and put up timeshares?" he said skeptically, rising from the couch.

"They have to get a change of use passed first, which shouldn't be too hard because money talks in this town. And they'll be 'required'—" Julie made quote symbols with her fingers as she said the word, "—to replace the affordable housing units they're destroying, but who knows when that might happen."

"That sucks." Sean shook his head slowly from side to side. "That's pretty much the way of the world these days, though, isn't it?"

"You say that as if it's something you just have to accept," Julie snapped as her brow creased with vertical wrinkles.

"What else can you do? You either learn how to play the game or you get run over by the guys with the ball."

Julie stepped toward Sean, stopping a foot away. "You can change your mind," she said and rapped her knuckles on the side of his head. "If you learn to open your eyes a little wider you might see that the only reason these people have power over us is because we let them have power over us. Once enough of us understand that, we can all just walk away."

Sean was again intoxicated by the scent of Julie's perfume. Still, her statement put a frown on his face. "What's that supposed to mean?"

The wrinkles slowly eased from Julie's brow, dissipating like ripples from a pond. "It means they cannot crush you if you don't crawl," she said, then turned and opened the door. "I need some fresh air. Let's get out of here."

Sean had always known Julie was intelligent, she just used to hide it behind the front of an air-headed blonde. Now, though, she didn't seem to mind smacking you upside the head with it—literally. The revelation both surprised and fascinated him.

Six

Julie inhaled the sweet scent of pine trees in the sun as she and Sean crossed the parking lot. The tree pollen had peaked for the year and all the cars were covered with the stuff. She stopped long enough to draw a large smiley face in the yellow dust on the rear window of her neighbor's Outback before they reached the well-used trail to the beach. Lecturing Sean on the tenets of changing the world was no way to start a relaxing get-to-know-you-again walk.

"So, how are your parents doing?" Julie asked. They left the pavement and walked under a thin band of yellow pines and Douglas fir separating the apartments from the sand.

Sean cleared his throat and kept his eyes forward, out toward the lake. "They were killed in a car accident," he said.

"Oh my God!" Julie stopped and turned to him. "How long ago?"

"That summer," Sean answered, halting. "After my sophomore year."

A bad year all around.

"That's horrible!" Julie said. She rested a hand on his shoulder. "I'm so sorry."

They stood in silence for twenty or thirty seconds, Sean watching the water, Julie watching Sean as his jaw clenched tightly then released.

"It's okay, it was a long time ago," he said. "Doesn't seem like it sometimes, though."

"I know what you mean."

Julie dropped her hand back to her side. Sean knew her father had passed away when she was nineteen, but some days it felt like yesterday.

As they walked on, Julie followed Sean's gaze along the surface of the rippling water and saw the M.S. Dixie—one of the lake's two sternwheelers—paddling along a mile or so offshore. Or was that the Tahoe Queen? She couldn't say for sure. The company that owned the Dixie had bought the Queen anyway, so what did it matter? Just another reminder of corporate politics stifling competition to increase profits at the expense of jobs and whatever else got in the way.

Ten steps onto the beach Julie already had sand between her feet and sandals. She stopped and leaned against a picnic table long enough to pull them off.

"How about your Mom?" Sean asked. "How's she doing?" There was a hint of hesitation in his voice as Julie slapped the sand from her footwear.

"She's doing good," Julie said. "She lives out in Dayton now. Got remarried a few years ago."

"That's great," he said, releasing tension from his shoulders. "What about your sisters?"

"Joan lives in Reno. She's married, three kids. Janine's in Las Vegas. Loves it there, I guess. She's still single." Julie's sisters were five and six years older than her and she had never been very close to them.

"I just went through Vegas last week," Sean said as they continued on. "It's amazing how much it's grown."

"I can't stand that town. Nothing but a huge monument to greed and arrogance."

"How do you mean?"

Julie glanced at Sean, trying to gauge his receptiveness to her preaching. He seemed genuinely interested, though he was probably only being polite. She pushed forward anyway. "Who would build a city in the middle of the desert like that except people who believe the laws of the natural world don't apply to them?"

They took a few steps before Sean replied. "And who believes that?"

"We do," Julie said, shaking her head. "We have met the enemy and they are us... or something like that."

Sean was quiet for another beat or two before asking, "And by 'us' you mean...?"

"This society. This culture."

"So, this country? The U.S. of A.?"

"Not just America. Industrial Civilization as a whole. Capitalism and the consumer economy we live in. The whole shebang."

"You just described everything on the planet."

Julie stopped and put an arm out to bring Sean to a halt as well then turned to look him in the eye. "Do you really believe that?" she said.

Sean pointed to the high-rise casino/hotels peering at them over the trees from two miles away near the state line. "What else is there?" he said. "We live in a consumer-driven, global economy. Our culture is *The* Culture."

"No, it isn't," Julie said, shaking her head slowly from side to side. "There are plenty of indigenous cultures hanging on around the world, we just need to stop killing them off long enough to realize ours is not the only way to live. These people can still teach us what we've forgotten. How to live in harmony with the Earth instead of raping her for profit."

Sean had changed more than Julie suspected. The guy she'd known years before had been concerned for the environment and the general direction the world was headed—more so than her at the time. She'd thought he would be more aware of the other ways of life still struggling for survival around the globe.

"Are you suggesting we go back to the Stone Age?" he said. "Live like savages?"

Julie set her feet in the sand, hands on hips. "First of all, living lightly on the Earth has nothing to do with being a 'savage.' Our society is infinitely more savage than any indigenous culture, we've just learned to ignore it. All I'm saying is that we need to consider alternatives to our way of life or we're going to end up back in the Stone Age, like it or not. We need to get over our superiority complex and understand what our true place is in this world. We are members—not absolute rulers—of this amazing web of life." As she finished she spread her arms wide and spun on her toes, offering Sean a physical display of humanity's connection to everything around them.

He stood silent, a skeptical frown gracing his puss. Julie stopped twirling and faced the lake. She wondered how much of his interest in the environment he'd lost. And if there was any hope of it being rekindled now that he'd spent nearly half his life in what she considered another soulless wasteland: L.A.

Anyhow, it was much too nice a day to let this descend into an argument—which was what usually happened when she discussed these topics with people unfamiliar with them. Sean surprised her, though, and changed the subject before she could.

"Are you going to school for all this stuff?" he asked.

"No, why?"

"I noticed the library at your place."

"Yeah," she said, "I like to read."

"Since when? It was nearly impossible to get you to crack a book in school."

Julie laughed. He was right, she hadn't really started reading until—

"How 'bout a swim?" she said, jolting herself from her own thoughts. Then she bolted off toward the water, heaving her sandals high into the air as she went.

* * *

Sean followed along behind, gathering Julie's discarded footwear as he went. "Isn't the water a little cold?" he said. He may have been wearing shorts, but he wasn't exactly dressed for a swim.

"Oh, come on," Julie said. "Has ten years in LA turned you into a wuss?"

She stopped ten feet from the water and stripped off her shorts, revealing a matching, turquoise bikini bottom. After unbuttoning her shirt, she pulled it off and dropped it in the sand next to her water bottle and shorts, then she waded into the lake up to her thighs. The Celtic tattoo he'd caught a glimpse of at the café was fully revealed. A stretched triangle with the short point facing down, it was a mass of intermingling vines with a softer, red center radiating warmth.

"Feels good," she said as she turned to face him.

"Yeah? You're not in very far."

With that Julie pivoted and dove, disappearing into the water. A solid thirty seconds later, she resurfaced some forty feet out from the water's edge. "Chicken!" she yelled back at him.

Sean flipped off his shoes and removed his socks with no intention of doing anything more than wading. If he had a bathing suit on he might have considered it, but probably not. It was only June and a big winter meant late snow runoff. He'd been waterskiing in a wetsuit the other day and the water was still an icy slap in the face every time he fell. Still, he pulled his phone, keys and wallet from his pocket and stuck them in his shoes before he continued down the beach.

He was four steps into the lake when Julie started back to shore with a crawl stroke. Her arms churned through the water with authority and, shortly, she stood in waist deep water ten feet further out than him.

"You're crazy," Sean said. "This water's got to be, what, fifty degrees?"

Julie splashed him. "It's not *that* cold," she said. "I can't take it for long, but it's good for a little clarity in the morning. Awakens the senses."

"You don't say." Sean looked down at his feet, clearly visible through two feet of water; his calf muscles were beginning to ache as the cold seeped into them. "I don't think I'm ready for that kind of clarity."

"Yeah, you're probably right," Julie said, advancing on him fast and splashing. "Sometimes it needs to be forced on you."

Sean hopped out of the water before Julie got to him, but she managed to soak him anyway. "I already had a shower today," he said, shaking water from his arms and legs.

Julie emerged, grabbed her things and headed up the sand toward a beached log. "Come on," she said.

Sean followed behind, pulling off his wet shirt and wringing it. "What's your tattoo supposed to be?" he asked.

She spun and walked backwards, sizing him up, a sly grin on her face. "It's a representation of the Celtic Earth Mother, Gaia."

"Ahhh," he said, not having any idea who that might be, but not at all surprised. So far Julie had proven to be everything he remembered. Spontaneous, energetic, interesting and odd—but almost always fun.

* * *

Sitting on the sun-bleached log, she fought hard to suppress the shivers. Though the day was warm and the sun hot, a breeze had picked up off the lake, chilling her wet skin. She wouldn't have been so bold these days to frolic in the surf in her bikini with a guy she'd just met, but this was Sean and even though they hadn't seen each other in years she still felt safe with him. Even so, she wished she'd brought a towel.

"You should come to the city council meeting with me tonight," she said, trying not to stare at Sean's bare chest as he approached.

"Sounds like something for locals to me," Sean said. He laid his shirt out over the log and sat down a couple of feet away.

"I don't think anyone will mind if you come. It's a public meeting."

Julie wanted Sean to understand the human side of the situation, not continue to see it in terms of "business as usual." It wasn't just a matter of replacing some old buildings, people's lives were being displaced—many of whom would have to leave the area they called home. "Do you have dinner plans or something?"

Sean stirred the sand with his feet. "I might," he said.

"With whom?" Julie said, fluttering her eyelids and tilting her head in his direction.

Sean turned, a small grin barely showing his dimples. "She's about five-six, blonde hair, green eyes, athletic build, currently wearing an itsy-bitsy, teeny-we—"

Julie punched him in the arm, blushing as she cut off his description.

"Alright, alright," he said and covered up to protect himself from another shot. "Might Milady accompany me to dinner before we attend her Gala Ball?"

"I'll think about it," Julie said. She folded her arms across her chest and shifted a quarter turn away.

This time it was Sean who hit her in the arm, though not too hard. Julie reacted quickly and pushed him backwards off the log where he flopped in the sand with a thud. A moment later his hand snagged her wrist and yanked her down as well.

*   *

She landed on top of him.

Chest to chest, their faces inches apart, she had him momentarily pinned.

As the laughter tapered off and their eyes locked he was sure she meant to kiss him. Instead, she rolled away and threw a heap of sand in his lap. He retaliated.

Once the momentary sandstorm subsided, Sean stood. He had sand in his hair, his ears and his shorts. Julie hadn't fared much better. She sat Indian-style on the beach grinning up at him, not even bothering to brush any of the sand off herself, as he was doing.

"You're crazy, woman," he said through a grin the size of the world famous snow cross on the face of Mount Tallac.

"You won't get it all off like that. Best thing is to just get in the water." She held her hands up for him to help her off the ground.

Sean obliged, took her hands and pulled her to her feet. They stood face to face for an instant, her eyes nearly melting him. A shiver ran through him that had nothing to do with weather and then she was running back to the lake, adjusting the bottom of her bikini as she went. She waded into the water without hesitation and disappeared under the rolling waves.

Sean followed, reluctantly admitting to himself that she was right. When his feet hit the water he took three steps and dove. The shock of the cold was nearly electric. He felt as though his rapidly beating heart stopped for a moment and he fought the urge to draw a breath. He managed only a few strokes underwater before he surfaced, gasping for air like a newborn.

Julie swam up and stood next to him in the chest deep water. "Feels good doesn't it?" she said, a shiver turning the last two words staccato.

"Yeah, sure," Sean said, his jaw clenched tight. He feared relaxing the muscles would cause his teeth to start clattering like an old diesel engine.

As he watched Julie drift away from him in an elegant backstroke, though, the silly grin found its way back to his quavering lips. He hadn't felt this good in a very long time.

Seven

They ate dinner at The Beacon. On the lake at Camp Richardson.

Out on the deck, under a post-mounted heater that resembled a small tree, they found a rhythm to their conversation. It turned out there was a lot to talk about and they reminisced about high school and caught up on some of the time they'd spent apart. Like two skaters avoiding the middle of a frozen pond, though, they skirted the issue at the center. Not knowing if that ice was thick enough to hold them, neither dared test it.

Sean continued to dance around the matter of his current employment. It was childish and it probably wouldn't mean anything one way or another to Julie that his business had tanked, but he liked the idea that he had a secret, too. He talked freely about everything else in his past, but when it came to his job he explained vaguely that he was "taking an extended vacation." The two times it came up, Julie dropped it quickly. She probably thought he'd been fired and didn't want to own up to it. That was fine with him… for now.

Sean enjoyed finding out what Julie had been up to for the last decade. She'd graduated from Lake Tahoe Community College with an Associate's Degree in General Studies then worked for a few years as a cocktail waitress at Harvey's before going to school to become a masseuse. Most of her twenties had flashed by in a blur of parties, outdoor activities and work at the casino. When she turned twenty-nine she decided a change was in order before she hit the big Three-O. So she went to the Sivananda Ashram in Grass Valley, California where she studied to be a Yoga instructor—something she'd already been practicing on her own for a number of years. Then, last year, she landed a small business loan and opened her own studio.

Julie suspected Sean was hiding something about his past. No matter how many times he said he was "on sabbatical" it was obvious to her that his most recent job had ended—and not well. But, seeing that he didn't want to talk about it, she tried to stay away from the subject.

Sean did explain how and why he had come back to the basin. And it turned out that Julie had heard it all before—most of it anyway—from any number of people she'd met who had relocated here. Sean had played the game, pursuing the so-called American Dream, and worked his ass off for the past ten years "in the software industry." He ended up with a status symbol in his driveway and a fat bank account, but instead of being happy he was stressed out, depressed, disillusioned and alone. He had no family (he was an only child and his parents were gone), or real friends (just work acquaintances, really), so he'd decided to get out of L.A. for a while. He didn't tell her all of this in so many words, but Julie was confident she'd filled in the blanks correctly.

Sean's first stop had been in Vegas. He'd only lasted two days before the mindless swarms of zombies blowing their rent money and wasting days on end at slot machines and blackjack tables had sent him running for the emptiness of the surrounding desert. He'd spent a week or so moving north and west on U.S. 95, basking in the relative calm and normalcy in the smaller outposts along the way.

According to Sean, he didn't really think about visiting his old stomping grounds until he rolled into Yerington and saw a sign for Lake Tahoe with an arrow pointing left—so he turned.

What truly amazed Julie was that Sean hadn't found anyone to settle down with. She'd always thought of Sean as a family man, even back in high school. Yet here he was, thirty-three and never married. He told her the longest relationship he'd had lasted a whopping ten months. Hell, she'd had two relationships longer than that, and one of her friends liked to jokingly refer to her as "Miss Noncommittal."

Sean was less surprised to find that Julie had never married. He was stunned, though, that she currently was not dating anyone—and hadn't been for over six months. For the Julie he used to know, not dating would have been like a bear kicking the hibernating habit.

Once most of the catching up was done, they sat side by side, forearms touching, as the sun sank behind the western rim of the Tahoe Basin. Alpenglow slowly turned the mountains from pink to purple while they listened to a local jam band and shared a rum runner with two straws, a magnetic field of charged silence tickling the air between them.

Eight

Julie waited in the passenger seat of Sean's Chevy Avalanche as he circled around to open her door. He'd gotten on her case at the restaurant when she'd opened it herself before he got there so, this time, she chose to let him feel chivalrous. She even took his hand for help down from the gas-guzzling behemoth as if she were dressed in a skirt and high heels instead of shorts and sneakers. The whole charade still stunk of chauvinism to her, though.

Such a large number had turned out for tonight's Special Meeting of the City Council that the main parking lot at the South Lake Tahoe Airport—which also housed the City offices and Council Chambers—was full and they'd been forced to park in an overflow lot to the north. Julie still enjoyed a modest buzz from the last Rum Runner they'd shared at the Beacon and the night hummed around her head like a swarm of gnats as she and Sean walked along the edge of the Airport's exit road, occasionally bumping shoulders.

Maybe what was really bugging her was how downright weird it was being on a date with Sean Connors. Not that either of them had bothered to point out that this was, indeed, a date.

Her slightly inebriated state of mind made it easier for her to ask a question she'd been dreading all evening, though. She reached out, grabbed Sean's swinging hand and said, "So, how long you gonna be around?"

"I think ninety is a good age to shoot for, but I wouldn't mind breaking the century mark," Sean said, not missing a beat.

Julie punched him in the arm with her free hand.

"Ow!" Sean said and rubbed the spot. "I need to get some sort of guard for that."

"I'm serious. What are your plans?"

They walked a few strides before Sean answered. "I guess I don't really have any."

"I see." Julie released his hand and stopped as they came to the main parking lot.

Sean turned back and halted as well. "What?"

"Nothing. That's just... It's not exactly the answer I was hoping for."

"I don't know what else to say," Sean shrugged. "This has all been so..." He waved a hand in the air, searching.

"I know." Julie sighed and looked down. She kicked the pavement behind her with the toe of one sneaker. "What were your plans before today, then? Before this morning?"

"Like I said, I didn't really have any. When I was waiting for my breakfast I remember thinking about heading up to Angora Lakes. Maybe jumping off the cliff into the water—if they still let you. Beyond that... not much. I haven't been thinking very long-term lately."

Julie studied him in the light of the overhead street lamp. He held her gaze, unwavering. She decided she would trust him. For now.

"Come on," she said, striding off along the edge of the road. "We're gonna be late."

* *

It was true, Sean didn't have an agenda. He'd been living day-to-day since he left L.A., doing whatever seemed the thing to do. For the last eleven hours the thing to do had become: "Find out where the thing with Julie is going." He knew it wouldn't take much for him to fall for her again—and maybe he already had—but with his mind reeling from all the recently dug-up emotions it was hard to think clearly. He was riding some sort of pheromone high and a general sense of paranoia was beginning to creep in as to just when and where this wave would break, slamming him face-first back into gritty reality.

Sean caught up with Julie at the front of the building where she'd stopped to speak with another of the attendees. As he approached he could see nothing but the man's back and Julie's eyes peeking at him over the stranger's left shoulder.

"Sean, this is Derrick Masterson," Julie said. "Derrick, this is an old friend of mine from High School, Sean Connors. He just got back into town the other day."

"Nice to meet you," Derrick said.

Sean stepped up and added the last point to their triangle, but when he turned to look at Derrick he found himself staring into the face of Brad Pitt. "Good to meet you, too," he managed as he shook the blonde Adonis' hand.

It wasn't really the movie star but Derrick should have been in pictures. His white, straight teeth gleamed in the outside lights and the five o'clock shadow on his jaw was the exact right length to give him the rugged—yet still sophisticated—look of a modern day mountain man. Sean returned Derrick's smile but noticed that the other man's expression didn't carry all the way to his steel-blue eyes, which assessed Sean with an icy glare.

"So," Sean said as he extracted his hand from Derrick's too-firm grasp, "you live at the Lake's Edge, too?"

Much to Sean's relief, Derrick replied, "No, my interest in all of this is on more of a professional level."

"Professional?" There was something about the man that Sean found familiar—other than the movie star association—but his mind refused to spit out the details. "Are you a lawyer or something?"

"Not quite," Derrick said. "Never got around to taking the bar." He issued a hearty, insincere-sounding laugh at what was probably one of his stock jokes.

"Derrick went to High School up here at Whittell," Julie said, checking back into the conversation. "His family is from Glenbrook."

"Oh yeah?" Maybe that was why he looked familiar. "So did you know each other back then?"

"No. We only met a couple of years ago at—"

Derrick cut her off with a stern look.

"Met at…?" Sean egged her on.

Derrick answered for her. "A rally."

"Yeah," Julie picked up, "a rally."

Julie had told Sean she hadn't dated anyone in over six months, but there had to be some sort of history between these two. What was he missing?

Derrick asked Sean, "What brings you back to Tahoe?" His eyes narrowed slightly, leaving very little white showing.

"Just back for a visit."

"Funny story." Julie wrapped her arm around Sean's waist. "Until this morning we hadn't seen each other in over thirteen years."

Derrick's jaw bulged as the muscles tightened under the skin. "Really?" he said, then forced a smile from clenched lips. Sean watched Derrick's eyes follow his left arm as he put it around Julie's shoulders.

"Yeah," Julie answered, apparently oblivious to Derrick's discomfort. "I ran into him at Sprout's. Weird, huh?"

"Yes it is." Derrick relaxed his jaw as he turned away toward the door. "I'm going to head in now. It was nice to meet you, Sean. Julie, I'll catch up with you later." Then he was gone.

Sean had suspected there would be a guy hanging around somewhere in Julie's life and he guessed he'd just found the culprit. "He seemed a little tense," he said, trying to keep his tongue in check.

"What do you mean?" Julie said as she pushed out of their embrace and looked up at Sean, confused.

"I don't know. Did you guys used to date?"

"No. Why?"

If they hadn't been a couple already then Derrick must have been hoping they would be in the future. "It's just…" Sean said. "He seems a bit overprotective. Jealous maybe?"

Julie crossed her arms. "Where did you get that from? He didn't say anything to give you that idea."

True. Derrick had said nothing to give Sean that idea. The communiqué had been meticulously non-verbal.

"We're just good friends," Julie added. "He knows where we stand." Then she, too, turned and headed into the building.

Does he? Sean thought as deep inside his skull a long-dark bulb flickered to life. *Does he really?*

Nine

CITY COUNCIL MEETING MINUTES
SPECIAL SESSION
CITY COUNCIL CHAMBERS, 1901 AIRPORT ROAD
SOUTH LAKE TAHOE, CA 96150

1. CALL TO ORDER/PLEDGE OF ALLEGIANCE TO THE FLAG:

Mayor Kordell called the meeting to order at 8:02 p.m. and led the pledge of allegiance to the flag.

2. ROLL CALL:

Present were Mayor Kordell and Councilmembers Compton, Karl, Lester and Strong. Also present were City Manager Jensen, City Attorney Van Leisen and City Clerk Alexander.

3. COMMUNICATIONS FROM THE AUDIENCE: (taken out of order by Mayor Kordell with Council consent.)

Jim Lexan, Lake's Edge Apartments Resident, spoke on the need for controls to reign in the development industry. Lexan noted a sharp rise in the local population moving out of the area during his 15 years of residence. Lexan expressed his hope that the council would take action to keep Eagle Development from forcing Lake's Edge residents out of their homes with exorbitant rent increases.

Yolanda Seres, another Lake's Edge Apartments Resident, also spoke on the need for help from city government. Seres expressed concern that "Big Money" was taking over the area and noted that the low-income residents who "keep the town running" cannot afford to live in the basin anymore. Seres stated her belief that the closing of two elementary schools the previous year could have been avoided if the City Council had acted in the past to protect or encourage more affordable housing.

At this point Mayor Kordell asked the audience if anyone had communications on other issues, as the Lake's Edge Apartments Issue would be open for public comment later in the meeting. No one else came forward with comments.

4. <u>CITY COUNCIL UNFINISHED BUSINESS</u>:

(a)   Discussion, Direction and Possible Action Regarding Residents of Lake's Edge Apartments Request for Emergency Rent Control

Lisa Armstrong, head of the Lake's Edge Tenants Association, presented an argument in favor of the Council's intervention in the matter:

Armstrong noted that the large rent increases being handed down by the new owner (Eagle Development) amounted to unfair evictions as most tenants could not afford the increases and were being forced out of their homes. Armstrong also pointed out that the lack of other affordable options in the community had forced a number of former Lake's Edge tenants to leave the area.

Armstrong spoke on the problem of large developers turning local's affordable housing into either tourist units or second home communities and the reality that the workforce is being priced out of the market. She argued that Eagle's high rent increases amounted to a "taking" of affordable housing units even though Eagle had not actually razed the buildings. Armstrong also noted that Eagle Development is well-known in town as a developer of timeshares and suggested that the company was planning a massive timeshare development on the parcel that the Lake's Edge Apartments currently occupies.

Armstrong argued that allowing Eagle Development to evict the tenants of the complex's 300 units with continuing rent increases would hurt the community well beyond any economic benefits that might eventually be realized from a new development. She closed with a request to the Council to take action to protect one of the last remaining affordable apartment complexes on the South Shore. She also noted that now was a perfect time for the Council to set a precedent that The City of South Lake Tahoe would take care of its citizens and "not allow outside money interests to run our town and ruin our community."

Applause followed.

Donald Eckhart, representative of Eagle Development, presented an argument against the Council's intervention:

Eckhart argued that any intervention by the City of South Lake Tahoe would amount to an illegal infringement on the property rights on the new owner. Eckhart also noted that any attempt to restrict Eagle Development's right to set rental rates as it sees fit for the Lake's Edge Apartments would also have to include other property owners of the same unit types.

Eckhart spoke on the supposed problems inherent in rent control situations, including: their interference with the free market; their tendency to cause a decrease in investment in rental units; and the observation that, instead of actually providing the community with more affordable housing, rent controls tend to decrease the overall affordable housing stock due to a decrease in new low-income housing starts.

Eckhart stated that Eagle Development had not currently finalized any plans for the Lake's Edge Apartments, but promised an announcement would be forthcoming.

Eckhart repeated that the Council would be infringing on Eagle Development's property rights by taking any action to limit what they could charge for the leasing of their property. Eckhart added that Eagle Development would have no choice but to take the matter to court if any intervention was proposed.

General discord from the audience was quieted by Mayor Kordell.

Councilmember Karl opened Council discussion by noting that it would be difficult for the City to find the funds to defend a lawsuit.

Loud discord from the audience was eventually quieted by Mayor Kordell who warned the audience that the chambers could be cleared if the spectators became too unruly.

Councilmember Compton asked City Attorney Van Leisen what the legal ramifications of any Council action might be.

Van Leisen noted that most rent control laws end up being challenged in court. She also stated that there are many communities around the country that have successfully defended their rent control legislation to put it into practice. Van Leisen spoke at length about the importance of writing any legislation intelligently and fairly. She also noted that placing the restrictions on just one property owner would be unprecedented and would, in her opinion, not hold up in a court of law.

Councilmember Karl expressed his opinion that the prospect of restricting only Eagle Development in the matter was not a feasible option.

Councilmember Strong agreed with Councilmember Karl's opinion. Strong also noted that the city still needed a better form of control over the affordable housing situation. He questioned whether some type of rent limitation might be part of the solution.

Councilmember Lester agreed, with reservations, that targeting one property owner was probably not the answer. Lester then spoke on the possibility of writing rent control legislation that would focus only on the lower income apartments around town.

Councilmember Compton also agreed with Councilmember Karl that the Council should not single out Eagle Development in the matter. Compton spoke again about the financial costs of defending a lawsuit against a Multi-National corporation.

Councilmember Strong noted that not proceeding with legislation that would benefit the community due merely to the threat of litigation by a profit-hungry corporation was essentially the same as bowing to extortion.

Applause followed.

Councilmember Karl pointed out that Eagle Development had been operating at Lake Tahoe for many years and had generally upheld responsible business practices.

Councilmember Lester noted that Eagle Development had been recently acquired by a larger company and that their practices appeared to be changing.

Mayor Kordell interrupted and pointed out that the Council was here to discuss possible action for protection of the Lake's Edge residents, not to argue about the standing of the property owner in the community.

Councilmember Strong noted that the issue now to be decided was whether or not to proceed with some form of City-wide rent control that would also benefit the residents of the Lake's Edge Apartments.

Councilmembers Compton, Karl and Lester agreed.

At 8:38 p.m. Mayor Kordell opened the public comment period.

Sam Gromley, owner of the Ski Run Apartments, stated that he believed a blanket rent control ordinance would unfairly burden owners of lower income housing. Gromley noted that he was "barely getting by" charging the low rents he did and restricting his right to raise his rent when he saw fit would essentially be a taking of his property rights by the City.

Dylan Bartleby, owner of Sierra Mountain Sports, noted that rent control legislation, when in effect, requires a department of its own for oversight. He questioned where the City would come up with the funds to run this new department.

Scott Newman, former Lake's Edge Apartments resident, spoke on the low quality and high price of the housing he had been able to find since "being evicted" from the Lake's Edge by a 50% rent increase. Newman noted that the choice of housing at the lake for a single working man who wants to live without roommates ranges from expensive closet space to exorbitantly priced studios and one-room cabins. He also noted that a number of people he knows are living on a week-to-week basis in motels with no kitchens—sometimes three or four to a room.

Sally Upton, 10 year resident and Economics instructor at Lake Tahoe Community College, noted that we live in a free market, democratic society. She pointed out that the market would eventually correct itself and said that any interference from the government would likely end up causing an economic downturn for the area. Upton also noted that rent controls tend to actually inhibit the construction of new affordable housing in an area.

Julie Thompson, Lake's Edge Apartments resident and owner of Tahoe Valley Yoga, stated that the science was suspect behind the studies declaring that rent control caused economic woes as they had all been financed by the real estate industry. Thompson also asserted that the free market does not operate in a fair and balanced matter, but requires regulations to force it to compensate for the extreme inequities of income and wealth in our society.

Thompson spoke at length about the issue of affordable housing and the need to offer incentives to private developers to get it built. She noted that private housing developers, with or without public subsidies, have consistently failed to provide a decent supply of affordable housing, regardless of the rent control status of an area.

Thompson proceeded to question why all of us blindly accept, and base our society on, the idea that it is acceptable for some human beings to withhold the necessities of life from others. She stated that food and—particularly in this instance—shelter are not things to be bought and sold, they are rights that every being on the planet is entitled to. She pleaded with the Council to "do something amazing, unheralded and unheard of: put people's faith back in government. Don't bow to corporate interests; support the people who support the community. Reach down—deep inside, down to your very core—and look at the human side of this situation. Then maybe you'll arrive at a humane decision."

An extended standing ovation followed.

No one else appeared to be heard. Mayor Kordell closed the public comment period at 8:53 p.m.

It was moved by Councilmember Compton, seconded by Councilmember Karl, that any action regarding the Lake's Edge Apartments Resident's Request for Emergency Rent Control be indefinitely postponed.

Councilmember Strong questioned the timing of the motion and noted that further discussion was necessary.

Councilmember Lester expressed his agreement with Councilmember Strong.

At this point the vote was taken, and the motion was carried as

follows:

Ayes: Kordell, Compton, Karl

Nayes: Lester, Strong

General discord from the audience and the dissenting

Councilmembers followed.

Mayor Kordell adjourned the Special Session at 9:41 p.m.

Hostility from the audience caused the Council Chambers to be forcibly cleared by security.

Ten

Julie was stunned.

She let Sean lead her out of the building by the hand as the place erupted into a free-for-all. They headed up the driveway to the north as more early exiters streamed out the doors toward the main parking lot.

What kind of a discussion was that?

Karl, Compton and Kordell had just steamrolled Strong and Lester with that motion from left field. Julie had noticed Compton fidgeting while listening to the public comments—like he had somewhere else to be. Compton was the one most suspected of having his hands deep in corporate pockets. Maybe he'd been worried any more comments like hers might end up swaying Karl or Kordell. That would explain the sudden motion to postpone the whole thing after she'd roused the place into a frenzy with her speech.

Once the vote was finalized, Harold Payne—CEO of Eagle Development—had sashayed up to the front of the room to shake hands with his henchman, Eckhart. She'd felt a sickness rising up in her, then and now still, to wrap her fingers around Payne's bloated neck and choke the bald, pie-faced son of a bitch until he turned bone white. Didn't these people give a shit about anything but money?

Close to where she had asked Sean about his plans before the meeting, Julie pulled her hand from his and stopped again. "Hold it," she said.

Sean pivoted on his heels. "What's up?" he said.

"Did you see what just happened in there?"

"Yeah, they postponed the decision and everybody went berserk."

Julie ran a hand through her hair. "I can't believe this shit! I am so tired of these money-hungry bastards plowing under the will of the people they're supposed to represent."

"They took a vote. And they're just postponing a decision, right? That's better than striking it down altogether."

"Yeah, right!" Julie barked. "That wasn't a vote, that was a joke. There's never going to be another vote. They'll just put it off until it doesn't matter anymore. What we just saw was the men who control this city sending out a message not to fuck with them."

Sean cleared his throat and eyed the pavement like she'd just flashed him. "Well, then... maybe I didn't see what just happened in there."

Julie turned back toward the building shaking her head. She was pissed off at Compton and Karl, Payne and Eckhart. She needed to get a hold of herself and stop yelling at Sean. Watching the other attendees wending their way through the parking lot like their team had just been whooped 55-10 in the Super Bowl, Julie realized the reality was worse than that: it wasn't just their team that had lost— fairness and basic humanity had suffered a serious beat down as well.

Julie was about to turn back and do her best to apologize to Sean when she saw Compton walking to his car. As he approached the rear of a large SUV, another figure stepped out of the shadows to shake his hand and give him a clap on the shoulder. Julie's rage ratcheted up another notch as the two men pivoted into the light and she was able to make out the plump, smiling face of Harold Payne. A split-second later her feet were carrying her across the asphalt as her hands balled into fists at her side.

"What the hell is wrong with you?" Julie hissed at Payne as she approached. "You like ruining communities? Throwing innocent people out of their homes? Do you get off on it?" As she closed the last ten feet Compton scurried away to the driver's door of his SUV like a startled lizard.

"And you..." she said as Compton fumbled with his keys. "How much did he pay you? What'd you make off this, huh?"

Eyes twitching, Compton slithered into his vehicle and slammed the door without a word. Julie turned back to Payne, her face no more than a foot from his. The guy was her height, maybe an inch taller, and the smile was gone from his face.

"I'm sorry, but I don't think we've met," he said.

"How many of the people whose lives you've ruined *have* you actually met?"

While he didn't appear scared, Payne squirmed slightly. He probably wished he could take a step or two away from her, but that wasn't possible with the way Julie had him pinned against the side of his car.

"You know," Payne said, a sly smile creeping back as he wet his lips, "when I find myself this close to a beautiful nameless woman she's usually a hooker."

Julie's eyes widened. She brought her arm up to slap the son of a bitch hard across the cheek, but she was abruptly yanked backwards by the very hand she was trying to plant on Harold Payne's smug little face.

"Julie!" Sean said as he pulled her off. "What the hell are you doing?" Then he was dragging her backwards across the parking lot, toward the driveway, as she tried to keep her feet under her.

"Ow, ow, ow," she cried, her shoulder trying to twist in a direction it wasn't designed to go. Sean released her long enough that she could get herself upright and facing forward then grabbed her other arm and continued pulling her down the street.

"You just can't go around accosting the City Council in dark parking lots. What the hell is wrong with you?"

"That was the CEO of Eagle Development and someone's got to stand up to him. For Christ's sake, Sean, he bribed them—he had to—and then the asshole had the nerve to call me a whore. Now would you please let go of my arm? You're hurting me."

Sean released his grasp, stopping short to look back at Julie. "He called you what?"

"He called me a hooker," she said as she tried to shake some blood back into her hand.

Sean's eyes narrowed and he looked back toward the CEO's vehicle, gears apparently turning in his head. After a long quiet moment he finally said, "Let's get out of here," then continued down the edge of the road.

Julie followed reluctantly, the anger still sizzling in her head like hot grease in a skillet.

* * *

Sean drove and Julie ranted.

By the time they stopped at the intersection where Lake Tahoe Boulevard joined Highway 50—know as the Y to Tahoe locals—she had insulted everyone in town in any position of power whatsoever. She finally quieted down as they cruised through the light at Tahoe Keys Boulevard. When Sean looked over he saw she was crying.

"Julie, it'll be okay. They just postponed the decision," he said again, then reached over and took her hand. "It's not the end of the world."

She lifted her head. On her cheeks, trails of tears glistened in the headlights of oncoming traffic. "You don't get it, do you?" she said, wiping her face with the back of her free hand. "You still don't get it."

Sean took his hand from Julie's and returned it to the steering wheel. "Don't get what?"

She shook her head slowly, eyes closed, tears still flowing. "Of course it's not the end of the world—"

"I didn't mean it literally."

"—that's probably a little ways off. It's just another symptom of this… dis-ease." She turned the last word into two.

"Disease?" Sean tried to clarify.

"Not De-Zeeze, DIS-ease." She shifted in her seat and faced him. "I know you can sense it, Sean. You told me how you were feeling back in L.A., why you decided to take this trip. You were lost, down, depressed. That's it… that's the DIS-ease. Your emotional state is a reflection of the sickness that's eating us—and this planet—alive."

Sean stepped on the gas and the Avalanche accelerated away from the light at Sierra Boulevard. It seemed to him that, in the years they'd been apart, Julie had developed a warped view of the world. But after reflecting on it he concluded she'd always been slightly warped.

"I guess I don't see what my emotional state has to do with Eagle Development taking away your home," he said. At least talking was now keeping her from crying.

"You sense there is something inherently wrong with the world we live in, don't you?"

"Yyyyeah," he said tentatively, "I suppose…"

Julie crossed her arms over her chest. "You suppose? So, what? You think Eagle has the right to throw us out if they want?"

"Look, I don't like it any more than you do, but…"

"But what, Sean?"

He glanced over at her glaring eyes, her set jaw. He didn't want to say what he was thinking, but he pushed ahead anyway. "Eagle owns the place now and they have certain property rights. They can pretty much do what they want. And if they want to charge more than market rate for rent, it's their business." Sean inwardly cringed, waiting for lightning to strike.

Instead, Julie looked out the passenger window, emitting a long sigh before she spoke. "What happened to you in LA, Sean? Did they brainwash you at that school?"

"What?"

"You used to care about the environment, human rights, all this kind of stuff. The guy I knew wanted to change the world."

Now Sean sighed as he pulled into the left turn lane for Lakeview Ave. "I wasn't brainwashed, Julie, I just grew up."

"Same thing," she said, letting her forehead bump against the window.

Julie's off-the-wall comments were starting to get under Sean's skin. It was the way she seemed so cock-sure of herself when she was tossing out these wacky ideas. Anger crept from his gut into his voice. "How can you equate growing up with brainwashing?" He said. "It's not the same thing."

"It is in this culture. People only participate in Industrial Civilization when they're forced. All these problems with our youth—depression, suicide, outright rebellion—are just resistance to being assimilated into this crazy society."

"What the hell are you talking about?"

"Sean." Julie spoke in a low, even tone. She still had her arms crossed, but was half-turned toward him in her seat now, eyeing him with great interest. "Are you siding with Eagle on this? Do you believe that Property Rights trump basic Human Rights? That some human beings have the right to withhold the necessities of life from others?" When Sean didn't immediately answer, Julie pivoted and sat back in her seat. Looking forward out the windshield as they cruised down Lakeview, she added, "I'll give you a minute to think about that."

He didn't know when or where, but Julie had definitely picked up the ability to verbally paint someone into a corner. Her question was a little like being asked if you thought killing small children was okay. No sane person would answer, "Yes." But if you said, "No," your Pro-Life interrogator would counter with, "So how can you support abortion?"

Another issue was that the question she'd asked made perfect sense to him. No, now that he thought about it, he did not believe anyone had a God-given right to withhold the necessities of life from another. He had just never considered his culture's way of life in those terms.

Is that what Julie meant by "brainwashing"? The inability to see what's right in front of you?

Sean decided he needed a little more than a minute to think.

Eleven

Back at the Lake's Edge, Sean didn't make it around the truck quick enough to open Julie's door. By the time he got there she had already jumped down and slammed it closed. Instead of taking the stairs up to her apartment, though, she bypassed the building and walked off toward the lake.

"Going for another swim?" he called after her.

"Just come on… you'll see," were the words that came floating back to him.

She left the pavement for a dirt path under the trees and Sean followed. The darkness away from the lights of the parking lot grew thicker. He tried to stay focused on the back of Julie's white sweater, the only thing he could make out in the gloom.

"What's happening with the Lake's Edge Apartments is only the tip of the iceberg," Julie said back over one shoulder. "Like I said before, just a symptom of this illness called Industrial Civilization."

Smaller trees and bushes closed in on either side and Sean realized this wasn't the same path to the beach they'd been on earlier. "I don't know if I would go that far," he said. "It definitely needs fixing, but an illness?"

"Yes, an illness. Some have even said that the human race is a virus—an infection that's killing the planet—but it's not the *entire* human race that's the problem, it's this dominant culture. And it all started thousands of years ago when some bonehead decided he had the right to lock up the food and force others to work for him."

Before Sean could ponder that too much he was struck in the chest with a branch that Julie had pushed aside when she passed. "Ow," he said. "Could you warn me about those, maybe?"

"Sorry," Julie said. She stopped, giving him a moment to catch up before continuing.

"How can you even see?"

"I know this path pretty well."

"And it takes us where?"

"You'll find out."

Sean lost track of her as the path wound through some leafy undergrowth, but his eyes had adjusted enough that he managed to follow it on his own. A minute or two later he emerged from the woods onto a basketball court. Somehow, Julie was already across the park climbing onto one of four swings. The lake lay on the other side of a small strip of grass and beach like a giant slab of obsidian glittering in the light of the just-rising moon.

As Sean approached the swing set he realized where they were. He and Julie had spent a number of evenings sitting at this park when they were younger, but they had always driven to the parking area nearby. "Still like to come out here and swing in the dark?" he said, taking the swing next to her.

"I guess so." She began kicking her feet, rising higher and higher as she swung back and forth. "You remember this place?"

"Yeah," Sean said. He kept his size tens planted firmly on the ground as he watched Julie swoosh back and forth past him. "So when exactly did you get the idea that all of our problems stem from withholding the necessities of life from one another?"

"It's not like I pioneered the concept. I've just read about it in the last couple years."

"But it's the way society operates. Without that concept how would it all work? It's like telling a drowning man the thing holding him above water is actually a snake. Who's going to actually let go of it?"

"Does that make it good? Or right? Or humane? So-called 'primitive' societies that lasted for tens of thousands of years held community and sharing tantamount—we've managed to turn that on its head. This culture reveres selfishness and accumulation of wealth. While a privileged few reign in comfort the rest of the world fights over the scraps."

"But those people—the ones you call the 'privileged few'—worked hard to get where they are."

"Ha! There's one of the biggest lies shoved down our throats by the corporate controlled media. Do you have any idea how many of the moneyed class actually accumulated their so-called 'wealth' themselves?'"

Sean stopped drawing circles in the sand with his toes and sighed. "I must have missed the reading assignment, Teach. I don't seem to have those numbers with me," he said, patting his chest and pockets.

Julie smiled a crooked smile. "I'm sorry. I can get a little confrontational sometimes."

Sean shrugged. "Why do you let it get to you? Even if what you say is true, what can regular people like us do about it?"

Julie went back and forth past Sean twice before she answered, ignoring the first question and answering the second. "We can get people to see the world differently, relate to life in a new way. Once enough of us understand what's really going on I think there will be some kind of revolution. Until then it's just a matter of trying to keep the damage to a minimum by whatever means we can."

Sean spun around slowly, winding the chains above him into a crude braid. "So just by changing people's outlooks you think you can start a revolution? I would've thought you'd be against violence."

Julie continued to push the swing higher and higher. "A revolution of thought isn't necessarily violent. The Industrial Revolution wasn't—at least not in the direct kind of way you mean. Anyway, I'm against *needless* violence, but everyone has to stand up for what they believe in. They only have power over us because we let them have it. If enough of us choose to we can just walk away and reject this hierarchy that's forced upon us every waking moment of our lives."

Sean considered that for a moment. "And what would we replace it with?"

"Nothing," Julie said as she approached the swing set's physical limits. "There's no need for a hierarchy. In the greater scheme of things, we're all equal. Rocks, trees, animals, humans—everything in this great, big, beautiful universe. We're all connected. All one."

It seemed Julie had talked around his question instead of answering it. He was about to say so when she jumped from her swing as it passed through the part of its arc closest to the ground. She sailed forward, a few feet off the ground, clearing the ten foot wide strip of grass separating the playground from the beach. She landed on the sand running, but her feet couldn't keep up with the rest of her and she tumbled, rolling down the beach four or five times before she came to rest in a heap.

"Are you okay?" Sean asked, lifting his feet off the ground and letting the wound chains above spin him like a top. When the rotation came to a stop, he stood up and walked toward Julie swaying slightly.

"Yeah, I'm fine," Julie said, giggling as she watched Sean approach. She sat up as he collapsed in the sand next to her then reached over and took hold of his right hand.

"I don't know what's going to happen, Sean," she said as they watched the waves lap at the shore the way they had since well before the dawn of modern man. "I know I can come off as a Little-Miss-Know-It-All about this stuff, but I don't know what will replace the hierarchy. It's probably gonna get ugly for a while when things finally crash, but that's no reason to stick your head in the sand and deny the crash is coming. Personally, I'd rather be prepared and help things along before we lose everything."

"And how, exactly, do you prepare for the fall of modern civilization?" he asked.

"Mentally you have to accept that our culture is just… wrong. Then you need to be ready to survive the crash physically. I'm still working on that. You know, learning to live off the land, that kind of stuff."

Sean was quiet as he absorbed Julie's words along with the night around them. He couldn't quite agree that this culture of ours would definitely crash. There were some very intelligent people working on the environmental problems industrial society had caused and he had hope that new technology would help reverse a lot of the damage— but he kept that to himself for now. After the drawn out silence had stretched itself into a finely-wound thread Sean changed the subject.

"I bet you're a great Yoga teacher."

Julie eyed him with curiosity. "Why would you say that?"

"I don't know. It seems like you're good at explaining things without making people feel like complete morons."

Her grip on his hand tightened and loosened in a constant rhythm and Sean wondered if she was keeping time with some song in her head. He listened to the sound of waves on the beach, breathed in the cool night air flowing off the water and squeezed her hand in the spaces between. The urge to lean over and plant his lips on Julie's was nearly overpowering, yet the multiple questions circling in his head kept him still: *Had Julie matured enough to want a real relationship or would she flake out on him again? Why all this talk about cultural ills and changing of minds? What was it that made her stop writing thirteen years ago? And where, exactly, did Derrick fit into all this?*

None of the answers were forthcoming.

Turning his view from the lake to the beautiful woman at his side, he found Julie already staring at him. He opened his mouth to speak, unsure what to say. It didn't matter because she leaned in and cut off whatever it might have been with a kiss.

*

Julie pulled back first, rose and ran for the swings. She couldn't let the kiss develop into an embrace out there on the beach or she feared the two of them would end up fondling each other in the sand. It had been long enough—and sufficiently passionate—for a first real kiss anyway.

She hadn't meant to do it at all. Although she'd been thinking about it since that afternoon, she'd been waiting to see if Sean might take the initiative first. Then, well…

Julie smiled and shivered as she sat back on her swing. Sean still sat where she'd left him. "You gonna spend the night out there?" she called.

He pulled himself from the ground and brushed sand from his pants before walking slowly back, eyebrows raised high on his forehead. "What was that for?" he asked and sat back down on the swing next to her.

"For being you," she said, swinging sideways and bumping into him.

"I see."

Julie swung in his direction again, but he shot back and to the left, whirling around her as she passed. Their chains crossed overhead and wrapped around one another as the two of them spun in, faster and faster, toward the center. Crashing together they held tight as the steel links above tried to weave themselves into a tangled, inseparable mass.

Twelve

"That was a bullshit meeting, eh?" Derrick said, emerging from the trees on the far side of the basketball court.

"Yep, it certainly was," Julie said, curious how Derrick had known where to find them. She and Sean had been sitting on their swings discussing innocuous things for a few minutes after untangling themselves. There had been no more kissing.

"Sean," Derrick said as he arrived at the end of the swing set nearest her. He leaned his forearms on the support beam between the two uprights.

"Derrick. Great to see you again," Sean said.

Julie thought she detected a hint of sarcasm in his voice.

"So, Julie," Derrick said. "I've talked to the others and tomorrow night's off. However," he rested his chin on his arms as he spoke, "I would prefer to discuss the new plan with you alone."

Julie looked at Sean. He shrugged. "Don't let me cramp your style," he said. The way he rolled his eyes belied his words.

"It's business, Sean," Julie said and rose from her swing. "I'll be right back."

Is Sean actually jealous? she wondered as she followed Derrick over to the edge of the trees where they sat across from each other at a picnic table. Julie spoke first.

"What's going on, Derrick? You're not cancelling the whole thing are you? Somebody needs to teach that son-of-a-bitch Payne a lesson. You can't call it off."

"Forget about tomorrow night," Derrick said. "Jean, Vic and I decided tonight would be better."

"Tonight?" Julie stared at him and blinked twice. "You're kidding."

Derrick shook his head.

"Shit. Tonight?"

"Look, that meeting was a joke. You saw what happened. Eagle has the Council in its pocket and as soon as they get all you tenants out of those apartments the change of use will go through just like Compton's bogus motion." Derrick's voice dipped, deadly serious. "The message will be stronger if we hit the Beach Resort tonight, while the general public is still seething. Then they can't help but understand what the driving force was behind the action."

"And you want me to help you tonight?" Julie said, glancing back at Sean. She ran a hand through her hair and exhaled through tight lips. "Derrick, I never even said for sure that I'd help tomorrow. I told you maybe."

Derrick turned his head and looked out toward the lake. "I know that. But Ziggy's out of town and I don't have anybody else that can do it on short notice."

"Wow." Julie shook her head. Now that the moment of truth was here she didn't know if she could go through with it. She had planned on deciding tomorrow morning, or afternoon… or evening even. "And you still think four people can take those buildings down?"

"The bombs have enough kick. If we place them right it should work."

"I don't know, Derrick, I've never done anything this… violent before."

"Julie, these people are taking away your home and ruining this community with their backroom deals. What happened to the anger I saw after the meeting? Right now, what better way do we have to let them know we aren't going to just bend over and take this?"

The image of Harold Payne's smug little face as he had calmly called her a hooker rose in Julie's mind and the heat of sudden, searing anger burned on her face. *Damn it!* Derrick was right. What else could they do? They'd tried the legal route—they'd done demonstrations, civil disobedience and lawsuits—but all of it had gotten them nowhere. She was going to lose her home. The South Shore was going to lose another chunk of affordable housing. What else did they have left to try?

Derrick reached his hand over and set it on top of hers. "Julie, this has to be done. We need to teach these pompous assholes a lesson."

She looked into Derrick's eyes, then down to his hand on top of hers. Once, when they'd first met, he'd asked her out and she had politely declined. She wasn't sure what it was about him that turned her off. It certainly wasn't his looks, she had just never been physically attracted to him.

She removed her hand from under Derrick's and looked over at Sean. He was swinging again, forward and back, rising higher with each kick. "What about him?" she asked.

"What *about* him?" Derrick parroted. "He has nothing to do with any of this. He's just your old high school buddy, right? What's he here for? Two, three days tops?"

"I think it might be a little more than that," Julie said, a smile creeping onto her face. She returned her gaze to the table and drew a circle in the pollen dust with her finger. She put in two eyes but hesitated before adding the mouth.

Derrick issued a heavy sigh. "Look, he doesn't matter. Jean, Vic and I will be at your place at 2:30, okay?"

"I meant what should I tell him about where I'm go—"

"Why do you need to tell him anything? Just keep it quiet. Tell him you're going to bed—or was he going to join you?"

Julie's eyebrows rose at the insinuation and she drew a frown below the eyes in the pollen. "Would that bother you?" she said. "You and I are just friends, right?"

Derrick bit his lower lip for a moment before he responded. "The only reason it matters to me is that it might throw a wrench in our plans."

"Really?" Julie said. She brushed the pollen face from the table then crossed her arms and let the word hang for a moment. "Let's just say I'll see you at 2:30 then, but make sure you knock first. You never know how many guys I might have in there."

Derrick rose and stomped off into the woods, leaving Julie sitting alone at the picnic table. Maybe she shouldn't have snapped at him, but it wasn't any of his damned business what plans she might or might not have with Sean for the night. And now she supposed she was committed to doing this… this thing. Making this statement.

As she stood to head back to the playground she saw that Sean had kicked his swing about as high as it would go. She stood watching him as he sliced through the air with each pass. Then, suddenly, he jumped. Soaring through the air a bit higher than she probably had, he landed hard in the sand and crunched to the ground.

Maybe he hadn't changed as much as she'd begun to think. Or maybe he was just learning to live again. She smiled as she ran over, jumped on him and rubbed some sand in his hair.

Thirteen

Sean didn't ask what Julie and Derrick talked about. He'd tried to tune out the murmur of their voices from where he sat on the swing, only catching occasional words here and there. When they got back to her place it was almost eleven thirty.

Julie stopped outside her door, key in hand, and turned to face Sean. "It's late and I've got to get an early start in the morning," she said. "Let me have your number and I'll call you tomorrow."

Sean was surprised she didn't invite him in. He couldn't think of a subtle way to say that, though, without sounding like he was expecting something more.

Maybe Derrick is inside waiting for her.

He dismissed the thought as quickly as it came. The way Derrick had stormed off Sean couldn't imagine the two of them hooking up tonight.

"I don't know the hotel number," Sean said, "but I'll give you my cell." Julie pulled a pen from somewhere but had nothing to write on. Sean remembered the few business cards he still had in his wallet. He handed one to her feeling like a door-to-door salesman harassing the lady of the house about a vacuum cleaner.

"Okay, well… goodnight," Julie said as she unlocked her door. She turned and gave Sean a quick peck on the cheek and then hurried inside.

Sean's reaction went from surprised to stunned. Was this the same woman who had kissed him so passionately on the beach barely twenty minutes ago? He took the next step in the salesman/homeowner exchange and stuck his foot in the door when she tried to close it.

"Julie, what the hell is going on?"

"What do you mean?" she said, her face a portrait of innocence.

"A few minutes ago we were having a great time. How did this turn into the end of a bad date?"

"I said I'd call you tomorrow, Sean. I'm really tired."

"Uh-huh." He knew she was lying. About what, he wasn't sure.

"Seriously, Sean. Please don't take this the wrong way. I do want to see you tomorrow."

He stood with his arms crossed as a wave of déjà vu washed over him like a hot flash. How many times had he heard that from her before?

Julie opened the door far enough that she could step out and pull him to her by the front of his shirt. They kissed for a long, delirious moment before she backed away into her apartment. "I *will* call you tomorrow. I promise." Before the door clicked shut she added, "Goodnight."

Sean took two steps back and leaned against the railing. What was it she was keeping from him?

* *

Julie fell back on the inside of the door and groaned. She hated lying to Sean. If she let him know what was going on, though, Derrick would kill her. She wanted to yank the door open and call him back—if she did it right now she could catch him—but she needed to get some sleep. If she didn't get at least a little rest she'd be a zombie by three a.m.

It wasn't that she didn't trust Sean. She didn't think he would understand. Maybe, given time, he might come around to her way of thinking, but he certainly wasn't there yet. All he would do now was try to talk her out of it.

* *

As Sean headed down the stairs he tried to figure out what bothered him most about the situation. Was it the fact that, minus the kissing, the whole thing stunk of high school? How many times had Julie told him she'd call when they parted ways? How many times had she actually bothered to pick up the phone? The kiss she'd left him with seemed to indicate a desire never previously involved, but it seemed odd that she hadn't invited him in.

He wasn't expecting anything specific. Hoping, maybe... but not really. It was too soon. And he certainly didn't want to add that to an already complicated situation. He guessed he should be thankful, then, that she had turned him away. Of course, she could just as easily be feeling the same way and that could be why she'd shut the door in his face. It occurred to Sean that back in the day Julie had always insisted she would be a virgin until she married. Could she still be holding out?

Naah, couldn't be, he told himself as he climbed in to his truck and started the engine. Those youthful ideals and beliefs tended to go by the wayside when one was introduced to the relative freedoms of adulthood. It had to be something else. Julie believed that she would shortly be thrown out of her home, she'd been flying back and forth from fury to tears most of the day, maybe that was all there was to it. She was under a lot of stress and she'd been quarreling with Derrick, too.

Sean was about to let it all go, head back to his hotel and try to get some sleep, when a few previously inconsequential snippets of Derrick and Julie's barely overheard conversation coalesced in his head. His eyes widened as he grasped the implications.

* *

Julie sat down on the couch without removing her sweater, keys still clutched in her hand. She needed to relax. This whole thing with Sean could continue tomorrow—must continue tomorrow. Tonight she needed to be able to concentrate on the task at hand.

She leaned her head back, closed her eyes and took a deep breath. Exhaling slowly through her mouth, she began running a chant through her mind to clear her thoughts. As she continued her deep breathing, concentrating only on the drawing and exhaling of breath, her hand slowly relaxed along with the rest of her body and the keys slipped from her grasp. She barely noticed as she rose above the whirlwind of her spinning mind. *As the heart beats, so the mind thinks. I am not my thoughts. I am everything and nothing at all.*

A knock on the door jolted Julie from her meditation and she opened her eyes as if from a deep sleep. Raising her head, she shook it gently from side to side trying to clear the fog that sometimes accompanied an interruption. Was it 2:30 already? She didn't usually lose time so easily while meditating.

Julie clawed her way up from the couch not feeling very rested. She looked at the clock on the kitchen wall. It read 11:05. She'd only been sitting for ten minutes. Glaring out the peephole, she saw Sean standing there and, completely ignoring the righteous anger in her head, her heart soared.

* * *

"What are you planning on doing tonight?" Sean said as Julie opened the door. He tried to keep his voice as neutral as possible.

"Getting some sleep," she replied. "Like I told you. Which is kind of hard to do with you pounding on my door."

"Uh-huh. Is that why you've still got your sweater on?"

"What are you getting at, Sean?"

"I'm not sure. I just know it's probably illegal, definitely dangerous and has something to do with Derrick and Eagle Development."

"You don't know what the hell you're talking about."

"Julie, don't do anything stupid. I know you're upset about the meeting and all, but you're gonna get yourself in big trouble."

"Sean, there's nothing going on. I'm just tired."

He took a step back. "So what I heard meant nothing? About the Beach Resort? Bombs? Buildings coming down?"

Julie's eyes widened. She leaned out the doorway and looked both ways. Apparently satisfied they weren't being observed she said, "Get in here," grabbed Sean by the shoulder of his jacket and yanked him inside.

Fourteen

Julie closed the door behind Sean before turning to face him. "What are you, a dog? How could you have heard us?"

"I think dogs are generally known for their sense of smell, not hearing."

"Whatever. Listen, eavesdropper, this is none of your business."

"None of my business? Weren't we just making out in the sand half an hour ago?"

Julie's lips tried to curl into a smile at the thought, but she gritted her teeth and forced them back into what she hoped was a menacing scowl. "Look Sean, this is something I have to do."

"And what exactly are you doing?"

"The less you know the better. Just pretend you never heard anything. Go back to your hotel, get some sleep and I'll talk to you in the morning."

Sean squinted at her, eyes piercing. "No," he said. "I won't do that."

Julie held his gaze. She hadn't expected Sean to openly defy her. She was continually being reminded that this was no longer the shy, timid boy she had once known. Pushing past him into the kitchen she said, "Just because I kissed you on the beach doesn't give you the right to waltz in here and tell me what to do. I can take care of myself."

"Really?" Sean said. "You've gotten better at that, then?"

She spun on him. "Yes, as a matter of fact I have! I've been doing just fine without you for a long time."

Sean released a lungful of air. "I'm sorry, I didn't mean that. It's just... I'm worried about you."

"Fine. Be worried about me. Don't you think I'm worried about you? Worried that you might up and leave? Worried that—"

You'll disown me when you find out, she almost said.

Instead, she changed course. "You understand what's going on here, right? You remember what's gonna happen to this place? What we're dealing with behind the scenes?"

"Yeah, but there's got to be a better response than... sabotage? Maybe one that's even legal. What's blowing something up going to accomplish?"

"It will send a message that we're not gonna stand for these dirty, backroom deals any more. That we're not gonna put up with this bullshit, this destruction of community masquerading as progress. If we continue to let these scumbags do what they want just because we can't prove they broke the law, where does that leave us? They're the ones making the laws for Christ's sake." When Julie finished her voice was close to a shout. She pushed some hair behind her left ear and paced the floor.

"Okay, I get it, I get it," Sean said, holding his palms up in a gesture of surrender. "There just has to be a better way."

Julie halted back it the kitchen. "There isn't a better way, Sean. We'll never beat the house playing by their rules because they always stack the deck in their favor. If we want to win we're going to have to start breaking the rules."

"I don't believe that. This country is ruled by the people, for the people. If you want something to change, you work within the system to do it."

Julie let her hands drop limply to her sides. "Can't you see that the system is fixed, Sean? Money is Power and together they do whatever they want. How do you fight that when you have neither?"

Sean sat on the arm of the couch and leaned forward, elbows on knees. "And there's another reason I'm worried about you. You're starting to sound like some paranoid freak in a mental hospital."

"Am I?" She considered that for a moment before continuing. "You know what? You're right. I'm sure there are quite a few people in mental institutions that would agree with me. Plenty of people who resist participation in this culture end up institutionalized. Either in mental hospitals or in prison... or just out on the street."

Sean raised his head. "What?"

"Come on, Sean, look around. People who disagree with the status quo are constantly labeled misfits and criminals—unless you're rich, then you're just eccentric." Julie pulled out a kitchen chair and sat down, wracking her brain for a way to make Sean understand. She tried a different tact. "You're coming at this from a very narrow perspective," she said. "You only believe what I want to do tonight is wrong because you've been taught by this culture to believe it your whole life."

"Sure," Sean said. "And why is that bad? Every culture has common values, right?"

"Sure they do. The problems start when people blindly follow those values without questioning them—or even being allowed to question them."

* * *

Sean sighed. This conversation seemed to be running in circles. Agreeing with Julie that her argument made sense wasn't the point here and, in his mind, was tantamount to rubber stamping the revolution. The simple fact that she was overlooking was that it was illegal and could mean real jail time if she was caught, but he continued to play along.

"So what values are you questioning by blowing things up?" he asked.

"All of them," Julie said. "You tell me that Eagle has certain rights because they own this property now. I question those rights. I question the idea of land ownership of any kind. I question a nation that supposedly holds property rights in such high esteem when the entire land base it occupies was stolen from others. Those property rights you put so high up on a pedestal really only matter for the people up on that pedestal, too. The rest of us are just chaff to be blown off in the wind."

Sean stared at the floor for thirty seconds before finally looking up at Julie again. She leaned back in her chair, arms crossed, eyeing him with a near-manic intensity. When he said nothing, she continued.

"This culture is based on lies and the deliberate avoidance of important issues. We lie to each other every day with all of our *niceties* and *manners*, pretending we're all happy, that everything's fine."

"But we *are* basically happy… aren't we? Basically content?"

"We're not happy; we're distracted. All of our little gadgets and trinkets—the internet, television, shopping—they all just keep us looking the other way while the planet burns."

Sean considered her words as he studied her face. Her lips were tightly pursed, her chin slightly lowered, she watched him with raised eyes under hooded lids.

"Are you trying to say that unhappiness justifies violence?" he asked.

"No," Julie said immediately. "Not my individual unhappiness anyway. But this blanket *dis-ease* of ninety percent of the population? Someone's got to send a wakeup call, Sean, because everyone else is too busy hitting the damned snooze button."

"Even if that's true, I don't see how it justifies what you're doing."

"I'm sorry you don't get it, Sean, but I have to do this."

Julie moved to the end of the couch opposite Sean and faced him. With her back to the arm, she pulled her legs into a lotus position under her. "You think I don't have reservations about this?" she said. "Mostly, though, it's a matter of fear. Even Ghandi said, 'Between violence and cowardly flight, I can only prefer violence.'"

Sean was surprised Ghandi had said such a thing, but he had to agree with the statement. You couldn't run from everything. Sometimes you had to stand and fight.

As he slid from the arm of the couch onto the cushions he sighed again. Leaning his head back, he looked at the ceiling and said, "Why risk everything you have—risk going to jail—just to send this Payne guy a message?"

Julie didn't reply for at least a minute. From the corner of his eye, Sean could see she had her own eyes closed. When she opened them, she spoke deliberately, "What does a cornered animal do when you threaten it?"

Sean raised his head so he could see Julie's face. "Fights back," he answered.

A sly smile formed on her lips. "Exactly," she said. "It doesn't matter if whatever has it cornered is ten times its size, it doesn't matter if the odds are against it, it will fight for its own survival. There are a lot of people out there feeling cornered, Sean, and if we all start to fight back things could change very quickly."

"So you're not going to change your mind about this, huh?" Sean said. He reached over and set his hand on Julie's right knee.

"I'm not," she replied, covering his hand with her own. "It's something I have to do."

Sean realized he needed to work on his powers of persuasion. He couldn't remember a single time he'd managed to talk Julie out of doing anything she'd made up her mind to do.

* *

"I need to get some rest before they get here," Julie said. It was after midnight and now she was riled up from arguing.

"You really think you're going to be able to sleep?" Sean said.

She hesitated. "Have you ever tried meditation?"

"Uh… no."

"Well, there's no better time than the present. Lean back and close your eyes."

Sean eyed her warily for a few moments before throwing up his hands in acquiescence and doing as he was told.

"Okay," Julie said, "breathe deeply. In and out." She followed her own instructions and lay back as she spoke. "Now, try and tense up every muscle in your body… Hold it for few seconds… Then slowly relax, from your feet to your head. Try to concentrate on your breathing. Focus on nothing but the breath, letting your true self— your essence—ride atop the running thoughts in your head, just observing, not controlling or directing. Let everything go and just be."

Julie glanced at Sean. His face was relaxed, his breathing slow and steady. Some people fell asleep their first time. She hoped Sean was one of them. Closing her own eyes and breathing ever deeper, Julie again let herself drift beyond thought.

Fifteen

◀

The moon is only a quarter full, but Sean's eyes have adjusted to the dark as he starts up the path through the snow. Away from the heat of the fire and the others the cold deepens and the breeze intensifies. He is on his way to the top of The Rock to check out the view and escape what has turned into a makeout-fest around the campfire—Sean being the only one without a partner. He'd been hoping to find Julie here, since her car is parked out on the road, but he has yet to see her.

The Rock sticks out of the mountainside at the northeast end of Saddle Road, not far from Heavenly's California base lodge. In the summer it's a well known party spot—one frequently cleared out by the cops. Sean doesn't know whose idea it was to have a bash up here in the middle of March with the temperature hovering in the mid teens.

Probably Glenn's, he thinks. Fellow high school senior—and used-to-be best friend—who was growing more reckless and distant as their June graduation loomed nearer.

Near the top of the granite formation, where the entire Tahoe basin is visible on a clear day, Sean comes to a small, flat area, sheltered from the wind by a few large boulders. Snow collected by swirling winds drifts up at an angle onto the rocks. A motionless person lying on the inclined bed of snow startles him as he rounds the corner. Then he sees who it is.

"Julie?" he says.

No response.

Her eyes are closed, head cocked to one side. A dark puddle nearby in the snow seems to indicate she's been sick. Most at the party have been drinking. Some more than others.

"Julie!" Kneeling next to her in the snow, he shakes her lightly. "Julie, come on… wake up."

His Health teacher had talked awhile back about the dangers of overdosing on alcohol. How was it again that you revived an unconscious drunk? He removes one glove and slaps her on the cheeks a few times with his bare hand, leaving it to rest there on her cheek.

Maybe smelling salts? Where the hell do you get smelling salts?

He grabs a handful of snow with his still-gloved hand and is about to place it on her forehead to shock her back to reality when he notices with the other hand that her face is already ice cold.

She's dead!

The thought rips through him like an electric current and he scoots backward on all fours like a crab retreating from a pot of boiling water. The nearest boulder halts his retreat and he is rewarded with a jolt of pain in his lower back. There he sits—frozen, hands to his face—trying to make his thoughts line up in some sensible order.

A minute passes before something from health class comes back to him: "Although excess alcohol slows the body's metabolism and lowers body temperature, the drinker will generally still feel warm and comfortable."

A shudder runs though him that has nothing to do with the temperature. Julie may have frozen to death thinking she was lying in a warm bed.

Sean tries to get his legs under him. He has to get back to the fire to tell the others that Julie is dead. He struggles to his feet and is about to head back down the trail when her left leg twitches. It's minor. Scarcely noticeable except for the tiny bit of dislodged snow that slides down the incline where she lies.

He scrambles back to her side, searches her neck with his ungloved hand for evidence of a pulse. Cheek to cheek, one ear close to her nose, he feels the very faint thump-thump of her beating heart beneath his fingertips before the whisper of a breath tickles his ear.

"Help!" Sean screams, standing up and slip-sliding immediately back down. There's no way he can carry her down this steep trail himself, but it will be a miracle if anyone besides the coyotes hears him yelling from up here.

"Damn it, Julie. Why?" He kisses her lightly on the forehead before skating down the hill to raise help.

*

Through a fine haze of alcohol intoxication, everyone Sean talks to assures him that Julie is fine, that she's "just resting." In the end, he manages to pull his friend Glenn away from a half-dressed, drunken blonde—who Sean belatedly realizes is Julie's friend Donna. He tells Glenn where Julie is and leaves him to get his own pants back on then retraces his steps up the hill. Coming up on the last bend before the flat where Julie lies, Sean hears scratching and scuffling ahead.

She's awake!

As he rounds the last rock and sees a figure looming over Julie's still prone body. Broad shoulders tell him it's a man. It seems the newcomer is struggling to lift Julie's limp body from the snow. "Here," Sean says, placing a hand on the guy's shoulder. "Let me help."

"Fuck off," the figure growls and rolls to the left. Julie is still unconscious, her head lolling to one side, but her jacket and pants are now unzipped. Underneath, her shirt has been pulled up, exposing her bare midriff and pink panties below. Recognition hits Sean like a body blow.

"What the fuck are you doing? She's passed out."

The stranger rises to his feet. "Take a hike," he says. "Before I kick your ass."

The brim of a cap keeps the guy's face in shadow, but Sean doesn't think he's seen him before. Sean sets his teeth as the stranger takes a step forward. He's got about thirty pounds and a couple of inches on Sean.

"What's wrong with you, man?" Sean says, shaky from either cold or adrenaline. "She's out cold. What were you gonna do?"

The fist nails him in the jaw before he can react, driving him backwards and spinning him to his knees.

"What'd I say would happen if you didn't get lost?"

Sean grabs his attacker's legs and uses his own to lift the guy up and push him backward. But he can't see where they're going and they slam into a three foot high boulder and roll over it, tumbling and thumping ten feet back down the trail. Sean ends up face down across the stranger's ribs, pinning him to rock.

"Get the fuck off me." The guy grunts and bucks like prized bull.

Sean reacts by pummeling his assailant wherever he can make contact. He lands a couple of shots to the chin and a few to the chest and body. A knee dead center to the groin draws a yelp and his assailant rolls away, hands to crotch.

Sean rises, blood rushing to his head from his galloping heart. He raises his foot for a swift kick in the ribs, but before he can follow through the sound of someone coming up the trail gets the stranger's attention. In an instant, he's up and loping off into the woods.

"I see you around I'm gonna kill you, fucker," the guy yells back as he disappears over the crest of the hill.

Glenn crunches up the trail behind Sean. "Who was that?" he says.

"Don't know…" Sean replies, breathing heavy. "I think he was gonna… rape her… had to pull him off."

"No shit?" Glenn says as he looks after the guy. "You okay?"

"I'll be fine."

"I think you're bleeding."

Sean puts a hand to his face. His lip is split, already swelling. "Son of a bitch sucker-punched me." Suddenly tasting blood, he spits. "Come on, she's up here." He leads the way to where Julie lies in the snow, then stoops to lower her shirt and zip her pants while Glenn looks on. Sean's eyes follow Julie's jacket zipper as he pulls it to her chin. Her face looks blue in the tree-filtered moonlight.

*

It takes the two of them—plus Glenn's re-dressed date, Donna—to get Julie out to the road and into Sean's Camaro. They load her limp body in the backseat with Donna and cover her with some jackets then Glenn jumps in shotgun. Sean navigates the winding series of turns down the mountain like an Indy car circuit, diving in and sticking every turn. He opens it up when they hit the straight shot to the lake on Ski Run Boulevard.

By the time they reach Lake Tahoe Boulevard snow is falling, the pavement turning wet. Heading west into the storm they quickly pickup a Police cruiser with cherries flashing as they streak though the red light at FairwayAve. Sean steps on it, pulls away into the suicide lane to pass two slow moving cars and runs another red at Rufus Allen. The traffic lights around the big bend by Eldorado Beach are green and Sean only lets up slightly on the gas to drift into the turn. There are audible gasps from the gallery, but the Camaro hangs on to the pavement and they rocket out of the turn past Rojo's.

Sean risks a peek in the rearview and notes he's putting distance between them and the cop as he accelerates to eighty down the straightaway toward Al Tahoe Boulevard. He has to tap the brakes to swerve around a slow moving Subaru at the intersection and he catches a peripheral glimpse to the left of more flashing cherries approaching from that direction. Luckily the road is mostly straight and the traffic in front is light. He nails it and the Camaro jumps forward with a roar as his vision tunnels down to a road-width corridor burrowing into the growing blizzard.

Through the red light at Third Street, coming in too fast to Fourth, he taps, taps, taps the brakes and turns, fishtailing through the intersection on the wet sheen of white flakes now coating the road. Donna screams and Glenn yells "Dude! Slow down!"

"Not gonna happen," Sean mutters.

He cleanly navigates the right to the last straightaway, but he's lost his focus and carries to much speed into the bend before the hospital. He can feel all four tires losing their grip as the entire car begins to shift to the left. He eases ever-so-slightly off the gas again. That tiny bit of braking force from the slowing engine is enough to break the rear wheels free, letting the floundering front end find a tenuous grip on the asphalt.

In the back seat, Donna screams again. In the front, Glenn has a death grip on the dashboard crash bar. Adjusting the wheel into the skid, Sean clenches his jaw and huffs once through tight lips.

In what feels like slow motion, the Camaro slides sideways into the hospital parking lot. Sean overcorrects and the back end skips around the other way, sending the vehicle skidding into the hard left at the rear of the building, back bumper missing the parked cars on the right by a coat of paint and a prayer.

They screech to a halt at the emergency entrance and Sean is first out of the vehicle, shooting around to the passenger side. Glenn barely has his door open when Sean gets there. His friend's face is ashen, eyes wide. The noise of police sirens grows louder as they close in.

"Well, get the hell out of there," Sean says, grabbing Glenn's arm and pulling him from the car. "You don't want to get caught, do you?"

Sixteen

Julie opens her eyes to a white, paneled ceiling in a semi-dark room. She looks around, taking a moment to grasp that she must be in a hospital. The last thing she remembers is being up at The Rock doing shots of 151 around the fire.

How the hell did I get here? And why am I so cold?

She pulls the blankets tighter around her and notices one of them is electric. She doesn't feel much heat from it, only the wires inside, like tiny little snakes under a tarp. She shifts onto her right side and sees Sean slumped in the chair beside the bed. His eyes are closed, his breathing slow and steady. On his cheek is a large, purple bruise and his upper lip is split and swollen.

Were we in a car accident? She does a quick check of herself and finds nothing broken. What was she doing with Sean anyway? She'd driven her father's car to the party with Mike and Tommy D.

"Sean?" she says, reaching out to shake him awake. Before she touches him, his eyes pop open and he sits up.

"Julie. You're awake."

"Yeeaahh," she says slowly, accentuating the obvious. "What am I doing here?"

"They weren't sure how long you were going to be out. The doctor said it could be days before you woke up." Sean stands and stretches, then leans over and hugs her. "Thank God you're okay."

As he steps back, Julie repeats herself, "What am I doing here?" A shiver shakes her from head to toe and she adds, "And why am I so cold?"

Sean looks at a readout on the wall behind her. "They said your core temperature dropped to eighty-six degrees. You're at ninety-six now. That's still a little low. That's why you're cold."

"Eighty-six degrees?" she says, eyes scanning the room in

confusion. "What happened?"

Sean blows air between his puffy lips. "You tell me. I found you passed out in the snow up near the top of The Rock. How long were you up there?"

Julie searches her mind for clues but finds only blackness. "I don't know," she says, turning away. "I remember doing shots around the fire. Nothing after that."

"The doctor said you're lucky to be alive. If you'd been out there another half hour you'd probably be dead."

Julie takes that in as Sean walks to the door and turns on the overhead light. She squints at the brightness and asks, "How did I get here?"

"I brought you. Glenn and Donna helped." Sean opens the door and is about to step out. "I'd better go get the nurse."

"Wait!" Julie says. "Come here a minute. I need to know what happened."

"I just told you," he says, but he steps back over to the bed anyway, letting the door swing shut again.

"What were you doing there?" Julie asks. "And what happened to your face?"

Sean looks down at the floor then back toward the door. Julie reaches out and touches his forearm.

"I saw your car—and the others—parked out on the road," Sean says, his attention now on the hand she keeps on his arm. "I stopped to see what was going on. I found Glenn, but nobody knew where you were. I…" He clears his throat, shuffles one foot on the floor. "I found you up by the lookout."

Blood rushes to Julie's face and her voice comes out in a whisper. "Was I naked or something? Is that why I got so cold?"

"What? No… Wouldn't you remember that?"

"I don't know." She withdraws her hand and wraps both arms around herself, trying to repress another shiver. "P-probably not."

"Look, I found you up there and went and got help and we brought you out to my car and I drove you here. That's it."

"What happened to your face?"

Sean touches his lip, winces and pulls his hand back. "I got into a fight," he says. "No big deal."

"A fight? With who?"

"Nobody," he says. "Don't worry about it."

Julie stares at the ceiling as another shiver shakes her body. "Are my parents here?" she asks. Since she isn't dead, she knows her dad will be looking forward to killing her.

"Your Mom was here before, but I guess I fell asleep. I don't know where she went. Your Dad is on his way back from Sac. Probably be here sometime soon—if they haven't closed the pass."

"What did you tell everyone?" Julie asks. "About what happened?"

"I told them the truth, Julie," Sean says. He locks eyes with her for a few seconds then turns away and puts one hand on the doorknob, as if to leave. After a moment he leans his other arm against the wall and lets his head hang forward. "When I found you up there lying in the snow in a puddle of your own puke I thought you were dead. What was I supposed to tell them? Should I have made up a nice little lie so you wouldn't get grounded? I thought if they knew exactly what happened, they might be able to save you."

Julie turns her head away. "I'm sorry," she says as tears pool in her eyes, spilling down her cheeks. "Sean, I am so, so sorry."

"I'm gonna get the nurse," he says. This time he pulls the door open and leaves her alone in the room.

As Julie curls herself into a ball under the covers, the shivers and the sobs threaten to tear her apart.

*

When the door opens again, Julie is engulfed in someone's arms before she can even turn to see who it is. "Thank God you're okay," her mom says. "Oh, thank God."

"Hi, Mom," Julie says. "Did you see Sean out there?"

"No, honey."

"Shit."

"Language," her mother says.

"I know. But I never even said, 'Thank you.'"

"I'm sure he'll be back, honey."

Julie can't imagine why. "I think he's probably h-had it with me," she says as another shiver wracks her.

Her mother stands back and shakes her head. Her light brown

hair is wild and unruly, her face free of makeup. A clear indication she was asleep when the call had come to let her know her daughter was in the hospital.

"He's not the only one," her mom says. "But, honey, he's just a good kid who loves you. You could do a hell of a lot worse than Sean. Besides, the police impounded his car. He can't have gone too far."

"They what?" Julie says, spinning back to face her mother. *Sean loves that car.*

"They claimed it smelled like alcohol, but he was clean. They wrote him a pile of tickets anyway and told him he could go to jail or they were taking his car. He decided to stay here with you.

"To jail?" Julie says, thoughts colliding in her brain like bumper cars. "Tickets for what?"

Her mom pats her on the shoulder lightly. "You're not too quick sometimes, honey. He drove like a madman down from Heavenly to get you here. Picked up two of the three units on duty on the way, but just flat outran 'em. I can't believe he didn't wrap that car around a tree. "

"Sean's a good driver," Julie says distractedly. Not only had he saved her life, he lost his car—and probably his license—doing it. Why hadn't he told her?

"Julie, why do you do this to yourself?" her mother says, tears in her eyes.

Her mom's crying gets Julie's waterworks going again. "I don't know," she says as her mother embraces her again. "I don't know."

*

Julie's mom has usurped the bedside chair and is flipping through a magazine when her dad appears at the door, all creased forehead and pinch-lipped. "You're awake," he says. "Praise the Lord."

With everyone showing so much appreciation for God's grace, Julie wonders if anybody has remembered to thank the person most responsible for her still being here. "You should thank Sean, too, Daddy," she says.

"They said he nearly got you killed bringing you in here." He gives her a cursory hug that lasts only a second and ends with a peck on the cheek before he pulls away.

"He saved my life, Dad."

"Well…" He clears his throat. "I can't believe we nearly lost you. What were you thinking anyway?"

"I don't know… I guess I wasn't thinking." Julie can't begin to count how many times this exchange has taken place between the two of them.

"Damn right you weren't, but thank God you're all right." He bends over and kisses her again, lightly on the forehead.

Julie's eyelids are growing heavy by the time her parents start discussing her punishment. Grounded for one month or two? Mom prefers the former, Dad the latter. No surprise there. She loses interest as her eyes close and her thoughts wander. She figures she must have really screwed up this time because she can't remember another time her father has kissed her twice in one evening.

She wonders, too, if Sean will ever forgive her for all he he's had to lose just to save her sorry life.

▶

Seventeen

A shift of weight on the couch brought Sean out of his doze. He'd slept in so many places in the past week it took him a moment to remember where he was, but he was becoming accustomed to the disorientation upon waking. Across the small studio apartment, Julie rummaged through one of her dresser drawers. Sean looked at his watch. It was 2:28 a.m.

"Still going, eh?" he said, sitting up.

Julie jumped at the sound of his voice and held a hand over her chest, as if trying to contain her startled heart. "You scared me—"

"Sorry."

"—and, yes, I'm still going."

A muffled knock sounded to Sean's right and Julie's eyes shifted to the door. "Your date, I presume?" he said.

Julie stuck her tongue out at him as she passed by and opened the door. Derrick stood on the deck smiling, a shorter figure behind in his shadow. They both wore all black. When Derrick's eyes found Sean on the couch his smile vanished, but a look of recognition flitted across his features—there and gone so quickly, Sean found himself wondering if he'd imagined it.

The newcomers shuffled though the door and Julie asked, "Where's Vic?"

"Change of plans," Derrick said. He glanced around outside before closing and bolting the door. "Vic's in jail."

"Jail?" Julie said, concern clouding her face.

Derrick jerked a thumb at Sean. "What's he doing here? I thought I told you to keep him out of this."

"He heard us talking on the beach."

"Shit!" Derrick closed his eyes and rolled his head back on his neck.

"What the hell is Vic doing in jail?" Julie said.

"The idiot got so blasted at Harvey's they had to call the cops to haul him off. They found out he owes a couple thousand in unpaid child support." He waved a hand in the air as if it didn't matter.

"You said we needed *four* people, Derrick."

The smaller figure behind Derrick spoke up. "The three of us can handle it," she said.

"Jean, this is Sean. Sean… Jean," Derrick said, finally remembering his manners.

"Nice to meet you," Sean said.

Derrick's accomplice had kept so quiet Sean hadn't even noticed that she was a she under the low-slung brim of her ball-cap. Her hair was artfully stuffed up under the hat, a few dirty-blonde strands sticking out at the temples. Though her height was about equal to Julie's, she was a little stockier in build with unwomanly broad shoulders and a jaw like a Marine's minus the five o'clock shadow.

"Well…" Derrick said, getting back to the issue at hand, "I think we can make do." He looked Sean up and down as if trying to decide what size pants he wore. "What about him?" he asked.

"What about him?" Julie and Jean said in unison.

"Yeah, what about me?" Sean added, rising from the couch.

"He's here," Derrick said, raising an index finger. "He knows." A second finger came up. "He could help." He finished with three fingers extended.

"Ohhh nooo!" Sean took Jean's place with Julie in the two-part harmony this time as Julie stepped over and wrapped an arm around his waist. Jean looked Sean up and down as Derrick had moments before. He was starting to feel a little like a male escort in a line up.

"It would be a good way for him to prove he's not some kind of narc," Derrick said.

Sean was growing tired of everyone talking about him as if he wasn't in the room. "I'm right here," he said. "And I have no interest whatsoever in participating in an act of terrorism."

"Whoa, Whoa, Whoa," Derrick said, one hand held up in a halt gesture as Julie pushed away from Sean. "Careful with the use of that word. We are not engaging in terrorism here."

"Really? What else do you call blowing up a building?"

"There's a huge difference between killing innocent people to strike fear in the heart of your enemy and destroying inanimate objects to make a point. Terrorists blow up a building at the busiest time of day in order to maximize the body count. We are doing this at night so that no one gets hurt."

Sean shook his head. "Is that really much of a difference?"

Derrick eyebrows popped up and he gave his head a little shake. "We're talking about killing people vs. not killing people, *Sean*." The derision in the way Derrick pronounced his name was palpable. "Or do you believe—as most of our present leaders apparently do—that the destruction of *property* is as heinous a crime as the killing of living beings?"

"No, *Derrick*," Sean answered, returning the disdain, "but I'm sure both crimes are prosecuted just the same."

Julie butted back into what was becoming an argument. "That's only because right wing conservatives have managed to cram environmental radicals and terrorists into the same pigeon-hole with their damn fear-mongering. If we didn't oppose the same capitalist and free-market values that Middle Eastern extremists oppose, that would've been harder to do. If you're going to call the disabling of a bulldozer or the burning of a Hummer dealership 'terrorism' you might as well label a barroom brawl a 'war.'"

"Okaaay," Sean said, "but if you could find a more peaceful way to make your point it would keep you out of that debate altogether."

"We went over this earlier," Julie said. "We've already exhausted the 'more peaceful' options."

"You could stage a sit-in or something. Won't getting yourselves labeled 'terrorists' just hurt your cause?"

Derrick tagged back in with a tap on Julie's shoulder. "Most of the things environmentalists have accomplished in the last twenty or thirty years would not have happened without the presence of the extremists. Pacifism doesn't work for the simple fact that the status quo condones it. Peaceful protest is only allowed by the powers that be because it doesn't have much of an effect in the long term. It is people like us that make the non-violent radicals look conservative. We allow their demands to look reasonable."

Sean felt like he was banging his head against the front of a slowly moving train. No matter what he said or did, the justifications just kept on coming. "Fine, fine," he said. "I get it, but that doesn't change the fact that it's illegal… and just plain wrong."

"Is it right that everyone in this complex will lose their home?" Derrick continued. "Is it right that, in the twenty-first century, we're still cutting old growth forest at an unprecedented rate? Is it right that species are going extinct on an hourly basis because of human activity?"

"Of course not," Sean said. He stared Derrick down. That familiarity was still there in his slightly crooked grin, but Sean just couldn't trust a man with eyes so cold.

Derrick continued, "We all know these acts being done to us— and our environment—are not right, yet they are all perfectly legal. At some point someone has to stand up for what's right, whether their action is legal or not."

Sean turned away and walked over to the bed, searching for a better argument against this insanity. It was late and he was tired. Were those the only reasons everyone else in the room seemed to be making perfect sense? After all, if men hadn't broken the law over two hundred years ago at the Boston Tea Party, the "Land of the Free" that they called home might have ended up as nothing more than an overseas suburb of the British Isles.

* * *

Julie understood the hard time Sean was having with all this. His innate defenses were up, struggling to protect the worldview that— just like everyone else in this culture—had been beaten into his head since the day he was born. But she could tell there were cracks forming in the foundation of those beliefs and some light was beginning to creep through. If he'd left earlier when she had told him to, this transition might have been a little more gradual.

Derrick turned to her. "This guy's going to rat us out."

"He is not," Julie said. "He's going to go back to his hotel and forget he ever heard any of this."

"Really?" Derrick pulled out one of the kitchen chairs and sat. "I find that hard to believe."

"You know," Sean said to Derrick, "I wouldn't give a rat's ass what you were doing tonight if it didn't involve Julie. And I'm certainly not going to do anything to jeopardize her welfare."

Despite the crassness of the gesture, Sean's masculine protectiveness left Julie a little choked up.

"What about my welfare?" Derrick asked. "Or Jean's?"

Sean's glare looked hot enough to etch glass. With teeth clenched he said, "It seems to me that if Julie's with the two of you, then your welfare is one and the same."

"I see," Derrick said. "But you could still rat the two of us out without implicating her."

Julie crossed her arms and set her own jaw as she let her eyes drift back and forth between Sean and Derrick. Sean wasn't her boyfriend and Derrick was just a friend, but it certainly appeared the two of them were fighting about more than tonight's action. And that ticked her off.

"Alright both of you, that's enough," she said. "Here's the way this is gonna happen: Derrick and Jean, I'll meet you outside as soon as I change my clothes. Sean, go back to your hotel."

All three faces swiveled toward her in disbelief before Derrick spoke up. "I have a problem with that plan," he said and pointed one finger at Sean. "I still don't trust him."

"Me either," Jean said.

"The only way this is going to happen is if he comes along," Derrick added.

"Not a chance," Sean said.

The four of them faced off across Julie's coffee table, an awkward ring of acquaintances and friends, strangers and lovers. Julie closed her eyes. It surprised her how much she actually wanted to do this now, but she could think of no terms that would be acceptable to everyone present. "I guess that's it then," she said. "Action cancelled." She opened her eyes.

"Well, shit," Jean said and turned to the door.

Derrick focused his attention on Sean. "You know, the only thing keeping this from happening is the yellow streak up your boyfriend's back."

Sean moved in a blur around the coffee table and Derrick rose to meet his approach. It all happened so fast Julie barely had time to get between the two men. She got a hand on each of their chests and pushed them back to arm's length.

"I'm not scared," Sean said.

"Right," Derrick said. "And I'm the King of England."

Sean tried to go around Julie to the right, but she cut him off, dropping her hand from Derrick's chest to keep Sean from attacking. She felt like the playground lady at recess. "Are we in fifth grade?" she barked. "Just knock it off—both of you!" She could almost smell the testosterone in the air.

Sean continued to push against Julie's palms as he looked down into her face. He held her pleading gaze for a moment before he closed his eyes, then abruptly turned and walked away.

A wicked grin formed slowly on Derrick's lips and he laughed. Julie was about to throw everyone out so she could get some sleep when Sean spun around, eyes ablaze with fury.

"You know what? I'll do it, *Derrick*," he said, spitting the name from his mouth like something foul. "Let's blow some shit up."

Eighteen

After the other two left Sean stood like a zombie, a fog of disbelief engulfing him. He'd let Derrick get under his skin and reacted without thought. He didn't know what the plan was, how it would be carried out, or even what his part in it would be.

What did I just get myself into?

Julie turned from the just-closed door with a sideways sneer across her lips. "What the hell do you think you're doing?"

Sean looked at her for a long moment. Her eyes were wild with anger, the set of her jaw an echo of her father's stricture. Unlike Jean, though, that hint of masculinity in her face only enhanced her beauty. The arguments he'd been listening to all day bounced around in his rattled brain, failing to coalesce into something decipherable. "I guess I'm going with you," he said.

"You guess?" Julie said. "We're not going to the movies, Sean. We're not going to egg someone's house or tear up a lawn. This is a big deal. You better do more than 'guess'."

Sean took a deep breath and held it, then shook his head slowly from side to side. When he finally exhaled it came out with a low grumble. "I know you don't understand. And I don't want to say it's because you're a girl, but…" his gaze fell on her, "it is. He called me out, okay?"

Julie stared at him with wide eyes, then shook her head. "Since when have you been one of those guys? One of the rock throwers, the chest pounders? Why does it matter what Derrick thinks?"

"It just does," he said, clenching his fists. "And people change. Besides, you told me how much this means to you. You heard him. If I don't come it won't happen. I don't want to be the reason for that." And if there was a little bit of rationalization in there then so be it.

Julie sat on the couch, lowering her chin to her chest and holding her head with both hands. Sean joined her and they sat in silence as the clock on the wall ticked like an impatient, tapping foot.

Without moving, Julie spoke quietly, almost under her breath. "If anything happens to you, I'll never forgive myself."

Sean reached over, put two fingers under Julie's chin and tilted her head up until her eyes met his. There were tears waiting there in the corners, yet to fall.

"You read my mind," he said.

II

Part II

One

The darkness behind the pile of lumber where they hid was in stark contrast to the brilliance of the searchlight roaming the beams of the wanna-be timeshare above. Julie pulled Sean's wrist closer to her face and eyed the numbers on his watch. Less than two minutes until this sprawling, four-story, monstrosity blew.

She tried to keep herself from shaking, but the excess adrenaline rushing through her veins, coupled with the chill from the cold concrete beneath her, conspired to induce a shudder. Sean tightened his arm around her, but she couldn't let herself relax.

What was the cop doing here anyway? They'd been careful. Derrick assured them they hadn't been followed, yet this guy had found them. A minute before, he'd started his car and the crunch of tires on gravel had let them know he'd pulled it into the yard. She hadn't wanted to risk a peek, especially once the engine abruptly cut out and the spotlight scanned the skeleton of the building again.

And where were Derrick and Jean? Had they gotten their fuse lit before that light split the night wide open? Were they hiding in the other building, waiting for the cover of explosions as well? Or had they already escaped?

Julie noticed the light had settled in one spot. Maybe the cop had left it and was approaching the building. She would go to jail before allowing an innocent man to be harmed. Placing a hand on Sean's shoulder to keep him from moving, Julie rose and peered over the top of the lumber pile. The beam shone to the left of their position, near the center of the building where the bombs awaited their six crawling sparks. The police car was an amorphous lump of shadow behind the bright light, but she heard the door creak as it opened and the silhouette of a man stepped out beyond the glare.

"He's out of the car," Julie said quietly and crouched again, next to Sean. "How much time?"

He checked his watch. "A minute fifteen."

Julie nodded and risked another look over the top of the pile. The cop was approaching the building with his flashlight on. He focused it on the slight haze of smoke that hung a few feet above the glowing fuses. She tried to estimate how long it would be before he reached the front of the structure, then had to duck down again as the flashlight beam flicked their way.

"When we're down to ten seconds we make a run for it," she whispered. "I'll yell to him to get back—that there's a bomb in the building."

"All right. Which way?"

Julie pointed west.

"Got it."

She shouldn't have let him come, but she'd been angry and he'd been so damned insistent in the end. Now that things had started going bad, though, she felt like it was her responsibility to get him out of here. The thought weighed on her as if someone had just added fifty pounds of rocks to her backpack and she tried to push it away.

* * *

Sean's thudding heart seemed determined to find its way out of his chest. Twenty seconds until their run for freedom. He felt like he should get into a track stance—maybe quick-draw a starting line in the dust on the floor since they were basically waiting for the crack of a starter's pistol. In the end he settled for rising to a crouch.

Sean was sure Derrick would find a way to blame the cop's arrival on him, but it had to be a fluke, didn't it? Most likely the guy had just been driving by and noticed the open gate. Who was it that had left the gate open anyway? Sean could swear he remembered closing it.

Behind them footsteps crunched in gravel. Sean fought the urge to rise, see what the guy was doing, and scream, "Get the hell out!"

On his watch the seconds dripped by like cold molasses, yet Sean still cringed inwardly at every change of digit, silently willing the clock to stop and speed up at the same time. *What if the fuses burn faster than Derrick thought?*

At four minutes and forty-seven seconds since Julie had lit the fuse Sean held up three fingers and began to whisper a countdown, "Three, tw—"

A series of deafening blasts cut him off. Instinct took over and he started to duck and cover, but Julie grabbed him by the arm and yanked, pulling him out of his crouch. As they took off running, Sean noted that the building was not collapsing in on them. It wasn't doing anything but standing there just as it had been.

"Get back, Officer! Get back!" Julie screamed toward the front of the building as she pulled Sean along. "There's bombs! Explosives! Get back!"

"They already went off," Sean yelled. He turned his head and caught a quick glimpse of the cop ten or twenty feet from the front of the building before the beam of the guy's flashlight swung their way. This time he turned his head before it hit him in the eye.

"Those were the other ones," Julie said.

"The other wha—"

Sean's toe caught on something and he hit the floor with a thud, slamming his hipbone on the concrete and dragging Julie down with him. Pain shot up his side as they slid to a halt, but he understood. If those explosions had been the other building—Derrick and Jean's—then—

Boom—Bah-BOOM—Blam—BAM!

Sean felt this nearly simultaneous succession of blasts deep in his chest. The thunder shook the ground and, almost immediately, splinters began raining down around them. Sean covered Julie's body with his own as echoes rolled away from them and back like ripples on a pond.

"We gotta get out of here," Julie said. She squirmed out from under him and rose to her feet.

Sean stood, too. Holding a hand on his smarting hip, he looked up at the partially completed roof, then back to the center of the structure. The six central support beams were now canted at odd angles and the rest of the framing was beginning to lean over in the direction he and Julie were headed. Jean and Derrick's building next door sat at an angle as well, but Sean was relieved to note that the cop had made it back to his patrol car. He was not so happy to see that the guy was screaming into his radio, no doubt calling for backup.

Sean turned back to Julie and was about to ask her which way she wanted to go when something overhead groaned, followed closely by a nasty, squealing pop. A second later the entire structure began to shift—an M.C. Escher painting set into sickly motion.

Sean seized Julie's wrist and bolted.

* * *

The squeak turned to a screech, splitting Julie's ears as Sean yanked her forward. The building was toppling over in the exact direction they were running. A sheet of plywood hit the floor to the right, blowing a cloud of dust in their path as splinters and nails rained down. Julie covered her head with her free arm as Sean did the same. A moment later a hardhat ricocheted off her elbow, tweaking her funny bone and bouncing off Sean's back—she barely noticed the pain.

Sean wove between posts looking for a straight shot to safety, but every time he changed directions something would hit the ground in their path and they would have to turn again.

A new groan joined the squeal, followed immediately by successive crashing explosions, reverberating like drums. Out of the corner of her left eye Julie saw a gigantic beam hit the ground ten feet away. Another twelve strides and they would be out past the side of the building. How much further they needed to go to avoid the lurching structure was anybody's guess.

Julie caught a hint of motion forward and above Sean's head and screamed, "Stop!" as she planted her heels and pulled on Sean's arm, bringing them to a halt as a twenty-by-twenty section of the floor above landed five feet in front of them. Sean held his arm over his face until the dust cleared slightly then ran straight ahead over the debris. Another beam knocked off something overhead and helicoptered to the ground a few feet away.

Tripping over the splintered edge of a shredded piece of

plywood, Julie would have gone down if it weren't for Sean's grip on her forearm, but the stumble slowed them. Sean looked back, terror on his face, and yelled, "Come on!" As Julie regained her footing they charged toward a rapidly deforming parallelogram in the outer wall that she could only hope was a door.

* * *

Sean shot forward through the mounting mounds of debris as the shifting, moaning timeshare-that-would-now-not-be crunched up against its neighbor to the west, abruptly stopping its groundward descent. A moment later a cool breeze off the lake hit him on the right side of the face as they finally passed the last beams of the exterior wall and emerged behind the next structure, which sat forward of their target and closer to the street.

Sean was about to breathe a huge sigh of relief—maybe even slow his pace slightly—when a loud snap from above was followed by an extended *wooooosh!* He glanced over his shoulder and saw a forty foot chunk of incomplete roof teetering, then slipping, off the top of the wall four stories up—and he knew they weren't going to outrun it.

A front-end loader sat fifteen feet to the right. Sean planted his left foot like a juking running back and changed direction ninety degrees, hauling Julie half off her feet. He swung her around and past him then pushed her down and under the yellow beast and dove in after. A split-second later, the huge slab of wood and shingles crashed down on the big machine with the sound of a thousand doors slamming at once.

* * *

We did it! Julie almost yelled as they passed through the collapsing wall. The next building had interrupted the other's collapse and only fifty more yards separated Sean and her from the cover of the trees— where they would be out of sight and, hopefully, home free.

But something snapped overhead and Sean made an abrupt right turn. He yanked, nearly dislocating her shoulder, and Julie stumbled forward and past him toward a huge bulldozer where he pushed her

roughly into the space beneath. She started to protest. "What the—"
was all she managed to get out before a head-splitting crash cut her
off and debris again rained down on them. As splinters and gravel
flew, Sean landed on top of her and pushed her head into the dirt,
covering her entire body with his own.

What the hell was that?

Once the roar subsided and the dust began to clear, Sean rolled
off. Julie brushed dirt from her face and hair before looking around.
The side of the bulldozer facing the building was now completely
blocked by rubble, some of it piled on the back of Sean's legs. The
machine itself lurched crookedly away from the structures. The other
side, previously clear dirt all the way to the trees, was now covered
with huge chunks of broken wood and bits of shingles.

"Holy shit," Julie said, moving to help free Sean's legs. "Are you
okay? Is anything broken?"

"I'm all right," he said. He pulled his legs out from under a few
shingles and boards then scrambled out the open side of the
bulldozer, reaching a hand down to help her crawl out.

She brushed at her clothing as she stood. "What the hell
happened?"

"Roof let go," Sean said and pointed up. "Let's get out of here."
He took Julie's hand and pulled her forward again like a rag doll
toward the tree line.

Once they were safely into the woods, Julie pulled Sean to a halt
and looked back at the destruction behind. Neither center building
had gone down completely, but they looked as though they had been
the victims of a large earthquake. The structures on either side might
have been ruined as well. Despite a slight pang of guilt, Julie wanted
to scream out in victory. Instead, she turned and kissed Sean.

"It worked," she whispered. In the darkness of the trees she had
trouble reading the emotions on Sean's face, but he had barely kissed
her back.

The squeal of approaching sirens got them moving and Julie led
the way through the woods. Though the area was unfamiliar, she
managed to find a path headed in the right direction. After a few
minutes, they emerged from the trees onto the beach and headed
west at a jog toward the silvery silhouette of Mount Tallac in the
distance. If things had gone better they would have headed east, to

rendezvous at Derrick's truck, but they had no idea where Derrick and Jean might be. She could only hope they were safe.

A couple of minutes down the beach, Sean stopped, planted his hands on his knees and asked breathlessly, "Where are we going?"

"My place," Julie said.

"Have to get past… Eldorado Beach… someone might see us," Sean said between gasps.

"Are you okay?" Julie asked.

Sean nodded but remained hunched over.

He was right, though. Highway 50 met the lake at Eldorado Beach. It would be difficult to pass there unseen if anyone was up on the highway looking for them. "You have a better idea?" Julie asked.

Sean pointed up the beach to the lights of a large building. "Yeah," he said. "I think that's my hotel."

Two

Sean flopped on the bed in his hotel room panting like a marathon runner after a sprint finish. As he rolled onto his back, he tried to remember how long it took the body to acclimate to high altitude. It was something like three weeks, wasn't it? No wonder he was still suffering after only two and a half days.

They'd left the lights off when they came in through the sliding glass door from the beach and Julie had pulled the desk chair over so she could sit and keep a lookout through a slit in the curtains. It sounded like her breathing had already returned to normal. "I don't see anyone out there," she said.

"I don't think we were followed," Sean said. All he could make out in the gloom was Julie's silhouette as she turned away from the door and faced him. The latest shot of adrenaline was fading quickly from his veins, fatigue settling in.

"You saved my life," Julie said. "Again."

"I don't know about that…"

"You did. No need to be modest."

"I was in just as much danger as you. I did what anyone else would have."

"You need to stop that. Saving me. I never even paid you back for last time."

"I have to stop…?" Sean trailed off more from exasperation than a lack of air. "Julie, we both nearly died back there. Who knows what happened to Derrick and Jean. And to top it off we're now wanted by the law. I thought this wasn't supposed to be dangerous?"

"I know, I know," she said, standing and pacing over to the TV. Even in the dark Sean could see her running a hand over her head as she turned back. "That wasn't how it was supposed to happen."

He sat up. "It never is, is it?"

"What's that supposed to mean?"

"It means you always manage to get yourself into trouble somehow. I wish—just once—I could get you to listen to reason."

"You know, I've been doing fine by myself all these years. And you didn't have to come with, Sean. I tried to keep you out of it."

"I tried to keep you out of it, too," Sean said as he stood, a little unsteady at first. "But I was constantly assured by everyone involved that it was no big deal, that we would be out of harm's way well before the bombs went off. Not to mention your good friend Derrick calling me chicken."

"You didn't have to give in, Sean. I told you flat out to go back to your hotel."

"Then what would have happened? Would Derrick have saved you? Would Jean?"

It was impossible to see Julie's expression in the dark of the hotel room, but Sean could still read posture. Her stance shifted, one leg stiff, the other out in front of her, arms crossed. "Maybe that damn gate would have stayed closed," she said.

"You're blaming me for the gate? I latched it. I told you that."

"You're sure?"

Sean was astounded she was actually grilling him about this. "Yeah. I'm sure."

Julie stomped away to the hall door. On the carpeted, concrete floor Sean heard only muffled thuds. "You have to understand that I have my own life here, okay? I'm not the same person you used to know. I *can* actually take care of myself now."

Sean breathed out his anger with a heavy sigh. It was like all the residual energy in his body left with it. His knees buckled and he sat back down on the bed. "Julie," he said. "All I've ever tried to do is keep you safe."

When she spoke again her words warbled, like she was holding back tears. "I'm an adult, Sean. It's not your job to keep me safe."

He could barely see her where she hid in the shadows by the bathroom. "Maybe it's not my job," he said, "but it could be, like... my hobby or something."

* *

Grinning through the tears streaming down her cheeks, Julie walked over, sat down next to Sean and kissed him. Emotions careened around inside her like lottery balls in a drum. Rage, exhilaration, fear, delight. Was there anyone else on the planet who could have her enraged and gnashing her teeth one moment then weeping with joy the next?

Out of the cacophony in her head a decision emerged fully formed.

I will tell him tonight.

She pulled back. Head tilted to one side, she looked him in the eye and allowed the thought to percolate. Yes, she would tell him tonight.

Not quite yet, though.

"Give me a minute," she said, then rose and walked away to the bathroom door. "I need to use the little ladies room." Closing the door behind her, she closed her eyes, flipped on the light and waited for her eyes to adjust to the brightness. When she could finally look at herself in the mirror, she thanked whatever gods there might be that they had kept it dark in the rest of the room. Except for the white trails of tears down her cheeks she was so covered with dirt she could have been in blackface.

Why am I such an idiot?

The unwelcome thought came out of nowhere. Maybe it was the stress of the long day talking. Still, she couldn't fathom how it had come to pass that Sean had saved her yet again. If she was still a believing Christian she might have concluded he was her guardian angel, sent down to Earth to protect her. But if that were true, where had he been back on that other fateful night.

Julie turned the water on and washed her hands. She was about to splash some on her face when she realized that would be like trying to hose off a muddy driveway with a squirt gun. Straightening up, she surveyed her clothing while the water continued to run down the drain. Her jeans were smeared with dirt and her sweatshirt looked like it had lain in the road for a week. What she really needed was a shower.

Suddenly it was all too much to think about and a heavy drape of exhaustion fell over her. She turned off the faucet, sat on the closed lid of the toilet and shook her hair from the ponytail she'd had it in all night. The spatter of dust and debris that hit the bathroom floor drew a weary exhale from her lungs.

"Sean?" she called through the closed door. "Do you have any clothes I can wear?" She couldn't see how she was going to get home in the morning in these things without drawing attention to herself. And waiting until morning seemed the only sensible thing to do.

"Uh... maybe," Sean said. "I have some sweats that might work."

"I'm going to take a quick shower then."

Under the stream of hot water Julie's resolve melted away. *What if he doesn't understand? Things are going okay, right? Telling him now might screw that up. Remember how bad it got at the café?*

She knew the two of them could only go so far without him knowing, but could she muster the courage to tell him on a night like tonight when she was physically and emotionally drained? Sean had proven to be the same great guy he was thirteen years ago—and so much more. Being friends with her love interest made much more sense to her these days than it had back then, but the quickness of her feelings and the whirlwind of the past eighteen hours was a little too much like a fairy tale—albeit a slightly twisted one. If she told him the reason she'd stopped writing the whole charade might come crashing down around her just like that damned timeshare.

All the sane voices in her head said that Sean would understand. But there was another one, tickling the back of her mind, that said he wouldn't. It was the same one that had kept her from dating him back then. The same one that always told her she wasn't good enough. Recently, Julie had begun to suspect it was her father's voice. Now it tried to cut through the din in her head to convince her that Sean would reject her if he knew. That he'd toss her right out into the night, like he'd done once before, and she would have to duck her head and walk home alone in her muddy jeans.

Three

◀

In the dark of the upstairs hallway Julie treads lightly, trying not to wake anyone. The five days that have passed since her father's death have been some of the worst of her life. Now that the funeral is over, though, she feels a bit lost. With all the preparations, things hadn't seemed quite real until the coffin had actually been lowered into the cold, hard ground.

After the prolonged, post-funeral gathering of family and friends had finally broken up around eight p.m., she'd slipped away to her room to change clothes. When she stretched out on her bed for what was supposed to be a few moments, six hours had passed before she woke. A few minutes ago, as she slipped out of her now-wrinkled dress and into her nightshirt, she couldn't even remember falling asleep.

Now it's two-thirty on this icy January morning and she feels like a bonehead for leaving Sean alone with her mother and sisters. Before Julie went to her room they had talked about Sean sleeping on the couch, or possibly in the rec-room, but no decision had been made. He'd driven all the way from Southern California on Christmas break from his sophomore year at USC to be here and she doesn't even know where in her own house to find him.

She pauses on the stairs as the third from the top creaks loudly under her weight. She's used to sneaking up the stairs in the dark when she comes in late, but doesn't usually worry about it in this direction. She places her sock-clad feet carefully the rest of the way down then pads silently across the wood floor to the living room. The couch is unoccupied.

Exiting the living room through the far door, Julie loops around the rear of the house to the kitchen. She opens the refrigerator and peers inside to see if there are any leftovers. Pushing aside a plate of cold cuts and one full of veggies, she finds half a bottle of pink wine and a couple cans of beer. For a moment she considers what her father will do if he finds out she's taken them. Then she remembers he's gone and emptiness pours into her gut like molten lead. She grits her teeth together to keep the tears at bay. Snatching the bottle and cans, she turns and heads toward the stairs to the rec-room.

The house sits on a steep hill that falls away to the rear of the lot so, essentially, the rec-room is a basement—even though there are full size windows on three sides and a deck on the back that sits ten feet off the ground. Past the pool table, Sean is asleep under a pile of blankets on the old sofa.

Julie sets the beer on the trunk that serves as a coffee table and sits in the green chair next to couch with her legs curled up under her. She works the cork out of the wine bottle and takes a long swallow. She prefers wine coolers, but wine is probably better tonight since it's more potent.

Out a side window she watches the huge three-quarter moon rising. It sits barely off the horizon and she can make out its entire circumference, the darker portion a lighter shade of gray than the black sky behind it. There seems to be a revelation stirring somewhere deep in her mind, a wisp of thought she can't quite grasp. When Sean suddenly grunts and sits up it drifts off into her inner stratosphere.

"Wha...?" he mumbles, rubbing at his eyes, then falls back on the cushions. "What are you doing down here?"

Julie sips her wine. "I brought you some beer."

"Beer? What time is it?"

"Around three, I think... I'm sorry I bailed on you."

Sean pulls himself back to a seated position on the couch. Kicking his feet free from the blankets, he grabs a beer from the trunk. "You're mom said you were sleeping." The can cracks open with a hiss.

"Yeah, in my dress. I don't know what happened. I guess I passed out."

"Hard day."

"Yeah."

They sit and drink and watch the moon in silence. The silvery light streaming through the window illuminates the room better than any nightlight would.

When Julie starts to feel a little cold she stands and moves around the trunk to the far end of the couch where she can get under some of Sean's blankets. She polishes off the last of the wine, setting the bottle on the floor next to her, then slides under the covers and leans back against the arm of the couch. The alcohol warms her stomach like freshly lit kindling in a wood stove as she crosses her legs Indian style under her and bumps a knee against Sean's thigh.

* *

Sean's eyes follow Julie's bare legs as she passes in front of him, her nightshirt barely making it a quarter of the way down her thighs. Once she slips under the blankets, he can feel the warmth of her bare skin as her knee touches his thigh.

"How come you're always here for me when I never am for you?" Julie says quietly, her eyes glistening in the moonlight.

Sean holds her gaze for a moment before he moves his eyes back to the window. "I don't know," he says and guns a bit more of his beer. "I guess because I care about you."

Julie lowers her head and lets her hair flop over her face. "I care about you, too," she says.

Sean would have chosen a better time to discuss their relationship if he could, since Julie had just buried her father earlier in the day. Keeping those thoughts to himself, he polishes off his beer and crunches the can in his fist. He comes close to throwing it across the room before leaning forward and placing it gingerly on the trunk.

Julie pushes her hair from her face. Her eyes flit to the crushed can then back to Sean. He holds his jaw tightly clenched and looks away as he falls back against the cushions. "I'm sorry I haven't been able to come visit you," she says. She pivots under the blankets and moves closer, her right knee coming to rest on top of his left thigh. A moment later she sets her hand there as well.

Sean barely controls an urge to squirm. "It's okay," he croaks and clears his throat. If she moves her hand a few inches to the right, she'll find out what kind of effect this is all having on him.

"It's not okay." Julie says, turning a bit more in his direction as she squeezes his leg with her fingers. "You need to just get mad at me sometimes." With her left hand she touches his chin and turns his face to hers. "Because I need to stop treating you like you'll always be waiting around for me." Then she leans in to kiss him.

Her lips touch his and Sean pulls back violently. "What are you doing?" he says.

The whites of her eyes glare in the moonlight. "Isn't this what you want?"

"I—I…"

Of course it's what he wants. He's wanted it for what seems like forever. But the place where it might end up scares him and this certainly doesn't seem like the right time. "Julie," he says as he slides out from under the covers and moves awkwardly to the chair, "I don't think—" He clears his throat again. "This isn't a good idea right now, is it?"

"Why not? I love you, Sean."

"W-well, for one," Sean says, "you have a boyfriend."

"He's an asshole," Julie says, her eyes on a frayed corner of the blanket she has begun fiddling with.

Sean ignores the comment. "And you just lost your dad."

Julie closes her eyes and turns away, burying her face in the covers. "I don't think I can cry anymore," she says, the soft fabric muffling her voice.

Sean moves back to the couch and wraps his arms around her, the blankets between them now. Julie shakes with huge wracking sobs as the anguish pushes its way out once more, but all he can think is: *What is wrong with me?*

*

Julie is lost. She's been lost for days. An empty shell, she needs to be filled with something—anything. As she climbs the stairs back to her room she realizes that, just to be held, she would have thrown herself at whatever guy might have been around. But at some point near the end of that bottle of wine she'd forgotten that Sean would hold her without expecting more. She'd nearly ruined everything. And if he hadn't stopped her…

Where might that have ended?

She closes her bedroom door behind her and stands for a moment in the dark. The bed beckons, but she doesn't think she'll be able to sleep. Instead, she walks to her desk and flips on the lamp. She wants to get her feelings down on paper—the things she'd been unable to find words for downstairs.

Opening her notebook to a fresh page, Julie writes, "Sean," at the top, but no other words seem forthcoming. She closes her eyes, tries to think how to put it, how to get her soul onto the page. She sits for a long while before she ferrets out the problem: she's trying to find a way to say this to Sean like he's standing right in front of her, like she can't take it back once it's out there. There is no reason to think like that since she can ball up the paper and toss it in the trash if she doesn't like it. With this thought in mind, the words pour onto the paper as if she's opened a vein and needs to get everything down before the last drop of blood runs out.

When she finishes, a smile graces her lips even as tears roll down her cheeks. She reads over what she's written, figuring she'll toss the sheets in the trash now that the catharsis has passed, but it all makes so much sense. She doesn't understand why she didn't see it sooner. Maybe she'll give it to him after all.

*

Standing in the road outside the driver's door of Sean's car, Julie keeps her hands stuffed in the pass-through front pocket of her sweatshirt. Sean sits behind the wheel with the window down, engine running. Breakfast had been an extended tug-of-war between tension and silence, both of them still reeling from the previous night.

"Have a safe trip," Julie says.

"Will do," he replies. "Oh, and, uh… thanks for letting me crash here."

Julie fingers the envelope in her hand, hidden in the pocket where Sean can't see it. "I, umm… I wrote you something last night," she says, looking away over the roof of the car.

"Oookay. What's it say?"

Everything, she doesn't tell him. *All of it.*

Sean revs the engine and Julie looks back at him. His eyes squint into the winter sun, but are no less intense for it. She takes her hands from the pocket, empty.

"I don't know," she says. "Lots of stuff."

"When do I get to read it?"

Putting one hand back in her pocket, Julie closes her eyes and tries to dredge up enough courage to put herself that far out there. She runs a finger back and forth along the edge of the envelope until it feels like it might break the skin. After a long moment she sighs, opening her eyes and looking up the street. "Not yet."

Sean sighs, too, turning his attention to the road ahead. He revs the engine again.

"Call me and let me know you got there, okay," Julie says.

"Yeah. Sure."

Julie leans into the car and plants a kiss on his cheek. "Thank you," she says.

"For what?"

"For knowing better than I do what's good for me."

Sean shakes his head slowly from side to side. "Julie Thompson," he says and shifts the car into drive. "Take care of yourself." Then he accelerates away, down the street.

"Bye," Julie says. She stands in the street, lost in a new world like Jack at the top of his beanstalk. Pulling the envelope from her pocket, she looks down at Sean's name writ in large, swirly letters on the front.

She wonders if she'll ever have the courage.

▶

Four

When Julie finally pried her eyes open the clock read ten fifteen. Sean slept peacefully next to her, his arm under her head. She vaguely recalled falling asleep cuddled up to him, but was surprised they hadn't rolled away from each other during the night.

In the end, she didn't have the nerve to tell him. They'd flopped down on the bed when she came out of the bathroom and that was about all they had the energy for. Now it was morning—late morning at that.

Julie slipped quietly from the bed and stumbled to the bathroom, pulling the T-shirt of Sean's she had borrowed down to cover her panties along the way. When she emerged a few minutes later Sean had rolled over on his side and begun snoring. She didn't want to wake him, but she needed to get to her studio for a one o'clock class and she couldn't just leave.

Sitting gingerly on the edge of the bed next to him, she tuned the clock/radio on the nightstand to the local FM station, wondering if there would be any news about last night's events. The sound of the announcer caused Sean to stir, then grunt and open his eyes.

"Morning, sleepyhead," Julie said.

"Huh?" he moaned. Turning away, he stretched his arms over his head. "What time is it."

"Ten thirty," Julie said.

"Why am I so damn tired then?"

"We didn't get to sleep 'til almost five."

"Ahh."

While she waited for Sean to get ready, Julie pulled on the sweatpants he'd loaned her, dug the walkie-talkie from her pack and turned it on. She sat in the chair by the door and tried to raise Derrick a few times with no luck. On the radio a "Rock Block" that didn't really rock stretched out toward infinity as Julie's gaze fell across the vast expanse of sparkling, blue water between her and the North Shore. A breeze had kicked up some whitecaps on the surface and she found that her mood was in the process of realigning with the rhythm of the lake: she felt unsettled, too.

Though this was a small room, Julie knew any place with a lake view and beach access would be expensive—especially this time of year. One thought led to another and she found herself wondering how much money Sean might have and how, if he was currently unemployed, he could afford this place. She *was* still guessing about his job and he, of course, was still in the dark about what went wrong thirteen years ago—

That thought jolted Julie's gold-digging train of thought squarely onto the relationship track. Another direction she didn't really want to be heading. There were so many things the two of them needed to get out in the open soon or this relationship would be as doomed as it had been in the past.

The previous night remained in her head more like a vivid dream than actuality. She felt like she needed to verify her own memories with Sean's to make sure she hadn't imagined it all. Just thinking about escaping from that falling skeleton of a building pushed her heart rate up. As she tried the two-way one more time she wondered what had happened to Derrick and Jean and whether or not the cops were looking for her and Sean.

Sean came out of the bathroom. "Do you think it's a good idea to be seen out and about today? I mean, what if they're looking for us?" he said, echoing her thoughts.

Julie turned halfway in the chair to face him. "It might look worse if I don't show up at my studio. I can't imagine that cop saw enough to identify us and I don't want to leave my students hanging like that." As she finished speaking, the music on the radio—The Moody Blues *Knights in White Satin*—mercifully wound down and the announcer came on with the news:

> *"The Big Story this morning is the apparent bombing of the unfinished South Tahoe Beach Resort being erected by Eagle Development. While still under investigation, police report that the perpetrators apparently used strategically placed pipe bombs to*

undermine the structures. No one was injured in the blasts, but the two central buildings have been completely destroyed and neighboring structures sustained extensive damage.

"Two people dressed in black were reported fleeing the scene as the explosions occurred around 3:30 AM this morning. Sources indicate the action may have been politically motivated and an initial estimate of the cost of the destruction is upwards of two million dollars. General Manager of Eagle Development, Harold Payne, has offered a $10,000 reward for information leading to the arrest and conviction of, in his words, 'the cowards responsible for this reprehensible act of terrorism.'

"In other news—"

Sean clicked the radio off and sat on the edge of the bed. "Wow," he said, staring into space. "I finally made the news."

Julie jumped to her feet. "This is great! Do you know what this means?"

The stunned look on Sean's face changed to confusion. "The cops should be here any minute?"

She sighed. "Come on, you heard him. They're only looking for two people."

"It was us that cop saw." Sean shrugged. "It's you and me they're looking for."

"How could he have identified us from that distance? He might know it was a man and a woman, but there's no way he could have seen us that well in the dark. Plus, there were bombs going off."

Sean narrowed his eyes. "What if the police are holding back information? What if they know who we are, but don't want to let the press know they know it?"

Julie jumped on the bed, tackling Sean as she went. "Now you're just being paranoid," she said and kissed him.

A few minutes later, she pulled herself off Sean and rolled away. She went back to the door and peered out at the lake as she caught her breath and let the flutter in her chest subside. To fill the sudden, roaring silence she said, "How can you afford this place?" and immediately regretted it.

Sean didn't answer right away and Julie resisted the urge to turn and look at him. "I have some investments," he said finally.

"Uh huh," she said, turning and trying to sound playful. "And what about your job?"

"Sabbatical... Remember?"

"You know you're a really bad liar, right?"

Sean shrugged as he sat up on the edge of the bed and looked at the floor, elbows on knees. "I'm not lying," he said. "Not a hundred percent anyway."

Julie let his words hang in the air. If he wasn't going to tell her, he wasn't and that was that.

After a minute or more Sean finally spoke. "I had a little software company that was doing pretty well until a couple years ago," he said as he picked at his cuticles.

"You mean it was *your* company?" Julie asked. "You owned it?"

"Basically," Sean said. "I had a partner. We started in a good niche market with a home fax program I wrote, then expanded from there into other utilities."

"Wow," Julie said. "I didn't realize you were such a Big Businessman."

"Well... I wasn't so much. I mean, I learned as we went along, but it was my partner who handled most of the business end. I took care of the technical stuff."

Julie nodded, urging him along even though he wasn't looking at her.

"I was smart enough to realize that I didn't know how to run a company so I got together with him. He was a business major. I guess I wasn't smart enough to pick someone with scruples, though. He screwed me and everyone else who worked for us. Pilfered at least five and a half million over six years by cooking the books. I never even had a clue until the payroll checks started bouncing. We ended up in Chapter 11 and I had to jump through hoops to prove I didn't know anything about it. In the end, the powers-that-be were nice enough to let me keep a little of the money I saved."

"So where's your partner now?"

"Eddie?" Sean said, looking up at Julie for the first time since he'd started his tale. "He's in prison doing a whopping four to six for embezzlement—and that's only because I testified against him. Probably wouldn't have gotten a conviction otherwise."

"I'm sorry, Sean," Julie said. She went to the bed and sat next to him, rubbing a palm along his back. "Where did you find this guy?"

"We were roommates junior year—it's not like he just walked in off the street for an interview. He was a friend and he stabbed me in the back for money, so I sent him to jail. What are friends for, right?" Sean stood up and retrieved his jacket from a hook in the corner. "We should get going, huh?"

"Yeah," Julie said.

*   *

Sean breathed easier now that he'd come clean with Julie. He did wonder, though, when she might reciprocate and let him in on her big secret.

As they walked out to the parking lot, he was surprised how much the whole thing with Eddie still hurt. He hadn't thought about it for a while—at least since he left LA—and now that white-hot rage was beginning to fester in his chest again. The knowledge that Eddie was paying for what he did didn't help much—they'd been buds. What he still didn't get, and probably never would, was how anyone could screw over someone they supposedly cared about for nothing more than money.

Sean was glad they had dropped his truck off last night on the way to their mis-deeds. Walking along Highway 50 to get it back would have been more exposure than he could've taken this morning. After they were both belted in Julie asked, "So what do you think you want to do now? Work-wise?"

"I don't know. I haven't been doing much of anything for months. My motivation has been lacking." He backed the big Chevy out of the parking space and put it in drive, rolling toward the street and keeping an eye out for anything resembling a cop car.

"Remember in high school when you wanted to be a rock star?" Julie asked with a giggle.

"Oh God, don't remind me."

"Why not? You weren't half bad," Julie said and punched him lightly on the arm. "Some of the lyrics you wrote were great! Do you still play?"

"I haven't picked up a guitar since college," Sean said as he pulled out of the hotel lot onto Lake Tahoe Boulevard.

"Well, I still remember that one song—what was it? Something about so-called 'Progress' killing the planet."

Sean shook his head, disbelieving. "How is it you remember that? You know it was horrible."

"It was not. It had a great message."

"Maybe. If I had a backing band or something."

"I suppose…" Julie drifted off and watched the lake out the window as they passed by Eldorado Beach. Sean put his turn signal on for the right onto Lakeview and slowed for the traffic light. He watched the rearview as they turned to see if anyone followed. No one did.

A little way down Lakeview, Julie spoke again. "Maybe you could get into something a little more green than software design is what I was getting at." She turned back to face him. "I mean, you're a radical environmentalist now."

"Whoa," Sean said holding his hands up off the wheel for a moment. "Don't go putting labels on me, Little Lady."

"Well, you did blow up a building."

"Technically, we blew up a construction site."

Julie laughed. "Yeah, well, whatever helps you sleep at night I guess."

"Hey, come on now."

"You're in a state of denial, aren't you?"

"No, I'm still in the great state of California." Sean turned into the parking lot of Julie's complex and headed toward her building, pulling up by the stairs to her unit.

Julie reached out and put a hand on Sean's where it rested on the seat between them. "We did a good thing, Sean," she said. "It's got to make a difference."

Sean stared straight ahead, feeling the heat of Julie's palm on the back of his hand. Yesterday morning in the café that hand had been stethoscope cold and he had recoiled from it. Now he flipped his hand under hers and returned the embrace, smiling in her direction. He hoped she was right—not only for her own sake, but for his as well. He didn't want to live the rest of his life knowing he'd committed a felony for no other reason than to show Derrick Masterson he wasn't chicken.

Five

Julie sat in the small office of her Yoga studio trying to clear her desk—and her head. The room was more of a closet, really, stuffed in a corner behind the front counter. The whole studio consisted of one large room for classes, a small entry foyer, a tiny little bathroom and the office. But at least it was all hers.

Her one o'clock class had finished a few minutes before and she had half an hour until the next one. Her entire body felt loose and quiet as she let herself sink into the chair. Physically, she was more relaxed than she'd been in days—if only she could get her mind on the same level. Her thoughts continually returned to Sean no matter what direction she tried to push them. She felt like a teenager. They'd been apart just a few hours and she missed him like the desert missed water. Maybe she should call him... just to say, "Hi!" She could make up something about how she'd forgotten what time they said for dinner.

Julie was digging through her bag looking for Sean's number when the bell above the front entrance jingled. She leaned back in her chair and saw Derrick approaching the counter. She wondered how he'd known she would be here before remembering she had class schedules posted all over town.

"I'm in here," Julie called as she found Sean's number and placed it by the phone. She had tried to call both Derrick and Jean before leaving her apartment and had gotten no answer from either.

Derrick's face appeared in the doorway. "Hey, I'm glad I caught you," he said. "Got a minute?"

"Hey," Julie echoed, jumping up. "You're okay!" She gave him a quick little hug.

"Yeah," Derrick said, "I'm here."

Julie stepped back as far as she could in the cramped office. "We did it," she said.

Derrick lowered his voice slightly. "Yeah, we did. It came down pretty well." His face showed no satisfaction.

Julie wondered why he wasn't happier. "Where's Jean?" she asked.

"Don't know." Derrick glanced behind him at the main door. "Probably home."

Julie grabbed his shoulders and shook him slightly. "What's wrong with you? We did it? Show me some emotion."

Derrick frowned, pivoted away. "They're looking for me," he said.

"Who's looking for you?"

He turned back, one eyebrow raised. "The law, who else?"

"Why?" Julie said, taking a moment to digest the information. "How could—"

"They know my affiliations, Julie. They also know my public stance on the project. And they know how I feel about Eagle." Derrick shook his head.

"So what? None of that proves anything. Just talk to them and tell them you had nothing to do with it."

"I would, but..."

"But what?"

Derrick sighed. "I can't be sure that cop didn't get a look at me."

Julie thought for a moment. She was pretty sure the two people who had been spotted were her and Sean and she said so.

"We can't be sure of that. They might be reporting that just to mislead the public. We have to operate on the possibility that all four of us were seen."

Julie pushed some hair back behind an ear and exhaled. "So what? You're going to run?"

"Let's just say that I feel like I should disappear for a while."

"That seems stupid at this point, Derrick. We don't really know anything."

"You might want to consider coming with me," he said, ignoring her comment.

She frowned. "What?"

"Your public comments at last night's meeting showed strong opposition to Eagle's plans—not to mention that you assaulted a councilmember afterwards."

Julie shot Derrick a sidelong look that could have singed hair before she turned to face him full on. "How do you know about that?"

"I know a lot of things, Julie. Not the least of which is that they will be looking for you very soon as well."

Julie held Derrick's gaze for a moment, trying to discern what was different in his eyes. She didn't know what it was, but something had definitely changed between the two of them. She narrowed her own eyes slightly before saying, "I'm not going anywhere, Derrick, and neither should you." She pulled her chair out and sat down, arms crossed. "I'll just talk to them when they show up. I don't believe they've got anything on us."

Derrick ground his teeth. "Well, I'm getting out of town regardless. Do whatever the hell you want." He walked back around the reception desk then turned. "Oh, and you might want to rethink your relationship with your little lover-boy there. Something doesn't smell right with him."

Julie sprung from her chair and through the office door. "What's that supposed to mean?" she said, hands gripping the counter's edge.

"It means you should distance yourself from him until this blows over. His allegiance is highly suspect at this point."

Julie started around the counter. "His allegiance? Derrick, what the hell do you know? Is Sean in danger?

"What? No…" He broke eye contact, spun away, then shook his head before turning back. "I just don't trust him. If the cops get a hold of him, he'll spill the beans in a second."

Julie had never seen Derrick look so frazzled. She had the feeling he was lying about something. "Why would the cops get a hold of Sean?" Julie said slowly. "No one but me, you and Jean even knows he's in town."

Derrick ran a hand through his hair. "Look they probably won't, but they might find him through you. Especially if he's *with* you."

The bell above the front door jingled and Derrick whirled around. The muscles in Julie's upper-neck and back tensed as she raised her eyes and saw it was only Mary Ellen—one of her regulars—with a Yoga mat under one arm. Julie relaxed, but Derrick still looked edgy. For some reason, Julie wondered if he was carrying a gun. She put the thought out of her head as soon as it occurred. This was Derrick, after all, not Ted Kaczynski.

"Hey," Mary Ellen said.

"Hi," Julie replied. "Go ahead in. I'll be there in a couple minutes." The woman smiled and walked into the studio. Julie faced Derrick as she said in a lowered voice, "I think you need to keep your damn nose out of my personal life."

Derrick sighed as he went to the door. "If you kept your personal life from affecting mine, we wouldn't have a problem."

Julie slapped a palm down on the counter and barked, "Damn it, Derrick. Sean is none of your business."

"We'll see," he said and opened the door.

"No, we will not see," Julie said through clenched teeth. She was sick and tired of all the male territorial bullshit. She and Derrick had never even been on a date, why would he think he had any claim on her what-so-ever? "Sean will be fine. Leave him alone."

"Whatever. Look, I've got to get out of here. I'm leaving tonight. If you want to come, meet me at the peanut bar at nine."

"I told you—I'm not leaving."

Derrick looked her up and down. "Fine," he said. "I'll be in touch." Then he was gone and the door swung shut behind him with a *whoomp*.

Julie went back into her office and sat, trying to slow her breathing and relax into a more Yoga-like mood, but it was hopeless. Her anger at Derrick simmered just below the surface, refusing to be quelled.

Six

Sean had wanted to get something to eat before dropping Julie off, but she was in a hurry so they'd agreed to meet for dinner later. He drove back toward his hotel feeling like the bubble he'd been living in since the previous morning had popped. Was he really involved with the girl who'd strung him along for four years back in high school and college like a kitten after a ball of yarn? The idea was absurd. That it had actually happened? Surreal.

Julie was great, of course, but they were both felons now. This whole ordeal had left Sean's brains mixed up like one of James Bond's martinis—shaken not stirred. Still, there was a warm feeling stirring deep down that his worries couldn't suppress.

I made out with Julie Thompson!

He couldn't wait to tell his friends. It took him a moment to realize he didn't have any—and that he was thirty-three years old, not thirteen.

The thought reminded him that the three people he was with the previous night at the timeshare were the only ones who knew he was in town, other than any number of anonymous service workers he'd interacted with. It was an empty feeling, but also freeing. If no one knew he was here, how could the authorities possibly be looking for him? With a fresh new outlook on the situation, Sean drove right past his hotel and on toward Stateline. He could just barely make out the tops of the remaining South Tahoe Beach Resort buildings above the trees as he passed by, but he resisted the urge to turn down the road leading to the development. He saw no point in tempting fate by returning to the scene of the crime.

The west side of town had actually changed very little while he'd been away. The business names might have been different, but they mostly occupied the same buildings that had been there in his youth.

It was at Ski Run Boulevard where you began noticing a transformation: a large timeshare resort had displaced a gas station and fast food joint and, further down the road on the right, a number of old motel sites had been turned into a park. But it wasn't until after Pioneer Trail, heading east, that the difference really made itself known. There, a massive Marriott timeshare complex and the new Heavenly Gondola had supplanted the row of low budget motels and shops that used to line the south side of the road. The opposite side was under construction, probably to eventually mirror the same image it faced.

Crossing into Nevada was another step back in time. Harvey's and Harrah's casinos turned the first two hundred yards of the Silver State into a Wall Street-like mirage to be outrun as quickly as possible. But the other two big casinos had definitely changed: Caesar's Tahoe into Montbleu and The Horizon to the Hard Rock. The Friday's Station property—a large, undeveloped land holding and an old stop on the Pony Express—still spread up the hillside between the casinos and Kingsbury Grade, lording over Edgewood golf course across the road like a smug, older brother.

Sean turned right onto Lake Parkway and looped around behind the casinos, back toward California. Just across the state line, gondola cars crossed conspicuously back and forth thirty feet above the road and the Forest Inn. The town had finally connected Heavenly ski area with the casino corridor like they'd talked about doing for years.

Continuing along Montreal Road, Sean passed behind the Crescent V Shopping Center that had been remodeled and renamed The Village Center. As he turned onto Rocky Point Road he finally realized he had a destination in mind. He followed the winding road up the hill, telling himself that he just wanted to check out the view. Of course, from what Julie had said about development around here, it was quite possible that the whole place had been paved over by a huge timeshare or some rich guy's ten thousand square foot mansion.

When he came to the stop sign at Keller he turned left and accelerated up the steep incline, noting, as he made another left onto Saddle Road, that Heavenly's California base had seen some updating. The number of houses lining the street seemed about the same and, as he arrived at the bend where the road began to loop back on itself, he saw that the area looked much as he remembered it.

He wondered if Julie had been back up here since that night—he knew he hadn't.

After parking his truck in the dead-end dirt road by a 'No Parking' sign, Sean walked out the wide path into the woods. The scattering of glass from broken bottles that littered the ground told him that the Rock still received plenty of partying visitors. After skirting the open area where the bonfire was that night, Sean wasted no time scrambling up and over boulders to the top.

The view of the basin was amazing and he found a comfortable place to sit where he could enjoy it. The casinos at Stateline, eighteen story behemoths that had towered above him only minutes before, now looked like children's toys. The new Gondola threaded its way through the trees to the right. All that was missing was a toy train. The lake—that vast expanse of shimmering blue, ringed by soaring, tree-covered peaks—remained the same.

Behind him was the spot where he'd found Julie. Now free of snow, of course. He did the calculation in his head and came up with fifteen years since he and Glenn had carried her limp body from this place. She likely would have died had they not. Last night he'd acted on pure instinct when he threw her under that front end loader at the last moment. He had followed that same instinct during the drive to the hospital back then. Afterward, he'd been just as surprised as everyone else that they'd gotten there in one piece.

There was a time a few years back when a work acquaintance had talked Sean into going rock climbing. The guy hadn't been wearing a helmet and took a fall, knocking himself out. Sean panicked. They were two miles from the car and he could think of nothing to do but sit there and slap his buddy's face until he came to. Luckily, he'd been okay. Afterwards Sean felt like an idiot—he'd frozen. What was it about Julie that put him in the zone in trying circumstances? And why did it also seem like the occurrence of said circumstances seemed to increase exponentially whenever he was around her?

Again, Sean found himself trying to untangle the present day Julie from the perfected memory he held in his head from years ago. It seemed to him that fulfilling an old, unrequited love required—at least in some way—looking at the other person as they had once been. And that's what he was doing, wasn't it? Playing out that unrealized teenage fantasy he'd never really given up on: dating the unattainable Julie Thompson?

Sean shook his head, disgusted with himself. Julie was an amazing, beautiful and complex woman in the present. He needed to accept her for who she was now and stop worrying so damn much about the girl she'd been in the past. That was a little harder to do since she still hadn't come clean about why she'd dropped off the face of the Earth, but he would find out about that sooner or later— he knew he would.

Sean looked at his watch. It was after two o'clock and he hadn't eaten yet. He rose from his perch, stretched and tried for a moment to enjoy the view without worrying about Julie, but she seemed to be stuck in his head for good.

*

After a nice lunch at a place called Freshie's, Sean parked back at his hotel and went for a walk on the beach. He thought about how he and Julie had fled in the other direction only twelve hours before and wondered if he maybe shouldn't be out this way. He saw no evidence of law enforcement though, so he continued on to the Pier at Timber Cove. At the end, five hundred feet out and above the water, Sean stood inhaling the fresh mountain air and facing the lake as if he rode on the bow of a ship. How had he managed to stay away from this place for so long?

On his way back down the pier, he stopped in the gift shop and wandered like a tourist, thinking it might be funny to buy something for Julie before he realized she would probably chide him for supporting child labor in Indonesia or some such thing. On his way out empty handed, the guy behind the rental counter caught his eye.

"Glenn?" Sean said. "Is that you?"

The guy looked at him for a moment, puzzled, before realization bloomed on his face. "Holy shit, dude. Sean Connors? No fuckin' way!" He came around the counter and shook Sean's hand like a whip, then gave that up and grabbed him in a crushing hug.

Glenn wore no shirt, just long baggy shorts, and his chest was tanned and toned like a body builder's. His blond hair still hung down around his shoulders and he smelled of marijuana smoke. "Where the fuck you been, man? I haven't seen you in fuckin' years. I figured you were dead."

"Nah," Sean said. "Not dead. Just down in LA."

"Same fuckin' thing, right?" Glenn said, knocking his head back and releasing a good loud laugh. "What the fuck you been up to, man?"

"Ah, you know, making a living, that kinda shit. What about you? You been here this whole time?"

"Mostly. Couple a years in Santa Cruz, surfin' and divin's about it. Tahoe's my home, man. Always will be."

"So you work here, or what?"

"Sorta... yeah," Glenn said and leaned in a little closer. "I kinda own the rental business here, man. Got a couple other places, too."

"No shit? That's great." Sean had been expecting that Glenn was working the rental counter for eight bucks an hour and sleeping in tent from the way he presented. "What do you rent?"

"Boats, jet skis, kayaks, canoes. I even got a guy who teaches scuba. You can rent the tanks and shit, too, if you got a card. Hey, you wanna go? If you never been down thirty or forty feet in Tahoe, you don't know what you're missin'."

"Thanks, man... maybe another time. I'll be around for a little while."

"Excellent! Anything you want, it's yours, man." Glenn took a step back and spread his arms again. "Dude... I can't believe it's you!" He hugged Sean again.

They chatted for a while about what they'd been up to and Sean mentioned that he'd run into Julie. Glenn said he saw her around now and then, but they didn't hang out. Sean finally managed to extricate himself from the little shop when a few customers needed assistance. He left with a promise that he'd be back to "run some jet skis or something" with Glenn before he headed back down south.

Sean wondered how many more times he would have to go through the *old friends reunited* routine. One of the reasons he'd lost touch with Glenn was that they hadn't seemed to have much in common anymore. It looked to Sean like that still held true, but he supposed it couldn't hurt to hang with the guy once or twice.

As Sean walked back to his hotel, a kite boarder with a colorful, parachute-shaped kite floated along the surface of the lake. The guy caught air off some of the larger waves as he cruised to the east over the afternoon chop. The breeze had picked up across the lake as thunderheads built to the west over Mount Tallac and Desolation Wilderness, sending rumbles though the basin now and then. Sean wondered if the threat of rain would come to fruition or if Mother Nature was just being a tease.

Seven

Julie didn't know if she had any fight left in her.

Louise, one of the students in her last class, had just left and she sat in her office feeling defeated and abandoned. It was a quarter to five.

Louise was an Eagle Development employee. She'd told Julie that the company was pursuing both the South Tahoe Beach Resort project—as well as the redevelopment of the Lake's Edge Apartments—with renewed vigor. The sabotage had apparently had the opposite effect on Payne than they'd expected: it had only pissed him off. They should have known Payne wasn't the kind of man who would understand their type of message. Maybe if Julie were to go on a ninja-style, ass-kicking rampage through Eagle's offices he would get it. She might even be able to pull it off. She'd earned her black belt in Karate the previous year.

Julie planted her elbows on the hard surface of the desk with a clunk, resting her forehead in her hands. Why was everything in this culture so broken? It didn't matter if the general public didn't want the timeshares built, as long as Big Money wanted timeshares, Big Money got timeshares. And it wasn't just a local problem. All around the country—every single day—there were examples you could point to that The United States of America was governed by the Rich, for the Rich. Anyone who cared to disagree with that would be figuratively hung from a tree—but only because the *actual* hanging of people tended to be frowned upon these days.

Julie let her hands slide down onto the cool surface of the desk and laid her head on her forearms. What could she do to stop these people? The ones who would destroy community, nature and all of life itself just to make a buck? The idea of Manifest Destiny had expanded from the American West to include the entire planet—hell, the whole universe. She just didn't know what she, and all the others who cared about preserving what little was left of the natural world, could do to stop the sickness of Industrial Civilization from spreading any further? At times like this it all looked so hopeless and so few understood that it didn't have to be this way.

She wondered if any good at all would come from last night's action or if it had been completely futile. She'd been so frustrated and angry about the outcome of that damned meeting that she'd wanted to hurt Eagle—and Payne in particular. But unless you had a large majority going against the system, the big guys always won because they had the money and the power of the state backing them. Sabotaging a bulldozer or pulling up survey flags on sensitive land did little more than annoy them.

The lyrics from the Corrosion of Conformity song she'd quoted the previous day floated through her mind. *"They cannot crush you if you don't crawl."*

She raised her head and laughed out loud, a harsh sound in the enclosed space of her tiny office. If the songwriter meant they can only crush your spirit if you let them, maybe he had a point, but in reality it didn't matter how tall you stood—if you got in the way of the ruling class' plans they would rub you out and toss you aside like a spent cigar butt.

Abruptly, Julie stood and wiped tear tracks from her cheeks. She had to get moving. Sitting around in a daze of self-pity accomplished nothing. She gathered her things and shut off the office light. As she walked into the foyer, a South Lake Tahoe police cruiser pulled up and parked in front of the glass entry doors.

"Shit," she said, her heart skipping to double-time. It appeared Derrick had been right.

*

"So you haven't seen Derrick Masterson since the meeting last night?" the suited man, who had introduced himself as FBI Agent Bartlett, asked.

"That's correct," Julie said. It was the second time she'd told him.

"No contact what-so-ever?"

"None. I told you, he had business off the hill."

Bartlett jotted something in his notebook. He wasn't alone, a uniformed South Lake Tahoe policeman stood sentry by the glass door—presumably to keep Julie from escaping. She sat in a folding chair in the foyer trying to look innocent. She wasn't surprised the FBI was here. These days any form of so-called "domestic terrorism" was their turf—especially when explosives were involved. She guessed the ATF was probably in town by now as well. The fact that Bartlett was with a local cop, instead of another FBI agent, gave Julie hope that maybe she wasn't considered much of a suspect.

"So what do you know about the terrorist activity last night?" Bartlett asked. He had pushed the only other chair in the area into position across from her and sat leaning forward, elbows on his knees.

Bartlett's use of the word "terrorist" raised the hair on the back of Julie's neck, but she managed to let it go. "Only what I've heard around town today," she answered.

"Which is…?"

"That someone blew up that new timeshare development over by Lakeland Village."

"Uh-huh." He wrote something else in his book. "That's it? Mr. Masterson never mentioned anything to you about plans to blow the place up?"

"Plans?" Julie said, raising her eyebrows. She crossed her legs and set her hands daintily on one knee before continuing. "Let's get a few things straight, Agent Bartlett. First of all, I may know Derrick Masterson, but I wouldn't say we're all that close. Second, I have no idea what plans he may or may not have had last night. And, third, I can't imagine Derrick would be involved in anything like what happened last night."

"Uh huh," Bartlett said, writing the whole time. "So he said nothing to you at the meeting about what he was doing last night?"

"Like I said, all he told me was he had business off the hill."

"Okay. What is your connection with the Eco-Militia, Miss Thompson?"

"The Eco-Militia?" Julie said, feigning surprise. "Isn't that a radical environ—oh, wait, I get it. You think they're responsible for this."

"Mr. Masterson has known affiliations with the Eco-Militia. Were you aware of that?" Bartlett didn't drop his gaze as Julie fought to maintain steady eye contact.

"Oh my God," she said. "You're kidding. Not Derrick. I mean, I knew he was concerned about the environment, but... No way would he be involved with a group like that."

"Uh-huh," Bartlett said, rolling his eyes as he flipped though his little notebook.

Julie saw the cop at the door hiding a grin. She needed to be a little more careful about her reactions.

"I have a statement here from a Mr. Harold Payne that says he 'was accosted by an attractive blonde woman in the Airport parking lot'—his words not mine—last night after the City Council meeting." Bartlett looked up. "That wouldn't happen to be you, would it Miss Thompson?"

Julie tried to fight the blush rising in her cheeks, but she saw no reason to deny it was her. "Yes, that was me. But 'accosted' might be a bit of a strong word for what happened. We had words."

"Yeah, well, here's the thing: How do you think it looks to me that you were seen screaming at the head of Eagle Development around nine p.m. and five or six hours later their little timeshare development goes kablooey? Especially since Mr. Masterson was the one who pulled you off the poor guy?"

"Mr. Mas—?"

Julie didn't finish. If they thought it was Derrick who pulled her off of Payne why tell them different? They were already looking for Derrick anyway. Maybe she could keep Sean out of this after all. She changed tact.

"What exactly are you accusing me of, Agent Bartlett?" Julie said as she uncrossed her legs and leaned toward him, forcing her eyes to stay on his. She figured if they had anything concrete on her they would have arrested her by now. Bartlett was just fishing for a confession, trying to get her to bite.

"I'm not accusing you of anything, Ms. Thompson... But I am wondering where you might have been last night?"

"I was with a friend."

"And that friend can vouch for your whereabouts?"

"So you're telling me that I need an alibi, Agent? That I'm a suspect?"

Bartlett scribbled some more in his book, ignoring her questions, then grunted to himself before standing. He searched through the pockets of his coat, pulled out a couple of sheets of folded paper and began smoothing them out, eyes pouring over them as he went. Thirty seconds passed before he whistled and said, "You're quite a vocal detractor of Eagle Development, aren't you Miss Thompson?"

Julie remained silent, looking quizzically from Bartlett to his sidekick and back.

The Agent held the papers up to her. "City Council Minutes from last night," he said and went back to reading.

"And this means what to me?" Julie said, annoyed at the abrupt turn into this line of questioning. "I'm aware that my statements are a matter of public record, but it's not as if I threatened anyone. You're going to have to make half the population of the South Shore suspects if this is what you've got for criteria."

"Here's a few more *criteria* for you," the Agent said, pulling a page off the back. "Says here you have two priors: one for trespassing and one for resisting arrest."

Julie leaned back and crossed her arms again. "You've certainly done your homework."

"Care to elaborate?" Bartlett said, waving the rap sheet at her.

"Not particularly. Though I will point out that those occurred during *peaceful* protests."

"Uh-huh." Bartlett refolded the papers and placed them back in his pocket. "Are you sleeping with Mr. Masterson?"

"Excuse me?" Julie sputtered, taken aback.

"I think you heard me."

"If I did I don't see how that's any of your business."

"Well, seeing that Mr. Masterson is suspected of causing a couple million dollars of damage last night, we think who he's sleeping with might turn out to be important."

Julie stood, folded her chair and carried it with her back behind the counter. "Let me put it to you this way, Bartlett," she said, purposely dropping the prefix before his name. "A few minutes ago this stopped being the friendly conversation you promised me when you came in. So you can either arrest me now or you can turn around and walk out that door."

The FBI agent sighed and turned to his sidekick. "Well," he said. "I guess we're done here."

When Julie didn't reply the city cop opened the door and stepped out. Bartlett began to follow, but before he let the door swing shut he turned back and pointed a finger at her like a gun. "You have a great evening," he said and winked. "I'm sure we'll talk again soon."

Julie watched as the two climbed into the police car and pulled away. Once they were out of sight she shut off the lights and locked the place up tight. On the way to her apartment, as fat raindrops spattered intermittently on the windshield of her beat up Subaru, she watched the road behind her for any indication she was being followed. She couldn't be sure because the car hung back, almost out of sight, but a black sedan matched her lane changes all the way home.

Eight

A knock sounded on Sean's hotel room door at 6:40 p.m. He had just finished shaving and was about to put on a shirt. He grabbed one from a hanger on his way to the door then peered through the peephole. Julie stood outside glancing nervously up and down the hallway.

Sean opened the door and said, "Hey, I thought I was picking you—" His words were cut off as Julie threw herself at him, engulfing him in a hug that would have knocked the wind out of old man winter.

"Thank God I caught you before you left for my place," she said, loosening her grip slightly.

Sean backed into the room, taking her with him, and pushed the door closed. His undonned shirt still hung from his left hand, down Julie's back. After another moment of this Sean peeled the woman off of him and asked, "What's going on?"

Julie took a deep breath and set her purse on the dresser as Sean stuck his arms in his shirt. "The cops are watching me," she said finally.

"What? I thought you s—"

"I know what I said but they know about me yelling at Payne last night and they know I know Derrick and I think they're trying to point the finger at me because of what I've said publicly about Eagle."

"But that's all circumstantial. It doesn't prove anything."

"I know. I guess that's why they haven't arrested me yet, but I couldn't have you coming to my apartment since I'm pretty sure they're watching it."

Sean raised one eyebrow. "If they're watching your place, wouldn't they have followed you here?"

"They didn't see me leave. I went out the bathroom window."

"From the second floor?"

"There's a tree."

"Ahh." Sean crossed the room to the couch and sat. This was not good. The reality of the situation was finally hitting home. As Julie had said at some point, this was not some teenage prank they'd committed. If they were convicted it would mean hard time.

Julie perched on the edge of the cushion at his side and turned her head to him. "I'm trying to keep you out of this, Sean. That's why I'm here."

Sean stared straight ahead. "Couldn't you just have called?" The words felt cold leaving his mouth.

Julie sighed. "I was afraid my phone might be tapped after what Derrick told me."

"When did you see him?"

"He came by the studio earlier." She relayed most of the conversation to Sean, leaving out Derrick's allegations at the end.

"So he ran? Maybe we should do the same."

"They don't know anything about you, Sean. No one even knows you're here."

"I was at that meeting last night. I pulled you off of Payne."

"They think it was Derrick."

"Really?"

"That's what Agent Bartlett said."

"Who...? You talked to the cops?"

"FBI actually. But, yeah."

Sean jumped up. "FBI? Shit. What the hell are they doing here?"

Julie let her head hang between her shoulders for a moment before looking up and tucking some loose strands of hair behind her left ear. "They have a satellite office out by the Y. And besides, the FBI handles cases of domestic terrorism—especially when explosives are involved," she said.

Sean spun away. "Fuck," he growled under his breath. He buttoned his shirt as he paced to the other side of the room. "If we're being investigated by the FBI it's only a matter of time before they figure this all out."

"Maybe. Maybe not," Julie said, then stood and crossed the space between them. "If you get out of here—in the morning if not sooner—they might never figure out you were even here."

"You mean alone? Leave you here?"

Julie closed her eyes for a moment before continuing. "Yes. Doesn't that make the most sense? You go home and I stay here. I keep everything 'business as usual' and we wait until this blows over before you come back. That's what I told Derrick to do. As long as they have no proof—and we didn't leave them any—there's no reason for me to run."

"So why should I?"

"Damn it, Sean, if the cops see us together they'll want to talk to you. Is that what *you* want?"

Sean ran a hand over his hair to the back of his head and left it there as he spoke. "Well, no…"

Julie reached up and moved his hand from his head then wrapped him in another hug. "This sucks," she said, one cheek on his chest. "Big time."

"Tell me about it," Sean muttered as he squeezed her tighter to him.

* *

When room service knocked Julie hid in the bathroom. This time she chose the edge of the tub as her perch as she tried to think of a quick way to make their troubles disappear. She didn't really believe the authorities could connect her or Sean to the bombings, but she wasn't so sure about Derrick. Julie didn't know Jean all that well, so she could turn out to be a wild card.

They had been careful not to leave any evidence at the scene, but one never knew what might have been forgotten. Police propaganda shows like "CSI" and "Law & Order" had the country believing the cops always got their man, but she knew that actual arrest rates were very low in relation to crimes reported, conviction rates even lower. Apparently the mainstream media thought it was in the best interest of the public that they remain ignorant of this fact—certainly the better to keep them in line. Derrick knew all of this, too, so it surprised Julie that he would run. But Derrick had been behaving strangely ever since Sean came in to the picture.

Julie shook her head, stood up in front of the mirror and looked herself directly in the eyes. No matter what she did, no matter how much she learned in the school of hard knocks, it seemed could never erase the remarkable amount of naiveté hiding behind those green irises staring back at her. Once again she'd been blindsided by the unexpected romantic feelings of a friend. Maybe she finally needed to admit that it just wasn't possible to be friends with a straight man.

The hall door closed and Sean rapped twice as he passed by, saying, "Food's here."

"Be right there," she called, still staring *at* her face instead of what she was trying to do: look right through it. Who was she, this woman looking back at her from the mirror? What did she have to show for her thirty-two years on the planet besides a miniscule sliver of enlightenment residing inside a bruised and scarred psyche? What business did this woman have seeking whatever form of imagined happiness there might be with someone like Sean? Especially when she continued to keep a secret from him that could destroy the very relationship they were trying to build?

She dropped her eyes, unable to hold her own gaze any longer. She was hungry, her thoughts muddled, but she knew she had to do the right thing and tell Sean. If she didn't, she might lose the nerve to ever look herself in the eye again.

Nine

Sean stood next to the couch, bottle in hand, ready to pour. "More wine?" he said.

"Why not?" Julie answered from where she sat ensconced in the overstuffed piece of furniture. "This *is* kind of a last supper for us."

Odd analogy, Sean thought and eyed her suspiciously as he filled her upheld glass. "I didn't know crucifixion was still an option these days?" he said. "California still frowns on cruel and unusual punishment, no?"

Julie opened her mouth to speak then closed it, sipping from her now full glass instead.

"And who's Judas in this little passion play anyway?" Sean added.

"Never mind," Julie said and tried to wave the topic away with her free hand. "It was a stupid thing to say."

Sean joined her on the couch—a loveseat, actually. There wasn't space in the room for a full-size sofa. "When are you planning on heading back to your apartment?" he asked. It was ten fifteen, they were halfway though their second bottle of wine and Sean was feeling a heady buzz.

Julie fell back on the cushions, raised her eyebrows and pivoted her head toward him. "Don't know," she said. "Depends on when you throw me out. And whether I can ever extract myself from this damn couch."

Sean poked her lightly in the waist with a finger and she giggled, "Hey!" Then he leaned in and kissed her.

When he pulled back he said, "Yeah, I think you better leave."

*

Julie punched him lightly in the arm then pulled him to her.

Alcohol flowed through her bloodstream like a rolling blackout on its way to her brain. She knew she shouldn't have even started on that last glass of wine.

Sean's hand was on her stomach, her side, her right breast. He was gentle, easing his way slowly, keeping the contact light but purposeful. She let her head fall back and suppressed a moan as he nibbled her ear. His lips followed a path from there, down her neck to her chest. Then a hand was on her thigh, moving slowly up the leg of her shorts. When his fingers hit the elastic leg band of her panties her eyes shot open.

"Whoa," she said and rolled away from him, accidently discovering that the secret to getting out of the couch was to throw yourself on the floor. She was up in an instant, but managed to spill some wine on her shirt in the process.

Not surprisingly, Sean looked at her from his seat as if she'd been possessed by demons. "What's wrong?" he said, a little breathless. Julie wouldn't have been surprised to see him ward her off with a finger-cross.

"I don't know," she said.

But she did. What was wrong was that this was all too suddenly soon. Too weird and yet... somehow too familiar at the same time. She was making out with *Sean* for God's sake. A moment ago her best friend had nearly had his hand in her panties.

Julie set what was left of her glass of wine on the desk and settled on the edge of the bed, head in her hands. She heard Sean shift on the couch, but he said nothing. What was her problem? She wanted this as much as he did. They were both adults who'd outgrown their Catholic upbringings and Julie knew that she, at least, no longer believed they were doing anything wrong here. Letting her hands slip from her face, she looked at Sean. His hair was shorter, his shoulders broader, but he mostly looked like she remembered him. He took a sip of his wine and waited patiently for her to figure this out—exactly like he'd waited for her in the past.

But he was not the same person. He was more confident. He was making the advances. The old Sean would have waited for her to make the first move. What would this all mean to him if they were to go forward from here? Would it end up being nothing more than a regrettable one-nighter, leaving her devastated and still alone?

Julie looked Sean in the eyes. He raised his eyebrows as he returned her gaze. That was one thing that hadn't changed at all: his eyes. There was kindness there. And concern. And—she hoped, still—love.

She opened her mouth to speak, not sure what would come out. "I think I need to tell you now," she said. "Before…"

*

"Tell me what?" Sean said after Julie trailed off. She had left him in the lurch and, although he had shifted on the couch, he was still uncomfortable about what must be an unsightly bulge in his pants.

"Tell you why."

"Why wha—?"

It finally hit him. She wanted to tell him the big Why. What had happened to her thirteen years ago. He lowered his eyes to the floor. His racing libido wanted to know: *Why now?*

"I was—" Julie started again, but a surge of emotion seemed to take her voice.

Sean looked at her: head down again, staring at the floor with shoulders slumped. She held one hand in the other as if trying to warm it. The brooder from breakfast the other morning had returned. Sean liked the bubbly, bright Julie much better, though this one did have a certain nihilistic beauty that tugged on another, darker one of his heartstrings. Ignoring the situation down below, he rose from the couch and sat next to her on the bed.

"It doesn't matter," he said as he put his arm on her shoulders. She flinched slightly at his touch and he let his hand drop to the bed behind her. "Water under the bridge, right?"

"No, you should know."

"Not if it freaks you out this much. You're shaking like you're in detox or something. Let it go for now, okay? Tell me when the thought of it doesn't… do this to you."

Julie lifted her head to look at him as if trying to gauge his sincerity. Tears welling in the corners of her eyes spilled over and trailed down her cheeks. A moment later she collapsed into his arms. "I'm so scared, Sean," she said into his shirt.

"Of what?" he asked when she didn't continue.

"Of the cops, of jail, that…" pulling back, she looked up at him again, still holding onto the front of his shirt with both hands. "That I'll never see you again after tonight."

He reached out, wiping a tear from her cheek with his thumb. "That's ridiculous," he said. "I found you again, why would I let that happen?"

"You might not, but other things might… interfere."

Sean sighed. "And the world might explode tomorrow. But what can we do about that?"

She searched his face again, his eyes. Then, as she leaned in to kiss him, he felt her body relax.

*

She let herself go.

Exhilarating, yet bone-wrenchingly frightening at the same time. It was like falling backwards from the high dive without knowing if there was any water in the pool.

In Sean's eyes she had seen the boy she'd known and she kissed him with an urgency built on too many years of buried feelings. Pressing her body against his, she ran a hand under his shirt, caressing his back. It was still happening too fast, too soon. Yet she understood now that it couldn't possibly be too soon or fast. They'd danced around this issue for as long as she'd known him. The fact that they hadn't seen each other in thirteen years had changed nothing.

After fumbling with the buttons on Sean's shirt for a moment she settled for pulling it off over his head. He returned the favor and, momentarily, she found herself in bra and panties. Her heart thudded in her chest and her breath came in gasps as she undid his pants.

They rolled up toward the pillows, losing the remainder of their clothing along the way. It was awkward at first, like two teenagers on a parent's bed, limbs flailing, bordering on frantic. But once locked together, their eyes met, nose to nose, and they began to move as one in rhythm and motion. Waves of bliss rose, slow and steady, to tsunami force and finally crashed down, submerging them—if only for a few moments—in a thoughtless sea of ecstasy.

Ten

◀

Julie turns to the railing and looks south, out past the little town of Meyers and into Christmas Valley. The decking of the old fire lookout on Angora Ridge groans beneath her feet. She stops short of leaning on the brittle railing.

"What are we doing up here?" she asks Sean.

"I don't know, I guess I like the view," he says. "Why? Where'd you want to go?"

Julie shrugs. "I don't know." She turns her attention to Freel Peak, Job and Job's Sister, towering over the South Shore to the southeast. The top third of the three mountain peaks is still lit by the rays of the setting sun, turning them a rich shade of pink, almost—but not quite—purple. Below, the lights of South Lake Tahoe twinkle in the gathering dark.

Julie can't believe it's August already. She'll be a high school junior in less than a month and, until Glenn had broken up with her two days ago, she'd thought she would be starting the school year on the arm of a senior.

"You should come over here and check out Tallac," Sean says.

Julie makes her way across the popping, creaking boards to the north side of the lookout. "Are we even supposed to be up here?" she asks.

Sean glances at her. "Probably not," he says. He raises his arm and points up at Mount Tallac.

From this angle, looking across Fallen Leaf Lake and up along the mountain's southern flanks, Tallac appears more like a long sloping ridge than a peak in its own right. The waning sunlight streams across the top in bands, reflecting off the low clouds overhead in a dizzying array of purples, oranges and pinks.

"Wow," Julie says.

"Killer, eh?"

Julie has never spent any time alone with Sean before today. She only knows him because he is one of Glenn's close friends. She'd been sitting at home feeling down and lonely so she'd taken a chance and called him—half-expecting him to hang up on her. Instead, they ended up cruisin' in Sean's Camaro. But hanging out with Glenn's friend is only making it harder for her to forget about Glenn.

For a few minutes the two of them quietly watch the colors shift in the waning light until Julie feels compelled to fill the silence. "So you're gonna be a senior this year?"

"Yeah," Sean answers, his elbows planted firmly on the wooden railing.

"One more year to go."

"Yep."

Another minute of silence.

"You know Glenn broke up with me, right?"

"Yeah." Sean picks at peeling paint on the railing with the index finger of his right hand. "I guess that kinda sucks for you."

Hot, fresh tears push into Julie's eyes. She closes them and takes a moment to compose herself. When she feels a little more in control she lifts her lids and looks at Sean. "Do you know why?" she says. "Did he tell you?"

Sean shrugs.

"It's because I won't put out. He didn't have to say it... I know. He must've told you that."

"Umm..." Sean looks away, out at the silvery, grey expanse of Tahoe's surface at twilight. "He didn't really tell me anything."

"Yeah, sure." Julie crosses her arms and leans back against the building. Why did she bring this up? She has never spoken to anyone but her friend Dawn and her mom about boys and their *needs*. Sean is just another guy and he'll probably end up telling Glenn everything.

The darkness continues to deepen around them. Sean's long hair keeps his face in shadows, making him hard to read. He turns and meets her gaze sheepishly for a moment before focusing his attention back on whatever he is picking at.

"You go to church don't you?" Julie asks.

Sean huffs. "Yeah, so?"

"I go, too, you know."

"I know."

"It's not something to be ashamed of. I just thought you might understand is all." Julie storms away, down the four steps to the dirt and gravel path. She crosses below Sean and sits on a bench halfway back to the parking area.

Why is it that boys never seem to care that sex is a sin before marriage? Doesn't matter if they're Roman Catholic, pagan or atheist, they always stand right in line like sheep, ready to damn themselves to hell in an instant.

After a few minutes Julie hears Sean's feet crunch in the gravel on the path.

"Understand what?" he says as he takes a seat at the other end of the bench. "What is it I'm supposed to understand?"

Julie looks over. "You're just gonna tell Glenn whatever I say, aren't you?"

"Is that why you called me? So I could be some kind of messenger?"

"No. I just thought… I don't know what I thought."

Silence stretches out again as the encroaching night pools slowly into shadows at their feet.

"You're Catholic aren't you?" Julie asks eventually.

"Yeah," Sean says. "I guess."

"You guess? So, what? You just go to church because your parents make you?"

Sean kicks a rock over the edge of the drop in front of them. Julie hears it rustle through the bushes as it rolls downhill. "I don't know," he says, shaking his head. "I mean, that probably is why I go. I went to Catholic School for eight years and I thought what they taught was just the way everything was. Now…? I don't know anymore."

Looking down six hundred feet at the huge, dark hole in the ground that Fallen Leaf Lake has turned into in the dark, Julie realizes she doesn't care if Sean tells Glenn everything. "I think it's a sin to have sex before marriage," she says. "I'll be a virgin until my wedding night."

Sean takes a moment before he replies, "Uh… okay." It's dark enough now that he is nothing more than a shadow at the other end of the bench.

"That's what I thought you might understand. You know, because you're Catholic and all?"

"Ahhh," he says.

Why am I so stupid! Had she really expected a guy to get this? She stands and walks toward the parking lot, wrapping herself in her arms against a sudden chill. She can hear Sean following behind and when they arrive at the car he opens the passenger door for her. They listen to the radio as they drive back down the bumpy, winding road. "Alive" by Pearl Jam comes on. Julie wants to sing along with the chorus, but she doesn't feel so alive.

A few songs later, as they roll into the Snowflake Drive-In, Sean turns the volume down and says, "Julie Thompson, you're kinda different... for a cheerleader."

Julie isn't sure how to respond to that. "Thanks... I guess," she says with a roll of her eyes.

"And I'm not gonna tell Glenn anything. He's kind of a dick when it comes to girls."

She looks at him, surprised as he pulls the car into a parking space and kills the engine. Before he opens his door, he meets her eyes momentarily, then looks away.

"I guess I am, too," he says and clears his throat. "You know... a virgin." Then he is out of the car and on his way around to her side.

Julie sits puzzled, waiting and wondering if maybe he does understand... if only a little. When he opens her door and offers to help her up from the low slung car she hesitates a moment before accepting a hand.

"You're kinda different, too, Sean Connors," she says. "For a guy."

▶

Eleven

Bright light brought Sean out of a disremembered dream. He sat up slowly and tried to shake it from his head, which only reminded him he'd had too much wine last night. After a moment sitting on the edge of the bed he realized he was naked and the sliding glass door out to the patio of his hotel room was standing open.

Julie?!

He looked behind him and found the bed empty. Turning back, his hand caught something under the covers and he held it up in front of his face: white lace panties.

Shit!

Was he not remembering things right? She'd seemed to want it as much as he had. You didn't generally repeat the act twice when you weren't into it. What had made her run off so quickly she couldn't even close the door behind her?

The scrape of a metal chair leg on the concrete outside startled Sean and he covered himself with the sheet. "Hello?" he said cautiously.

Julie stepped into the room. "Oh, hey, you're up." She looked away as if she'd just walked in on a naked stranger.

"I thought for minute you'd left," Sean said.

Julie glanced at him then dropped her eyes. "Don't be ridiculous," she said coming over to the bed. "I was just out enjoying the view." She leaned down and gave him a quick kiss. "You should get dressed."

"I think these are yours," Sean said, dangling her panties on the end of a finger. Julie's cheeks flushed and she tried to snatch them from his hand. Sean grabbed her wrist and pulled him to her. "Does this mean you're going commando?" he said as she fell in his lap.

"Cut it out, Sean." She rolled away, grabbing the undergarment from him as she stood, then she stuffed it in her pocket and went back to the door. "It's late."

Sean was confused again. He looked at the clock and saw that it was 8:30. Not exactly high noon. To say that things had turned awkward would be an exuberant understatement. "You got another hot date?" he said.

Julie crossed her arms. "No, I've got a class at eleven."

Sean considered leaping up on the bed and bouncing around in his birthday suit to see if he could shake Julie out of the doldrums, but thought better of it. He'd stopped her from coming clean last night to avoid this side of her, but here it was again anyway. Maybe he should have let her talk.

Sean grabbed the sheet and pulled it around himself as he stood up. "Perhaps you'll excuse me for a moment so I can find some clothes," he said.

* *

Julie stepped back out on the patio and tried to shake some life into herself. When she'd awakened naked next to Sean half an hour ago she'd wanted to reach out and stroke his bare skin, but had been struck by an irrational fear that if she touched him he would vanish. Instead, she'd slipped silently from the bed and into the bathroom. After a quick shower she had dressed in the clothes she could find and let herself out onto the patio for some fresh air.

What had happened last night was huge! It paled in comparison to the cops and the sabotage and even the looming loss of her home. Sean had been back in town two days and she'd already hopped into bed with him. What could he possibly think of her now?

She had an urge to leave. To try and escape a foreboding that had slid into her head like an ocean tide. She and Sean would have to part regardless of his reaction to last night and that reality, she thought, was the driving force behind the itch to kick up her heels and run. She considered a quick dip in the lake to shock her to her senses, but she doubted it would work. She was good at bailing out on people quickly and quietly, the loving and tearful goodbye was not one of her fortes.

What about being honest with him?

Julie wasn't sure whose voice that was in her head, but it certainly wasn't her own. How could she be honest with him when she couldn't even tell him why? And the longer it went on, the harder it got.

I'm sad, she told herself, *that's all*. Sean had to leave again. And even though they'd only been together a couple of days it felt much longer—almost as if the thirteen intervening years had vanished. But she had to get it together. She couldn't let her shame and depression manifest as anger. Honesty was the only answer... about some things anyway.

"So you want a ride home or are you gonna hoof it?" Sean said as he stepped onto the patio behind her.

Julie turned and hugged him.

* *

Sean returned the embrace, his head spinning. Was she bipolar? Had she developed multiple personalities over the years? Was that what she had to tell him? That she'd been institutionalized?

That thought brought on another: What a horrible comment he'd made about mental hospitals the other day if it turned out to be true.

Julie pushed back a foot or two and said, "You shouldn't be seen with me."

"Yeah, I remember. I'm just trying to be a normal guy asking if his girl needs a lift home."

Julie's eyes turned up to him. "So I'm your 'girl' now, huh?"

Sean immediately wished for his words back. "W-well—" he stuttered. "I mean, yeah, sure... if you want to be..."

Real smooth, Ace.

He'd been presumptuous, he knew, but after the previous night it was just an assumption his brain had made. Who knew what assumptions Julie was making about the status of their relationship. Maybe not even Julie.

Instead of responding to him, she turned her head and rested it on his shoulder. "I don't want you to go," she said and burst into tears.

"So I won't."

"But you have to. Don't you get it? They'll be after you and it'll all be my fault."

"That's not true," he said gently. "It wouldn't be your fault. We'll be together after this all blows over. It's not like you'll never see me again."

Julie's words were muffled, spoken into his shirt. "That's what I told myself last time," he thought she said.

Twelve

Julie walked slowly along the beach, sandals in hand, kicking up sand.

So Sean thought she was his "girl" now. If that was true, then he was also her "man." She guessed last night had sealed the deal. While her heart soared, her intellect still scoffed at the idea. So possessive. She didn't like feeling owned.

And why was her head always looking for reasons to bail on a relationship? She knew on a rational level that Sean didn't think he owned her, so why not let the thrill she'd initially felt when he'd said it continue to flourish?

Because you're a tramp and you know it. What do you think he'll do when he finds out?

She recognized her father's voice this time. She had loved her father, but he'd had the strange idea that berating her regularly was the way to let her know he cared. It hadn't left her with the best impression of herself, something she'd spent the better part of the years since he died trying to overcome.

Julie looked out over the lake at a flock of waterfowl taking flight against the crystal blue sky. The day was gorgeous—yet another example of why Tahoe drew so many tourists—but she was miserable. Maybe it would be better to live as a hermit and not get involved with men. Two days ago she'd had no one to miss and was relatively content. Now she felt like she'd had her left arm removed. Something she could physically live without, sure, but the phantom pains could be hell.

She and Sean had decided that three weeks with no contact ought to suffice. Then, if no one had come looking for him, he would return as if he hadn't been here in years. But considering that, at the moment, the past two days felt like two months, three weeks might as well be eternity.

As Julie shuffled along, intentionally dragging her pace to slow their separation, she remembered the last time she'd spoken to Sean before the other day at the café.

◀

"It's *Communications*, dork," Julie says into the phone.

She sits at the kitchen table, the late afternoon sun cutting though the window and reflecting off the linoleum floor. The phone cord stretched across the room from the wall-mounted base casts wiggling shadows on the wall as she swishes it back and forth across the floor like a jump rope. It's the first day of Daylight Savings Time. The sun hasn't been up this late since fall.

"So that means you're majoring in what? Talking?" Sean says from the other end of the line—somewhere in that mythical land down south that Julie has never seen: SoCal.

"It's not talking. It's, like, you know… studying media and public relations and stuff."

"Ahhhhh," Sean says. "So it is talking… just to the press."

"Shut up."

Sean laughs. "Sorry."

She knows he's just kidding around, but sometimes he makes her feel like a second-class student because she goes to community college while he's three-quarters of the way though his sophomore year at USC.

"Are you coming home this summer?" she asks as she twirls her finger in the coil of the phone cord. Her mom looks over. She's been quietly preparing dinner at the counter, but now seems quite interested in Sean's answer to her question.

"Home?" Sean says. "I'm going back to my parents' if that's what you mean."

"Come on, home is Tahoe."

Her mom frowns and turns back to her cooking as Sean says, "I guess."

Sean's parents moved from Tahoe to San Diego last August. The only time Sean had been here since was for her dad's funeral a few months back.

"You guess?" Julie says. "You grew up here, Sean Connors. You've been gone, what? Like eight months? How can this not be home?" When he doesn't answer right away she adds, "Besides, I'm here." Her mother turns a wry smile her way.

Julie's mother has never kept her preference that she and Sean get together a secret.

The mother daughter relationship between them has always been very open, with Julie sharing most of the details of her love life. The older she gets, though, the less prudent that seems.

One of the things Julie has kept to herself is the letter she wrote to Sean the cold January night of her dad's funeral. She'd tried twice to send it since then, but each time she'd arrived at the mailbox she hadn't been able to make her fingers let it go.

"You could come visit me?" Sean says. "You've never been to San Diego."

"How would I get there?"

"They have these things called planes," Sean says. "You get on 'em and they fly through the air—like birds—and when you get off you're right where you wanted to be. It's amazing—"

"Sean."

"—if you look up in the sky you can sometimes get lucky and make one out."

"Cut it out."

Julie's mom mouths, "I'll pay," and points at herself with a spatula.

Julie waves her off with her free hand and says to Sean, "Besides, I was gonna take a couple summer classes so I could catch up."

"Whatever... I'll see if I can get up there. Glenn's been bugging me to go see him, too. Something about surfing."

Julie's heart sank. "If you can't make it, then I'll come there. How's that?"

"Sounds wonderful."

"It's a date then."

Julie's mom smiles. Since January things had been tough for the Thompson clan, but they were starting to come out of it. Her mother had loved her father very much, even though he frequently made her furious. Ever since he died, though, Julie could swear her mom had been pushing her even more toward Sean. Almost as if she needed to see her daughter with someone she loves, since she no longer had the love of her life. And Julie had definitely grown closer to Sean. She'd begun to think of him almost as a boyfriend and hadn't been dating anyone else since she dumped the bozo she was with who couldn't even make it to the funeral. She can only hope he understands she really isn't kidding this time, but she knows he'll get it when she finally musters the nerve to send him the letter.

"I've got to get this paper done," Sean says. "It's due tomorrow."

"Yeah," Julie says, smiling. "I've got a test tomorrow, too."

"Alright, then."

"Alright."

Silence rules the line for thirty seconds before Julie breaks out in giggles.

Sean laughs, too.

"Bye," Julie says.

"Alright, bye."

"Talk to you soon."

The line clicks and she finally takes the receiver from her ear, pressing and holding the button to hang it up. Her mother opens her mouth to speak and Julie stops her with an open hand. "Don't say a word, Mother. Just don't. You'll jinx it or something."

Her mom shrugs, a smile beaming from ear to ear. "Whatever," she says as she turns back to her cooking.

As Julie swings the phone cord back and forth, watching it kick up miniature dust devils that glitter in the shaft of evening sunlight, a silly grin tickles her lips.

And that the was the way they had left it.

Just like that, with plans for the summer. Then she hadn't spoken to him for thirteen years. Four days later, at that stupid party—

"Julie!"

The voice came from behind. She turned to look up the beach and saw Derrick trotting across the sand toward her.

Thirteen

Sean needed coffee.

A double Americano might do the trick. Caffeine to wake the brain. A veil of fog filled his head, turning reality into pea soup.

When he arrived at the coffee cart in the lobby, he found that they served alcohol as well. He hesitated only an instant before deciding it could never be too early to start drinking when you'd just run into your high school sweetheart, blown up a timeshare with her, slept together for the first time, then had to part ways because the cops were on her tail. It was that same old story of love found and love lost. Such a cliché.

He headed back to his room, large coffee with a double shot of Bailey's in hand, newspaper under one arm. In the hall a maid said, "Good Morning," with a thick Mexican accent. He grunted a reply, an ogre lumbering back to his cave. When Sean stepped into his room the first thing he smelled was Julie's perfume. Had she put some on in the bathroom before she left? He went out and sat in a chair on the patio to get away from the reminder.

Sean wasn't surprised to see the bombing of the South Tahoe Beach Resort had top billing on the front page of the Tribune—it had happened too late to make yesterday's paper. "Activists Take Aim at Developer," the headline read. A picture below showed the site, the two center buildings canted and leaning against their neighbors.

He read the short article and found that it basically repeated the radio news report—no new info. Flipping through the rest of the front section, he came to the Op/Ed page. After a Letter to the Editor about the speed limit being too low on Lake Tahoe Boulevard, Sean came to one entitled, "Terrorists Must Be Stopped:"

In regards to the destruction wrought at the South Tahoe Beach Resort development the other night, I wanted to say that I know who is responsible.

The accused has repeatedly spoken out against progress in this community, has defied law and order in illegal protests and, just last night, accosted a high-standing member of the community in a dark parking lot. All of this in addition to the terrorism perpetrated at The South Tahoe Beach Resort Thursday morning.

As I said, I know who you are and I have reported you and your thug boyfriend to the police. Justice will only be served when you—and the rest of your kind with no respect for the laws of this country—are behind bars.

Jessica Compton
South Lake Tahoe, CA
(Wife of City Councilman Mark Compton)

Sean let his hands fall in his lap, crumpling the paper and nearly spilling his coffee. "Shit," he said out loud. Two people passing on the beach looked his way but he ignored them. Did Mrs. Compton know who he was? Or was she the one who had him confused with Derrick? And when had she told the police what she supposedly knew?

Sean stood up and went back inside. He paced the carpet from the sliding glass door to the hall door and back. Mrs. Compton couldn't know who he was, right? As far as he knew there were only four people who knew he was in town, not counting the hotel staff. And how could she be so sure that Julie had been involved in the sabotage? It had to be some sort of smoke screen to catch them off their guard. The only person who could have seen them at the site was the cop. There hadn't been anyone else there, had there?

Sean stopped at the open slider and leaned on the doorjamb. He had to admit that he knew next to nothing about Derrick and even less about Jean. Julie swore they wouldn't rat out her or Sean, but how could she be so sure? Had anyone cared to ask him at the time, Sean would have said his business partner wouldn't screw him over for money. The simple fact was that people did things you thought they were incapable of each and every day.

So Julie was right: Sean needed to get out of Tahoe. He grabbed his suitcase, tossed it on the bed and began throwing clothes from the dresser drawers into it. Everything lay in a heap—half in, half out of the suitcase—when he realized that Julie needed to know about Jessica Compton's letter.

Fourteen

"What are you still doing here?" Julie said to Derrick as a breeze off the lake blew her hair across her face. "I thought you were leaving town."

"Yeah, well…" Derrick said, his eyes flitting around suspiciously as he approached her. "I'm getting around to it." His posture seemed different. His shoulders slumped more than usual maybe?

"How did you know where to find me?"

He dropped his gaze to the ground before pointing up the beach. "I was at, uh… Regan Beach. By the swings. I saw you pass by."

"Uh-huh," Julie muttered, wondering why he was lying to her.

"Hey," Derrick continued, "I stopped you because I thought you should know, your friend is in this a little deeper than we thought."

Julie raised an eyebrow. "What are you talking about?"

"Your boyfriend. The one you spent the night wi—"

"Have you been following me?"

Derrick frowned. "What? No, of course not. I…"

"Yes?" She crossed her arms.

"I came by your place early and you weren't there. I just assumed."

"Uh-huh."

Derrick straightened up and seemed to pull himself together. "Anyway, he might be compromised."

"We're talking about Sean here?"

"Who else? Turns out he holds a shitload of stock in Eagle Development's parent company, QTC Inc."

Julie's jaw dropped. "And you know this how?"

"I checked him out. Unfortunately, I didn't get this info until last night."

She felt a jitter in her stomach. Not as much at the information, more that Derrick had actually dug into Sean's background without her knowledge. "Why would you do that, Derrick? Did I—or did I not—ask you to stay out of my business?"

"It's my business, too, when I'm doing an action with the guy."

"You pulled him into it," she said, exasperated. "Couldn't you have just trusted me? Did I go digging into Jean's past to make myself feel better that I wouldn't be betrayed? No, I didn't, because I'm not paranoid. What is wrong with you?"

"I'm in a more sensitive position than you are, Jules," Derrick said and turned away. "The cops are constantly looking for a way to get to me. I have to know who I'm working with."

Julie groaned. "So why did you taunt him into helping us then?"

Derrick took a moment to answer, his back still to her. "We were desperate."

"Look at me, Derrick," Julie said, her voice hard. Once he had turned back she continued, "I told you who you were working with. If I didn't absolutely believe he could be trusted, I wouldn't have let it happen."

Jaws set they stared each other down in silence for ten seconds before Derrick broke eye contact and stalked off a few feet, hands stuffed in his pockets. A moment later he brought one out and held something orange and white up to look at it, shook it, then put in back. It happened so quick she couldn't tell what it was. She was about to ask when another voice called her name from behind.

Julie pivoted and saw Sean running along the beach from the direction of his hotel. All she could do was sigh. Why were these two men having such trouble doing what they said they would and getting the hell out of Tahoe?

Fifteen

Sean couldn't believe his eyes. Was that Derrick standing with Julie on the beach? As he approached them at a trot, suspicion rose in his head. Why would the two of them be meeting out here? Especially after she'd told him that Derrick had left the basin?

"Hey," he said breathlessly to Julie as he came to a stop, ignoring Derrick completely.

Julie looked around the beach, scanning the treeline and playground. "Sean, why are you here? You know we shouldn't be seen together."

"I know... I know," he said, still catching his breath. "I needed to tell you... about the paper."

"The paper?"

"The newspaper... The letter."

Julie shook her head. "Let's get out of the open until you can talk." She took Sean's hand and led him to the edge of the sand where they were less visible in the shadows of the trees. Derrick followed like a forlorn dog.

Sean sat on a log and waited until his breathing slowed. He kept forgetting he'd only been back at altitude a few days. When he felt a little less like a fish out of water he said, "Listen, there's a letter in today's paper from that Councilman's wife. She says she knows who we are—that she knows who did it."

"What?" Derrick said.

"How could she know?" Julie talked over him.

"Which Councilman's wife?" Derrick added.

Sean looked back and forth between the two, finally settling on Julie. "I don't know," he told her. To Derrick he said, "Compton. The one with Payne when Julie attacked him in the parking lot the other night."

Julie and Derrick stared each other down for a moment before Julie shrugged. "What?" she said, raising her eyebrows slightly. Derrick clenched his jaw, narrowed his eyes and turned away. The tension between the two was palpable, like standing next to an electrical transformer. Sean wondered again what he'd interrupted.

Julie turned back to him. "So she wrote a letter to the paper actually naming us?"

"No names," Sean said as he pulled the torn out strip of newspaper from his pocket. "But she obviously knows who you are. And maybe me, too." He handed the letter to Julie and she scanned though it quickly.

"I don't know," she said and handed it to Derrick. "I don't think this changes the plan."

"Me either," Derrick said when he'd finished reading.

"I wasn't talking to you," Julie said. "As far as I can remember you had your own plans." To Sean, she said, "I don't see how she could know who you are. She might even be the one who told the cops it was Derrick who pulled me off of Payne."

"Told the cops what?" Derrick said.

Sean and Julie turned to him.

"The FBI Agent who came to question me yesterday thinks it was you in the parking lot with me the other night… not Sean."

Derrick looked dazed. "And where did he get that idea?"

"We don't know," Julie said. "Maybe the wife."

"But you corrected him, of course?"

"Well…"

"Fuck!" Derrick said. He closed his eyes and ran a hand over his head. "You should have told me about all of this. No wonder they're looking at us so closely."

Sean chipped in. "But none of this proves anything about the sabotage."

"Of course it doesn't," Derrick said. "But you don't understand the way these people think. It's virtually impossible to pin these kinds of actions on anyone, so they start at the end and work backwards. Instead of following the evidence where it leads—which is nowhere, we made sure of that—they begin by picking someone they want to pin it on and then fabricate the evidence to make it stick."

"That sounds a little paranoid," Sean said.

Derrick narrowed his eyes. "I suppose it does," he said. "But that doesn't mean they're not out to get me."

Sean watched the waves roll up the beach for a minute or two as no one spoke. A woman in a bikini strolled along near the water, leading a little girl by the hand. It was Derrick who finally broke the stalemate.

"I'll reiterate my previous suggestion," he said to Julie. "You should get out of town. I know any number of people we could stay with if you come with me."

"Running now makes me look even guiltier, Derrick," Julie said. "Sean and I already decided he should get out of here, but only because we didn't think they knew who he was."

Derrick glanced at Sean. "I still doubt they're looking for him. They would have found him at his hotel by now."

"You think so?" Sean asked.

"They got to Julie yesterday afternoon. They would have found you by now if they were looking."

Sean hoped he was right.

"Stick around us much longer and they'll definitely be onto you, though."

Julie widened her eyes and gave Sean a knowing look.

Derrick turned his back and walked away. "I'm getting out of here," he said. "I suggest you two do the same."

"Whatever," Julie said, shaking her head. "Do what you want."

"I will," he said over a shoulder. "I will."

"See ya," Sean said, resisting the urge to flip him the bird.

Derrick waved a hand in the air as the trees enveloped him.

Sixteen

"What's wrong with him?" Sean said.

Julie sighed again as she mulled over what she wanted to say. Could Derrick be trusted? What if he'd made up the stuff about Sean's investments just to get her to confront Sean? And how did this whole thing keep turning into some stupid love triangle no matter how hard she'd been trying to keep it from doing so?

She sat down on the log next to Sean, shoulders slumped. "I think maybe Derrick has turned out to be the guy you think he is."

Sean looked at her askance. "What does that mean?"

"I think he was following me," she sighed. "And he seems obsessed with proving that you're not who you say you are."

"That I'm not—" Sean cut himself off. "What?"

Julie took a breath and turned toward him. "Maybe you can tell me. He says you own a lot of Eagle Development's stock."

Sean squinted and shook his head slightly. Again he said, "What?"

Julie waited a moment to see if he was just surprised or really didn't understand. When he didn't reply she started to repeat herself, "Derrick sa—"

"Yeah, I got it." Sean stood up and took a few steps away from her. "You and Derrick did a background check on me?"

Julie rose, too. "No, Sean—"

"Now I get why you two were out here on the beach together."

"—it was just Derrick."

He turned his angry eyes on her. "So you asked Derrick to check up on me? How do you even get that kind of information on somebody?"

"I didn't ask Derrick to do anything." Julie closed her eyes tight. "I wouldn't do that."

"Uh-huh," Sean said as he paced the sand.

Julie sat back down on the log. Why had he come after her? They'd left things well when they said goodbye before—as good as could be expected, anyhow. Maybe she should have given in to the urge she'd had earlier to run for the hills.

* * *

Acid ran through Sean's veins. He was so furious it was probably out of proportion to the offense, but he still wanted to go after Derrick and take the son-of-a-bitch down in the woods like a mountain lion on a lame deer.

"So… what?" he asked Julie. "You think I'm a mole or something? A spy?"

"No. I don't think you're a spy, Sean. I haven't had time to figure any of this out. It's all falling apart right here in front of me." She rested her head in shaking hands.

It seemed to Sean it had taken her half a beat too long to answer him.

"I don't own any stock in Eagle. I never even heard of them before a couple days ago."

"Their parent company is QTC, Inc.," she said, timid as a mouse.

Sean thought it was a tad late to bring out the sad little girl act. He knew he held a sizable interest in QTC, but he'd had no idea they owned Eagle. "It doesn't matter what it's called," he said. "Even if I owned a million shares of Payne's fat ass, it's not really any of your business—and it's certainly none of Derrick's."

Julie raised her head. Eyes narrowed, jaw set, there was a different edge in her voice now. "You're right, it's none of his business," she said. "But it might be mine. I am your 'girl,' after all."

Sean winced. "I don't see why my investments should have anything to do with our relationship at this point."

Julie stood up. "How can they not have something to do with it? When it turns out you own stock in the company that's trying to toss me out on the street!"

"And what would you like me to do about that? Go to the next shareholder's meeting and complain?"

They stared each other down across ten feet of sand like two gunfighters with itchy trigger fingers. Sean waited for her to flinch.

"I hope you know what you should do," Julie said finally. "Because I'm certainly not going to tell you."

Sean laughed. "Maybe you could be a little more enigmatic?"

Julie turned, picked her bag out of the sand and walked away from him.

"So you're just gonna leave?" Sean said to her back, arms out at his sides, palms up. "That's your answer? Again?"

A hand went to her face in a wiping motion, but she kept walking and said nothing.

"Julie, come on," he said, letting his arms flop to his sides.

"You need to go," she screamed back over her shoulder as she broke into a run. "Get the hell out of here."

He took three steps in her direction then stopped. He was too pissed off. He needed to cool down—literally. The anger seethed hot under his skin. His face, neck and shoulders felt sunburned. He took in a breath, about to yell down the beach after her, but forced himself to do nothing more than release it in a long, aggravated sigh. Kicking sand high into the air, Sean turned away from Julie's receding back and headed toward his hotel.

* * *

Julie ran as hard as she could. By the time she reached the apartment complex her breath came in ragged gasps. She skirted the back of her building then scaled the tree to her window, wiping tears from her face as she went.

She wished she hadn't brought up the stock. She'd known Derrick's digging would raise Sean's hackles. She just wanted to know if it was true—which it apparently was. Maybe he was surprised to find out that QTC owned Eagle, but that didn't change the fact that his money was supporting a company that was helping to ruin this community. If he couldn't figure out that he should sell, it wasn't her job to tell him. What had really blindsided her was his accusation that she and Derrick were conspiring against him. How could he even think that after last night?

The tears subsided a bit as she shimmied through the window into her bathroom and anger took over. Why couldn't people understand that all their actions had consequences? That if they held stock in Shell Oil, they were endorsing the company's genocidal policies abroad and their ecocidal activities at home? Everyone in the country was so damned oblivious that she could probably sit and explain it to all of them face to face and still no one would get the message.

This was all Derrick's fault. The bastard had actually done a background check on Sean. She wondered if he'd done the same with her before he'd deemed her co-conspirator—or girlfriend—material. The man seemed dead-set on keeping her and Sean apart and, at this point, he was certainly succeeding on that front.

Julie stormed into her kitchen and pulled a bottle of cold water from the fridge. She guzzled half the bottle in one long pull, her thirst suddenly unquenchable. Then she slumped to the floor, the ice pick pain of a brain freeze stabbing into her right temple as she wrapped her arms around her knees and the wracking sobs now came in earnest.

Seventeen

The clock on Sean's dash read 7:01 p.m. when he pulled back into his hotel parking lot. In direct defiance of Julie's wishes for him to leave town, he'd spent the afternoon and early evening circumnavigating clockwise around the lake. In between cathartic climbs to the top of Eagle Rock on the West Shore and Cave Rock on the East he'd even found time for a late lunch at a Mexican restaurant in Incline Village.

After fighting with Julie he'd been so angry he couldn't sit still. He'd wanted to hit someone—preferably Derrick. He knew he needed to calm down, but the seething anger seemed a better option than what he'd expected was waiting in the wings: a crushing depression ready to envelope him like a heavy, wet blanket.

Ever since Sean first got his license, driving had been his best escape. When he was behind the wheel of a moving automobile, his body and subconscious occupied with keeping the vehicle on the road, the rest of his mind was free to work out life's problems. But even the inspirational scenery he'd been privy to all day hadn't helped him come to any useful conclusions about the current morass his life had become.

The hotel parking lot had gotten much more crowded since he left earlier. It was the Friday before the Fourth of July so he shouldn't have been surprised, but he couldn't even get around to the back lot where he'd been parking all week—it almost looked blocked off. He took the spot of a departing car up by the road and hoofed it across the lot into the main lobby.

The front desk clerks were both occupied as Sean passed and entered the hallway leading back toward his room. He was thinking he might have to locate that tree up to Julie's bathroom window after dinner. The timing had just been wrong for him to leave earlier and he'd feared that any hope of reconciliation might have been lost if he left the basin before talking to her. Anyhow, his anger had cooled over the course of the day and he really wanted to see her.

The hotel was laid out like a lightning bolt with the front to back hall making up the connecting center piece between the two long, jagged ends. Sean's room was in the wing to the left, about ten doors down. As he rounded the corner into that hallway he came to a nearly screeching halt. Two police officers in what looked like full riot gear stood directly outside of his room.

Sean instantly backpedaled into the main corridor and ducked behind a fake tree, then scanned his surroundings for escape options. If he continued toward the back of the building for another fifty feet, he would come to the hallway on the right, leading to the other wing. He risked a glance around the corner. The cops remained by his door, apparently they hadn't noticed his blunder into plain sight. Glancing fifty feet behind him to the lobby, he spied another officer in a regular uniform who appeared to be casing the joint.

"Shit," Sean mouthed. His neck and shoulders tensed as he breathed in. Across the hall, windows looked out on the pool. Children splashed and played in the water while Sean stood, back to the wall, on the verge of panic.

How the hell did they find me?

Had someone overheard the scene on the beach with Julie and Derrick and led the police here? And why the battle gear? If they were only here to question him, they wouldn't be dressed like that, would they?

Sean looked up toward the lobby again. The cop was talking to one of the women at the front desk. Even from this distance he could see her point down the hall toward him. Without hesitation he broke from the cover of the fake-plastic tree and marched purposely across the ten-foot gap between the left-hand hallway walls.

Traversing that vast emptiness felt like parading naked across an arena stage. He forced himself to turn his head and glance toward his room anyway. The heads of the cops turned slowly, their attention drawn by his movement down the main corridor. Sean tried to maintain a normal pace, but the distance across the gap seemed to stretch out and the urge to sprint was nearly overwhelming. A moment later he passed the far wall, out of the officers' line of vision.

No way they could have ID'ed him from that brief glimpse, right? In a few seconds he hoped to be home free, around the corner and into the other side hall.

"Hey you, hold on there."

The strong voice came from the direction of his room. Footsteps thundered on carpet as Sean increased his pace to what used to be called speed-walking.

What evidence could they possibly have against him? The indictment of a councilmen's wife seemed pretty insubstantial for a judge to issue a search warrant. Or could they enter the room without one since it was a hotel? Sean didn't know about that. What he did know was—like Julie had said—running would make him look guilty, but this turnout of force seemed to indicate they had something solid to go on.

Sean reached the hallway on the right, turned and accelerated. He made it about five doors down the hall when he realized there was no way he could possibly make it to the exit at the far end before his pursuers turned the corner behind him. The door to the parking lot looked a mile and a half away to him and he'd reached a point of no return, about halfway down the hall. The cops' footsteps pounded on the carpeted floor back in the main hall—they would round the corner any second.

Coming up one door down was a fully loaded maid's cart against the left hand wall; the guest room door next to it sat partially open. Mexican mariachi music blared from inside and seeped out into the hallway through a two-inch gap between door and jamb.

Sean looked once more behind him. The cops had yet to make the corner. He wheeled and ducked behind the cart, his body blocking the room door. Eyes on the floor, he waited for the inevitable thudding footsteps that would find him.

Eighteen

Julie hung a quick left across two lanes of speeding traffic into the Harvey's driveway and cruised under the casino bridge. At the stop sign she checked her mirror. The black sedan that had followed her from home turned in behind. She steered her battered Subaru right and headed for the "Self Parking" arrows that pointed into the garage. The car's balding tires screeched around every corner up into the bowels of the structure.

She disliked visiting the casinos, but her mother had insisted they meet at Harvey's. Earlier, between her Yoga classes, her mom had called to say she would be in town for the evening and Julie had jumped at the opportunity to get her mind off Sean and Derrick and the cops, at least for a little while. It was Harvey's this time because her mother had yet to eat at Cabo Wabo—Sammy Hagar's tequila club/restaurant that served an Americanized version of Mexican food. Turned out her mother was a Sammy Hagar fan. Who knew?

Julie parked in the open air on the fourth floor of the garage and checked her face in the rear view before hopping out of the car. She rarely wore makeup, but had applied some before leaving her apartment in the hope that her mother wouldn't notice that she'd been crying off and on all day.

The feds had been staying in their car at least, not following her on foot, so she hoped to have a little privacy at dinner. She managed to get the car door latched closed after only three tries, then entered the nearby stairwell and clomped down the metal stairs to the ground floor. Exiting into the driveway near the road, Julie risked death by distracted, rental-car-driving tourist as she jogged across the drive to Harvey's corner entrance. She came in half a floor below the main level and descended the side stairs, avoiding the casino floor entirely. Over the years Julie had charted many routes in and out of restaurants and nightclubs in the Stateline area with the absolute minimum time spent on any casino floor. It was one of her talents. She'd even considered putting it on her resume.

After skirting the edge of the arcade and hoofing it down the hall past the restrooms, Julie found her mom seated at the bar inside Cabo sipping a frozen margarita. Her mother had gone through a period following her father's death where she'd spent too much time and money in these four casinos. Julie suspected one of the reasons her mom had moved out to Dayton was to get a little further away from the glitz of Tahoe.

"Hey, Mom," Julie said as she walked up behind her mother.

"Julie!" Her mother leaned over and hugged her from her seat. "Look at you," she said. "You're positively glowing! Who is he?"

"It's probably just sweat," Julie said, taking the next stool. "I practically ran from the car. Anyway, can't I be happy without it having to do with a guy?"

"I suppose you could," her mom said. "But you've never been any good at it." She smiled a knowing grin and sipped her drink.

Damn.

Julie had never met anyone so able to read people as her mother and she really didn't want to spend all evening venting about Sean. In fact, she hadn't even decided if she was going to tell her mother that Sean was back in town. The way her mother had sung Sean's praises in the past, Julie wasn't sure she wanted to hear the woman's opinion just yet on where she and Sean currently stood.

"Did you tell anyone we need a table?" Julie asked.

"They'll call when it's ready. So, who's the new man? How long have you been seeing him?" Her mother sipped again at the frozen concoction in front of her as the bartender approached.

"What can I get you?" he asked Julie.

"Whatever she's having is fine." She had a feeling that alcohol was going to be in order tonight. Her mom had been her confidant growing up, never one to judge her. But, like an old hound dog, she could also sniff out when Julie was hiding something.

Seemingly disinterested, her mom said, "You don't have to tell me if you don't want to." She patted Julie's hand where it sat on the bar then launched into a long-winded description of the real estate seminar she had attended that day in Harrah's convention center across the road. A few pages into the rundown, she was interrupted by a call for their table—none too soon in Julie's view.

Despite being in her late fifties, her mom was still slim with a shapely figure that she had—as usual—accented with a well cut business blazer and knee length skirt. Julie noticed that her still-light-brown hair showed not a strand out of place and she wondered if her mom had it done on the way over from Harrah's. It wouldn't have surprised Julie if she did. Her mom had been raving about Allison at Lulu's for over a decade now.

Once seated, Julie's mother dove back into her monologue with a description of the jacket one of the speakers at the conference had been wearing. Julie knew her mom was doing it on purpose, but it worked nonetheless.

"Mom, it's Sean, okay?" she blurted from behind her raised menu. "Sean Connors."

Her mother's hand appeared at the top of the menu and pulled it down so she could see Julie's face. "I'm sorry, did you just say 'Sean Connors' or am I hearing things?"

"That's what I said, Mother. Stop being so dramatic."

Her mom raised her own menu, though not enough to obscure her eyes. "So, Sean is back in town?"

"Yes."

"Hmmm… The shrimp fajitas look good."

Julie fought the urge to snap at the woman. She decided on the veggie burrito and set her closed menu on the table. "Go ahead, ask away. I know you can barely contain yourself."

Her mother's eyes met Julie's with feigned surprise. "Why, what do you mean, child?" she said.

"It's Sean, Mom… your Prince Charming, your Knight in Shining Armor."

Julie's mother made a show of folding up her menu and setting it aside. "Julie," she began, then paused for a sip of water. "I always liked Sean. And, yes, I thought the two of you would make a great couple. But there was always something in that pretty little head of yours—" she tapped a finger on the side of her own head, "—that kept you two apart. And just because a mother knows what's good for her child doesn't mean her child knows what's good for herself."

Julie gritted her teeth and looked away. She didn't think her mother had ever quite understood the situation between her and Sean. Of course, that was then. Julie wasn't sure she understood it herself now. Was complete confusion a normal reaction to love or had she gone totally insane?

The waiter arrived, took their orders and left them sitting in silence. Julie stared blankly at the tablecloth in front of her. After a few moments her mother spoke in a quiet voice. "What happened?" she said.

The tears came slowly and Julie lifted her napkin from her lap to wipe them away as they ran down her cheeks. "It's so stupid, Mom," she began. Then the words came out in a flood, "I ran into him at Sprouts a couple of days ago and he was back in town for the first time in years and we were talking just fine and then—like, immediately—we got into this huge fight."

"A fight? Why?"

"He wanted to know why I broke it off."

"Ahh."

Her mother was one of the few who knew what that was about, so she, at least, could maybe understand. Back then her mom had tried to convince her that Sean wouldn't walk away from her, but Julie hadn't listened.

When she didn't continue her mother said, "So that was it?"

"No. I stormed out because I didn't know what else to do."

"What about telling him?"

Julie gave her a look that she hoped would burn.

"Anyway, I ran out so fast I forgot my sweater and he…" Julie shook her head and smiled through the tears. "Of course he, being Sean, found my place, brought the sweater and apologized for being an ass—when it was me who should have apologized."

"Did you?"

Julie held her head up defiantly. "Yes, as a matter of fact I did."

"So you told him what happened."

She bit her lip. "Not exactly."

"Julie!"

"I couldn't think how to do it, Mom. It still scares me, alright? And now… it just keeps getting harder."

Her mother reached across the table and put a hand over hers. "It's okay," she said.

Julie tried to compose herself. When their dinners arrived, she ordered another margarita. She suspected it would take no effort at all to drink herself into oblivion on this early summer evening.

Nineteen

Crouched behind the maid's cart, Sean heard nothing from the end of the hall.

He pivoted, slowly and quietly, and found a line of sight through the piles of towels and rolls of toilet paper. Two cops in regular uniforms stood at the hallway intersection looking this way then toward the beach exit at back of the building, apparently determining which way to go. After a moment Cop #1 motioned silently to Cop #2 and the latter disappeared down the other hallway. Cop #1 then advanced on Sean's minuscule hiding spot at a slow pace.

Shit. Sean kept the obscenity to himself this time.

He had two options: 1. Wait to be found; or 2. See what kind of Mexican dance party was raging in the room behind him. He made his decision, leaned back into the door and slipped into the room, then quickly returned the door to its original position.

He'd expected to find a housekeeper staring at him in disbelief—or even screaming at the top of her lungs—but was surprised when he saw no one. The volume of the distorted music through the tinny speakers of the bedside clock/radio was headache inducing. Sean sat in a crouch for a moment with his back against the wall behind the door before peering into the bathroom and vanity area. The housekeeper faced away from him, on her knees, scrubbing the bathtub. Her rear-end bopped along with the beat of the song.

Unseen, he stood and stepped quickly past the opening and across the room to the sliding glass door, which stood ajar. Just as he was about to step out onto the small patio, a shadow appeared on the ground. Moving quickly back and behind the drapes, Sean managed to get out of sight before Cop #2 passed by at the rear of the building.

Well, what now?

He stood like a wax statue, back to the curtain, facing the hall door. It would probably open any second and Cop #1 would burst in with gun drawn. Sean hoped the man wasn't trigger-happy.

A flicker of movement in the light from the bathroom caught his eye. The housekeeper standing? Coming out? He caught her reflection in the mirror above the dresser as she switched off the light. Before she could round the corner into the main room, Sean wheeled through the open slider and onto the patio. He looked quickly from side to side, expecting Cop #2 to deck him, but there was no one there. He slumped into the corner next to the door and tried to catch his breath. The air came in and out too fast and he felt on the verge of hyperventilating. The triple-time mariachi music wasn't helping matters.

Every patio here was separated from its neighbors by solid walls. Sean felt like a horse with blinders. He rested against the right-hand wall, facing away from the exit at the far end of the wing—where he hoped the two cops had met up again by now. He had a great view of the beach and lake, but in order to see anything to either side he would have to stick his head out past the end of the wall.

Straining to hear any footsteps over the blaring music, Sean slid closer to the edge and leaned out. He looked left first—the direction he and the cop had come from. Seeing no one, he ducked his head back in, turned and popped it out again. No one that way either. Cop #2 was either around the corner of the building or up on one of the patios.

Sean considered the vast expanse of sand in front of him. Should he make a run for it? Out to the lake and up the beach?

He quickly nixed the idea. He would have to cover upwards of seventy-five feet of open ground before he came to any cover. But he had to figure out something quick. The housekeeper had started up the vacuum and it was only a matter of time before she would get to the door and spot him standing here. With all that in mind, he took a deep breath and crept around the dividing wall to the next patio, watching for bodies in riot gear as he went.

The curtains in the next room stood open, but the door was locked. With a rapid side-to-side glance, Sean continued on to the next patio. He feared he would step into the middle of some guest's barbecue if he kept this scheme up too long. The glass door to the second room stood wide open, but the screen and curtains were closed—occupied. Sean slid to the next patio with still no sign of his pursuers.

He'd thought the best thing to do was go toward the end of this wing and away from his own room, but did he really expect to find a vacant room just standing open? What was he going to do if one of the cops came back this way or more came from the other direction?

At about the sixth patio—he'd lost count and didn't know why he'd started counting in the first place—he tried the door and found it unlocked, curtains pulled wide. Willing the door not to squeak in its track, he slid it open and stepped inside. The beds were both made, but open suitcases sat along the wall and personal belongings littered the nightstands and dresser.

Another curse nearly escaped his mouth, but before he could turn and exit the room he heard footfalls approaching from the right. With no time to close the patio door, he pivoted out of sight beyond the open curtain. The footsteps stopped close by as Sean's eyes flashed to the gloom over near the hall door. He could only pray that the tenant wasn't currently in the bathroom.

From his vantage point next to the curtains, Sean could see a foot or so of the partition wall outside the door. Gravel crunched between shoes and concrete just out of view. Sean looked again to the hall door with longing. He would have to cross twenty feet or so in full daylight to get there—damn these people for leaving their curtains wide open. He tried to push himself further into the wall.

A shadow fell on the glass as one of the cops leaned in toward the open door. Sean was only slightly relieved to see that he didn't have his gun drawn. Taking one last step forward, the guy rapped his knuckles lightly on the glass three times and said, "Hello, anybody home?"

Sean counted ten thuds of his racing heart as the cop stood three feet from him waiting for a reply, so close he could clearly see a bead of sweat as it rolled down the guy's forehead and disappeared into his eyebrow.

Then he stuck his head in the room.

Twenty

Julie's mom cut her second enchilada into neat little bites. "Well," she said, "has he run back to whence he came? Is he married? What?" The table had been soothingly quiet for a few minutes as they dug into their food.

"Sean's not married," Julie said. "Never has been."

Her mother didn't look surprised. "That boy always had it bad for you. You probably ruined him for life."

"Mom!" Julie said, though she couldn't keep the blush from rising in her cheeks.

"Well, it's true, dear."

"I don't think I've ever 'ruined' anyone."

"Never underestimate the power you hold over men, honey. They may have brawn, but we have beauty and guile." Her mother grinned a sly grin and took another bite from her fork.

"Anyway…" Julie cleared her throat. "After last night, we kind of—"

"What happened last night?"

Damn it.

Could she let nothing slide? Julie had been hoping to slip last night past her. She'd always been frank with her mom when it came to her sex life, but this was different somehow. She kicked around what to say as she chewed, then, through a mouthful of rice, just blurted it out. "I slept with him."

"Excuse me?" her mother said, the look of shock on her face almost comical.

Julie made a production of swallowing her rice down then followed it with some water. She met her mother's inquisitive eyes and repeated, "I slept with him," clearly enough that heads turned toward her from adjacent tables.

"After two days, honey? That's not like you." Her mother's voice was louder than her own had been. Julie closed her eyes and lowered her chin to her chest, trying to fold in on herself and deflect the disapproving eyes.

The clap of her mother's hands brought Julie's head back up. "But you two knew each other before," her mom said. "And I knew it! I knew you were meant for each other. Haven't thought about it for quite a few years, but I knew it. See how things come back around and work out in the end?"

"Mom," Julie said.

"That explains the glow."

"Mother! You're missing the big picture here."

"Big picture?" She looked bewildered for a moment. "Oh, the unhappiness. Sorry. Continue." Her mother went back to her food.

Julie guzzled more water, ignoring her second margarita completely now. She'd been wrong about the alcohol. All it had done was make her tired. "We didn't exactly leave things well," she said.

"Why did you leave things at all?"

"It's a long story," she said, looking away. "He had to go back to LA for a while."

Her mother's smile remained unshakeable. "I'm sure he'll be back."

"I don't know… Things aren't that simple."

"They are if you let them be. Love's not easy to find—I assume you've figured that out by now—when it comes around, you do what you can to keep it."

Julie sighed heavily. "Listen, Mom, don't get me wrong, Sean's still a great guy and all, but…"

"But what? He's turned into an ogre?"

Julie shot her mother another evil look. "No. It's just… we're having trouble seeing eye to eye on a few things."

Her mom's face drooped. "Julie, you have trouble seeing eye to eye with everyone on everything."

"Not *everyone*."

"Just about. You're on the fringe, dear. I take it he has more of a mainstream outlook?"

"Yeah, you could say that, but…" She wrung one hand with the other. "I guess he's big on investments, but he doesn't even know what his money is supporting. Turns out he owns some of Eagle Development's stock."

"Eagle Development?"

"The company that would like nothing more than to toss me out of my home? The one that bends all the rules to their advantage. The one that's ruining this town."

"Oh, that Eagle Development." Her mother sipped her drink. "How could he have known what they were doing here?"

"He could have checked."

"And how many people actually do that kind of thing?"

"Just about none," Julie said, crossing her arms. "That's the problem, isn't it?"

Her mom set her knife and fork on her mostly empty plate and pushed it aside before settling her forearms on the table, hands clasped. "Julie, honey, you can't realistically expect anyone to ever completely share your point of view. You can try and help him understand the way you think, but he may never see the world the way you do."

Julie released an aggravated sigh.

"And there's the bottom line," her mother said under her breath—just loud enough for Julie to hear—as she retrieved her purse from under the table and began digging in it. "Listen, dear, you're never going to agree with anyone one hundred percent of the time. You're thirty-two. It's time to grow up and realize you don't live in Fantasyland." She pulled her wallet from the purse and set it on the table. "Fairy tale relationships only exist in fairy tales. They're imaginary. If you want to have any kind of meaningful relationship at all you have to learn to compromise."

Julie leaned back in her chair and set her jaw. Her mother seemed to be growing more and more motherly as she aged. "I'm not looking for a fairy tale relation—"

"Yes, you are," her mom said forcefully. "Do you think your father and I saw eye to eye on everything? That Max and I do? Would you have been able to have conversations like this with me back then if I held all the same views and beliefs that your father did? Look, it's a matter of accepting the other person for who they are and loving them for it, not trying to turn them into a carbon copy of yourself."

Julie looked away. "I just want us to get along."

"I suspect that Sean is more than willing to 'get along.' That it's you who are not."

Julie sometimes felt like her mother could see directly into her soul. "But Mom, he doesn't even know wh—"

Her mother held up a hand in the universal stop gesture, then leaned forward again, elbows on the table. "Julie," she said. "If Sean is anything at all like I remember, don't you think you should try and *not* let him go this time? A man like that doesn't come along very often and I'll bet he's not naïve enough these days to wait around while you sort out those demons in your head—even if he does still love you."

Does he? she wondered as she stared into her melting margarita. *And, if so, just who is it he loves?*

Twenty One

Sean willed himself invisible as time stretched out like a frayed bungee cord. Breath caught in his throat, he stood next to the sliding glass door with his eyes closed, as if maybe the cop wouldn't see him if he couldn't see the cop.

The wheels of the door moved slightly in their track and Sean braced himself for discovery. A moment later, from somewhere outside, a voice called, "Can I help you officer?"

Sean opened his eyes in time to see the patrolman withdraw his head and upper body from the doorway. He stepped from Sean's view and turned away. "Is this your room, sir?" he asked.

"Yeah," the other voice said. "What's going on?"

Sean seized the opportunity and pushed away from the wall. He crossed the room, honed in like a laser pointer on his goal. He didn't look back until he was safely in the gloom of the vanity alcove.

Out on the patio the cop stood with his back to the door, blocking the guest's entrance to the room. The tourist said something about how his kid must have left the door open. Sean didn't wait for the cop's reply. He opened the hall door a couple of inches and peered out in the direction of the exit—he was four doors from the end of the hall. But where was the other cop?

Sean glanced over at the patio. The one out there still had his back turned. Pulling the door open further, Sean risked a peek up and down the hall. Nothing but the maid's cart cluttered the corridor. In one swift motion he slid out and pulled the door shut behind him. The heavy steel *clomped* shut and echoed through the empty hallway. Like an Olympic sprinter off his blocks, Sean bolted down the hall as some words Julie had been saying a lot lately ran through his head, "Running only makes us look more guilty." Which, of course, he was.

Too late now, he thought, teetering on the edge of full-blown panic.

He hit the exit door at full speed, cracking the glass as it slammed open with a crash. Into the parking lot he stumbled and nearly tumbled forward to the pavement. One hand down to steady himself, he regained his balance and charged forward toward the trees on the other side, expecting to hear a harsh, "Stop or I'll shoot," any second.

When Sean reached the edge of the lot, he ducked behind an SUV that was backed in under a tree. No one called out after him. He crouched in the shadows wheezing, trying to catch his breath. After a minute or more—he really couldn't tell how long it was—he raised his head enough to peer back at the exit through the tinted rear window of the vehicle.

One cop stood outside the cracked hotel door speaking into his radio, just out of earshot. A second later the other one appeared from around the front of the building and joined him. They surveyed the parking lot, trees and beach, then walked to the corner of the building and peered around the back to the west.

Sean seized the moment and scurried along behind the row of cars in the direction of Highway 50 hunched over like the guy from Notre Dame. He paused momentarily and looked back as he passed every car to make sure he hadn't been spotted. When he heard an engine racing and a vehicle appeared from the direction he was heading, he ducked behind a large wagon. Peering out from the side of the car, he just caught sight of a black and white Ford Expedition shooting past.

Here comes the cavalry.

Turning from the lot, Sean looked across the fifty feet of open grass to the trees behind him. Just into those trees a six-foot high fence separated this property from the next. It ran nearer to the parking lot the closer it got to the highway. About thirty feet from his position Sean saw a break in the fence where a walkway passed through. If he could get down the row of cars to that walkway, maybe he could get through it without being seen. He was loath to leave his truck in the lot, but, at this stage of the game, he could see no way of getting to it without being caught.

He raised his head just enough to see what the cops were doing at the rear of the building. Their attention was still focused toward the lake. Ducking down, he slipped across to the cover of the next vehicle.

Twenty Two

Julie's mother snatched the check from the table as soon as the waiter set it down, insisting, over Julie's protests, that she was paying. Once that business was done they took their time wandering through the arcade and down the hall to the hotel lobby, making small talk about Julie's yoga studio and her mom's real estate business. Her mother, of course, had her car in Valet. Julie sometimes wondered how she had ended up so down to Earth when her own mother always had such aspirations to luxury.

After handing her car claim check to an attendant out front, her mother said, "I wish I'd had a chance to say hello to Sean. Is he gone already?"

He damn well better be, Julie thought.

"Yeah, he left this morning," she said. "Angry." She felt tears trying to push their way out from behind her eyes, but refused to let them.

"Honey," her mother said wrapping an arm around Julie's shoulder. "You two used to be such good friends... I know you can work this out."

Julie considered her mother's words. "But isn't that part of the problem?" she said. "That we were such good friends?"

"That's a blessing, dear, not a problem. Your father and I weren't friends—didn't even know each other before we dated. It's so much harder to get to know the other person that way because your defenses are always up. Max and I, we were friends for years before we ever dated."

"So how did you justify risking that friendship by getting physical?"

"If it's time for a relationship to move forward, it will. If you're not on board then you've missed the boat anyhow," her mother said as an attendant pulled up with her car. "Besides, after last night you two are way past friendship anyway."

Ain't that the truth.

What direction had they gone, though? This was unfamiliar territory. She didn't know if it was all over or just beginning.

After giving Julie a peck on the cheek, her mother climbed into her car, closed the door, lowered the window and said, "Call him, honey. Don't let him get away again."

"I'll try, Mom," Julie said.

"We'll do dinner," her mother said as she pulled away. "The four of us."

At present, Julie couldn't even begin to picture that happening.

*

Ten minutes later, sitting at the stop light at Highway 50 and Ski Run Boulevard, Julie let her forehead rest momentarily on the top of her steering wheel. How had everything fallen apart so completely in only three days? She'd been doing fine by herself. She was feeling more at peace than she ever had without having a man in her life. Then she'd run into Sean, sitting at that damned table at Sprouts. Now Derrick—who she'd thought was a good friend—had lost his mind and the fight to save the Lake's Edge looked mostly lost. She felt like her life had been tossed in a blender set on Frappe.

The honk of a horn brought her out of her reverie. The light had turned. She shifted through the gears, getting the car back up to speed, and wondered if this was all in her head, like her mother had suggested. Julie wouldn't even know about Sean's investments if Derrick hadn't pried where he shouldn't have. Maybe she was just using this as an excuse to back away from a relationship that had always been too scary for her.

She regretted walking away from Sean on the beach and leaving him angry, but she hadn't known what else to do. It had seemed better to leave than let the fight escalate—especially out in public. Now the situation left her unable to contact him. Although... she did have his cell number, what if she called him from a payphone?

No. I can't risk leading the authorities to him.

Julie checked her rearview mirror for the black sedan. She didn't see it right off, but she assumed it was back there somewhere.

Twenty Three

Sean huddled against the front grill of an older model sedan, shaky from pumping adrenaline. The car sat adjacent to his path to freedom—the sidewalk leading to that break in the fence. About twenty feet separated him from the cover of the first tree, but it was a wide open twenty feet. All that was left to do was sprint for it.

At the rear of the building the cops were fanning out in a new search pattern. The more immediate thing in his line of sight, though, was a group of seven or eight college-age kids walking directly along his intended escape route from the front of the hotel. One or two pointed toward the police out back, but they still continued forward in his direction.

If he stayed where he was the kids would see him when they passed by. How could they not figure he was the one the cops were looking for? Why else would he be crouched behind a parked car? As the group approached he slid around to the driver's side of the vehicle, the SUV next to the sedan obscuring him from the cop's view at the rear of the building.

By this point Sean had become accustomed to his galloping heart, but as he watched the group approach—and saw through the widows of the neighboring SUV that the cops had taken an interest in them—it cranked up to a previously unmatched thundering. With the police attention focused this way how could he make a run for it now?

When the kids were ten feet from the sedan, a last ditch idea surfaced in Sean's head. As the group arrived at the rear bumper and continued up the passenger side of the car, he slid down the driver's side opposite them to the trunk. The SUV on his right was a behemoth—and poorly parked as well—leaving the rear sticking out five feet past the back of the smaller sedan. Sean scrambled around to the back bumper, in plain view of anyone in front of the hotel. He could only hope no one was looking from that direction—and also that the ass end of the SUV was enough to shield him from the cops' view.

Rounding the corner of the car to the passenger side, Sean stayed in a crouch as he came up behind the kids. The first few were already past the front end of the car and out in plain view of the curious cops. Sean stood as he passed the front door of the vehicle and moved up along the right-hand side of the group—putting the tallest guy between himself and the cops.

Eight heads turned in unison as Sean appeared next to them from out of nowhere. "Hi," he said, keeping pace with the group as they approached the fence.

"Hey," the tall one said, an eyebrow raised in confusion. Two of the girls Sean had startled eyed him warily, like they might a cute, but rabid, dog. They all kept walking, though. Sean focused past the kids, on the cops. A number still looked this way, though none seemed to be raising any alarms.

"Can we help you with something, man?" the tall kid asked. He looked about nineteen with a patchy beard still struggling to cover his chin.

Sean considered the question. Before he decided what to say they passed behind the fence and out of view of the police. "No thanks," he answered. "You've done more than enough." Then he picked up his pace and speed-walked away from the kids, forcing himself not to break into a spastic run through the trees.

The path wound in a useless manner through the forest and eventually dropped Sean exactly where he didn't want to be: on the sidewalk at the edge of Lake Tahoe Boulevard. If a police cruiser were to pass by there was nowhere to hide. Looking down the highway to the west, Sean saw the stoplight between him and his hotel entrance turn red. As he turned back the other way—thinking he would cross the road to get behind the buildings on the other side—he noticed a battered, gray, Subaru wagon slowing down for the light. Sean released a pent up, slightly crazy laugh as he recognized the driver.

It seemed Julie owned a car after all.

Twenty Four

Someone pounded on the passenger window and Julie jumped in her seat. She immediately revved the engine and started to release the clutch, thinking she was getting carjacked. She was about to take off through the red light before it occurred to her that she was in Tahoe, not Oakland.

The guy kept pounding on the closed window then began shouting something. Julie concentrated on the muffled sound of the word and realized it was her name. The man ducked down so she could see his face and Julie immediately knew why she hadn't recognized him sooner—he should have been halfway back to Southern California by now.

Julie reached across and unlocked the passenger door without really deciding to do it. Sean climbed in and immediately reclined the passenger seat until it touched the rear bench. "Don't turn into my hotel," he said. "Drive right past like everything is fine."

"Hello to you, too," Julie said as she accelerated away from the now-green light. "What the hell are you doing here? You're supposed to be gone—again!"

Sean let out a pent up breath. "I needed to talk to you."

"So you've been—what?—standing on the side of the road hoping I'd come by?"

"You know," Sean said, pointing both index fingers at her like two pistols, "that's *exactly* what I've been doing. I've been waiting since noon. What took you so long?"

Julie let the sarcasm slide. "Sean, what's going on?"

"Take a look to your right… It appears the police have found out about me after all."

"How…?" Julie trailed off as she took in the scene outside Sean's hotel. Lining the lot were five or six police cruisers, at least three vans, a number of unmarked federal cars and—were those ATF vests some of those guys had on? "Jesus Christ."

"Yeah," Sean seconded. "I passed 'Jesus Christ' a while back, I'm leaning more toward 'Holy Fuck' at this point."

Julie laughed out loud at Sean's deadpan delivery, despite the circumstances. She looked over at Sean's face to see if he was serious. He wasn't smiling so she lost the grin and checked her mirrors for the black sedan as they rolled past Rufus Allen Boulevard. She still didn't see the car back there. Could be her pals were currently occupied at Sean's hotel. Otherwise they probably would have roared out of obscurity to pull her over once she'd picked up her fugitive passenger.

"Don't go back to your place either," Sean said. "We need to get somewhere more secluded."

"What did you do today?" Julie asked. "How did they find you?"

"Nothing. I don't know," he said, his delivery short, words clipped. "I drove around the lake. Didn't see anyone following me. When I got back—there they were."

Julie passed Lakeview and continued west on Lake Tahoe Boulevard, trying to think of a safe place to go—somewhere she could be sure they weren't followed. "What about Sawmill Pond?"

"Yeah," Sean said. "Sure."

She thought it would be easy to tell on the open road west of the Y if they had a tail, but she wondered why his reply had a hint of reluctance in it. As they cruised in silence, Julie kept one eye glued to the rearview.

The only constant is change.

The thought came unbidden. Ten minutes before she'd been trying to come up with a way to contact Sean without tipping off the cops. Now he sat right beside her and she couldn't think of a single thing to say. As they approached Third Street she came at the problem from a different angle.

"What did you want to talk to me about?" she asked.

Sean shifted in his seat before replying. "You know, I had this whole apology speech worked out in my head earlier, but at some point when I was running from the cops my remorse seems to have evaporated."

Julie squinted at the road ahead, confused. "Excuse me?" she said.

"I'm still stuck wondering why Derrick has it in for me. And whether you've got anything to do with it."

"You're kidding, right?" Julie tried to keep her eyes peeled for cops as they cruised straight through the light at the Y. She found it difficult to do with Sean accusing her of conspiring against him. "How could you seriously think that?"

"You two obviously had something going on when I caught up to you on the beach —and he seems awfully jealous for somebody you keep insisting is 'just a friend.'"

Julie slapped the steering wheel with her palm. "I don't believe this. After last night you have the balls to accuse me of betraying you? What do you think I am? A whore—like Payne said—who hops into bed with every guy I meet?"

Sean crossed his arms and clamped his jaw firmly shut. As she brought the car to a halt for the stop sign at D Street, Julie restrained an urge to punch him.

"I don't know what to think anymore," he said. "You've got information on me that you shouldn't even be able to get. Which, for some reason I can't fathom, makes *you* mad at *me*." He sat up, voice rising as he continued. "Derrick is a jealous freak hell-bent on keeping us apart. The cops are rifling through my stuff even as we speak. And there are federal agents probably tailing us right now, ready to shoot on sight. So tell me what I should think, Julie. Tell me, *please*!"

"Don't get all high and mighty with me!" Julie yelled back.

"It was an elaborate set up. The two of you pulled me right in."

"For what? So we could pin it on you?"

Sean lowered his voice. "Apparently."

Julie popped the clutch and the Suby screeched away from the stop sign, throwing Sean back into his seat. She pushed the old beater up to sixty miles an hour out on the gently-swooping, divided, four-lane through the trees and the steering wheel wobbled beneath her fingers like a warped record.

"No one was supposed to get caught," she said. "No one."

Twenty Five

The Subaru screamed around the corner onto Sawmill Road and Sean pinched his eyes shut. He prayed Julie was a better driver than he remembered. The car careened through the ditch at the entrance to the parking area and bounced into the lot by the pond. She yanked the emergency brake while it was still moving then jumped out almost before it slid to a stop. The driver's door banged against the latch once and flopped back open.

Sean lay in his seat: arms crossed, jaw set, blood boiling. After listening to the rattle of the idling engine for more than a minute, he reached over and shut it off. A primal scream echoed from somewhere in the trees behind the car. If it was Julie, she was already a long way off.

Sean returned the seat back to its full upright position and looked around. The place was different. The parking lot had been paved and there were restrooms in the center. He could only see a portion of the pond over the tall grass.

He climbed out of the vehicle. Four other cars sat in the lot, but there was no one around them and Julie was nowhere in sight. He found a path heading toward the water and wandered down it, breathing deeply as he walked, trying to calm down. Adrenaline and fear had conspired to turn him into a lunatic. He'd been planning on apologizing to Julie, yet ended up accusing her of using him as the fall guy for the sabotage. Now that he had a moment to think, he didn't actually believe Julie would do that and he wished he hadn't said it. But that still didn't clear up the questions about the background check.

Julie was still nowhere in sight as Sean arrived at the edge of the pond. He sat down on a bench and leaned back, watching a father and son cast fishing lines into the water. Purposely, he pushed his mind to other thoughts, trying to recall the last time he'd been here, in this place, Sawmill Pond.

The only thing his stubborn brain offered up, however, was the last time he'd been here with Julie.

◀

The night is warmer than it should be, even for July. A half moon lights up the hillside, glinting off the water of the pond as a light breeze ripples the surface. In the crowded dirt parking area, Sean leans against the driver's door of his Camaro. He had headed back to his car for a drink after the game of Manhunt that he and a bunch of others had been playing had broken up. Some have been drinking beer, some hard liquor. Tonight Sean is sticking with Pepsi.

A rustle from behind catches his ear and he turns. Julie and her friend Dawn stumble out of the bushes, giggling. When the two girls look up and see him the laughter stops. They whisper dramatically back and forth for half a minute before Dawn says, "Just go," and pushes Julie toward him. She lurches forward, regains her footing and hesitates a moment before walking a beeline for his car.

Sean hasn't seen Julie around much lately. After the fiasco at the Rock back in March and the mad dash to the hospital she'd been grounded for two months. Once that passed, he'd heard that her father had warned her to stay away from him.

That was fine with Sean. Once he'd finally raised the cash to get his car out of impound his parents had taken it away from him until after high school graduation. Spending his last three months of high school without a vehicle had left him more than a little pissed off. The only thing he had to be thankful for was that Julie's mom was old friends with a South Shore judge and all the charges against him had been quietly dropped. Regardless, since that night in the hospital he hadn't spoken to her other than to say, "Hey," as they passed in the halls at school.

Julie slows as she approaches. "Hey there, Sean Connors," she says. "How've you been?" She leans against the front fender, three or four feet away, with her wrists twisted, hands locked together backwards.

"Alright," he says then polishes off his soda. "What's up?"

"Nothing… I didn't know you were here."

"Yeah, me neither."

Julie pushes out a forced laugh.

"Haven't seen you around much lately," Sean says.

"Summer school sucks. And I went to Florida with my stupid family for two weeks," Julie says then hops up and sits on his hood.

"Yeah," Sean says, even though he hadn't known. He can tell Julie is sober. He hears she's been off the sauce since the hypothermia. He looks over at her, notices the moonlight tickling the top of her head, shimmering in her hair.

She turns to him then, meets his eyes. "Thank you," she says.

He looks away. "For what?"

"What do you think? For saving me."

Sean eyes silver ripples rolling across the pond's surface, shuffling off to oblivion. She hasn't thanked him before now.

"You're welcome," he says. A breeze kicks up some dust in the ensuing silence. "Thanks for taking care of the tickets."

"That was my mom," Julie says.

"I heard."

"Why didn't you tell me at the hospital about the guy you fought? The one who split your lip?"

Sean doesn't answer for a moment, wondering himself why he hadn't told her. "I guess I didn't see how your knowing would help anything," he says.

Quiet returns, interrupted only by intermittent shouts in the distance. It sounds like another round of Manhunt has started up.

Sean clears his throat.

Julie crosses her arms.

When he can't stand the empty air between them any longer Sean says, "I can't believe I'm leaving for college in less than five weeks."

Julie slides off the fender and walks over to him. She takes his hands in hers, looks up into his eyes and opens her mouth as if to speak. Instead she collapses into his chest and hugs him fiercely. "You're not going anywhere," she says into his shoulder.

Sean hugs her back, hesitantly. "I'm going to USC," he says. "Next month."

Julie leans her head back and searches his face, though her body remains pressed against his. "I can't let myself believe that," she says.

"It'll ruin my whole summer."

Sean frowns. "It's gonna happen wheth—"

She cuts him off with a finger to his lips. "Just don't say it, okay? If we don't talk about it, it doesn't have to be real yet." She buries her face in his shirt again, squeezing him tight.

"But—"

"Please Sean?"

Sean lets out a long, heavy sigh and returns her embrace as the light of the moon spills silently over them in a fine mist.

▶

Sean rose from his bench after fifteen minutes. Julie still hadn't materialized.

He walked back to the parking lot the way he'd come and saw her sitting on a boulder thirty feet from the car. Out of sight at the edge of the trees, he stopped. She had her feet pulled up, arms wrapped around her knees, head turned slightly away. In the evening light, and from this distance, she could easily have passed for seventeen. The age she'd been that last time here.

As Sean walked out of the trees confusion rushed in, replacing the remnants of his anger. Julie shifted her gaze toward him and the way her hair fell across her face in a wave nearly turned his legs to jelly.

Twenty Six

Julie watched Sean cross the dirt parking area, her left ear resting on her knee. She'd managed to push the anger down into her gut, where it now churned like a nasty heartburn, but at least she'd quit screaming at the hills.

Sean's shoulders slumped slightly and he wore a sheepish look as he approached. The height of the rock on which she sat put the level of her head two feet above his. "There you are," he said.

"Here I am." Julie narrowed her eyes and stared him down until he turned away. There would be no apologies for now. They needed to focus on getting Sean off the hill. Letting the anger take over was dangerous and would likely lead to both of them getting caught.

"So," she said and slid down from the boulder. "How are we gonna get you out of here?"

"Get *me* out of here? What about you?"

"We've been over this, Sean. I'm staying."

"Oh no. That was before they found me."

"Yeah, but the cops aren't busy ransacking my house. They're after *you*."

"They've been following you, spying on you."

"Exactly. They're trying to catch me doing something. As long as I don't do anything suspicious, I'll be fine."

"You don't know that. What if Derrick fingered you, too? How do we know they aren't going through your place right now?"

He had a point. She hadn't been home in hours, but— "Derrick? You think Derrick ratted you out?"

"Come on, who else could it be? How would they have found me otherwise?"

A couple approached from the pond and Julie leaned back against the rock. She waited until the strangers were safely in their car before she continued.

"I can't imagine Derrick doing that, Sean."

"Can you imagine him digging into people's backgrounds without permission?"

"That's—"

She was about to say "different," but was it? Was it possible that Derrick had turned on them? Trying to save himself maybe? She shook the thought from her head. "Can we forget about how the cops found you for now? I've got a friend who will probably let me borrow her car for a few days."

"Where the hell am I gonna go, Julie? I can't go back to LA. They're probably tearing my condo apart right now."

He was right. She racked her brain for an alternative. "How about my Mom's?"

"What'll we tell her? I ran out of money and just need to crash on her floor for a while?"

Her mom was cool and all, but they couldn't tell her the truth. And any story they came up with would be flimsy at best. Either they needed to stick with like-minded people or Sean needed to head for the wilderness. Not a bad idea if he had the backcountry gear to make it for a few days, but she guessed he didn't. As she watched him stare off into the distance across the pond a thought occurred to her.

"I know somebody," she said. "He's a caretaker at a place on Upper Kingsbury. Maybe you could crash with him for a few days. He's sympathetic to the cause and, as long as the owners aren't around, it should be cool."

Sean eyed her suspiciously. "Somebody would see me. Those places are pretty close together up there."

"Not this one. It sits out in front of Boulder Lodge on the bluff. Twenty acres or so."

Sean paced away from her and back. "Then we should both go. I don't know this guy… I don't want to get him fired."

"Who's gonna be around up here to clear your name and find out what's going on if we're both in hiding?"

"Clear my name?" Sean laughed. "And how, exactly, do you plan on doing that?"

Julie didn't know. That didn't stop her from feeling like she owed him, though. "I guess I'll just have to think of something," she said and walked back toward the car, her mind as empty of ideas as a burned out light bulb.

* * *

Sean didn't like Julie's solution at all. Derrick was still on the loose and he wouldn't trust the guy to tie his shoes. Now that he and Julie were back together he thought they should stay together, the anger roiling beneath the veneer of civility they'd painted on notwithstanding.

"Listen," he said, following her to the Subaru. "How about we swap out your car for your friend's and at least check your place out to make sure the cops aren't there? You know, before I go... Just in case."

Julie eyed him across the roof of the car, then nodded her head as she climbed into the driver's seat. "All right," she said and started the engine. "But we need to be careful."

Sean climbed into his seat, a glint of hope crossing his lips in slight a grin. "No need to overstate the obvious," he said.

Twenty Seven

They got the car from Julie's friend, Leigh. It was another beat-up Subaru wagon—this one maroon and not quite as ancient, but just as ailing. Leigh had lost her license and wasn't currently using the vehicle. Her only request was that they have it back to her "in a week or so." Her father was coming to town and he would be driving it.

Julie called Jake from Leigh's place. The owners of the posh retreat on Kingsbury where he was caretaker were spending the summer in Europe and he had no problem with Sean crashing in one of the guest cabins for a few days. She couldn't help that Sean was uncomfortable staying with a stranger and she knew he wasn't done trying to talk her into coming along. After leaving her car hidden behind a Dumpster at Leigh's condos, Julie drove out Tata Lane and made a right onto Lake Tahoe Boulevard, heading back to check out her place.

Having to deal civilly with Leigh had allowed Julie's anger to cool further, but it still simmered deep within. As they rolled to a stop at the Y, she said to Sean, "You never answered my question."

He looked over, puzzled. "What question was that?"

"Do you believe that some human beings have the right to withhold the necessities of life from others?"

Sean sighed, long and heavy. "Do we really need to get into this right now?"

Her timing could have been better, but with the amount of arguing they'd been doing she really wanted to know where he stood on this topic that she considered so basic. "Yes," she said. "We really do." Julie scanned the other cars at the intersection while she waited for Sean's reply.

"When you put it the way you put it," he said and crossed his arms. "It's impossible for anyone to answer, 'Yes,' to that question."

Julie pulled away from the light with the rest of the traffic as she tried to keep a rising smile from forming on her lips. "Not if they truly believe in the foundations of this society," she said. "If they truly have faith in the way this culture runs they would say, 'Yes.' If for no other reason than to protect their precious worldview. The fact that you can see the conflict there means you're starting to understand that our way of life is based on the cruelty of letting fellow human beings suffer while you have more than you need."

Sean sighed again. "I don't know what to believe anymore. You guys have been pumping me so full of ideas these past couple days my head feels like it's going to pop."

Julie resisted the urge to point a finger at Sean's head as if she meant to pop it like a balloon. Why was it so damned hard to stay mad at him?

He continued, "I have to say that I don't believe any person has the right to withhold food or water or shelter from another, but the fact that I don't believe it changes nothing. Six billion other people still do believe it—and that just makes me the odd man out."

This time Julie couldn't keep the huge smile from blooming on her face and she grabbed his left knee with her right hand and squeezed. "The fact that you believe it changes *you*, Sean. A movement can begin with a single thought and we're far from alone in this idea. If you accept that the dominant worldview is out of whack you'll eventually understand that there's nothing wrong with you—it's this culture that's gone insane."

They cruised through the light at Third Street, but got caught by the yellow at Tahoe Keys Boulevard. Julie had to remove her hand from Sean's knee to downshift.

"So I get to be, what, one of the sane people running around in the lunatic asylum?" Sean said. He appeared to be eying a man on the side of the road who looked like he had everything he owned strapped to his back. "Maybe I'd be better off staying one of the inmates."

"No!" Julie said so suddenly that Sean jumped in his seat. His stubbornness was continually aggravating. "Never say that. Never!" She punctuated the last "never" with the heel of her hand on the steering wheel. "You can't turn your back. Once you've seen the truth the easy way out is no longer an option. Now that your eyes are open don't you ever think about closing them again!"

* *

Sean stared at Julie's profile against the passing lights of the Motel Six. Her passion was palpable, a third passenger in the car. "Julie, I'm wanted by the cops, my business is dead and my whole world is collapsing around me. Dealing with these... philosophical issues? Right now, it's beyond me."

"But this is the best time to deal with this stuff. When your world gets turned upside down it's easier to notice all the things that were hidden before."

What passed for the City of South Lake Tahoe flashed by in the gathering dusk, a litany of towering trees interspersed with old buildings and the occasional meadow. Maybe Julie was onto something. Since he had no true "normal" to return to, might it be easier for him to readjust his baseline?

Twenty Eight

It was almost full dark by the time they reached Julie's apartments, but Sean still felt warranted reclining his seat back so he was out of sight as they approached.

"Not much going on here," Julie said, "but there's an unmarked car in the street. I'm turning off."

Sean felt the vehicle swerve left and accelerate. He started to sit up, but Julie put a hand on his chest, holding him there.

"Wait a minute. Let's make sure they don't follow us," she said.

He acquiesced, staring at the tattered headliner of the borrowed car as Julie slowed and accelerated through three stop signs. At least the cops still weren't on to her. Unfortunately, that gave him less ammunition to convince her to stay with him.

"Okay, I think we're clear," Julie said finally. She took another left hand turn as Sean sat up and adjusted his seat.

"What now?" he asked.

Julie looked over at him, the frown on her face evident in the light of the dash. "Like we said—we go get my car and you go underground."

"You should really come with me."

"How many times do I have to say it, Sean? I can't disappear. As long as they're not onto me I have to just plug along like everything's normal."

"Just like you always have," Sean said under his breath.

"What?"

He groaned and turned to her. "Why is it always me who has to leave? You've been pushing me away the entire time I've known you."

"Is that what you think? That I'm trying to get rid of you?"

"It's not like it hasn't happened before. Right when I thought everything was going fine."

Julie jerked the car over to the side of the road and slammed on the brakes, pitching Sean forward against his seatbelt. "And you think everything's fine now, huh? We've been fighting and bickering all damn day."

Sean rubbed his shoulder where the seatbelt had bitten when she stopped. "Maybe if you were a little more forthright we wouldn't be."

"You want *me* to be forthright?" Julie pointed a finger at her own chest. "I'm not the one hiding where my interests lie."

"I never hid anything. I told you, I didn't know QTC owned Eagle. Should I get out the rest of my portfolio so you can double check it for me?"

"Maybe. Who knows what other horrendous acts you're supporting with those investments."

"Horrendous acts? I'm just trying to make a little money!"

"And for all you know you're financing Shell's genocidal policies or Monsanto's deforestation in the process."

"I don't believe I hold any of their stock," Sean said, staring straight ahead. "And we were talking about what *you* were hiding, not me."

"I'm not hiding anything," Julie grumbled under her breath.

"Oh, really?" Sean held out his hands and checked points off on his fingers as he continued. "You didn't tell me about the extensive background check required to be in your little circle of friends; you didn't tell me about your involvement with the Eco-Militia—until I dragged it out of you; and then there's that little matter of, oh... I don't know... why you blew me off thirteen years ago."

Julie bit her lower lip and turned back to Sean, her eyes slowly narrowing as indignation rose within, followed closely by fury. "You said it didn't matter what happened back then," she hissed.

"Well, surprise, surprise," he said and held his hands up in a you-caught-me gesture. "It does. Did you really think I'd forget the whole thing? I was crushed, completely useless for months."

He was crushed? For months? After all these years she was still dealing with the fallout from that spring. "You know what?" she lashed out. "If you hadn't been such a wuss and just kissed me back then, things could've turned out a lot different."

Sean recoiled against the inside of the door. Reaching down with his right hand, he found the door handle and pulled it open, releasing the seatbelt with his left. "When did I ever have a chance to kiss you? Your lips were always surgically attached to some jerkoff's."

He hopped out of the car and starting walking toward Highway 50 in the distance, leaving the door ajar. Julie's last words buzzed around in his brain like a haywire circuit, popping fuses. Why did it seem to hurt most when others pointed out something you'd always suspected, but never fully admitted to yourself. He made it two blocks before Julie pulled up beside him with the passenger door still hanging open.

"Get in the car, Sean," she said.

"No." He kept walking.

She idled along beside him. "You're going to get us both thrown in jail."

"I don't care."

"Damn it, Sean, don't be stupid."

He stopped and the open door pulled even with him. "Why do you care what I do, Julie? You don't give a shit about me. You don't give a shit about anyone. You're always too damn busy protecting yourself."

Julie yanked the parking brake and was out of the car in an instant. "How the hell can you say that after last night?"

They eyed each other warily across the roof of the borrowed vehicle in the wash of a yellowing streetlight. Sean said, "I'm sure you've fooled around with a shitload of guys you didn't care about over the years. What's so different about me?"

Julie could barely believe her ears. "Sean," she said slowly, purposely lowering her voice. "I have never—*ever*—made love to anyone I wasn't in love with."

Sean opened his mouth to reply then did a double take. "What?" he said.

"Look, I don't just hop in bed with every guy who shows up on my doorstep. I—" Julie's lips kept moving for a moment after her words failed her.

What did I just say? Did I really just tell Sean I'm in love with him?

She hadn't meant for it to come out like that. Sean knew how she'd been with guys in the past and she'd only intended to explain that, in the intervening years, she hadn't begun sleeping with every man she dated. As she gazed over the roof of the idling Subaru and into Sean's quizzical eyes, though, she realized that—regardless of how horribly they were currently getting along—the words that had found their way out were absolutely true.

"Did you just sa—"

"No," she cut him off, flustered now. "Forget it, okay?"

How the hell could he forget that? She'd just said that she was *in love* with him. He'd heard the word *love* from her mouth hundreds of times in the past, but—as he was acutely aware—the big difference was that little *in* that had come before the all-encompassing *L-O-V-E*.

"You know what? Why don't you take the car from here," Julie said. "I'll walk." She turned, reached through the open rear window and grabbed her purse from the seat. Then she started walking back the way they'd come.

Breaking his paralysis, Sean slammed the passenger door before running around the front end of the idling car. "Hold on. Get back here, you. You can't just run off after dropping a whopper like that on me. And I don't even know where I'm supposed to be going."

Julie stopped and turned to him, staying put twenty feet away. "Just forget it," she said. "Please, Sean? For now anyway?"

"Why would I want to forget it?"

She walked slowly back toward him and stopped at the rear bumper of the car. "Because my timing is just amazingly... ridiculously... desperately wrong. You're wanted. I'm being followed. A minute ago we were screaming nasty things at each other like evil little children." She leaned against the rear fender and closed her eyes. "I need some time to think, Sean. You go to Jake's and relax, hang low for a couple days. I'll try and find out what's going on around here."

Sean looked away, fists clenched tightly at his sides.

"We can't ever seem to get our timing quite right, can we?" he said.

Julie kicked a stick across the road and into the bushes.

"No," she said. "I guess we can't."

III

Part III

One

◄

"There's a difference between loving someone and being *in love* with them," Julie says, trying to get her thoughts straight in her head. She sits on the side of Sean's waterbed, the edge of the wooden frame numbing a stripe across her rear end. She's on her fourth wine cooler and God knows how many shots of Goldschlager she's downed.

"I guess I don't get it," Sean says and drains the last of his own drink. "If you're *in love* with someone, then you *love* them." He stands in front of her swaying slightly back and forth.

"Yeah, but it doesn't go both ways," she says, unsure if it's him or her doing the swaying. Sean shakes his head, still not getting it.

Julie is in big trouble. It's four thirty in the morning and she was supposed to be home by twelve. Sean is home for the summer after his freshmen year of college and having a 4th of July party. Although she told her mom where she was going, she'd failed to mention that Sean's parents were out of town.

"I don't know how to explain it any better," Julie says. Unable to take the wooden bed frame creasing her butt any longer, she flops back on the mattress. Water sloshes from one end to the other like a wave pool and she rides it out. She hadn't known that Sean had a waterbed, since she'd never been in his room. How is it she's known him for two years and has never even been on the second floor of his house before tonight?

After lying with her feet hanging over the edge of the bed for a few moments, Julie remembers that she's wearing a skirt and pulls her legs up onto the bed as well. She wonders briefly if Sean has enjoyed the peep show. She keeps her eyes closed until the bed stops moving, though, afraid the motion might make her sick.

"Are you *in love* with Kevin?" Sean asks.

"We've only been going out for, like, two weeks," Julie says, turning her head toward him. Now in the chair at the foot of the bed, Sean is a tangle of long limbs and angst draped over the armrests. If she were to reach out a hand she could touch his thigh. *Why is it we only talk about this kind of stuff when we've been drinking?*

And what is she doing in Sean's room again? Oh yeah, his friend Doug had dragged Sean and her up here going on about how the two of them are "so obviously in love with each other" they just need to "do it and get it over with already." But Doug is a man-whore, he couldn't possibly understand her relationship with Sean. She doesn't much like Doug.

Julie raises herself up on her elbows long enough to polish off her wine cooler then lies back, eyes closed again. The waves inside the mattress move her body like the surface of the ocean and she decides that the motion isn't so bad after all. Sean takes the empty bottle from her hand as she lies there imagining another place. She half expects him to join her on the bed—any other guy would.

The quiet in the room stretches out and the only sound is the slight swooshing of the water in the mattress as Julie rocks herself to keep the waves coming. She finally opens her eyes to find Sean still sitting, staring blankly at the opposite wall, his empty glass in one hand, her empty wine cooler bottle in the other. It takes her a moment to remember what they were talking about.

"I love my sisters," Julie says eventually. "But I don't want to date them." She watches Sean's face. He clenches his jaw but doesn't look her way.

"So what does that make me? Your brother?" He brings his glass up to his mouth, notices it's empty and lowers it back to the armrest.

Julie reaches over and puts her hand on Sean's arm. He looks first at her hand, then her face. "Sean, you're my friend, don't you get that? You're, like, the best friend I've ever had and I don't deserve you at all." A few tears are forming in the corners of her eyes. She tries to blink them away. "You look out for me and you listen to me and... I don't know what I would do if I lost that."

He turns away again. "What makes you think you would lose it?"

Julie laughs. "You're aware of my dating record, right? How long do I ever stay with guys? Weeks, right? How would I not screw it up with you?"

"You just don't date the right kind of guys."

"Maybe, but you're gonna be going back to college and…"

"And what?"

"Nothing… You'll be gone is all."

The bed sloshes as Julie crawls closer to Sean, wraps her arms around him and squeezes. "I miss you so much when you're not around," she whispers.

He sits silent, rigid as a post. After a moment he shrugs her off and stands up. "I need another drink," he says and stalks out of the room.

Julie lies back on the bed, quiet and still, until the motion of the waves ceases beneath her. Closing her eyes, she tries to ignore the tears running down her temples and dampening her hair.

* * *

Fifteen minutes later Sean sits in the living room staring blankly at the images flickering by on the television screen. After leaving his room, he'd stumbled down the stairs to the kitchen looking for something else to drink. Something hard. Something to help obliterate the memory of what Julie had just said. He'd found a bottle of Everclear and mixed some with Pepsi.

Now, as he polishes off a second drink, the stringent, medicinal flavor of pure grain alcohol still burns in his throat beneath the syrupy sweetness of the cola. He relishes it like a minor tooth pain that's hard to quit biting down on.

Julie isn't the first girl he's had this problem with. There was Helen back in high school… and Barbara, too. Same old crap. "I just want to be friends." After they'd been the ones supposedly interested in him.

"Whatcha watching."

It's a guy named Joe, beer in hand and barely an acquaintance.

"I don't know," Sean says, feeling a slur encroaching on his words. "You can change it if you want."

Joe studies him for a moment then shakes his head. He looks

about to speak then just throws himself on the couch and snags the remote. "Is Headbanger's Ball on?" he asks.

Sean shrugs and stumbles to his feet, wavering toward the kitchen. Out of nowhere Doug appears to help him on his way. "Dude, what'd you strike out up there?" he says.

"Wha...?"

"With Julie? She shot you down, right? Or did she do you first? 'Cause her and Glenn are up there on your parents bed sucking some serious face right now."

Sean pushes away and sways for a moment before steadying himself with a hand on the kitchen table. He shakes his head and glares at Doug. "She's doing what? With who?"

"Makin' out," Doug says louder. "With Glenn."

Glenn hasn't wanted anything to do with Julie for almost two years and Sean thought Julie had sworn him off, too—said that she hated him, in fact.

What the hell?

Sean reels around the corner to the stairs and pulls himself up by handrails that creak under the strain. His parents room is at the top on the right. As he pushes open the door and barges in two startled faces turn toward him. Julie's skirt is hiked up above the white lace panties he'd glimpsed earlier and Glenn has one hand under her shirt.

"Dude, a little privacy, huh?" Glenn says as Julie's face pales.

Sean leans on the open door to avoid falling over and locks eyes with Julie. Her face shows confusion mixed with the twitchy-eyed recognition of the trapped. She squirms out from under Glenn, stumbles as she stands and pulls her skirt down to cover herself. For a moment her head hangs between her shoulders, then she looks up and approaches Sean slowly, like he might be dangerous.

"Sean, I—" she starts.

But he seizes her by the upper arm—snapping her words off like a brittle twig—and pulls her from the room and down the stairs. Nothing but a tenuous hold on one railing keeps the two of them from tumbling to the bottom in a heap. They arrive at the front door and he jerks it open, yanking her lithe form over the threshold with him. Then, without a single word, he turns and leaves her swaying on the porch like a willow in the wind.

Behind her, the door thuds closed and Julie finds herself alone in the dark. The loud *schuck!* of the locking deadbolt pushes through the vibrating tendrils of night swirling around her head and hits her ears like a slap.

►

Two

Rays of sun slipping through the partially closed blinds over the kitchen sink stabbed into Julie's retinas like two hot ice picks. She slammed her lids closed again and rolled onto her back. Rubbing her temples, she tried to focus on something other than the strobe-like throbbing in her head.

What the hell did I do last night to end up with this kind of hangover.

There was the fight, of course. Julie remembered that. And her ineptly blurted profession of love. Yep. Remembered that, too.

Then Sean had headed for Upper Kingsbury and she'd started walking home. But on the way she began to feel like she didn't want to be alone. So she made her way over to the edge of Barton Meadow and followed the vague trail that skirted the back of the Al Tahoe neighborhood out to Highway 50 near Meek's. From there it was only a quick trot up the road to Whiskey Dick's where her friend Heather tended bar.

These days Julie usually shied away from the nightclub scene around Tahoe. The lopsided ratio of men to women in the area turned every bar into a meat market, the men into starving wolves fighting over every last scrap of female flesh. Whenever she did venture out she usually ended up feeling like the teacher that every schoolboy in the room had a crush on.

She couldn't remember any guys from last night, but she did remember Heather insisting on pouring her a free drink—or five. At some point Julie had lost count of the ridiculously strong, frozen margaritas her friend kept feeding her. Any memory of the rest of the night's events had been lost in a deluge of top-shelf tequila.

Julie kicked her blanket off and sat up, placing her bare feet on the floor. Her head swam and she steadied herself with a hand behind her on the mattress. She vaguely recalled dancing but the memories were all too hazy and didn't make any sense. It had been a long time since she'd gotten blackout drunk—at least five years. At some point in her mid-to-late twenties she'd finally learned that the best way to avoid alcohol-induced stupidity was to not drink so much of the damned stuff in the first place.

She rose to her feet slowly and gave herself a moment to find equilibrium before heading across the room to the kitchen. There she filled a large glass with water from the tap and downed half of it as she leaned back against the counter.

I've never made love to anyone I wasn't in love with.

She still couldn't believe those words had slipped from her mouth so non-chalantly, but there was no point in denying what the statement implied. Sometime in the past three days she had fallen *in love* with Sean Connors, it just hadn't been something she'd consciously considered until that moment.

It was the oddest thing, her voice spouting her feelings before her head had time to concur. Rationally she knew it was too soon to feel this way—too soon to sleep with him, too soon to bring up the "L" word regardless of context—but things were happening so fast. Reality had accelerated to Mach 6 and her life was blurring around her. She was having a hard time making sense of any of it.

The problem Julie always had with men was that the *in love* was either one sided on her part or it never ended up translating into the longer lasting *love* needed for a relationship to stand the test of time. She yearned for this thing with Sean to work out, but they'd both come into it with so much baggage. And not just individually, their whole past relationship was a matter of contention now. She'd been rolling along on the naïve belief that he'd meant it when he said he didn't care if she told him what happened back then, but now she knew the truth. If they were to move forward everything would have to come out. Somehow she needed to find the strength to tell him.

Then there was Derrick. She didn't know what to make of him, digging up Sean's background and acting like a jealous boyfriend. It seemed out of character for the man she thought she knew. Was he having some sort of breakdown? Could he have set Sean up? If he had been following her around, he would have known where Sean was staying. Yet, no matter how she spun it in her head, she couldn't see him doing it. Derrick was her friend. She needed to talk to him so they could sort this all out.

As Julie's attention came back to the present she noticed her place was a wreck. Books from the shelves were strewn across the floor and couch like she'd been looking for something. The clothes she had on last night were scattered about like she'd lost them on her way from the door to the bed. A half-empty bottle of vodka sat on the counter next to two empty glasses. She closed a couple of kitchen cabinets that were hanging open and walked around the living room picking things up off the floor. Her heart sank as she imagined possible explanations for the disarray, but her mind still refused to pony up any details.

She had retrieved her discarded clothing and reshelved most of the books when she noticed The Box. It sat innocently on the floor between the coffee table and the couch. She hadn't thought about it in quite a while. In fact, the last time she moved she had seriously considered tossing it in the trash. Instead, it had been relegated to the rear of her bottom shelf of books where she would be unlikely to happen upon it accidentally.

The Box was square and dark brown with a faux-leather covering. Two fat but now fraying rubberbands held a cap-style lid in place. The Box contained all the letters Julie had ever received from Sean and she hadn't opened it in over six years. But now, even though the lid was secured in place, a few of the letters lay scattered about on the carpet.

Julie retrieved the wayward correspondence, sat on the edge of the couch and picked The Box up. She rested it gingerly in her lap and ran a palm over the dusty lid. After a moment's hesitation, she began removing the old, brittle rubberbands. One of them snapped, stinging her wrist like an angry bee, and she dropped the lid to the floor. The scent of old paper filled her nostrils, bringing back a sudden memory of her father's office from the house of her childhood.

She placed the loose envelopes back inside and flipped through the rest. All the letters were still there—even that pesky last one from Sean that she'd never opened. It was addressed in his jagged print to that same old house and she picked it out and stared at it. Whether it was Sean pleading with her to call or telling her to get lost, she'd managed to convince herself she wouldn't be able to handle it. And she was apparently still convinced.

As Julie looked at the letter then back into The Box she noticed something missing after all. Down at the bottom she should have found the letter she'd written to Sean the night of her father's funeral, but it wasn't there.

She set The Box aside and ripped through the tiny apartment again, looking in every nook and cranny. She would know it on sight. It bore only Sean's first name, writ large across the front in her juvenile, flowery script. She had never found the courage to just put the damned thing in the mail.

As her heart fluttered in her chest like a busy hummingbird she whispered to the empty room, "Where the hell did it go?"

Three

Sean swallowed the last dregs of his coffee and stared out the window into the trees. Sweeping lake views were apparently reserved for the main house up the hill, down here in the guest quarters all he got was woods.

Not that he was ungrateful for the roof over his head. The little one bedroom cabin was cozy. It had a small kitchenette complete with coffee and coffee maker. Unfortunately, it didn't sport a television or computer. The owners must have been trying to provide a rustic feel for their guests. The place did have a phone, though, and with nothing to distract him from his thoughts, he was having trouble steering them away from Julie and all the possible reasons why, at half past ten, she still hadn't called when she had so explicitly said that she would.

Was it because of what she'd blurted last night in the heat of their argument, or had the authorities caught up with her? Or—he had begun to think most likely—had she completely forgotten? Was Julie just being Julie?

Before they'd parted ways the previous evening she'd given Sean directions to The Estate—as Jake referred to it—then she took his cell phone from him, turned it off and tossed it in the bushes. He obviously wasn't used to thinking like a fugitive, he'd forgotten about the ability to track a phone by GPS and even just plain old cell towers. Julie had promised to call in the morning then they'd said goodbye with a quick, non-chalant kiss before Sean climbed back into the borrowed Subaru and headed for Kingsbury Grade.

He still questioned whether splitting up had been the best solution. They'd both been angry and agitated when he left and he wished he'd said something more. What, exactly, he wasn't sure. He was still having trouble believing what had happened. It wasn't as though she'd looked him in the eyes and whispered sweetly, "I'm *in love* with you." The words had slipped out sidelong in the middle of a nasty fight filled with stupid insults and accusations. That they were stupid didn't make them any less true, but if she really didn't sleep with guys she wasn't *in love* with… then what?

Sean winced as he remembered her "if-you'd-only-kissed-me" remark. Yeah, maybe he should've kissed her, but she had always been the one holding him at arm's length back then. He'd just been trying to do the right thing and not come off as another pushy jerk.

No matter how angry she'd made him, though, he kept coming back to those two little words: *in love*. Was Julie really *in love* with him? Was he *in love* with her? Infatuated sure, but they hardly even knew each other. Sure they'd been close in the past, but they'd been having one hell of a time recreating that in the present. Maybe all the fighting they'd been doing spoke to some sort of passion? He didn't know, but worry about what might have happened to her had mostly eclipsed any lingering anger in his emotional universe at this point.

He shook his head slowly and looked around the room. What were people supposed to do for entertainment here anyway? A shelf on the wall held a few books and games and a deck of cards sat on the coffee table in front on him. He picked up the cards, shuffled a few times and attempted to deal himself a hand of Solitaire but couldn't seem to remember how. Who used an actual deck of cards to play solitaire anymore? Everyone used a computer, or their phone.

Frustrated and annoyed, Sean brushed the cards onto the floor. He needed a damned television—or computer or video game—to take his mind off his problems. Sitting here without those distractions, there was no escape from his own thoughts. He hadn't watched any TV in days and he felt lost, disconnected from society, an outcast banished to the wilderness of his own mind. The realization flooded him with shame, like a needy addict.

Luckily the phone rang, making him start. He picked it up on the second ring.

"Sean, it's Jake," the voice on the line told him.

"Hey," Sean said. "What's up?" He'd only met Jake briefly the previous night when he'd arrived, so his acquaintance with the man was like that of innkeeper and guest.

"Not a lot. I just wanted to offer you the Grand Tour… if you're interested. It's a pretty cool place."

Sean didn't want to miss Julie's call, but he was going a bit stir crazy and the phone did have an answering machine. "Sure, why not," he told Jake. Might as well have a look around if he was going to be here a few days.

Four

Julie picked up her phone, started punching in a number, then slapped the receiver back on the counter. She couldn't call Sean at The Estate from here. What was she thinking? The missing letter had her all discombobulated.

She took a deep breath, pushed a few loose hairs behind one ear and began straightening the apartment again. When she was done, she showered and dressed and headed out the door with her still-wet hair hanging limply against her neck.

The unmarked cop car sat in the street facing the apartments, but a glare on the windshield made it difficult to tell if there was anyone in it. Down the stairs and two buildings over, Julie knocked loud and harsh on Heather's door. Before her bartender friend had the door open two inches Julie assaulted her with a question: "What did we do last night?!"

"Well, good mornin' to you, too," Heather said, a cheery grin on her face. "Come on in." The twang of her Texas accent was like sugar to Julie's soul.

"I'm sorry," Julie said, entering the apartment then giving her friend a quick hug. "I just woke up to a complete mess, clothes all over my place and I can't remember a damn thing."

Heather closed the door. "Slow down, hon. Relax. We'll figger it out."

"Just tell me," Julie said. "Did I take somebody back to my place?"

Heather's grin turned mischievous. "Yeah, actually you did…"

Julie's stomach sank and she stopped breathing. "Wh—what?"

"Oh, c'mon girl, it was me." Heather laughed. "I'm just joshin' you."

Eyes closed, Julie let out her pent up horror in one long breath.

"Don't do that to me."

"Babe, you think I'd let you shack up with some half-wit after listenin' to you wax poetic about your true-love half the damn night? You know I always got your back." Heather smiled and embraced Julie again.

As the other woman released her, Julie said with a smile, "You know, I probably wouldn't be having so much trouble remembering if you hadn't fed me all those margaritas."

Her friend waved a hand at her. "Uh-huh. Like I don't hear that one all the time."

Heather was tall, blond and brash with a heart the size of her home state. Texas born and raised, she'd only moved to Tahoe after high school. Her persistent southern drawl always had a calming effect on Julie, but today she could have done without Heather's teasing—good-natured or not.

"So, what exactly did we do last night?" Julie asked as she took a seat on the couch.

"Well, let's see… You danced the night away with just about every guy in the place until I fine'ly got off work, then we hit the Brothers, then Steamers—were gonna stop at the peanut bar but you nixed that one, said 'Uh-uh, No way,'—then we headed on back to your place and knocked back a few more. By that time you were fit to pass out, so I put you t'bed and headed on home. You want some water or somethin', girl?" Heather asked as she wandered away to the kitchen.

"Yeah, thanks," Julie said, distracted. She was relieved there were no men involved, other than the dancing, but Heather's tale still didn't expl—

"Oh, sometime in there we delivered that letter, too," Heather called from the other room. "And you told me about the other night."

Julie's breath caught in her throat again. "Delivered what?" she squeaked.

"That letter to Sean. The one you wrote him from way back. You said he had to see it—was pretty damned adamant about it. You added a page or two first, though. Said it would fix ever'thing."

Julie wracked her brain trying to remember doing anything of the sort. "Oh my God," she said, a palm to her forehead. "*The* letter? Tell me we didn't deliver that letter."

"Don't worry, hon, that old letter was great," Heather said, reappearing with two glasses of water. "Even made *me* a little misty-eyed. Don't know what you added to it, but I'm sure that was fine, too."

She felt a haze descend over her as she accepted her glass. "Where did we deliver it?"

"The place he's hidin' out. Up on Kingsbury?" Heather said it like it should have been prefaced with a "Hellooow?"

"I told you about that?"

"Told me? We spent most of a half hour sneaking around in the pitch black up there just to stick a letter in a mail box. And damn if you didn't make me drive around and around in circles for whatcha call forever just to make sure we wasn't followed."

Julie felt shell-shocked. "What else did I tell you," she asked sheepishly.

"Most ever'thing, I guess. The sabotage. Gettin' with Sean the other night. Derrick's shenanigans."

Julie stared down into her water and decided she would drink no more alcohol until this situation was well over, lest she do something even more stupid.

"One thing I'm not too sure of, babe, is who this Sean character is. I just don't remember him one little bit."

"He was before your time. We were friends in high school, but he went to USC and his family moved to San Diego and…" she trailed off, fidgeting with her water glass.

"And?"

Julie raised her head slowly and met Heather's eyes. "And we lost touch … let's leave it at that." Heather wasn't *that* close of a friend—regardless of everything else Julie had apparently told her last night.

The bartender looked back at Julie for a long moment before letting it go. When she continued she said, "Is this the guy who saved your life that time? In the snow up at The Rock? With that crazy drive to the hospital?"

A blush rose in Julie's cheeks as a smile stretched across her lips. She was helpless to stop either.

"Oh, girl," Heather said, rushing over. "It's like a fairy tale." She took both of Julie's hands in her own and knelt in front of her. "Did he sweep you off your feet this time?"

Julie may as well have been sixteen again, talking about boys in her bedroom with Tina and Shelley on top of the flowered quilt her grandmother had made. "Sort of," she said. "He kinda saved us both the other night. You know, at the timeshare."

Heather slapped her on the knee. "Oh, he's a keeper. You gotta hold onto this one… So what's the problem?"

Julie dropped Heather's other hand. "I don't know," she said. "We can't seem to stop fighting."

"'Bout what?"

Julie looked into Heather's eyes, mouth working, no sound coming out.

"Can't be that important," Heather said, standing up. "Looks like you two are destined to be together, so y'all just need to get over it. Fate only smiles on some, babe, and them second chances are few and far between."

A bartender's quick advice, but Julie thought there might be something to it. If someone was your destiny it was best to get along. Did that mean there was only question that truly mattered?

Is Sean my destiny?

And the letter? On the way back to her place, she couldn't stop beating herself up for delivering that letter. It was nothing but teenage mush, how would Sean react to that? And what, exactly, had she added to it?

As she approached the stairs to her apartment, Julie slowed. Someone was knocking on a door up there. She took the first three risers slowly and saw Agent Bartlett standing at her door like a hungry cat eyeing a mouse-hole.

Five

Jake was a relatively short man, stocky and fit. The scuffed up Teva sandals on his feet looked well used and Sean wondered if Jake was the kind of guy who wore the things year round. He thought he might be that type, the shorts-and-sandals-in-the-snow type. There used to be plenty of them around the lake that seemed to flaunt it like a badge of honor.

Sean took in the grandiose surroundings as he and Jake climbed the stairs bordering the long sloped drive up to the main house. The center section of the monstrous building stood two stories above the drive and was flanked by one story sections that extended out at angles, helping to create a circular reception area under a large porte-cochere. The style was what Sean thought of as Early 21st Century Mountain Chic, meaning it was built with enough wood and granite to refill the Cave Rock tunnels. The place could have passed for another Marriott Timeshare building, right at home next to the Gondola base. Up over the rooftop, the steep, treed slope of East Peak's flank rose like a wall, elevation difference between the summit and the lake: over three thousand feet.

Pulling his attention back to Jake, Sean asked, "So, how does one become a caretaker at a place like this?"

Jake laughed. "I fell into it really. A buddy of mine married the owner's first wife's daughter. He put in the good word for me and I got a call. I started out part time, helping the full time guy. When he left, I took over. Now here I am, Lord of the Estate." He laughed again and shook his head. "Never thought I'd be living like this, working for the wealthy elite."

"Yeah, right," Sean said, trying to sound affable. He didn't care to let on that he currently belonged to that same class. "So you and Julie are good friends?"

"I wouldn't go that far. We went on a few dates way back when.

We're mostly just activist buddies. You know, we see each other around at protests, meetings and what-not."

Sean breathed an unintentional, but silent sigh of relief as they arrived at the front doors: two massive hunks of wood that looked like they'd been hewn from Giant Redwoods. On either side, floor to ceiling glass stretched out at least twelve feet in both directions. Through the windows Sean could see that the entry way on the other side of the glass dropped down into a sunken living room. Across this great room, opposite from where they stood, was a two story wall constructed of almost nothing but glass. The only thing Sean could currently see through those west-facing windows was Tahoe's famously blue sky.

Jake punched a security code into a panel mounted to the doorjamb, being sure to block Sean's view with his body while he did it. The right hand door creaked slightly on its hinges as Jake opened it. "Guess I'll need to take care of that," he said.

Inside they were welcomed by the scent of freshly refinished wood floors that matched the doors. A grandiose staircase with twisted knotty pine railings curved up to the right onto a landing overlooking the Great Room on three sides. The interior decoration mirrored the outside: dark, rustic wood furniture, western blankets and patterns, and a huge granite fireplace that looked big enough to stand in.

"Whew," Sean exhaled. "Quite some place."

Jake nodded. "You ain't seen nothin' yet," he said. "Come on."

Jake descended the four stairs down to the Great Room and headed for the window wall. Sean followed and felt a moment of vertigo that made him slow as he approached the glass. The view that met him was startling. The ground dropped sharply, two or three hundred feet into a gully, only to rise back up to another shorter ridge before falling away again. It was a rollercoaster for the eyes, dropping—down, down, down—to lake level where the late morning sun glittered and danced on the deep blue surface of Tahoe like a disco ball on steroids.

The entire South Shore—as well as the west and most of the north—could be seen from this vantage point. To the right, the ridge that began near lake level with the treed knob known as Round Hill rose up toward the crest of the Carson Range with Castle Rock sticking out of the trees a little below them. To the left was that wall of East Peak broken up only by a fire scar that drew a horizontal swath of brown through an otherwise green forest speckled with granite.

Sean could imagine watching the sunset from here. Fifteen miles away, the western lip of the basin looked lower than where he currently stood. He'd experienced the effect a few times before, the sun seeming to shine up from below as it slipped behind the horizon, casting shadows on the ceiling.

As he speechlessly took in the wonder of the lake, Sean's eyes caught an anomaly of perfection in the natural world. The tops of the trees on that ridge across the gully—the ones still standing anyway— were all cut in a straight line the length of the ridge. A number of others looked like they had been cut down or blown over and left to lay where they fell. The still living ones were all short and fat, the upper twenty feet or so missing. Sean noticed that the line those tree-tops now traced was a perfect match to the curvature of the south shore of Lake Tahoe behind them.

"What's up with those trees?" he said to Jake.

"Haven't you heard?" Jake answered. "There's a bit of an uproar going on around here about all that." He went on to explain that the owners had been denied a permit to cut—or even trim—the trees across the way. The land use restrictions being what they were at Lake Tahoe, the Tahoe Regional Planning Agency had a say in just about anything people wanted to do, even on private property. The owners had gone ahead and done the job even though they knew the fine would be in the $100,000 range. It was a small price for them to pay for the view they would get from it.

"So they just paid the fine and that was the end of it?" Sean said. "The powers that be are okay with that?"

Jake shrugged. "Yep."

"That's hardly even a slap on the wrist for someone with enough money to afford a place like this. What's your boss do anyway?"

"He's the CFO of one of those international conglomerates. The umbrella corporation goes by the name QTC, Inc."

Sean's breath caught in his throat. Julie couldn't possibly have known. Derrick? Yes, probably. But not her. Sean wouldn't be up here right now if she knew. He decided to let the issue pass for now and got back to the subject at hand. "There needs to be more of a deterrent for people like that."

"But that's what money gets you in this world, right?" Jake said. "The ability to do as you please—right or wrong."

A phrase ran though Sean's head: *It's only wrong if you get caught.* He thought maybe his old partner had said it a few times. He'd gotten caught, of course, and was currently vacationing behind bars. But if getting caught only meant a meager fine, then where was the real penalty? He supposed that was the point. Julie was certainly right that money is power and the wealthy are the ones making the rules.

Sean looked over at the mess left behind across the way once more. The needles on the downed trees and branches were already brown and dried out. "Why'd they leave it like that?" he asked.

"Boss told me the tree guy said it was better for the environment. My guess? He didn't want to pay the guy to haul the slash out."

Sean found himself shaking his head again. Maybe being immersed in Julie's world these last few days had skewed his outlook, but this all seemed so wrong. "I can't believe someone took down all those trees just so they could see the lake from their house. What were they thinking?"

"They were thinking that nothing else on this planet has any worth other than what humans assign to it. If it's in your way you either cut it down or run it over." Jake launched into a lecture on the difference between that worldview, called Anthropocentrism, and an alternate one that Sean was sure Julie would agree with: Biocentrism. The latter held that everything around us had worth regardless of any human uses for it. So rocks had worth as well as bugs and lions. Jake didn't seem so sure of the worth of a lot the beings that passed for human these days, though.

As the caretaker trailed off Sean eyes moved past the devastated ridge and down to lake level. He spied the scar through the trees where Highway 50 ran through town and followed it, snaking from the Y north and east toward Stateline, until it came to the five towers of the big casinos. If the Earth and all of its creatures had worth outside of any human uses for them, then who had decided it was all here for us to create or destroy as we pleased? And if you assumed dominion over all of non-human creation wasn't it just a hop, skip and a jump to the right to rule over other humans as well?

Six

"To what do I owe the pleasure, Agent Bartlett," Julie said as she gained the landing to her front door.

Bartlett didn't appear startled by her approach. "Good morning, Ms. Thompson," he said. "Do you have a few minutes?"

Julie slipped in front of the man and unlocked her door. "Actually, I have an errand to run. Can it wait?"

"I'm afraid not. We need to find your boyfriend ASAP."

She opened the door enough to step in and set her purse on the couch, then turned back to him, blocking the entrance. "I'll say it again Agent: Derrick is not my boyfriend."

"Not talking about Masterson. Though I'd be ecstatic if you could tell me where the hell he flew off to. I'm talking about one Sean Connors of, uh …" he consulted his notebook, "Corona, California."

So they'd finally managed to connect the two of them. She wondered how as she donned her best puzzled look. "What do you want with Sean?"

"We just want to ask him a few questions."

Julie sighed deeply. "Have you tried his hotel?"

The agent rolled his eyes. "Uh, yeah, we looked there. Would it be alright if I came in for a moment?"

"I would prefer that you didn't."

"Well, we could do this back at the station."

"Are you going to arrest me, Agent Bartlett? Am I being charged with a crime?"

"No, Ma'am. I just want to talk."

"Fine," Julie said. She pushed the door open and walked into the kitchen. "Leave it open, it's kind of stuffy in here."

Bartlett stepped into the room and quickly scanned the place.

Julie watched as his eyes fell on the partially closed bathroom door and lingered there a moment. She guessed that all he'd really wanted was a look inside her place—maybe more than the opportunity to ask his questions.

Julie pulled out a chair and sat down at the kitchen table. "Can we get this over with?" she said. "I've got things to do." As the words left her mouth she realized she hadn't chosen them with enough care.

Bartlett remained standing. "I bet you do," he said. "Anyway, tell me again where you were three nights ago?" He flipped back through the pages of his notebook as he spoke. Behind him the same uniformed officer from her studio stepped into view out on the deck.

"Three nights ago?" Julie said, shifting her eyes from the uniform back to Bartlett. "I told you, I was with a friend."

"And might this friend have been Mr. Connors?"

Julie held Bartlett's gaze steadily as she spoke. "I fail to see how that's any of your business."

"If it was Mr. Connors, then it's my business because he's suspected of—among other things—blowing up the South Tahoe Beach Resort."

"Excuse me?!" Julie said and laughed. She stood up and paced into the kitchen, buying a moment as she tried to figure out what the "other things" might be. "You can't seriously think Sean had something to do with that?"

"Let's just say we're looking at a pretty airtight case."

Julie turned back. "Really? Are you aware that, until five days ago, Mr. Connors hadn't set foot in the Tahoe Basin for over ten years?"

"Or so he apparently told you."

Julie couldn't imagine what evidence they had against Sean. But if they thought they had an airtight case, and she told Bartlett she wasn't with him, it would leave Sean with no alibi at all. Then again, if she admitted being with him, she might be implicating herself as well. A thin sweat broke out on her palms as she decided she had to trust that whatever evidence the police thought they had could be proven wrong and put herself on the line for Sean.

"Look," Julie said, crossing her arms. "I was with Sean all night. He couldn't have had anything to do with it."

Bartlett's eyes narrowed. "I don't think that will help Mr. Connors much at trial... And, come to think of it, all it does is make it look like you helped him."

Julie met the man's piercing gaze. "Again, Agent, are you charging me with the commission of a crime?"

Bartlett sighed his weary sigh. "I'm not charging you, Ms. Thompson, but telling me you were with the guy that we suspect of bombing the place just makes it look like the two of you are in cahoots."

"Cahoots?" Julie said, trying for a calmer demeanor than she felt as she sat back down at the table. "Listen, why don't you sit down for a minute and let me tell you a little about my evening with Mr. Connors?"

The detective hesitated a moment, looking like he might protest, then he pulled out the chair opposite Julie and sat. Julie told the tale of running into Sean in the café and spending the afternoon and evening with him. She said that, after the meeting, they had walked to the beach and played on the swings, then gone back to her place. She only deviated into lie for a few moments when she told the cop that she and Sean had had one drink and then gone to Safeway for ice cream. Then, she said, they went back to his hotel room and didn't leave again until the following morning.

Bartlett sat quietly finishing his notes. When he finally looked up, one eyebrow was raised high on his forehead. "So you expect me to believe that you two were doing what all night?"

"Again, I don't see how that's any of your business," Julie said. Still, his insinuation left her feeling slightly ashamed.

Bartlett stood up. "All right then, Ms. Thompson, when was the last time you saw Mr. Connors?"

Julie put on a thinking face. Theoretically Bartlett didn't know about her trip to Sean's the other night and she saw no reason to tell him. "Two mornings ago," she said. "When he dropped me off here." She had her fingers crossed under the table as Bartlett flipped through his little book looking for something.

"Where was he headed?"

"I think he said he was going for a drive around the lake."

"And you haven't seen him since then?"

"No."

"So you two slept together and you haven't seen him since?"

Julie shot to her feet, indignant. "Agent Bartlett, I'm beginning to take offense at what seems to me an unprofessional interest in my sex life. If you can't keep your questions to things that actually pertain to your case I may have to file a complaint."

Bartlett squinted his eyes slightly and stood his ground. "But it does pertain to the case, Ms. Thompson. If we can just get straight that the two of you were packing pipe bombs in that hotel room instead of bumpin' uglies."

"Alright, if you can't stop spewing accusations and sexual innuendo this conversation is over," Julie said, shaking off the nasty comment like a glass of water to the face. She took Bartlett by the elbow and ushered him toward the door. As they arrived at the threshold she added, "Have a wonderful afternoon, Mr. Bartlett. And don't forget to keep a look out for that formal complaint I'll be filing."

To stop himself from being forcibly ejected from the apartment, Bartlett put a hand on the doorframe and turned to face Julie. "Regardless of what you were doing in that hotel room, Ms. Thompson," he said, a sly grin perched on his lips, "you must have noticed all the explosives at some point."

Despite her best effort to stop it, Julie's jaw flopped open like she'd just been hooked.

"Explosives?" she said. She tried to regain some semblance of calm while still looking surprised as her thoughts screamed: *They found explosives in Sean's hotel room!!?*

"Quite a stockpile," the agent said. "Mr. Connors must have been planning something else big." He filled the doorway, one hand on the jamb, blocking exit from the apartment.

Julie stepped back and crossed her arms. "That's crazy. Sean doesn't have any explosives."

"The bomb squad begs to differ."

"I don't know what to tell you. There were no explosives in that room when I was there. Someone must have planted them."

"Ah-ha!" Bartlett laughed, though his face showed no trace of humor. "The ever-popular plant. And who might be responsible for that? The FBI? ATF?"

"I don't know who it was, but Sean wouldn't have that kind of stuff."

"And how do you know he didn't bring it all in after you were there? Until a couple days ago you hadn't seen the guy in how long?"

Julie stared him down but said nothing. She wasn't going to get into an argument with the man over Sean's supposed inclinations to anarchy when she knew absolutely that the explosives were not his. There were only two people who could be responsible for their appearance in his room—unless there *was* something he wasn't telling her.

"People change, Ms. Thompson," Bartlett said. He sounded like her father, trying to get her to open up. But with Sean well-hidden, Julie figured it might help if Bartlett thought his tact had created a hint of doubt in her.

"Sure, it's been a while," she said. "But Sean's not the type— never has been."

Bartlett issued another long sigh as he flipped through the pages of his book. "By the way," he said. "What happened to your car?"

"My friend borrowed it," Julie answered immediately. When she saw a grin forming on the agent's face she added, "Not Sean."

"Uh-huh," Bartlett grunted and finally stepped out onto the deck in front of Julie's apartment. She used the opportunity to grab the open door and begin closing it behind him, but he spun back on her again, leaning a shoulder against the doorframe. The uniformed police officer had retreated to the top of the stairs.

"Ms. Thompson," Bartlett said, leaning his head back into the apartment. "You seem like a nice girl. You might want to rethink the type of people you've been associating with lately. They might just wear off on you."

"I'll take that into account, Agent." Julie closed the door a bit more, trying to get the man out of her home once and for all.

"Again, if you think of anything that might be helpful—or if you hear from Mr. Connors or Mr. Masterson—don't hesitate to call."

"I'll be sure and do that, Agent Bartlett."

"You still have my card?"

"Of course. I'll need it when I file that complaint, remember?"

The agent's eyes dropped and his head turned toward the couch as he pushed back out of the apartment. Julie thought she saw his eyebrows rise with recognition as he stood upright, but his face quickly returned to a neutral expression. "All right, Ms. Thompson," he said. "We'll talk again soon."

"Bye," Julie said. She closed the door and locked it, then waited in silence as the two cops' footsteps receded down the stairs. When she was sure they were gone she turned her attention to the couch. There was nothing of interest sitting on the seat, but when she looked behind it—down along the wall—she saw a sweatshirt on the floor. It was the sweatshirt she had worn the night of the sabotage and that, in itself, meant nothing. The problem was that the black piece of clothing was covered with dirt and the sleeve that reached out toward the corner of the sofa like it had keeled over during an escape attempt looked scorched. The reason for that had been holding her arm too close to a candle, but she was sure Bartlett wouldn't believe that.

Julie bent down and pulled the thing from its hiding place. She must have set it on the back of the couch when she unpacked her bag yesterday and sometime since it had fallen back there. She stood and looked around for anything else she might have overlooked. There was nothing incriminating sitting out, but she'd made sure she didn't have anything all that incriminating. Was the grimy, scorched sweatshirt enough for them to get a search warrant? Enough for Bartlett to come back and arrest her?

Julie thought about the agent's last words. "We'll talk again soon," he'd said. She didn't like the implication there and decided it might be unwise to wait until he showed up back at her door.

From under the bed, she pulled her large backpack and began filling it with supplies she hoped would last a couple of days. It was mostly full when she spied The Box sitting on the bookshelf where she'd left it. On impulse, she tried to cram the whole thing in the pack, but it wouldn't go. With a grunt of aggravation, she pulled off the top and dumped the heap of letters in loose. Then she grabbed the scorched sweatshirt and headed for the bathroom window, leaving the empty box and its lid scattered on the bed like two just-rolled dice.

Seven

Sean stopped for a moment and leaned back against a large boulder to catch his breath. The crest of the hill he was climbing had disappeared again as the faint trail he followed grew steeper. Based on how long he'd been hiking uphill, his estimate of the height of this ridge where the trees had been cut was substantially flawed. Either that or he was in a lot worse shape than he'd previously thought.

After the mansion tour, he had retired to the front porch of the little guest cabin while he waited to hear from Julie. It was early afternoon and she still hadn't called so he read some of a book called *Ishmael* that Jake had given him.

A number of the ideas in it paralleled things Julie and her friends had been telling him the last few days—the author's "Mother Culture" always whispering in our ears, our conviction that our way is the only "right" way to live—but he couldn't seem to get into it. Maybe it was the telepathic gorilla.

When his restless legs had ruined his concentration even further, Sean fetched a bottle of water from the fridge and marched off to nowhere in particular, feeling like a hike might do him good. Not far from the cabin he thought he caught a sideways glimpse of someone passing through the dense trees off to his left, but when he stopped for a moment and quietly watched the area nothing moved. *Maybe it was Jake*, he thought. But still, what with Derrick creeping around out at the beach and the cops at his hotel, perhaps he should investigate. There did seem to be a faint path headed that way, so he followed it.

Now, down into the deep gully and up the other side by this boulder, Sean still hadn't found anyone, but his thoughts were telling him that the figure he thought he saw had been more Derrick-sized than Jake-sized. He eyed the skyline as he swigged some cold water from his bottle then continued along as the trail switched back up the steep slope—once then twice—before he gained a rise and it leveled out.

An instant later he realized that "leveled" was an apt word for what he discovered at the top of the ridge. The trail had dumped him in the epicenter of destruction. Where he now stood, *all* the trees had been felled—and not in any controlled manner or pattern that he could discern. The result was an impenetrable mass of tangled Pic-Up-Stix with branches on them. As if someone had just hacked haphazardly away with a chainsaw, paying no heed to what direction the trees would fall.

Shoes sloughing in the duff and pine needles left from the havoc, Sean slipped along the east side of the ridge as the elevation dropped down to where only the tops of the trees had been cut. The drying chunks—ten to twenty feet tall—lay between and around the bases of the still living upright sections that were now more like tall evergreen bushes. Some of the tops hadn't completely detached and hung from the sawed-off trunks like dangling windsocks without a breeze to give them life.

Sean stopped and wiped beaded sweat from his forehead with the tail of his shirt. This whole scene was unbelievable. That the trees had been cut? Yes. That they hadn't been cleaned up? Sure. But the real sticker in his mind was the reason Jake had given him for all of it: to improve the view from a single home. That monstrosity across the gully clinging to the side of the mountain like a bloated tick on a dog's ear.

And how improved was the view anyway? Sure you could see the lake from the house now, but you had this eyesore of a devastated ridge to look past in the foreground. To Sean it was a selective subtraction. The annihilation of one type of beauty for another.

Sean didn't know how to put a stop to this sort of thing. If the only penalty was financial then those with money could do what they wanted and pay the fine—the costs factored in beforehand. In order to have teeth, the punishment for things more likely to be perpetrated by the rich needed to be anything but monetary. Maybe forced community service or mandatory jail time. If not, then some sort of public humiliation was certainly in order.

Sean had some money—a lot actually—but, thankfully, he'd never acquired the drive to control others and subjugate the world to his will. He wondered what Julie would think when she found out exactly how much he was worth—if she didn't know already.

And what would she think when she found out Jake's boss—the owner of the Estate giving Sean refuge—was the CFO of the company that wanted to bulldoze her apartments? Sean still didn't know what to make of that coincidence. Strange things were afoot and he didn't know yet if he was a player in the game or just a pawn, but he currently supposed the latter.

Tired of looking at the destruction, Sean, just like everyone else, wanted a peek at the lake. He looked down the ridge for a break in the detritus, but heading in that direction would take him further from the cabin, the phone and Julie's awaited call. He had turned and started back uphill when he heard a clatter of rocks from below, somewhere toward the bottom of the gully.

His first instinct was to look and see who or what might be moving around down there, then he remembered he was a fugitive. Quickly and quietly, even as the thought flitted through his head that he was being overly paranoid, he made his way into a shadowy, cave-like area created by a hanging treetop and a couple of fallen trees. He was able to squeeze around the trunk of the still standing tree at the center and crouch down out of view. When he leaned out to take a peek, he saw nothing moving in the shimmering heat and hoped if anyone was there they wouldn't see him back here in the shade.

For what felt like five minutes Sean stayed there, crouched down, listening and peeking. In that time he neither heard, nor saw, anything else. *Probably a squirrel or coyote kicking down some rocks.* Still, in the time he'd spent under the tree he noticed that there might be a way through the mess to the west side of the ridge. *Better safe than sorry*, he thought and started out in a crouch in that direction.

Before he'd gone very far a rustling off to his left froze him in his tracks. Through a tangle of branches, he saw three ottoman sized bear cubs playing in the duff. Each probably weighed thirty or forty pounds. They were little balls of fluff, their fur fuzzy and thick, jumping and rolling and having a grand old time. Two were dark brown in color, but the third was a golden bronze that lit up in the rays of sunlight reaching the forest floor like staccato bursts of yellow flame as he tumbled and tackled one of his siblings.

Even in the painful half crouch he held, Sean was mesmerized.

He had never been this close to a bear in the wild—let alone three cubs. But where was Momma Bear?

A crash from behind gave him his answer. He half-turned and saw a large brown bulk advancing on him along the path he'd followed in. The cubs to the left, Momma to the right. Sean was stuck between. A sudden rush of adrenaline brought a flush to his face.

Momma emanated a low chuffing sound like a chugging choo-choo train and accelerated along the path. Sean took off and began breaking his own trail. Branches tore at him as he pushed his way through the deadfall. He ducked under a couple of two foot thick trunks suspended like high jump crossbars in the branches of live trees on either side. Up ahead bright sunshine and blue sky were visible through the trees, but the way below looked completely blocked by a ten foot high wall of rocks that was half buried in slash.

He risked a glance back, hoping momma bear would have peeled off to check on her cubs once he was out of the way, but she was still back there, huffing and grunting—and gaining.

To the left a long-dead tree had fallen up against the wall of rocks, it's upper portion balanced along the edge like a teeter-totter. Sean saw no other option for escape and ran up it like an escalator in the off position, using scraggly branches poking up along the way as handrails. At the pivot point, where safety dictated he should debark, Sean stopped. The tree straddled more deadfall atop the wall that looked impossible to navigate. But if he continued up the tree as it thinned and cantilevered out, he thought he might be able to make it to safer ground on the other side.

Sean looked back. Momma bear had paused at the base of the dead tree, having reached a decision point of her own. Hers was apparently less of a quandary than his. It took her only a second before she lifted her front paws and plopped them down on the trunk. Sean grabbed another spiky branch to keep from being thrown off into the debris as Momma Bear chuffed again and hopped all the way onto the dead tree. Then she was on her way up, shaking the log as she came.

As quickly as one would expect to climb an inclined, eight-inch-wide balance beam in an earthquake, Sean sidled up the narrowing, creaking, dead tree. He looked down past his feet for a jumping off point, but saw that the ground he'd hoped to land on disappeared over a cliff. How big a cliff? Didn't matter and he couldn't tell in his excited state anyway. He was only sure of one thing: it looked too far to fall.

He stopped and turned. Momma bear had reached the pivot point. He remembered something about making a lot of noise and trying to look big if confronted by a wild animal. Problem was he couldn't remember if it applied to bears or mountain lions or something else. *Oh well.* He raised his hands, waved them around over his head and yelled loud enough to strain his throat, "Stop right there, Bear. Stop, stop, stop!"

To Sean's surprise the bear actually stopped, startled for a moment. He was encouraged so he followed up with some loud growling and incoherent babble. The bear eyed him with a savage intensity, then tilted her head ever-so-slightly to the left, as if puzzled. Gently, as if reaching for one of her cubs, she moved her right paw forward a step and shifted her weight onto it. Sean felt the tree under his feet begin to tip slowly in his direction.

"No! No! Stop! Stop! Stop!" he screamed as she brought one hind paw forward to match the front. Then his breath escaped him as his entire world dropped out from beneath his feet.

The tree tipped faster than Sean thought possible, crunching onto the rocks below. His feet lost purchase on the trunk as he was thrown backward toward the cliff. He turned as he fell, searching for something to grab hold of, but found only empty space. A moment later he slipped over the edge with nothing more than an angry kiss from the rocks below.

Eight

DEAR JULIE,

HOW'S IT GOING?

I DON'T KNOW WHY YOU WON'T RETURN MY CALLS OR LETTERS. I'VE BEEN TRYING TO GET HOLD OF YOU FOR A WHILE NOW AND I'M ABOUT TO GIVE IT UP. I TALKED TO GLENN AND STEVE, BUT THEY DON'T KNOW WHAT'S UP EITHER. I THOUGHT THEY WOULD KNOW IF ANYTHING BAD HAPPENED.

I GUESS I HAVE TO ASSUME YOU CHANGED YOUR MIND AGAIN. AFTER THAT LAST TIME WE TALKED ON THE PHONE I THOUGHT THINGS WERE FINALLY MOVING FORWARD. REMEMBER HOW WE SAID WE'D GET TOGETHER THIS SUMMER?

I REALLY DON'T KNOW WHAT TO DO HERE. I'M HANGING IN LIMBO LIKE THE RUG'S BEEN PULLED OUT FROM UNDER ME BUT I STILL HAVEN'T HIT THE FLOOR. IT'S THE MIDDLE OF FINALS RIGHT NOW, BUT MAYBE I'LL TRY AND HEAD UP THERE WHEN THE SEMESTER IS OVER AND FIND OUT WHAT'S GOING ON.

ANYWAY, SCHOOL HAS BEEN TOUGH THIS YEAR, WHAT WITH MISSING YOU AND ALL. I HOPE TO PULL OUT OF IT WITH A B AVERAGE, BUT I JUST DON'T KNOW. THEY'RE GONNA MAKE ME DECLARE A MAJOR NEXT YEAR AND I STILL DON'T KNOW WHAT IT WILL BE. I WANT TO DO SOMETHING THAT MATTERS, YOU KNOW? I'M NOT REALLY SURE WHAT THAT MEANS, MAYBE

Environmental Science or something, I don't know.

The problem is that You are what matters most to me right now, You know? and I don't understand why I can't get You to talk to me. If I did anything to make You mad I'm sorry, but I can't think of a single thing that would have set You off. Even Your mom won't tell me a thing. She just says that You don't want to talk to me.

If something's wrong I just hope You can remember all the good times we've had. You are my soul mate, Julie, and I'm willing to wait for You if You're still a little scared of that, But I can't keep hanging on out here in left field with no word from You at all.

I love You.

You know that—I know You do—but You need to believe it. I'll always love You no matter what You do! I want to marry You! I want to spend the rest of my life with You!

I guess I'll say goodbye for now cos I really don't know what else to say. I need to see Your face, hear Your laugh, watch You smile, but none of it will happen if You don't talk to me.

You have the number. You know the address. The ball's in Your court because I can't go on like this anymore.

I love You,

Sean

*

Julie placed the letter back in its envelope and wiped tears from her cheeks with the backs of her hands. Her first inclination was to find a payphone as quickly as possible. She needed to talk to Sean—had told him she'd call—but that wasn't going to happen out here on the side of this dirt trail behind Sierra Tract.

Would things have turned out differently if she'd had the courage to open his last letter thirteen years ago? Sean would have forgiven her then. The sentiment in the old letter made that clear. But now? Their current situation had gotten complicated, to say the least. All the yelling and screaming; Derrick's prying; Sean's ridiculous assertion that she'd had something to do with setting him up; hers that he'd been a wuss for not trying to kiss her; and, of course, her blurted profession of love.

A hot flash of fear ran through her as she wondered if Sean had read her letters yet. What would he be thinking? The same thought had pushed her to finally open his letter a few minutes before as she was kicking through the woods. If he was going to get a look at hers, she figured she might as well buck up and take a look at his. Tit for tat, so to speak.

And now she knew that he'd certainly shown more courage than her back then by mailing that last one. It had taken her over thirteen years and a blackout drinking binge to finally release her death grip on the one from the night of her father's funeral, so who was the real wuss here? The fear still tightening like a boa constrictor around her ribs gave her an unequivocal answer to that question.

When she returned the letter to her pack her eyes caught on the others in the bottom and she was tempted to go on an old letter reading binge. She remembered the ones from his first year away at college, when he'd dated some red-headed hussy. And the larger stack from his second year, after he'd moved for good with his family to San Diego. That fall, through nothing more than words scrawled on paper, they'd somehow managed to patch up the gaping wound in their friendship inflicted by her indiscretion with Glenn and Sean's reaction to it. It was that exchange of thoughts and emotions that had begun to push her feelings for Sean to the next level. Well, that… and Sean just being there for her on that long ago night when she'd thrown herself at him.

Julie rose from the log she'd been sitting on and shook the past from her head. Instead of another letter, she pulled her water bottle from the pack and took a long swallow, leaving the paper bundle of regret and remorse in the bottom of the bag where it belonged. She needed to focus on the present. Her current plan was to find Derrick. She'd made a few stops and inquiries here and there since climbing out her bedroom window, but none of her contacts had anything useful to tell her about Derrick's whereabouts.

At any rate, her one-Clif-bar lunch was over so she replaced the water bottle, shouldered her pack and continued down the trail. She headed for the bridge over the Upper Truckee River that would take her over toward Barton Hospital. The gym where Jean worked was in a small plaza near the corner of Highway 50 and Third Street and this had been the most indiscreet way she could think of to get there. Talking to Jean seemed like the next logical step since she and Derrick were currently Julie's only suspects for setting Sean up.

A sound from behind like nylon scraping brush caught her ear as the trail rounded a bend through the trees. She turned her head, expecting to see a runner or mountain biker coming her way, but there was no one there. There were numerous trails running through this area—so many it was easy to get lost if you didn't know the way—so the noise had probably come from a side trail she couldn't see. Still, her awareness ticked up a notch as she continued along toward a clearing.

When the dirt track widened and the forest opened up Julie felt suddenly exposed. In the middle of the open area was a crossroads, a four-way intersection where her trail crossed another. They had both been dirt roads at some point in time when vehicular traffic wasn't restricted out here, now they were four feet wide and sandy. She needed to head straight on through, where the path would wind back up into the trees, but a blur of motion turned her attention to the trail approaching from the right.

Up the intersecting path a man approached, his face shaded by the brim of a floppy Columbia hat. Probably just another hiker, but she still picked up her pace so she would clear the intersection before he reached her. She glanced again at the figure as she crossed the trail then came to an abrupt stop in the middle of the X.

"Derrick, what the hell are you doing here?" she said. An uneasy relief flowed through her like a shot of Demerol, leaving her a little queasy.

"Julie?" Derrick said, pulling the brim of his hat lower. "Holy cow. I can't believe I ran into you out here."

Yes, what a coincidence, she thought as she watched his shadowed eyes. He looked as surprised to see her as she was him. Or was he too surprised? Overacting? She immediately chided herself for being paranoid. After another beat of silence with her staring him down he seemed to recall her question.

"Oh, I'm camping over there," he said with motion of his head past her. Then he patted an overstuffed backpack hanging off one shoulder. "On my way back from a supply run. What are you doing out here?"

Julie was cautious. "On my way out to my studio," she said. "Thought I'd take the scenic route."

"Ahhh," he said shaking his head slowly from side to side. "Are they looking for you, too, now?"

"I'm not sure," Julie answered as more doubts resurfaced in her head. "But they're definitely looking for Sean. Something to do with explosives turning up at his hotel. You wouldn't know anything about that, would you?"

Derrick held her gaze, unflinching. "I heard about it, if that's what you mean." He raised an eyebrow. "Is that what you mean?"

Julie hesitated, pushing a few strands of hair from her face. She still couldn't see Derrick setting Sean up and turning him in. Yes, she questioned his motives in digging up Sean's past—and she thought the trust lost there would be difficult to overcome—but, before Sean had shown up, he'd been nothing but a friend to her for over a year. Her conscience wouldn't allow her to abandon him now that things had gotten a little rough.

"Yeah," Julie finally answered. "That's all I meant. If you'd heard."

As if she'd blown a relaxing breath his way with her reply, Derrick's entire being visibly relaxed.

*

Julie sat on the ground opposite Derrick, knees to chest, arms wrapped around her legs. A small pot steamed on a portable cook stove between them. He hadn't been lying about camping out here, his camouflaged tent was to her back. When he'd invited her to join him for a late lunch she'd agreed to come mainly to see if he was telling the truth.

"So how have you been getting around?" Julie asked.

"Haven't been much. When I have to get out I've been sticking to neighborhood trails... like you."

"How did you hear about Sean, then?"

Derrick fussed with the burner for a few seconds before answering. "A couple of friends I talked to when I went for supplies."

"Ahh." Julie fidgeted with the toe of her right shoe. "Any other news?"

Derrick opened his mouth to speak, closed it again, then finally continued. "I hear Eagle's mostly cleaned up our mess and they're going to pursue the Lake's Edge project with renewed vigor. Seems our little nighttime escapade did not have the desired effect."

"They've cleaned it up already?" Julie thought of the canted buildings leaning on their neighbors. "How many did they lose?"

"Only the two we hit. The others were... salvageable."

Julie kicked that around in her head. She, Sean and Derrick were on the run and probably looking at jail time for taking down a couple of unfinished buildings that would most likely be rebuilt before the snow flew. "Why did we do it again?" she said.

Derrick bit his lower lip. "We did it to make a point, but our point was misconstrued."

"More like ignored."

"Yes." Derrick frowned and scratched his chin before adding quietly, "I think the ante needs to be upped."

Julie didn't know what he meant and didn't ask. If he wanted to do anything more spectacular than the other night she didn't want to be involved. She changed the subject, "So what's your plan? I thought you were getting out of the basin?"

"That was the plan," Derrick said, looking up toward the top of the ridge to the south. "At first, anyway. Now... I decided to take care of some other business before I get out of here."

"Business, huh?"

Derrick turned his attention back to Julie and waved a hand in dismissal. "Something I've been thinking of doing for a couple of years. I figured, 'Why not take care of it before I disappear.'"

"So why not take care of it and go? It's gotten pretty hot around here for you."

He screwed up his lips, seeming to ponder the question. "It's something I've had to wait a bit for… but I'll be able to shove off after the fireworks tomorrow night."

Julie dropped her knees into a semi-lotus position. "Derrick, what is going on? You lied to me about leaving the other day and now you can't even tell me what you've got going on?"

Anger flickered across Derrick's face like a mirage, there and gone. He sighed heavily—maybe forcibly—before saying, "Look, Julie, you're already in enough trouble, the less you know at this point the better."

"I see," she said and pivoted ninety degrees away from him. Annoyed, she looked up at the mountain he'd been eyeing a minute before. She didn't know this side of Derrick. He'd always kept his emotions under control, always been very even tempered. But after the way he'd been acting with Sean and his twitchy demeanor the last couple of days she wondered if he had some deeper problem. Since he'd gone on the lam he was behaving a bit like a mental patient off his meds.

Out of the corner of her eye she saw Derrick pick up a stick, fidget with it for a moment, then toss it over his shoulder. A few seconds later he spoke in a more subdued tone. "Julie, listen, I…" She turned her head to him but he kept his eyes on the stove. "I'm just trying to protect you."

Julie barked out a laugh and pushed herself to her feet. "Why is that? Why is everyone always trying to protect little old me? I can take care of myself, for god's sake." She stalked away from the hissing pot of water between them, running a hand through her hair. Before she left the campsite entirely she stopped and whirled back on Derrick. "You know it doesn't work don't you? In the end you can't protect me any more than my parents, or Sean, or anyone else ever could."

Derrick looked confused. "I don't know what you're talking abou—"

"I'm talking about everyone wanting to decide things for me," she said and took three steps back toward him. "I'm not twelve years old and I'm not an idiot."

The water was boiling now, over the edges of the pot to splash on the ground. Derrick reached out, but before his hand got there Julie snatched it off the stove. "I've got it," she said. She filled their two cups of dehydrated noodles as steam rose up in her face, leaving a hot flash of condensation there. It felt a lot like rage and she wished she understood why.

Nine

Like a fish slipped from the hook, Sean flopped from the earth to the sky, squirming for a handhold somewhere—anywhere. His right fingertips scraped bare rock and came away with nothing. Sagebrush grazed his left cheek and he was upended again. The impossible blue of the sky flitted by and the sun caught him directly in the eyes just before it disappeared behind the lip of the cliff he'd gone over.

The improbability of the moment flashed through his mind as he floundered in midair. He'd survived an exploding building a couple of nights ago, but here he was now, being taken out by a bear. And for no good reason either. He'd made for the hills when Momma Bear had come back to her cubs. The damn bear was just holding a grudge.

Sean's left hand felt leaves. Something brushed his forearm and he flailed at it, catching a grip on a branch. The plant held and he flipped again then slammed—full along the right side of his body—into the cliff face. His hip took the brunt of it, sending an arc of pain down his leg to the tips of his toes, but his right hand remained deadlocked around the branch as he bounced into the rock once, then twice, his left hand scrabbling for and finding a grip there as well.

Dangling, his feet searched for purchase. No foothold presented itself as his shoes scuffed back and forth across the stone. He tried to look down, but leaves in his face blocked the view. The bark of the branch six inches from his eyeballs was the shiny, reddish-brown of Manzanita.

After some more flailing around, his feet finally found a tiny crack, about knee level, where he could wedge the toe of one shoe. He crammed his right foot in as far as he could and shifted his weight onto it, pushing himself up further into the bush.

Now that his weight was off his arms he had the ability to look around. The top of the cliff he'd gone over looked to be twenty or thirty feet above his head. Below, it was another near-vertical thirty feet until the rock face began to develop into a bit of a slope. Another flash of adrenaline shot through Sean as he realized he was now in the middle of a sixty foot free-climb in his street clothes.

He took a deep breath and tried to steady himself. The pain in his hip became a dull roar on the back-burner of his consciousness. Sean had only been rock climbing once in his life. This was going to take all of his concentration. Based on the two available options, the look of the steep run-out at the bottom of the vertical cliff helped him make a decision: up looked easier than down. The first problem would be getting out of this bush.

And what the hell was a Manzanita doing here anyway? Sean didn't think they usually grew on vertical walls. Of course, if he wanted to accept Jake's bio-centric worldview, the bush might be wondering the same thing about him.

He shook off the crazy thought. Maybe the adrenaline was affecting his head. The toes on his right foot had gone almost completely numb and he needed to move.

Out to the right a horizontal crack looked deep enough for hand and maybe even footholds. That crack appeared to run over to a vertical chimney of sorts that might take him all the way to the top. He would need to get to the horizontal one first across five feet of smooth rock. Sean squinted as he surveyed the surface with forced diligence. As he eyed it more carefully, smaller ridges and pocks revealed themselves. A couple might be large enough for brief handholds if he could somehow get a toe into a crevice three feet over that looked even tinier than the one his club of a right foot was currently wedged into.

Sean tightened his grip on the Manzanita and tested it with his weight again. It still seemed well-rooted into the rock. He slowly lifted the weight off his numb right foot and had to wiggle it back and forth to remove it from the slot. The toe of his left shoe was just as hard to wedge back in, but he was finally able to settle his weight on that leg and give his arms another rest.

After allowing a minute for the blood to find its way back into his right toes, Sean felt ready to make his move—as ready as he was ever going to feel anyway. He released his right hand and slowly leaned over in that direction, reaching out for the closest nub he could see. With his left arm stretched out behind him and pulling at the bush he heard a rustling creak that was not entirely encouraging.

When his right hand reached the protrusion on the rock it felt woefully inadequate to hold his weight. He tried to get a grip on it, but he might as well have expected to pick someone up by grabbing onto a lump on their head.

Moving quicker now, he swung his right foot over to the lower crevice. That, too, was smaller than hoped for and he'd only managed to get the very tip of his shoe in there when the Manzanita behind him snapped like a wet towel.

His toehold didn't hold and his foot slipped from it. He swung across the rock face by thumb, middle and index finger grasping a stone lump, half a bush dangling from his other hand. He was so focused on not releasing his tenuous grip on the granite with his right hand that, try as he might, his left hand would not let go of the broken branch.

As his body reached the apex of the swing to the right, the force ripped his fingers from the stone. He was falling again, but drifting right and spinning slightly. He swung his left hand around as his body pivoted and he stretched toward a vertical fissure running down from the bottom of the horizontal crack, the branch still stubbornly in his grasp. A moment later he jolted to a halt.

Getting his bearings once more, he saw that he was only five or six feet below where he'd been hanging onto the bush. He'd somehow managed to wedge the trunk end of the broken branch into the vertical gap. Quickly, Sean found footholds below and took the weight off the branch that had now saved him twice. Releasing his grip was like prying open a nutshell. He had to flex his hand over and over to get it to loosen up.

After a good bit of deep breathing and shaking of his limbs, Sean started methodically up toward the horizontal crack and over to the larger chimney. From there it was a much easier climb and within a few minutes he found himself back up top. The bear was nowhere in sight as he headed east along the ridge, toward the estate.

Ten

Julie and Derrick had eaten in silence before she excused herself. She'd told him that she had a class to get to. When she asked Derrick how she might be able to reach him he only shrugged and said, "If it's meant to be I'm sure we'll meet again." She'd never thought of Derrick as the type to leave things up to fate, but maybe his predicament had turned him a bit more philosophic lately.

As she made her way across the South Upper Truckee River footbridge she tried to get out of her own head and focus her awareness on the present moment. The late afternoon sun shone hot on her skin, birds sang in the bushes, the water gurgled and swished around the bridge supports as it found its way through the narrow gap. A perfect Tahoe summer day, but her problems wouldn't let go. Their claws were dug in deep, ingrown.

Tears leaked from her eyes, borne more of frustration than sorrow or regret. What if Jean had nothing to tell her? What would she do then? Sean was counting on her and she was about to play her last card. With the authorities likely after her it would be a huge risk to go to any of her other friends for help and Derrick had turned out to be useless.

On the far side of the bridge, Julie stopped and closed her eyes. She wished in that moment that she was with Sean. They would have made up by now if they were together, she fantasized. She could picture the two of them cuddled up in the cabin at the estate sipping a cool, white wine while they waited for this storm of idiocy to pass—never mind that she had sworn off alcohol until that happened.

"Enough," she said aloud and opened her eyes. Enough self pity. She had things to do—well, one at least. And if that didn't pan out something else would. She continued up the trail, determination renewed. It wasn't too far to the gym where Jean worked.

*

Julie leaned her head in through the partially open door to the back office of the health club. "Hello?" she said. The freakishly athletic guy at the front desk had pointed her back this way when she'd asked if Jean was in today. As she began to push the door open she heard a toilet flush. A moment later Jean emerged from the bathroom wiping her hands on a paper towel.

"Julie?!" Jean gushed in a loud whisper when she spotted her. "Holy crap, where have you been?" She pushed the office door open further, pulled Julie in and closed it behind them. They stood in a tiny room with a small, overloaded desk, a corner piled with boxes and a few lockers. No sooner had Julie gotten a look around then Jean was hugging her fiercely. "I'm glad you're okay," the other woman said.

"Yeah," Julie said as they separated. "I'm fine. How are you doing?"

"Me?" Jean said. "I'm good." Then she lowered her voice further, her eyes darting around the room, before she added, "But I'm not the one wanted by the cops here."

Julie wondered how Jean knew they were looking for her. "What do you mean," she asked.

Jean shifted from one foot to the other. "Well, they're after Derrick… So I just assumed…"

"That they'd be looking for me, too?" she said and leaned back against the front of the desk, letting it take some of her weight.

"Well… sure," Jean said.

"Are they looking for you?"

"No. I mean… I don't know. But the cops have been by to talk to me twice."

"By here?"

"No, my place."

"Were they asking about me?"

"A little bit, yeah. Mostly about Derrick, though. The second time about Sean."

"So they still don't suspect you?"

"Doesn't seem like it."

Julie sighed. "At least one of us got away with it."

"Maybe."

Maybe was right, but until the authorities found some evidence that hadn't been planted Julie couldn't afford to give up.

"What about Sean?" Jean asked. "Where is he? How's he doing?"

"He's… somewhere safe."

"Good, good," Jean patted Julie on the knee as she sat on the edge of the desk next to her.

Julie didn't think the level of their friendship warranted such closeness and she inwardly shied away. "So, have you seen Derrick since the other night?" she asked.

"I saw him for about two minutes yesterday and that was it."

"Where was that?"

Jean eyed Julie from the side before saying, "You checking up on him or something?"

Julie didn't know what Jean's true relationship was with Derrick, so she needed to be careful here. She still had to entertain the possibility that the two of them had planted the explosives at Sean's hotel together. But how to get any information Jean might have about Derrick's plans?

"I'm worried about him," Julie said finally, figuring a half-truth was better than an outright lie. "I saw him earlier and he seemed… I don't know… off."

"Off?"

"Fidgety and purposely…" she waved a hand as she searched for the right word. "Evasive, I guess."

"Huh… He was a little stressed out when I saw him, but mostly okay."

"Did he say anything about having big plans for tomorrow, or what he might be doing?"

Jean eyed her with suspicion again. "Tomorrow?" she said as her eyes focused farther away. "Tomorrow is the 4th of July."

"Yep," Julie said, unsure why she felt the need to agree with Jean's statement of the obvious.

Jean stood, walked over to one of the lockers, opened it and began digging around inside. Without turning to face Julie she said, "I don't know anything about what Derrick might be doing tomorrow."

Was Jean intentionally hiding something? Or was she just hurt that Derrick hadn't confided in her? Regardless, she'd made it abundantly clear that she wasn't in the mood for dishing any more dirt. Julie pushed up from the desk and went to the door. As she placed her hand on the knob Jean spoke.

"You know, he's always been after you."

Jean's tone made Julie's heart kick up a beat. Her words weren't just an observation, there was accusation and vitriol in them.

"A-after me?" Julie stuttered as she turned her head.

Jean stared back hard for a moment with her jaw set before rolling her eyes away. "He likes you, you know? He's got the hots for you?"

Julie only relaxed slightly. "Yeah, I just found that out the other day."

"A lot of women would be glad to have him, but you're too good for him, aren't you?"

Julie let her hand drop from the doorknob and fully faced Jean, puzzled why the other woman had brought this up now. "What's this about, Jean?"

The other woman's hand flitted to her head as if she had an itch. "Do you have any idea how long I've loved him? And all he ever does is chase after you: Little Miss Perfect. God damned Miss America. And you never even notice." Tears dribbled from the corners of her eyes.

"Jean, I'm sorry, I—"

"You're not sorry. Just look at you. You're probably not wearing any makeup at all—been out wandering in the woods all day—and you're still gorgeous. How could you not get any guy you want?"

Julie could think of no good response to that. Apparently this truly was "Return to Adolescence" week. She wished she hadn't missed the memo. "Jean, I—" she began again.

"You should go," the other woman said and turned back to her open locker. "I don't know where he is or what he's doing, but it's probably got something to do with you."

Julie shook her head as she opened the door and stepped out. Instead of illuminating anything, the whole encounter had just muddied the water. She felt bad and yet she didn't. It wasn't her fault she looked the way she did and it wasn't her fault that Derrick liked her. But, at the same time, she could completely understand the way

Jean felt because—whether Jean would believe it or not—she had been in that position herself once or twice. And what, as a woman scorned, might Jean be capable of? Planted explosives, perhaps?

Julie was exiting the gym thinking about the possibility of Jean setting up Sean when she noticed a South Tahoe Police cruiser slowing to make a right into the parking lot. She immediately moved in the opposite direction, maintaining a normal pace, and scooted around the corner of the building. Once out of sight she accelerated to just short of a run and headed for the trees at the back of the lot.

Eleven

Back in the guest cabin again, Sean toweled off gingerly in the tiny shower of the tiny bathroom after a hot shower. He was scraped and bruised and was careful not to reopen any of the slowly scabbing cuts. His fingers on both hands were raw and tender and his hip throbbed like a pulsing disco beat even after the five Ibuprofen he'd swallowed twenty minutes before.

As he winced his way across the bedroom to look for some clean clothes he checked the bedside clock. It was 6:25 p.m. and Julie still hadn't called.

I have the time to nearly get killed by a bear and do some advanced free climbing, but Julie can't find a minute to pick up a phone.

Almost as soon as the thought entered his mind he realized it wasn't fair. He didn't know where she was or what she was doing, but he did know that finding a payphone could be difficult—the things had become scarcer than honest politicians these days. And he knew it was really his worry about her safety that this new anger was trying to cover up.

When he was once again positioning himself out front with a beer, a book and the phone, the thing miraculously rang in his hand just as he was setting it down on the table.

"Sean?" Julie said, slightly breathless, before he could even say hello.

"Thank god it's you," he answered. "I've been worried sick."

There was a brief hesitation from the other end before Julie responded. "Sorry, I was dialing the number from memory, I forgot to write it down when I left my place this morning and I've been all over South Lake and haven't been able to find a payphone that wasn't broken or completely exposed and now I'm at the Tahoe Keys Shopping Center and I'm not sure if the cops are following me and I thought I should call you real quick while I had the chance because I don't know the next time I'll be around a secure or public line and—"

"Whoa! Whoa!" Sean broke in. "Take a breath. The cops are after you?"

"Right." Julie breathed for a moment. "Listen, I can't talk for long, this phone is way too exposed. And, yeah, I think the cops are looking for me. It looked like that FBI Agent saw my scorched sweatshirt this morning when he came to question me again. I wasn't going to wait for them to come back with a search warrant so I bailed out the bathroom window. I've been talking to people and trying to keep a low profile, but I haven't found out much."

"He questioned you again? About what?"

"About all the explosives they found in your hotel room, believe it or not."

Sean half-squeaked, "They found *what* in my room?" and nearly fell out of his chair.

"Explosives. He didn't go into detail and I told him it was crazy, that there was no way it was your stuff, but I'm sure he just thinks I'm covering for you."

Sean thought about the situation for a moment. With only a few people knowing he was in town… With Derrick apparently stalking Julie and him…

"It had to be Derrick," he said through clenched teeth. "Who el—"

"That's where my mind jumped, too, but there might be another player or two involved here. Jean for one. I still can't see Derrick doing that."

"Julie, what do you really know about these two? How can you not see what's going on here? They set me up to take the fall."

"I know that's how it looks, Sean. But I'm trying to stay positive here and believe in these people until I have some concrete proof."

Sean let out an aggravated sigh that travelled down the line with a strange, accompanying hiss.

The sound made Julie grit her teeth and take a deep breath. She did not want to get into an argument here, but she could feel the animosity building. This was the first time they'd spoken since the big fight and Julie decided abruptly that the subject needed changing.

"Sean," she blurted, without giving much thought to the words to follow. "I'm sorry about last night, all that stuff I said, I didn't mean to hurt you, we just… " Not sure where to go from there, she trailed off into silence.

A moment later Sean filled it. "Yeah, we just," he said, his voice softened. "Don't we always? I mean, find a way to screw up a good thing."

She laughed. That was good to feel, that he could still make her laugh in spite of everything. She wanted to ask about the letters—if he'd gotten them, if he'd read them—but she didn't. Maybe the fact he was talking to her at all told her he hadn't. She kept quiet as more static crackled across the line.

"And I'm sorry, too," Sean said finally. "We… I…" He stopped and let out a short, exasperated breath, annoyed at his inability to find the right words. "I want to…"

What? What did he want?

To make up? Sure.

To have this whole fairy tale work out in the end? Definitely.

But there was a giant roadblock in his head and there was only one way to break through it: he needed to know what happened thirteen years ago. He'd thought he could let it go at first, but he was wrong. It had become a burr in his mind. A constant irritation demanding resolution.

Julie filled the void left hanging after his cutoff stuttering. "Me too," she said quietly.

And he knew exactly what she meant. That right there was why he wanted this to work out. There was a connection between them that he had never experienced with anyone else. Two minds on the same wavelength? Two hearts beating in the same time signature? Soul mates? Sean didn't know what it was. All that mattered was that it felt so right that goose bumps popped up on his arms and a shiver ran through him. And, for now, he was able to let the past go once again.

*

They talked quickly about what they'd been doing for the last eighteen hours. Sean left out his bear encounter and who owned the

Estate; Julie failed to mention her drunken blackout and the accompanying idiocy. After a minute or two the subject came back around to problems at hand.

"So Derrick was acting strange earlier, huh?" Sean asked.

"Yeah."

"Does the guy have a condition?"

"Not that I know of," Julie said. "I've never seen him be anything but professional and committed to the cause. He's acting completely out of character lately."

"Any idea what he might be planning?"

"Nope. I figured I'd check out his place in a little bit. Maybe I'll find something there."

Sean digested that for a moment before speaking again. "You need to be careful. You have no idea what he's capable of. And the way he seems to be following you around… I don't know, sounds like a stalker."

Julie breathed heavily, in and out, the aggravation building yet again. "Sean, he's not a stalker, he's my friend. If he needs help, I want to help him. He's not going to hurt me, if that's what you mean."

"You don't know that," Sean said. "And you need to think about the police, too."

"I know what I need to do. I can take of myself."

Sean backed down. "I know, I know. Just be careful ple—."

"Gotta go, there's a car coming this way," Julie said, a little panicked. "I'll call when I can."

"Okay, bu—"

"Bye."

Sean started to speak again but she was already gone. He let the phone drop from his ear and pushed the end button as the color seemed to drain from his world.

Twelve

Julie trotted along the canal behind the houses on the south side of Venice Boulevard trying to look like she belonged there. This was the best way she'd come up with to get to Derrick's house without walking right down the road. The approaching car that had caused her to cut Sean off—and basically hang up on him—had turned out to be nothing more than a lost tourist that Julie was able to point in the direction of the Tahoe Keys Marina.

Regardless of the way their conversation had been going when Julie ended it, the words, "I love you," had rolled around in the back of her mouth and she was glad they hadn't fallen out. Once in eighteen hours was quite enough when it came to unprovoked professions of love, thank you very much. And there were still the letters to think about. Maybe he'd never gotten them at all. Heather said they hadn't been completely sure they were leaving them at the right cabin last night. Her and Sean would just have to burn that bridge when they came to it.

Maybe she'd been on her own for too long, but it grated on her nerves to have so many people telling her what to do lately. She needed to do better at shrugging these things off, let her Zen mind prevail and turn the other cheek.

Yeah right. In her experience, turning the other cheek usually just ended up getting you slapped on the ass.

*

It always seemed odd to Julie that Derrick lived in the Tahoe Keys, one of the biggest environmental disasters in the history of the Lake. An entire wetland marsh had been turned into a neighborhood of multi-million dollar homes with canals and boat docks. The construction of the subdivision had required the straightening of the Upper Truckee River which, in turn, had reduced the filtering of sediment from Tahoe's largest tributary. Over the years, the extra silt finding its way into the lake had contributed to a drastic drop in the lake's clarity.

But now wasn't the time to worry about that and Julie stayed alert as she approached the back of Derrick's house, well aware that the authorities might be watching the place. Derrick kept a hide-a-key under the deck and she fished it out then let herself quietly in the rear door. She crept up to the living room window that faced the street and peered out from the side of the curtains. There were no vehicles parked on Venice Drive within a couple hundred feet on either side of the house. That didn't necessarily mean no one was watching, just that—if they were—they were being more discreet than at her place.

Julie slid out of her pack and dropped it by the front door. She left all the lights off and didn't bother to grab her flashlight. There was still enough daylight filtering in that she could see and she didn't want to draw attention to her presence. Not having any idea what she was looking for, she wandered in and out of rooms aimlessly, staying away from the windows as much as possible. It didn't look like the cops had been through the place, so they'd apparently never come up with enough evidence for a search warrant. She didn't think Derrick would be stupid enough to keep anything incriminating here anyway.

In the kitchen she noticed a calendar on the wall that had the Third and Fourth of July circled in red with no accompanying explanation why. The house was a four bedroom, probably over three thousand square feet, and she didn't find anything else of interest until she entered one of the spare bedrooms on the ground floor behind the garage. It was a room Derrick seemed to be using for storage, but what caught Julie's eye was the gun cabinet in the corner—guns weren't something normally associated with environmentalists. She'd never imagined that Derrick would own guns.

She approached the glass front of the wooden case and noticed that it wasn't completely closed. The door stood ajar by a couple of inches and she opened it the rest of the way. Julie knew next to nothing about guns—hated them, in fact—but the ones in the case didn't look like what she thought would be your average home protection pieces. The bigger, rifle types looked like they had places for large magazines and most of the pistols were large and threatening. All in all, Derrick's weapons cache looked more suited for military use than, say, hunting.

At the bottom of the rack, where the bulk of the pistols sat, were four empty spaces, but Julie couldn't tell if they had ever held guns. On the shelf beneath, though, something was painfully obvious, even in the encroaching gloom. At least four boxes of ammo were missing, as evidenced by the number of square, empty spaces in the accumulated dust.

Sudden recollection of a conversation she'd had with Derrick months before made her gasp, "Oh my god!"

On the South Shore of Lake Tahoe, the Fourth of July fireworks were set off above the water. The shells were staged on barges then pulled out into the lake for the show. A while back, she and Derrick had kicked around a hypothetical plan to hijack the barges in order to make a point. Julie was against it because she didn't think it could be accomplished without the use of force. She also thought that security and the timing of the launch would make the logistics a nightmare. Now she found herself staring dazed into the gun cabinet at those empty spaces in the dust, thinking about those two red circles on the calendar in the kitchen and wondering how hypothetical Derrick's proposal had actually been.

But he wouldn't. How could he?

Something else he'd said earlier at his campsite popped into her head: "I think the ante needs to be upped."

Whether it was a recent change, or she'd been wrong about him the whole time, Julie could no longer put aside the mounting evidence that Derrick had gone rogue. The realization made her blood boil anew. Just how long had the son of a bitch been lying to her? And about how much?

Brashly, Julie reached into the gun cabinet, but hesitated when her hand touched a cold pistol grip. *What the hell am I doing? Do I want to be just like him?*

But how could she not? If she wanted to stop Derrick—and help keep Sean out of prison—she needed to be able to confront him as an equal. The idea that the master's tools couldn't be used to dismantle the master's house had never held much water with her anyway.

With that in mind Julie grabbed hold of the pistol, snatched a box of ammo from the shelf and slogged out of the room like a loaded freight train. She didn't remember what message the hijacking of the fireworks was supposed to send, but she did know where the loaded barges currently floated. The same place she'd sent those tourists not long before: Tahoe Keys Marina.

Thirteen

Sean stood in the kitchen of the caretaker's cabin, wincing a little at the pain in his hip as he watched Jake plate a meal that would have looked at home on a Friday's Station table at Harrah's. Turned out Jake had trained as a chef before his current stint as a caretaker.

"How'd you get all banged up?" Jake asked.

Sean took a moment to respond. He'd already hemmed and hawed his way around the "What did you do all afternoon?" question without revealing where he'd been. Truth was, he felt like an idiot for having fallen over a cliff, but he was also still kinda ticked at that bear for chasing him down.

"It was the damned bear, okay?" Sean said, grimacing again as he lifted his leg off the floor. He had to lean on the counter for a little more support. "The damn thing tried to kill me."

"Bear?" Jake said, surprise on his face. "You were attacked by a bear? Do I need to take you to the ER, man?"

Sean laughed, releasing a little of his pent up stress. "No, I think I'll live."

Jake handed Sean a plate, grabbed the beer he'd been working on and led the way to the dining room. Sean did the same and followed as the caretaker asked, "So, what the hell happened?"

Forty-five minutes before, Sean had been going stir-crazy in his cabin again, wishing for some escape from his own thoughts when Jake had called and invited him up for dinner. He'd figured, *What the hell, I'm hungry*, and didn't want to turn down a homecooked meal. So here he was, hesitantly launching into a curtailed version of his misadventure on the mountain. He got a little more into it as he went along. They were well along in their meals before Sean wound down and said, "I don't know what the hell was wrong with that bear. It just kept on coming."

Jake put down his fork before replying, "For one, you got between her and her cubs."

"At first, yeah. But I got right out of there. Why keep chasing me?"

"Well, maybe there something actually wrong with her. Probably not physically, but…" Jake paused and took a long pull off his beer. "Look at it this way. How would you be feeling if someone had come in and leveled your home a month ago? You might still be a little pissed off, no? And if one of those responsible happened to return to the scene of the crime?"

Sean was incredulous. "Are you trying to tell me that bear chased me because I look like the ones who cut down all those trees? You seriously think that's a thought process a wild animal can follow?"

"Yes, I do. But I wouldn't really call it a thought process. That bear has certainly seen humans around. She probably saw a number of them trashing her home, putting her family in danger and generally scaring the shit out of her. Then, after she thought they were all gone and she was adjusting to life in her new surroundings, she comes back to her den and finds you hanging around her kids. Again, what would you do?"

Sean set his own fork down and stared at Jake. What the other man was suggesting was ludicrous. Wasn't it? Sure, he cared about animals as much as the next guy, but if they could really think like that… What would that mean? Julie had said something the other day about everything being connected. And about humans only being members of the web of life, not absolute rulers. The idea of bears and mice and eagles all having families and homes and, well, lives, meant that they mattered as much as humans, right? His mind boggled at the thought and he swallowed some more beer, trying to beat back the cascading implications.

"Then again," Jake said, perhaps noticing Sean's discomfort. "Could be she's just got rabies."

"Bears get rabies?"

"I don't know… maybe."

Sean thought Jake did know and just wasn't saying.

*

Later, in the middle of the main drive of the Estate on the way back to his cabin, Sean stopped and tilted his head back. Through the canyon in the trees the driveway had created was a swatch of sky peppered with brightening stars. The sun had been down for half an hour and they grew brighter by the minute as everything else faded to black. Down here on the ground, with no moon yet, the dark was quickly sliding from partial to absolute. One too many beers had left him with a buzz in his head as he tried to find the path to his cabin, navigating mostly by feel.

Jake had turned out to be an interesting guy. After they talked about bears they moved on to other, more esoteric topics like sports and women. They found that they were both Giants fans—of different sports. Jake, a native of the East Coast, was a New York Giants football fan. Sean loved the Giants of the San Francisco baseball ilk. The rest of the big four sports broke down roughly along the same lines. Sean also found out that Jake's brief flirtation with Julie had been ended by him, not her.

"We dated for about a month," he'd told Sean, "but it always seemed like there was someone else. I didn't like feeling like I was the second fiddle."

Sean didn't know if Jake was inferring that the other guy might have been him, but whatever Julie had said, he seemed to have the idea the two of them were serious now. The thought that she had given an old flame that impression warmed his insides even as a cool breeze trickled up under his loose shirttail and made him shiver.

He wondered where she was right then, what she might be thinking, what kind of scar she'd been carrying around this long that the mere thought of revealing it scared her more than bombs and falling buildings. And he wondered if there was anything he could do to help her in that regard.

Truth was, after talking to her earlier this evening, his mind was pretty much made up. Julie was his girl. Always had been.

Fourteen

Julie crouched behind an earthen berm a hundred feet from the fireworks barges and peered over the top, trying to see what was going on. *Nothing*, pretty much summed it up. Through two rows of boats in dry dock she could see a lone security guard reclined in a chair on the dock by the barges. It was full dark now and she hadn't seen any other guards since she'd arrived. Derrick was nowhere in sight.

Before she left his house she had stuffed the gun and box of ammunition in her pack. Forcing herself to load the thing was another matter and she hadn't been able to do it. She knew how guns worked in general—had even fired one a few times in her younger days—but she couldn't imagine ever using one to shoot a living being. Having it in her bag did give her what was probably a misplaced sense of confidence, even if it was just for show.

She'd exited Derrick's house the way she came in, then skirted the glorified puddle behind the residences on that side of the street. Once she crossed Tahoe Keys Boulevard it was only a couple of minutes to where the fireworks barges were docked near the boat storage yard that backed on Venice Drive. The shells for the show were staged on two barges, one of which was the original M.S. Dixie sternwheeler stripped of its fore-cabins. Tomorrow morning they would be tugged a mile out into the lake behind the casinos.

Julie didn't have any idea how long she might have to wait so she tried to get comfortable by removing her pack and sitting in the grass, legs folded in a lotus position. She waited for what felt like an hour while nothing continued to happen at an agonizingly slow pace. She kept herself occupied by counting the cars coming and going from the Tahoe Keys Marina visitor's parking, another quarter mile down Venice Drive toward the lake. As another oversized SUV passed on its way out she changed the total in her head to seventeen. When she finally pulled her watch out of her bag it was ten fifteen.

What if Derrick isn't coming?

She'd acted on a hunch and was beginning to lose faith in her intuition. It was just a lark that she'd remembered that conversation anyway. They'd only been imagining a *possible* action, something someone could maybe do given the right support and circumstances. That didn't mean Derrick was going to hijack these barges tonight. What worried Julie the most, though, was the guns. The very real possibility that Derrick was packing had been a game changer for her.

Another car passed. There couldn't be that many people left at the restaurant out there. The security guard had slipped down in his chair and pulled his hat over his eyes. Had to be hired help. She figured anyone with a stake in the goings on would be paying more attention.

Things stood like that for fifteen or twenty minutes more as Julie practiced her deep breathing. She heard a few cars passing out near Tahoe Keys Boulevard a couple hundred yards to the west. A minute later the sound of vehicle doors opening and closing reached her ears. Probably over in the shopping center on the corner where she had called Sean earlier. Some more time passed before motion off to the west brought her out of what had been developing into an open-eyed trance.

A hundred feet away, two people in black carrying full packs gained the crest of the berm separating the boat storage yard from the road. From this distance, and with so little light, they were only silhouettes. From the shape and size, though, they appeared to be a man and woman. In a half crouch, the two figures crossed the sunken boat storage yard as Julie slid down her own berm to lessen her profile. They approached the passageway into the main yard headed directly for her, but when they reached it they veered off to their left, skirting the fence and approaching the barges. Julie was pretty sure the man was Derrick. A ball cap, brim pulled low over the eyes, shaded the other face. Based on the build, though, Julie could make a pretty rock-solid guess that the accomplice was Jean.

She lost sight of the two as they passed behind a huge cabin cruiser. She used the opportunity to check on the security guard. He was still slumped in his chair like a dead thing, eyes covered.

Some security.

Now that the suspicions she'd been harboring appeared to be true, Julie realized she hadn't thought this through. She had no plan and couldn't seem to get her thoughts moving. If she'd been right about one thing, though, she was probably right about another: these two were armed.

I am, too, she reminded herself. But what good would it do when she knew she couldn't pull the trigger?

She couldn't let that matter. She had to do *some*thing. This was crazy. Hijacking fireworks barges with loaded weapons. This kind of thing would only cement the greater public's view of so-called "radical environmentalists" as actual terrorists.

Quietly, Julie shouldered her pack and rose to a crouch. She moved in the direction the two shadowy figures had approached from, and skirted the twenty-foot-high boat storage racks that separated her from the fireworks barges. When she rounded the end she found the only thing blocking her entrance to the yard was a single chain strung two feet off the ground. She hopped over it and continued on. Keeping to the shadows, she approached the guard cautiously from the left.

She was twenty feet away when she saw movement to his right. She momentarily panicked before melting further into the darkness behind a cabin cruiser and peeking out around the front. Derrick and his accomplice ran from behind a house boat with pistols in their hands. When they reached the dock they slowed and crept like cops, guns in both hands pointing up above one shoulder. Had Derrick been in the military? If so, he'd never mentioned it to her.

Julie waited. She couldn't imagine them injuring the innocent guard and didn't want to startle them into doing something even more stupid. She could clearly hear Derrick as he said, "Alright, buddy, stand up slowly and put your hands behind your head."

The guy jerked upright and his hat tumbled off. It bounced once on the dock before splashing into the water. "What the hell?" he said.

"No talking," Derrick's accomplice barked. A female voice. The brim of her hat still covered her face as she pointed her gun at the hapless security guard. He complied and stood, lacing his fingers behind his neck. Derrick pulled a radio from the guard's belt, turned it off and pocketed it before patting the guy down for weapons.

"All right, now move! Onto the barge."

The guard turned and stepped from the dock and Derrick followed. His accomplice did not. She tossed her bag onto the deck of the craft, but continued to stand guard, scanning the surrounding area for danger. Julie doubted she could be seen, but she ducked back behind the boat anyway as the other woman's head swiveled her way.

When she risked looking out again, Derrick had dropped his bag and pulled something from it. "Hands behind your back," he said. The *zzzzzip* that followed told her he was using a plastic zip-tie to bind the guard's hands. "Alright, get on the ground." The guy did as instructed and his feet were bound as well. Derrick pulled something else from the pack and proceeded to stick a strip of duct tape over the guy's mouth.

Adrenaline flushed Julie's face and her heart moved into her throat. She could think of no reason to take the guard along. This whole thing was so far outside the boundaries of any environmental action—radical or otherwise—that she had no frame of reference. (1) They weren't supposed to have guns. (2) They weren't supposed to confront anyone. (3) They certainly weren't supposed to take hostages. This had turned into an actual act of terrorism, plain and simple. If she had a cell phone on her she would have called the police then and there.

But she didn't. And as she searched her head for a plan, Derrick's accomplice removed her hat to scratch her head. It was Jean. The one who had sworn she didn't know what Derrick was planning. The one who was jealous of Derrick's feelings for Julie.

Still, Julie couldn't fathom either of these two actually shooting her. But, to be safe, she decided to let them know it was her approaching. She also wanted to appear unarmed, so she left the pistol in her pack and spoke before showing herself, banking on the hope that they wouldn't just fire wildly in the direction of the sound.

"Derrick? Jean?" she called out, intentionally using their names. "It's Julie."

"Shit!" Jean muttered, spinning toward the origin of the voice. "How the hell did she find out?"

Derrick seemed less surprised. "Ah, Julie," he said as he turned and raised his arms in a grotesque attempt at a welcome. "Glad you could join us. Come on out, hop aboard. We need all the help we can get."

"Derrick!" Jean said, chastising. "This isn't part of the plan."

"The plan must always remain fluid, Jean. One can't be dead set on every detail lining up perfectly."

Julie stepped from behind the boat and approached slowly. "What the hell are you guys doing?" she hissed. "This is crazy. You're carrying guns. Attacking people." Julie noted that Jean tracked her with her weapon, yet Derrick had lowered his when she stepped into the light.

Looking down at the gun in his hand, Derrick laughed. "It's not loaded," he said. "Although... I'm not sure about Jean's. I haven't been watching her all that close."

Julie looked over at Jean again. The other woman's sight was still set on her. "Stop pointing that thing at me," she said.

With an air of disgust Jean lowered the pistol. "Derrick, we don't need her," she said.

After a moment he replied, "Need is a relative term."

Jean sighed.

Julie stepped between the two of them, her back to Jean, facing Derrick. "You guys have to stop this right now," she said. She looked down at the guard on the deck. His frightened eyes pleaded for salvation. "One step further and you've gone past the point of no return. You're going to get caught."

"Maybe," Derrick said, taking two steps toward her. "But think of the publicity."

"Publicity for what? Stupidest environmental action of the year?"

Derrick's gaze flitted past her and he nodded his head slightly. In that instant Julie knew she had badly misjudged these two. She started to turn—to run? to scream?—but Jean's gloved hand came around from behind and clamped over Julie's mouth with boa constrictor like force.

A moment later, the barrel of the other woman's gun jabbed her in the ribs.

Fifteen

◀

Julie hesitates in the dirt at the edge of the pavement, half a block from Sean's house. The moving truck still sits in the street, closed up now like a shuttered cabin. She'd decided to walk over today, not only for the exercise, but because it would give her more time to chicken out if need be.

It's been six weeks since Sean kicked her out of his party and she hasn't spoken to him since. The first couple of weeks she'd sworn him off like a bad habit; the next few she'd begun to waiver. Now, after forty days of missing him terribly, she knows she screwed up and can't let it end this way. Even if the drunken memory of him locking the door behind her still makes her furious.

She'd known for six months that he would be moving with his parents to San Diego this August, but it hadn't sunk in until recently. His leaving seemed more like a dream. Something so far outside the world of her imagined future that it couldn't possibly happen. Then yesterday, while doing recon in her dad's Suby, she had rounded the corner onto Sean's street and seen two burly men loading his living room couch into the moving van. The dream had quickly become reality and she'd turned off before anyone could spot her.

She still couldn't believe he'd thrown her out. Sean had been her friend and confidant—as close as she'd ever had to a soul mate—and he'd just tossed her out into the dark like a bag of trash on garbage night.

Maybe that's all you are… trash.

No. She can't go there. Feeling down on herself is no way approach Sean. It saps the anger she still feels. Without letting herself reel it in, Julie starts up the road at a quickened pace.

* * *

Sean hears the knock, but doesn't initially budge from his sleeping bag on the living room floor. His mother is mopping in the kitchen and he hears a splash in the bucket before her feet clomp down the hall to the front door. Even though he has been awake for a good half hour he's been having trouble mounting the enthusiasm needed to get up. A lot needs to be done. Not least of all, leaving the only home he's ever known.

His mother's sing-song voice drifts back to him as she exchanges greetings with someone. He can tell the visitor is female, but can't make out any words. From where he lies on the floor near the back of the house he can't see the door.

Footsteps plod across carpet and his mother's face appears around the corner. "Get your butt off the floor, mister," she says. "Julie's here... and she's not happy."

Sean sits up and a shiver runs through him, despite the warm August morning air blowing in the window. "Julie Thompson?" he says.

"Do you know any other Julies?" his mom says as she returns to the kitchen.

What the hell is Julie doing here?

Beth had told him three weeks ago that Julie never wanted to see him again. He'd spent much of the last six weeks trying to get it through his thick head that that is a good thing. Throwing her out was the best thing he'd ever done, he kept telling himself, even if he was so drunk he barely remembers doing it.

Sean struggles to his feet and makes a stop in the bathroom on his way to the door. He swishes some Scope around his teeth and gums and considers not jumping to her beck and call. But when he gets to the front door and peers out past the curtain, his breath catches in his throat.

She sits on the stoop, back to him. Her blonde hair is pulled up in a barrette yet it still falls past her shoulders—longer than the last time he saw her. He tries to muster the anger he felt the night he pushed her out this very door, but it fails to materialize. Pulling the door open, Sean steps out into the hot sun.

* * *

She doesn't acknowledge his presence as he sits down beside her without a word. The sun on her head, arms and legs is a bonfire. She's a roasting turkey, her brain shriveling inside her skull as the heat intensifies. Without turning she says, "Hey," her eyes open and alert behind dark glasses.

"Hey," he answers. Not without a slight hesitation.

This was a bad idea. She shouldn't have come. Sitting out here in the hot sun, her anger has melted away like a scoop of ice cream in a pot of boiling water. She could have written to him at school. Or just... not.

* *

Like her, he keeps his face forward, looking out at the moving van but not really seeing it. He squeezes the fingers of his left hand with his right as the heat of the sun tries to bore into his brain through the top of his skull.

He says, "So, what's going on, Julie? Why are you here?"

She fidgets. "I..." she begins, but leaves it at that.

He looks at her then, keeping his unshaded, squinting eyes on her face, but his mind flashes to an image of her and Glenn on his parents bed that night. As he turns back to the moving van, he shakes his head. "I didn't think I'd see you again," he says.

"You were almost right," she answers, gravel in her voice.

He clenches his jaw and grits his teeth.

*

She pivots, finally laying eyes on him. While she has let her hair grow, he cut his—shorter than she's ever seen it. He looks older, more grown up. Confusion rushes in as a quiver shakes her, but she pushes it away with a breath.

"I'm sorry," she says to break the tension.

Elbows on knees, Sean lets his head droop between his shoulders. "Why would you do that? Get with Glenn like that? I thought you two were done."

"We were… I mean are—done."

She wants to reach over and touch him, but she restrains the urge. Instead she turns her head away and studies a hundred foot pine in the next yard. Softly she adds, "I just wanted someone to hold me. That's all."

"I would've held you," he says, quieter even than her.

She turns back. Sean's head still hangs between his knees like his plane is crashing. "I didn't want you to get the wrong idea," she says. "If I asked you, I mean." But as the words leave her mouth she knows that's not the whole truth. She'd also been terrified of rejection. It had been the thought of him pushing her away that stopped her. She could live with that from Glenn. Not Sean.

He stays silent as she looks out at the moving van. She can feel tears brewing, getting ready to bubble up at the slightest provocation. But this time she takes the leap and slides across the step, wrapping her arms around him and resting her head on his shoulder.

"I'm gonna miss you so much," she says.

He doesn't hug her back.

An eternal minute passes before he finally says, "I'll miss you, too."

With the way things have gone can she really ask for anything more?

▶

Sixteen

"You're not gonna believe this," Jake said.

It was early afternoon and Sean, happy to be out of his little abode that had begun feeling like a prison cell, had just returned from the bathroom after enjoying lunch at the caretaker's cabin. Jake sat at the kitchen table with a coffee mug in front of him as talk-radio babbled from an under-cabinet stereo.

"Believe what?" Sean said, heading for a refill from the steaming coffeemaker.

"Someone hijacked the fireworks barges last night."

It took Sean a moment to remember it was the Fourth of July. He turned to face his host, coffeepot in hand. "They did what?"

"Just heard it on the news. They drove 'em out into the lake sometime last night. They've got hostages, too."

Sean tried to make sense of that. "Do they know who did it? What they want?"

"Not yet... At least nothing they're telling the public, anyway."

"Huh," Sean said, turning and finally pouring himself some coffee. Julie wouldn't be involved in something so stupid, would she? He hoped not, but there certainly was a lot more going on around Tahoe than he remembered from growing up here.

"This thing," he said, trying to assuage his concern, "you think it might have anything to do with the Eco-Militia?"

"Oh, shit!" Jake jumped up and disappeared into the living room. "Forgot something."

Odd reaction, Sean thought.

From the other room Jake called, "Sorry about that. I just remembered I had something for you." A minute later he returned to the kitchen and reclaimed his seat. "Here you go." He dropped an envelope on the table in front of Sean. "I found that yesterday in one of the other cabins. Somebody must have stuck it through the mail slot thinking you were staying there. I had to come back here for a call. I must've set it down and forgot about it. Guess it's a good thing I'm not a mailman."

"Who the hell knows I'm here?" Sean said, puzzled.

"I can only think of one person," Jake replied.

Julie.

On the front of the thick envelope his full name was writ large in a curly script he hadn't seen in over a decade. He wondered when she could have delivered it—and why she hadn't mentioned it on the phone. When he turned it over and saw that she'd drawn a small heart with a smiley face in it at the point of the flap he excused himself to the living room.

Perched on the edge of the couch, he tore the letter open. There was another envelope inside, along with a few loose pages. A Post-It on the inner-envelope read, "*This one first.*" Under the note his first name was written in larger, even more garish letters. He set the loose pages aside and pulled three more from the second envelope then unfolded them and began reading.

Dear Sean,

I don't know how I can ever thank you for stopping me tonight. For that, or for any of the other things you do for me all the time. I'm sitting here at my desk, crying as I write this, while you're just two floors down probably lying awake and wondering why I'm such a crazy freak, but I know if I try to say any of this in person it won't come out right.

Sean stopped reading, confused. He flipped through the letter looking for a date. There was none. Neither envelope had one either. He picked up the loose pages again, unfolded them and saw that the first page was dated two days earlier. He also noted that the loose paper was different than the other and that, although they were very similar, the handwriting didn't quite seem to match. He shook his head and read on.

> *I love you!*
>
> *I love you so much, it hurts sometimes. But I'm so scared. Every guy I've ever been close to has ended up hurting me or leaving—or both. And I know I can't actually blame my father for dying, but he's gone now too, isn't he? And you're the only one who came to be with me through the whole thing. I guess death can really show you who your true friends are.*

Sean now understood what he was reading. This was the letter Julie had written the night of her father's funeral, after she'd thrown herself at him and he'd pushed her away in what now seemed to him a misguided and naïve attempt at honor. The memory washed over him like a vision: sitting in the car outside Julie's house the next morning just before driving off; Julie saying she'd written him a letter but didn't want to give it to him yet. Sean couldn't believe she'd kept it all these years. He'd tossed all of Julie's letters out in a fit of rage that summer when she'd refused all contact from him.

> *I hope you know that you're much more than "just a friend" to me, Sean. You're my confidant, my guardian angel, my soul mate. I feel safe when I'm with you. Safe from bad guys and car crashes and heartbreak and—most of all—safe from myself.*
>
> *I don't know why I do the stuff I do, it just seems like a good idea at the time. Sometimes I think I really must be crazy. I've kept you hanging on by a thread all this time and then I throw myself at you when you're just here to comfort me.*
>
> *And it dawns on me now—after all this—that*

maybe you really do love me. That you don't just say it as a way to get in my pants. I guess I never actually believed it before, but you stopped me! No other guy ever did that. No one else has ever looked past their own wants and needs and realized that what I was doing wasn't good for me.

I love you so much, Sean, and I want to be with you. I'm sure you know, for me, that means marriage. Someday, Sean, I will marry you and you will be my first...

My first—and only—True Love.

I Love You,
Julie

Sean set the letter aside and dabbed a couple of welling tears from the corners of his eyes. He could understand, given Julie's hesitancy to commit back then, why she hadn't given him this letter, but he wasn't one hundred percent sure what she meant by it now? Would she have sent it to him if she didn't still mean all of it? Shaking his head, he picked up the other pages.

Sean,

I'm a little drunk, sitting here at the bar waiting for my friend to get off work. After we split, I just didn't want to be alone with my thoughts, so I hoofed it over here.

Anyway, I guess I'm just stalling. I wanted to tell you how I felt and where we stood, but after reading that old letter, I decided it still said it all. That's the way I still feel—again! Now there's only one really important thing left to sort out and that's what happened 13 years ago. So here goes...

I was raped—

He feels a sharp stab of pain in his chest and his breath catches like his heart has stopped. The papers shudder in his hand and he nearly drops them. He closes his eyes and reminds himself to breathe again. Why had she thought she couldn't tell him that? And who was the son of a bitch who did it? At that thought his eyes snap open and return to the page as his horror begins to turn to rage.

I still don't think I would be able to put that down on paper right now if I wasn't drunk. As it is, my hand is shaking. There aren't too many people who know this and I have never written it down before, but reading my old letter to you brought home to me why I was—and still am—so scared to tell you about it.

I was still a virgin then... and I thought you were, too. In the aftermath I managed to convince myself that I was damaged goods and didn't think you would want me anymore. I also believed for years that it was all my fault. I was so sure of both of these things that I broke it off with you.

That was a long time ago and I know rationally now that I wasn't completely to blame—that it's just what this patriarchal society likes to teach. No one ever has the right to take something that isn't given regardless of the circumstances. The problem is that seeing you maybe caused some sort of regression in me. Suddenly my gut started telling me the same things it told me years ago.

"If Sean finds out, he won't love you anymore."

All I can say is that I hope it isn't true.

I love you, Sean—after all these years I'm IN LOVE
with you!—and I can't wait to see you again.

Love,
Julie

Sean's hand falls into his lap, still clutching the letter. He looks down again at those three words leaping off the page:

I was raped.

He can't understand why Julie would ever have thought he would shun her for that. The anger growing in his chest isn't at her, it's at the bastard who took not only what she didn't wish to give, but a large chunk of his life with her as well.

"Holy shit!" It was Jake's voice from the kitchen. A moment later the caretaker stood in the doorway. "Sean, they're saying it's Derrick that hijacked the barges. Derrick Masterson and Jean Naples."

Sean turned and looked at Jake, dazed. "Derrick?" he said. He had to pull himself back to the present moment to remember who Derrick was.

Ah, yes, Julie's jealous friend.

Sean stared blankly at the wall. He'd thought maybe he caught a glimpse of Derrick in the woods the previous day, but that was unlikely if he and Jean were hijacking fireworks barges and taking hostages doing it. Sean wondered why the news didn't surprise him.

Jake returned to the kitchen as the radio announcer continued to drone on just out of Sean's range of comprehension. The phone rang. Sean looked at the letters again. Old in his right hand, new in his left. Julie's girlish handwriting on:

My first—and only—True Love.

Giving way to the shakier, angrier lines of:

I was raped.

The ultimate loss of innocence.

"Oh no," Jake said from the kitchen, "you've got to be kidding." Then, louder, "Sean."

Like the instant a 3D Magic Eye image becomes clear, a number of things click suddenly into place in Sean's head and his eyes widen. He turns and looks at Jake as the other man appears in the doorway again, phone in hand.

"It's Julie, Sean. Julie is one of the hostages."

Sean's eyes move to the floor as his mind takes in the new information. It was Derrick, he now realizes. Derrick was the one he'd fought with, the one he'd pulled off Julie's limp body up at The Rock fifteen years ago, that night of Julie's hypothermia and the wild ride to the hospital. Derrick was the one who'd split his lip, the one with the Whittell hat. It had been Derrick this whole time. That was why he looked familiar. And Derrick must have known for days who Sean is—that might explain the background check, the set-up, the explosives planted in his hotel room.

But what about Julie?

Derrick's world must be spinning more than a little off axis for him to still be pursuing her after all these years. He must be completely obsessed with her. And now Julie is his hostage on a barge full of fireworks out in the lake.

A sense of purpose fuels Sean like a rocket and he jolts suddenly to his feet before he realizes he has absolutely, positively no idea what to do.

Seventeen

In the extended quiet the only sound comes from waves lapping against the hull of the barge. Derrick and Jean have ceased their yelling. They'd been fighting over whether or not to release their hostages and their words had filtered down from the bridge loud and clear.

Jean said, "Yes."

Derrick, "No." It would leave them with no leverage.

So far Derrick's only demand to the authorities has been that all boats and aircraft stay at least a quarter mile away. Now the two linked barges float in a huge circle of open water ringed by a solid line of boats. Coast Guard and police craft patrol the edges to keep stray tourists from floating into harm's way.

Julie wishes she could remember what this action was supposed to prove as she flexes her fingers behind her back, trying to keep the blood flowing in her bound hands. She sits atop a three foot high wooden crate in a storage area of the converted M.S. Dixie that would once have held passengers. She has a view through the windows to the west of dark thunderheads building on the horizon. By the position of the sun she guesses it's around one p.m.

Off and on through the night and morning she dozed, but never truly slept. Her butt is sore from sitting on the hard, uneven surface of the crate and her wrists feel like they're clenched in a tiny vise. She rests with her back against the wall, knees up, bare feet flat on the crate's top. Unlike the security guard, Derrick hadn't bothered to gag her and had even removed the tape from the guard's mouth after they'd gotten under way last night. Once they were out on the lake it was unlikely anyone would have heard them scream anyway. Derrick had bound Julie's ankles, though, just like the guard's—whose name, she has learned, is Jason. Since then he and Jean had proceeded to ignore their two hostages.

Julie has tried reasoning with them whenever they are within earshot, but she knows it's too late for that now. She figures they'll probably see just as much jail time if they give themselves up as if they follow through with their plans—whatever they are. Unless, of course, those plans involve killing anyone.

To Julie's left, Jason stirs and awakens from a doze. "How are you doing?" she whispers.

He shrugs. "Hanging in there, I guess."

Jason is twenty three and this is his first stint as a security guard. There were supposed to be two of them on shift last night, but his support had called in sick. Julie can tell Jason doesn't trust her. It must be obvious to him that she knows his attackers and she wonders if he has concocted some elaborate reason in his head why they have tied her up just to trick him.

Julie moves sideways and manages to slide off the crate to the floor. She hops her way over to the stairs and yells up to the bridge. "Hey, can we get some water down here?"

Derrick's head appears in the stairwell opening. "Sit down," he says. "Do you want to get shot?"

"By who?" she asks.

"Whom," he corrects her and points out toward the police boats.

"Why would they do that? I'm an innocent hostage."

"Hostage? Maybe. Innocent? Certainly not. They'd do it by accident."

Derrick moves quickly down the stairs and gathers her up like a ragdoll. She notices how he uses her body to shield himself from the windows as he pushes her back into the more protected area at the rear of the cabin.

"They've got snipers trained on us by now," he says as he lifts her back onto her crate. "You should be a little more careful."

"Ow!" Julie says. "What's your problem, Derrick? I thought we were friends."

He barks out a laugh. "We've never been friends. You've just been leading me on since the first time we met." He pops the top on a water bottle and puts it to her mouth.

When she has finished drinking she says, "When did I ever lead you on?"

"You're an incessant flirt, Jules. It doesn't matter if you love or hate someone, you still flirt with them." Derrick offers water to Jason, but he shakes his head. "You sure? Don't want to get dehydrated." The guard turns away. Derrick shrugs and sets the bottle aside.

Julie doesn't know what to say. That he has never considered them friends stings.

Derrick continues, "I have to admit you surprised me with the high school crush, though. Jumped right into the sack with him after what? Two days?"

Julie struggles against her binds, wanting to slap him. "How the hell do you know that?"

Derrick shrugs. "Motel curtains don't close as tightly as they should."

"You… You saw us?" Julie says, mouth gaping.

A grin forms on Derrick's lips. In lieu of the slap, Julie reels back and spits in his face. He recoils, wiping the saliva away on the shoulder of his shirt, but his smile remains.

Julie closes her eyes and tries to repress the revulsion growing in her gut. A moment later her eyes snap back open as he touches her upper arm lightly. As if bitten by a snake, she flinches and scoots to the back of the crate. "Don't," she says. In his eyes she finally recognizes what has always turned her off about him. The shade of blue is too cold, too icy. Like the winter sky in January, it's inhuman. And she is sure about something else now, too.

"You planted the bombs in Sean's room, didn't you?"

"Maybe…" He moves closer and caresses her thigh until she squirms free again. "Maybe not."

"You're jealous? Is that what this is all about? Digging into Sean's past? Setting him up to take the fall?"

Derrick's smile fades and his gaze falls past her, out the windows up front. "Julie," he says, "humans are a disease on the face of the planet. For the Earth to survive, we have to go. In those terms, individuals don't matter much. A few gone here and there aren't going to change anything, but a larger storm is coming to blow the world clean."

"What the hell are you talking about, Derrick?" Julie says. He should know better than to blame the entire human race for the scourge of just one culture, but his cryptic comments also have her worried about something else. "Are you going to kill someone? A lot of people? Have you lost your mind?"

"Au contraire," he says. "I'm thinking quite clearly." His eyes return to focus on her. "Relax, dear Julie, I'm not planning on killing anyone. But things need to escalate soon if we want to see any progress. Today we're just putting on a show. An Extravaganza of Liberty, so to speak."

"Couldn't you have let the fireworks people handle that?"

Derrick sighs. "Remember when we talked about this? The point is to hit them where it hurts—this celebration of their supposed Independence. That laughable idea that this is free country. And what better show of Independence than hijacking the symbol itself? The extravagance that symbolizes the whole?"

Julie sits speechless. She vaguely remembers their old discussion, but the logistics problems had superseded talk of the overall message. They'd basically concluded that the ends didn't justify the means and she'd thought nothing would come of it because it wasn't doable in any reasonable, nonviolent way. But it appears that Derrick has shifted his outlook since. Or maybe he's felt this way all along and has just kept it to himself.

Julie starts as Derrick suddenly jerks upright and rises. He neglects his own warning to stay out of sight and crosses the room to the stairs in full view of the windows.

To Julie's infinite dismay, no one shoots him.

Eighteen

In the kitchen of the caretaker's cabin, Sean paces the floor like a smoldering wildfire before a heavy wind. Jake is at the counter spreading a topo map of the South Shore out in front of him.

"This is a bunch of crap," Sean says. "I'll just take the bike and run the roadblock."

"It'll never work, man, they'll be on you like wolves. That motorcycle's a two-fifty. You can get through no problem if you just follow this trail."

Sean stops pacing long enough to see where Jake is pointing on the map and follows his finger as the caretaker continues. "Here's where Old Kingsbury drops out of the Boulder parking lot. Once you get down on Palisades here, you follow Easy Street out to this path and just stay left. That'll put you on this trail where you'll run into the Van Sickle Connector. A right and a quick downhill and you're out behind Raley's on the loop road. Just watch out for hikers."

"Easy Street?" Sean says. "Seriously?"

"Yeah," Jake chuckles. "Like I said, couldn't be any easier."

So this is the best we can do?

Sean doesn't know how much time has passed since the news about Julie being a hostage, all he knows is that it's been too much. First Julie's friend's P.O.S. Subaru wouldn't start. Then, before Sean could even ask to borrow another vehicle, Jake heard through the activist grapevine that the authorities had some sort of roadblock/checkpoint set up on Highway 50 between Kingsbury Grade and Lake Parkway, right where 50 is the only road that runs through to the casino corridor. Apparently there are roadblocks set up at similar choke points on the west side of town, creating traffic jams of epic proportions as tourists and locals alike try to get to the lake for what is usually billed as the "biggest fireworks display west of the Mississippi." Which—depending on Derrick's plan—probably isn't going to happen anyway.

The motorcycle had been Jake's idea. It's an old dual sport that was holed up in the big house's huge garage. Jake has ridden it around the property a couple of times and says it runs okay, but Sean hasn't been on a dirt bike since he was a teenager. How is he supposed to navigate sandy, rocky, singletrack trails on a motorcycle only half suited for dirt roads?

"I don't know about this," Sean says, looking out the window into the forest. "I wish there was another way."

Jake leans his elbows on the countertop, lowers his head and shakes it. "Me, too," he says. "But I can't think of any."

*

Blasting down Easy Street, Sean leans into another bend in the road and sees the pavement up ahead coming to an end. He downshifts into third gear and slows the bike a bit, though not as much as he probably should. After crossing a small cul-de-sac, he hits the dirt at about forty.

The ride down the old road—what was the original Kingsbury Grade in Pony Express times, but is now a mostly abandoned, sandy doubletrack through the woods—has given him a little more confidence on a looser surface. The one thousand feet of elevation he'd just lost had disappeared under his tires like a steep ski run on a powder day. It couldn't have taken him more than three minutes from the Boulder parking lot until he hit pavement again on Palisades. Now, as the dirt lane narrows to five feet in width, he takes the 250 down another gear, slowing it another ten MPH, and watches for the fork in the path Jake said to look for. A few seconds later he has to tap the brakes as he peels off on a continually narrowing trail to the left.

Small tree branches begin encroaching on the right of way, slapping against the full face helmet he'd found hanging by the bike in the garage. The thing is at least two sizes too small, making his head feel like it's being squashed between two extra firm pillows. Jake had also told him the trail would be a bit less travelled and maintained from here to the Van Sickle Connector.

After a couple of minutes spent fighting his way through the duff around a fallen tree blocking the trail, Sean idles along in first gear as he approaches the fence Jake had also told him about. Eight feet high, chain-link, barbed wire on top, but with a pass-through hole cut out of it that includes a step-up over an oversized railroad tie half-buried by years in the woods.

Eyeing the size of the hole, Sean decides he can make it, guns the engine and pulls up on the handlebars. Instead of lifting the front tire off the ground as he'd intended, the rear tire—with a street knobby on it—spins in the sand and he rams right into the step. Luckily, the front suspension sucks up the impact and his forward momentum propels the tire over the obstacle, but the bike also bounces him upward as it bucks like a bronco over thing.

With a loud crack his helmet slams into the upper crossbar of the fence and wrenches his head back. Pain shoots down his neck and he loses hold of the right handgrip, but as his hand slips from the bar the throttle twists, revving the engine. This time the rear tire bites on the railroad tie and the front end leaps up. The bike flips over backwards and throws him, tumbling, downhill from the trail a dozen feet. The motorcycle coughs and sputters out where it comes to rest on its side, handlebars twisted around, rear wheel still spinning.

"Fuck!" Sean's yell is loud inside the helmet even though his ears are ringing from the jolt to his head and neck. He struggles to his feet, slipping and sliding on the steep hillside below the trail. Luckily there were no rocks or downed trees were he fell, it's just his head and neck that took the blow. He pulls the helmet off and tosses it uphill where it bounces off the gas tank of the downed bike and rolls to a stop against the railroad tie.

Sean grunts, sways and closes his eyes. Multi-colored sparkles and flashes haunt the darkness behind his lids. *Concussion?* he wonders. Regardless, he's got things to do. He opens his eyes and struggles back up through the pine needles and sand to the trail surface.

The motorcycle is leaking gasoline from the carburetor into the dirt. He grabs the handlebars, lifts it up and leans it on its kickstand where he can look it over. The bars are a little bent on the left side and he has to brush dirt and debris out of the chain and rear suspension. A few cables are also out of place up front, but he manages to push them mostly back into position. By the time he's done with that the gas seems to have stopped dripping.

As Sean mounts the bike a mantra of, *Please still work, please still work*, runs through his head. He finds neutral and pushes the electric start. Nothing happens. Not even so much as a click. He examines the area around the button and sees the wire is ripped from the back of the switch. There appears to be no way to reattach it without removing the cover. He doesn't have any tools and has no idea where to look for any on the bike. Instead, he flips out the kick start and starts pumping—swearing like an Army private on PT. After a minute or two of stomping on the thing he is out of breath with sweat beading on his forehead and nothing more than a sputter coming from the engine with each kick.

"Son of a…" Trailing off he collapses against the handlebars banging his forehead on his forearm and sending another jolt of pain down his neck.

A minute of self pity passes before he looks up and steps off the bike, looking around for an idea. Through an opening in the trees to the right the lake stretches out to the north, the big four casinos sprouting from the trees like alien towers a few hundred feet below and to the left of him. There is an open circle out on the water formed by the hundreds of boats gathering for the fireworks show. In the center of that circle float two dark, lonely shapes: the fireworks barges.

Julie is on one of those—

My first—and only—true love.

—along with the now deranged Derrick.

Sean's face flushes and his breath catches in his throat as her words float through his mind. The thought of losing her now is like a stake through the chest. Ignoring the pain wracking his skull, he marches over, retrieves the helmet and jams it on his head.

Back on the bike, he flips the kickstand up, pulls in the clutch and gives himself a push down the slightly inclined trail. The bike picks up speed slowly at first, but begins to accelerate as the slope increases into a dry runoff channel, then he clicks the transmission into first gear and pops the clutch.

The rear wheel locks up and skids in the sand and he pulls the clutch back in. He'll only have one more shot before the slope bottoms out and the trail heads back uphill. He waits for an upcoming rock about four feet long before trying again. This time the rear wheel bites. The engine coughs and sputters as the bike begins to slow.

"Come on, come on," he yells into the facemask.

One final buck as he hits the bottom of the hill and then the engine jumps suddenly to life, nearly throwing him off the back again. This time, though, he clings to the handlebars with a death grip born of hot-blooded determination. He even twists the throttle a little more as the motorcycle rockets up the narrow trail leaving a rooster trail of sand in his wake.

Nineteen

Julie turns her head, trying to make out Derrick and Jean's current argument, but the wind gusts under the approaching clouds and drowns out their voices. She looks over at Jason, still sitting on the floor to her left, but he appears to be dozing. When the debate upstairs suddenly turns into a screaming match his eyes pop open.

Jean yells, "She doesn't want you, Derrick. Don't you get it? She never has."

"Sit down," Derrick commands.

"No! I'm not listening to you anymore. You're just using me you son of a bitch."

Jean storms down the stairs and halfway across the room toward Julie with a pistol held in her shaky, right hand. Wet tear tracks trace lines down her cheeks.

"Jean, come on," Derrick says, climbing down after her. "You're going to get one of us shot." He stops at the bottom of the stairs, just out of sight of prying eyes and rifle scopes.

The other woman's face scrunches up, squeezing more tears from the slits of her eyes. She raises the gun and points it directly at Derrick's forehead then takes a deep breath. She lets it out in hitches, but her face relaxes somewhat. "Stop telling me what to do," she says.

"Easy now, Jeanie. Let's not forget the plan," Derrick says as he raises his hands up to shoulder height. Somehow Julie doesn't find the universal sign of surrender believable on him.

"Can't you just shut up for one God damned second?" Jean says, shaking the revolver as she speaks. Derrick closes his mouth and rests his hands atop his head.

"Jean?" Julie says in her best calming voice, cultivated from years of leading yoga classes. "What are you doing?"

The other woman's eyes flicker over to Julie and she blinks twice. Then her eyebrows twitch into a deeper V of rage. "You," she snarls. "You shut up, too, Little Miss Perfect. This is all your fault." She keeps one eye and the gun on Derrick as she sidesteps over to where Julie sits on her crate.

"Jean," Julie begins, "I—"

The gun swings around, settling six inches from Julie's forehead. "Didn't I just tell you to shut up?" The other woman's eyes quiver in their sockets. The animal brain pushing its way up through layers of civility? Or a bit of outright insanity seeping out?

Julie doesn't know, but she tries to keep a rising panic at bay by closing her eyes momentarily. When she opens them the gaping, black hole at the end of the gun barrel threatens to swallow rational thought and leave her blubbering for her life. A deep breath silences the demons—for now.

"I bet you were a cheerleader, weren't you?" Jean says. "Girls like you always are."

Julie continues to breathe deeply as she attempts a silent entreaty with her eyes, assuming the 'no talking' rule is still in effect. She doesn't think she'll changing Jean's mind about anything at this point anyway. Jean seems to think she has it straight in her head who Julie is and proving otherwise at gunpoint would be a miraculous feat.

"You drift through life with your looks and your perfect little body," Jean says. "And all the pretty little men line up in a row. Where does that leave people like me?"

The gun shakes violently in the other woman's hand and Julie flinches. Her reaction makes Jean smile.

"Yeah," she says. "Who's in the driver's seat now? Huh?"

"Jean."

The voice comes from the other side of the cabin. It's Derrick.

"Didn't I tell you to shut up?" Jean says without turning.

Julie hears a quick inhale of surprise from Jason as her eyes focus past the gun at the end of Jean's arm. They fall on another at the end of Derrick's.

"Jean," Derrick says more forcefully, "leave Julie alone."

A mushroom cloud of fury boils up in Jean's face and she spins away from Julie. Her empty left hand comes up and closes around her right, steadying the gun. Three quick explosions—deafening in the small space—coincide with bursts of blood from Jean's back and Julie yelps as the woman collapses in a heap across her legs.

"Oh my god, oh my god, oh my god," Julie repeats as the panic pulls her under.

He shot her! Holy shit! Derrick shot Jean!

Blood bubbles from the other woman's mouth as her body slips from the crate to the floor like a sack of beans. Julie scoots away, off the crate, hopping backwards to the interior of the room, but something trips her up and she tumbles down. Flat on the floor, she turns her head and stares into two lifeless eyes.

Not Jean.

Jason.

The innocent Security guard on his first assignment.

On his forehead, slightly off center, is a black hole beginning to seep blood. How had he been shot? She could've sworn she'd seen all three bullets hit Jean.

This time the only reason Julie sucks in a deep breath is to help push out a bloodcurdling scream. She rolls over Jason's legs, screaming again, and flops onto her stomach. Her bound wrists and ankles leave her crawling across the floor like an inchworm.

Away. Have to get away.

No idea where that might be, she only knows she has to get there.

She's nearly to the opposite wall, heading for one of the sliding doors out onto the deck, when Derrick's shadow falls on her. "Where do you think you're going?" he says. His hand snags her shoulder, turning her onto her back in one quick flip.

"Get back. Get away from me," Julie grunts.

She kicks up with her bound legs and lands her feet in Derrick's crotch. He collapses on top of her, pinning her to the deck. The crushing weight of him sets off another wave of panic and she bucks and writhes like a wild horse, her wrists grinding into the deck beneath her, but Derrick is too heavy and she can't escape.

He sits up, straddling her waist with his knees on the floor. "You've got more spunk than any girl I have ever met," he says.

Searching his eyes, Julie looks for some hint of the man she thought she'd known. She finds nothing but anger and madness behind his cold blue irises. Narrowing her own eyes, she reels back and spits in his face a second time.

Then the gun comes down, butt first, bringing with it a sudden, relaxing darkness.

Twenty

The rest of Sean's trip is unexpectedly uneventful. He pisses off a few hikers on the Van Sickle Connector trail, but other than that no one even looks twice at him as he makes his way out to Lake Parkway and through the back streets heading toward Bijou.

When he has to ride up the shoulder of Fairway Drive just to get over to Johnson Lane from Glenwood because of the dead stopped traffic on Highway 50 he decides to leave the motorcycle in a parking space at the Safeway grocery store on the corner. From there he hoofs it to Glenn's shop at Timber Cove, hunting for a favor from his old friend.

"Okay, dude, what is it you need again?" Glenn says after finishing with a customer.

The plan had formed slowly in Sean's head over the course of the trip. "Some scuba gear and a boat," he says quietly.

Glenn laughs and shakes his head. "Dude," he says, "it's the Fourth of fuckin' July. There ain't no boats." He isn't angry, just stating the obvious. "Besides, don't look much like the fireworks are happenin' anyway, with some fuckin' lunatic hijackin' the barges and takin' people hostage."

"Shit," Sean slaps a hand on the counter top. His friend has shot the only plan he's come up with out of the air on the first pull.

Glenn leans in closer and drops his voice to a whisper. "What is it you're tryin' to do here anyway, man? Fill me in."

Sean considers how much he wants to reveal. He decides to go with a bit of the truth. "Julie is one of the hostages on the barge," he says.

Glenn does a double take and ends up looking at Sean sideways. "How would you know that, man?"

"Let's just say 'a friend of a friend'," he says, surveying the room.

No one appears to be paying them any undue attention.

"Ohhh-kaaay," Glenn says, holding his hands up, palms toward Sean. "So what are you gonna do about it anyway? I'm sure the cops got it under control."

Sean sighs, running a hand through his hair. "Remember the guy who tried to r—" The R word sticks in his throat. He clears it. "Take advantage of Julie? Up at The Rock that night when we carried her out?"

Glenn looks at Sean like he's crazy—maybe even dangerous—before recollection slowly dawns on his face. "Yeah…. I guess I remember. So what?"

"So that's the guy who's holding her hostage."

Glenn's jaw drops. "No way, dude! That's trippy. How could that happen? And how the hell could you know that, too?"

Sean sighs again. "I just know, okay."

Stepping back, Glenn gives Sean a quick up and down then shakes his head. "Man, you still love her don't you?"

"I do," he answers without hesitation, holding Glenn's stare.

"Well alright then," Glenn says, laughing. With a nod of his head he raises his voice to address the customers milling around the shop. "Sorry folks, looks like we'll be closin' a little earlier than planned this evening. True Love calls."

*

Sean keeps his head down as Glenn pilots the fifteen foot skiff gingerly through the maze of boats clogging the water a quarter mile out from the fireworks barges. The boat is a runabout that Glenn keeps around for things like rescuing stranded jet skiers—or shuttling crazy old friends out to their doom.

As they near the police line, Glenn brings the craft to a halt three boats back from the circle of empty water surrounding the barges. Out in the middle, the barges sit like mirages atop the gleaming surface of Tahoe as the sun nears the end of its afternoon trip to the horizon, maybe thirty or forty minutes from disappearing behind the mountains.

They have taken the extra time to steer around to the western side of the circle on Glenn's advice. With the cops patrolling—and who knows who watching from the barges—he thought it likely someone would notice a swimmer thirty or forty feet down in Tahoe's famously clear water. Even at over sixty feet beneath the surface, a white disc the size of a dinner plate is still visible. Glenn's idea was for Sean to approach the barges from the west. That way, with the setting sun behind him, the glare off the water will have a better chance of concealing him.

Sean has only been scuba diving once, on a trip to Aruba a few years back, so he can't argue much with Glenn on diving issues. In theory, coming in that way should be a good idea. In practice, though, the dark clouds currently blocking the sun might negate the whole concept. Their only hope is a gap between those clouds and the western mountains that is rapidly brightening as the sun continues to sink lower in the sky.

They had gone over all the basics when Sean slithered into the rental wetsuit back at the shop. Now, sitting on the side of the boat, he slips the tank onto his shoulders and cinches up the straps. The three boat buffer is meant to avoid detection by the cops when Sean enters the water. They figured driving right up to the police line and swan diving into the forbidden zone might draw some unwanted attention.

"Alright, dude," Glenn says as he checks Sean's work on the straps and tank. "Just do like I told you and you'll be fine."

"Until I get to the barges you mean."

"Well, yeah. You're on your own then, man. Hope you got a plan."

"Me too," Sean says, wondering when he might come up with one. "And thanks, man. I'll pay you back some day."

"Don't worry about it, dude. Just don't get yourself offed out there."

Sean looks to the west and Glenn's eyes follow. As the bottom of the sun slides out from behind the clouds, rays of sunlight stream down to the mountain tops in golden sheets.

"Told ya it would work, dude."

Sean smiles. "Yeah, you did."

Sean reaches out to shake Glenn's hand, but his old friend instead leans in and gives Sean a big hug. Before he can return the embrace Glenn pulls away.

"Alright then," Sean says. He pulls on his goggles and sticks the mouthpiece between his lips. With a thumbs up, he rolls backwards into the lake. The cold water is like a slap in the face and he can't suppress a mighty shiver that shakes him from head to toe. Once it passes, he spins around and flippers his way deeper into the lake, his neck, head, hip and fingers throbbing again from this new insult of cold and pressure.

The depth gauge on his wrist rises quickly to thirty and he stops, the ballast and buoyancy Glenn setup keeping him there. Shadows from the boats above block a large portion of the sunlight where he now floats, but out to the east it's broad daylight. Floating like driftwood in the icy water, Sean' resolve waivers. The sun reaches further down into the lake than seems possible and he can't imagine how he's going to get across that quarter mile of still, clear space without being seen.

This is crazy. What the hell was I thinking?

Derrick has to be armed. You don't go around hijacking a boat without guns. What does Sean think he's going to do? Swim up out of the lake like some Navy Seal and snap Derrick's neck with his bare hands? He'll be lucky if the cops don't nab him before that. He's gotten this far on adrenaline alone and now that it's being siphoned off by the cold—and the pressure of thirty feet of water—he can't think of a thing to do.

A boat moves out on the open water, running down the police line. Would the authorities have someone in the water? He doesn't see anyone around, but it occurs to him that the cops can't really do anything even if they see him swimming past the line down here. If they go any closer to the barges up on the surface they'll be breaking the quarter mile limit and risking the lives of the hostages—and Julie is one of those hostages.

A new determination takes over. He can't turn back now, he's come too far. He'll just have to wing it. Figure it out on the fly, so to speak.

Sean waits for the police boat to move off down the line before he swims out into the vast, empty light. He keeps an eye on his depth gauge, follows his compass and increases his pace as he goes. With every flick of his flippers his right hip sends a shot of pain up to his throbbing head.

Twenty One

Julie opens her eyes to the glare of the setting sun screaming off the surface of Lake Tahoe like a searchlight. The undersides of the low clouds are lit up like Joseph's Amazing Technicolor Dreamcoat. Reds, yellows, oranges and purples reflect off the water, turning the lake into a giant stained-glass window. Most days the gorgeous light show outside would have lifted her spirits. The only thing likely to do that at this point is a full-blown SWAT assault on these barges she's stuck on.

In a heap on the floor she lies, legs curled up beneath her and mostly asleep. When she lifts her head it throbs along with the beating of her heart, particularly prominent at the left temple. As the haze in her brain begins to clear, she realizes she's been out cold for quite some time and the reason for that sets her heart racing again.

She scans the room. Jason and Jean's bodies are gone. She guesses Derrick has hidden them somewhere.

Unless I imagined the whole thing.

Looking down at herself, though, she sees crimson stains on her shirt, smears on her legs. Nearby, in the growing shadows on the floor of the barge, is also what appears to be a drying pool of blood.

A noise from the other side of the cabin widens Julie's circle of attention. Derrick is hunkered down in the back corner working intently at something, his back to her. As she watches, he pours liquid from one bottle to another and sets the second aside. Even with the sliding doors to the outside deck wide open, the whole room reeks of gasoline. They are close to the engines and Julie can't recall if the smell was there before.

As quietly as she can, Julie struggles to a sitting position and leans back against a crate. Through the open doors she can see that the quarter mile gap to the police line still appears intact. Apparently the gunshots earlier were not enough to draw in the cavalry. She wonders if Derrick has had any more contact with the authorities and, if so, what kind of demands he might have made.

Not that it matters. She's stuck out here with him. Alone on what might as well be a desert island.

The reality of her predicament hits her with such immediacy that her breath catches in her throat and her stomach turns. She swallows to push rising bile back down her throat but panic pulls again at conscious thought, threatening to send her writhing to the deck uselessly pulling at her bonds.

Somehow she forces herself to inhale and draws a deep, hitching breath. She holds it for a moment and then releases it as evenly as she can. Oxygen is food for the brain, she tells herself. Breathing, the seat of relaxation.

After a minute of repetition Julie decides to try talking some sense into Derrick again. It seems a pretty weak plan, but what else can she do? With her ankles and wrists bound escape is unlikely and she can't fight back, but he still hasn't gagged her. Words are the only weapons available. Unless…

Julie looks around for her pack. It leans against the wall in the corner, ten feet in the opposite direction from Derrick. The gun is probably still in there, but she's not sure she can get to it without drawing his attention. Even if she can, how would she load it or manage to point it at him with her hands bound behind her back?

She closes her eyes and rests her aching head against the crate. *What's the point?* she wonders. She simply can't imagine herself shooting Derrick. Sure he's gone nuts, but does that give her the right to pop a cap in his ass? She has to do something, though. Sitting here waiting to die doesn't strike her as a viable option.

When Julie opens her eyes she looks Derrick's way without lifting her head. He's still dealing with his bottles. What the hell is he doing? A chemistry experiment? He's very focused on the task. Almost too focused. After a moment of searching for an explanation she realizes that if she's going to take any action, now is the time, while he's distracted. A breeze in the eaves of the cabin is even creating some cover for her movements.

She slips back down onto her back, hoping her Yoga practice has made her limber enough to pull off what she has in mind. Lowering her shoulders as she slides her hands down under her butt, she brings her knees up to her chest and stretches. The plastic zip-ties bite deep into the flesh on her wrists, feeling like they might take her hands right off. But her hands won't go past her hips. Her wrists are strung too tightly together to make it around. She strains, pushes and pulls but makes no headway. After a few moments of this she relaxes and lowers her legs back to the deck.

Flat on the floor, breathing oxygen into every corner of her body, she tenses than lets her muscles go. She visualizes her body as water—fluid and malleable—sinking through the barge and into the lake beneath. With eyes closed she tries moving her hands downward again and her shoulder blades follow—a shift that might normally cause pain—but the now-relaxed muscles let it flow easily. She raises her legs again and her wrists slide past her hips and up behind her knees. In another second her hands are in her lap as she returns to a sitting position.

If Derrick turns now her escape attempt will be over. She has to move fast. The wind gusts and she crawls with the sound over to her pack. Opening the zipper is another matter. She slides it down slowly—almost one tooth at a time—willing it to be quiet, but the thing insists on *tick-tick-ticking* all the way down. Looking behind her, she watches Derrick's back as she pulls. He remains intent on his task.

The gun lies in the bottom of the pack and Julie eases it out carefully, along with the ammo. A feeling of unreality washes over her like a bad scent. She can't believe she's doing this. She considers not loading the gun but the memory of Derrick shooting Jean and the ricochet that hit Jason—it had to be a ricochet—is too fresh in her mind, too graphic. Slowly, she lifts the lid from the box of bullets.

The gun is a revolver. That's as far as Julie's knowledge of firearms takes her in identifying it. The thing feels awkward in her hands, especially with bound wrists. After a moment of fiddling she manages to get the wheelie thing that holds the bullets to swing out. It makes a distinctive *clink* as the latch releases and, from the corner of her eye, she sees Derrick turn and begin to rise.

"What are you doing?" he says. "Get away from there."

Julie stuffs one bullet in the gun, but her fingers fumble trying to grab more and the box of ammo spills from her lap onto the deck.

She manages to catch hold of only one more as the rest scatter across the deck, rolling in every direction.

"Hey," Derrick says. "What the hell have you got there?" He starts toward her, pulling his gun from his belt.

Julie crams the other bullet into the revolver and snaps it closed. "Stop right there," she says, voice shaking right along with her hands as she points the gun at Derrick's advancing form.

He stops halfway to her, kicking rolling bullets out of the way as a grin creeps slowly across his lips. "Or what?" he laughs. "Little Miss Passivist'll shoot me?" He takes another step and brings his own gun up, aiming it directly at her head. "You couldn't hurt a fly, Jules."

The patronizing names enrage her as they spill from his mouth and steady her quivering hands. "Don't push me, Derrick," she says through clenched teeth.

Derrick tilts his head back and spouts a derisive, "Ha!" enjoying the situation immensely. When his attention returns he comes at her quickly, a wolf on its prey.

Until then Julie hadn't known if she had the balls to pull the trigger—to actually shoot another human being. As Derrick bears down on her, though, his sick grin twisting his handsome face into an evil-clown mask, her finger contracts. She hears the clap of the hammer falling. Not once, but—*snap-snap-snap*—three times in quick succession.

But Derrick's body doesn't jerk back and drop. The gun doesn't fire. The hammer only falls on empty chambers.

Then Derrick is upon her. Yanking the pistol from her grip, straddling her, pinning her to the deck. Her hands are caught beneath him as well.

"Well, well, well," he says as Julie again writhes under him, trying to get free. "You've got more fight in you than I thought. Amazing how personal mores go straight in the toilet when faced with your own mortality, eh?"

Derrick sets her gun atop the crate next to them and puts the barrel of his own to her right temple. He pulls something else from his belt and, as he raises it, Julie is blinded by the reflection of the setting sun off the shining surface of a long, sharp, hunting knife.

Her kicking ceases. The gun, the man—the world—disappear. Body limp, eyes wide, she stares transfixed at the glinting, cold steel of the blade. Serrated on one edge, honed outward to infinity on the other, it holds her attention like a hypnotist's watch and there is no question why.

The first bastard had used a knife, too.

Twenty Two

Sean looks up at the bottoms of the two connected barges from forty feet down in the lake. On approach he'd become paranoid and decided to risk going ten feet deeper. Now he floats face up while he searches for the buoyancy control on his belt.

He's cold. The water in Lake Tahoe never really warms up as a whole. Surface temperatures in some areas can reach the low seventies in the middle of summer, but down here, out away from the shore, he feels like he's encased in ice. Below a few hundred feet the temperature never strays from a constant thirty nine degrees. *So what does that make it at forty feet?*

Increasing the pressure in his BC, Sean begins to ascend slowly. Glenn had assured him that the gas mixture in the tank is sufficient for quick, low-depth dives, but Sean isn't taking any chances, he's heard that the bends are more painful than childbirth and has no idea how far down you have to go, or how quick you must come up, to get them. As he rises, he heads for the larger barge—the one that looks like it towed the other out—hoping that's where he'll find Julie.

As he wafts up toward the surface like a feather on a current of air, he wonders who else might be on the barge. He only knows for sure that Derrick, Jean and Julie are up there. He has no idea how many other hostages there might be—or if Derrick's posse consists of anyone other than Jean.

He floats up directly under the center of the hull and pushes along the bottom of the boat with his hands. At the rear of the front barge a ladder sticks a few feet into the water. He surfaces slowly, keeping the splashing to a minimum, and pulls himself up two rungs. As quietly as he can manage, he turns off the air feed from his tank and spits out the mouth piece. One by one, he removes the flippers from his bare feet and hooks them around his wrist. He expects more pain from his right hip, but the cold water seems to have numbed his aches and pains for the moment. The deck of the barge is six feet over his head as he starts to climb.

Like a lurking crocodile, he peeks over the edge of the deck. He has come up behind the main cabin and the wall in front of him runs the width of the craft, entirely blocking his view in that direction. Twenty feet back, and slightly to the right, the other barge floats, still tethered to the front with a couple of heavy cables. There is no cabin on that one and there doesn't appear to be anyone on it. The fireworks racks are spread out in rows like the dark squares on a checkerboard, leaving hardly any place to hide.

Sean pulls himself up with stealth in mind and sits on the deck with his feet hanging off the side. He releases his shoulder straps, sets his airtank aside and lays everything down carefully, then crawls the six feet to the wall of the cabin. There are no windows at the back, but not wanting to draw undue attention to himself, he remains on hands and knees as he makes his way left to the only visible doorway. When he risks a quick look around the corner he can see all the way through the cabin to the front of the boat, which is set up with fireworks racks much the same as the barge behind.

He leans back and considers his options. Rush the cabin or approach with a bit more stealth? There might be any number of people hiding in the shadows inside, but he has to get in there to see what's going on. Julie must be in there somewhere. Where else could they be keeping the hostages?

Sean decides to toe the middle ground—move quickly and pay attention. He rises to his feet and rounds the corner into the cabin, not wanting to meet his death on hands and knees like a beggar. His adrenaline kicks up a notch, heightening his awareness as he searches for anything remotely resembling a weapon.

* * *

Catatonia.
That's what they call it, right?
Her eyes refuse to blink as they trace the edge of the blade in Derrick's hand. The barrel of the gun digs into her temple but it's the razor-edged knife that holds her rapt. A deer in the headlights, she is

frozen to the floor like a shallow, winter puddle.

"What's wrong, Jules?" Derrick says, following her eyes to the shining blade. "You giving up? We've hardly even started."

He lowers the knife to her belly and slips it under her button-down shirt. The cold steel moves slowly toward her neck, slicing loose each button in turn. When the last one skitters away across the hard floor he flips the fabric back with the sharp tip.

She lies motionless. Mesmerized. The only thing covering her above the waist her white lace bra.

In her mind's eye she sees Him—her First. Just like the The Box, He's taken on capital letter significance in that locked up safe of horrors she sometimes calls a memory. He'd held His knife to her throat while He jammed his cock into her and she'd known then that the pain would have been less if He'd just slit her jugular. Death is a singular loss. Rape an ongoing, eternal hell.

She'd known Him, too. His first name, at least. She'd flirted with Him at the party—maybe teased Him a bit. But that didn't give Him the right to follow her out into the dark, throw her down in the bushes and stick it to her. To take what was left of her innocence with that quick, inelegant violation of her very core.

Movement from Derrick brings her attention back to the present moment as he slides his weight down onto her legs. The gun moves away from her temple, but remains pointed at her face. He slides the knife under the left leg of her shorts, slicing the fabric all the way up to, and through, the waistband. He rends the other side just as easily and yanks the ruined garment from under her, tossing it aside. Like road kill beneath a vulture she lies there, her bound hands resting across her bare stomach between her horseshoe shaped belly-ring and the waistband of her low-cut panties, but she still can't move.

Derrick reaches quickly behind him, the knife disappearing from her view momentarily, and slits the zip-tie holding her ankles. Then the blade comes up again and slips under her bra strap, in between the swell of her breasts. She closes her eyes just before Derrick jerks the blade upward, slicing the undergarment in two.

Elastic snaps and her breasts are suddenly exposed, nipples tightening as they meet the cooling evening air. It's enough to snap her out of her stupor, but it feels like waking from a deep sleep and she struggles to drag her consciousness out of the cellar in her brain where it's gone to hide. No matter how hard she's tried, she's never forgiven herself for not fighting back that fateful night so many years ago. Better to die than go through the rest of her life feeling the same way about this very moment unfolding before her.

Julie shakes her head to clear the fog and opens her eyes. Derrick has set the knife on the deck so he can unzip his fly. He still holds the gun pointed at her face with his other hand. His own pants undone, he reaches for the waistband of her panties. A thought swims into her head unbidden:

Live in the now.

It's something she teaches—time to own it. With a grunt and a growl she jolts upward, bashing her bound wrists into Derrick's arm. She jars the gun, but it doesn't fall and his other hand comes up to steady it. As the weapon swings back toward her head, Julie lets loose a banshee's shriek.

* * *

Sean works his way down the corridor until he comes to a doorway on the right. There's a commotion going on somewhere, but the acoustics in this place make it hard to pinpoint. Everything sounds muffled. Maybe it's just the hood still covering his ears. Next to a couple of new-looking scuba tanks in a corner, he finds a two foot piece of pipe. Not his ideal choice for a weapon, but better than nothing.

Sean holds the pipe over his head and steps through the doorway, ready to strike. He finds himself facing a row of crates stacked floor to ceiling. To the left is another opening. As he turns his head to the right what lays there stops his breath and he recoils against the wall, every muscle in his body tensed.

In a dark dead end two lifeless eyes stare up at him from a slackened face. It's a young man with what looks like a bullet hole in his forehead. He forces himself to look closer and sees too many limbs splayed out beneath for just one body. Blond hair protruding from under the man's legs causes his stomach to clench even further into a ball.

I'm too late.

Steadying himself, he draws a deep breath and holds it. Flashes of Julie, cold and nearly lifeless in the snow up at the Rock, roll through his head.

"Julie?" he whispers as he pushes the guy's leg aside. He cringes and barely contains a scream as the second head flops forward. He has to reach down and push the blond hair out of the way to see her face. As suddenly as before, he retreats again, back against the crates.

It's Jean. Someone killed Jean.

And some other guy Sean doesn't know.

What the hell is going on out here?

A grunt and a thud pull Sean's attention away from Jean's open, glazed eyes. He doesn't know how long he's been staring into them. He lifts the pipe to his shoulder and skitters away to the other end of the crates like a startled mouse. As he nears the corner the overpowering smell of gasoline hits his nostrils in a wave.

Before he can determine where the scent originates, a deafening scream fills the cabin.

* *

It's a warrior's battle cry.

An eagle's diving screech.

Not the frightened scream she'd released when surprised by the death-stare of the security guard. This comes from her gut, her heart—her soul. The kind of fearless lioness' roar mustered when there is absolutely nothing left to lose.

Julie bucks under Derrick like an epileptic in a full-blown seizure and lashes out with her bound hands at his face, chest and arms. The gun flies from his grip and he rolls backwards off of her, covering his head and face with his arms. As he begins to rise, Julie kicks, flailing her unbound feet wildly. She catches him in the leg, the side, the head and he flops back down to the deck where his hand falls on the hilt of the knife. Freshly armed, he advances on his knees, holding the blade down as if to stab her with it.

Through clenched teeth she growls, "Get away from me," and draws her legs up to her chest.

"Don't know when to quit, do you?" Derrick says. "Never seem to know when you've crossed the line."

He raises the knife over his head in both hands and Julie strikes.

Kicking straight out, she lands her feet squarely in the center of his chest and heaves with another Amazon's howl. Derrick careens rearward and thuds to the deck on his back.

Julie sits up and rolls around quickly onto to her knees. Her revolver sits atop the crate to her right—exactly where Derrick left it a minute or two before. She snatches it with her bound hands and points it at him as they both regain their feet. He holds the knife; she, the gun.

Then—like an apparition from the depths of the lake—a figure in a wetsuit appears behind Derrick holding a length of pipe in one hand. The shadow from the diving mask still perched on his forehead obscures his features. If Julie fires at Derrick now she's liable to hit the newcomer, too. She starts to speak but the apparition cuts her off.

"Julie, are you okay?"

Why does this guy know her name? Or, for that matter, why did he come to rescue her carrying nothing but a pipe.

Derrick turns his head toward the stranger. "Stop right there or she gets it," he says, waving the knife at Julie while still looking back.

"Derrick," the new guy says. "Drop the damn knife. She's got a gun on you."

He knows Derrick's name, too.

"She won't shoot," Derrick says without taking his eyes off the newcomer. "She's not gonna risk hitting her high school sweetheart, too. Right Jules?"

High school sweetheart?

Julie finally pieces it together.

"Sean!"

*

Sean drops to the floor behind Derrick. "Shoot the son of a bitch, Julie. He's the one I pulled off you that night at the Rock."

"Wha…?"

Julie looks dazed, standing there in her panties, her tattered shirt and bra hanging off of her.

"Pulled who off… What?"

Shit. Sean doesn't want to risk rushing them, but it looks like Julie is freezing up. He takes a crouching step toward Derrick, but the other man follows suit, stepping closer to Julie.

"You know," Derrick says. "I've wanted to kick your ass ever since that night."

"Ditto," Sean replies. Then to her, "Julie, shoot him. Wing him in the leg if you don't want to kill him."

"She won't do it. Too risky. We already have one dead from an unfortunate ricochet."

Sean notes the state of Julie's clothing again. "What the hell did you do to her, you bastard? I'll kill you with my bare hands if you—"

"Relax, Romeo," Derrick says, taking another step toward Julie. "Juliet here fought me off with the wrath of a demon."

Julie comes around with a shake of her head. "Get back," she says to Derrick.

"Go ahead, shoot. I dare you. You miss me and Romeo here gets it." Ten seconds tick by in the stalemate before he adds, "I told you she wouldn't."

Julie's right foot comes up so fast Sean barely gets out a spluttered, "Don't!" before it connects with Derrick's outstretched hand and jars the knife loose. The momentum of the kick spins her around as she plants that same foot on the floor and leaps into the air. Derrick turns his head back just in time to meet her rising left foot as it slams into his jaw. The ferocity of the blow rocks his head back and sideways and his body follows. He flops over a short crate and lands in a heap on the deck, unconscious. Julie completes the most graceful roundabout kick Sean has ever seen by landing solidly with both feet flat on the floor.

"Holy shit," Sean says. "You're like a ballet ninja."

Julie looks shell-shocked. Her bound hands still hold the gun out in front of her. She turns her head from Derrick's fallen body to Sean as if seeing him for the first time. The gun slips from her grasp and clatters to the floor. Shuddering, she follows it down.

Twenty Three

And then Sean is there. Wrapping his wet, neoprene-clad arms around her.

She loses control and starts blubbering. From Princess Warrior to sobbing heap of Damsel in Distress in under ten seconds. Has to be some kind of record.

Sean tries to get her on her feet and drag her away from where Derrick lies, but she latches onto him like a drowning woman. Face buried in his chest, she refuses to move. He manages to get her arms out from between them and slices the ties that bind her wrists—she doesn't care to know with what. Finally free, she wraps her arms around him with renewed vigor.

Eventually Sean manages to hoist her into his arms and carry her out of the cabin to the front of the boat. When he lowers her to the deck she finally releases him and leans back against the high wall of the ship's bow where she is out of sight and sheltered from the wind. He unfurls a blanket he's found somewhere and covers her. Once swaddled in the warm fabric, she realizes her skin is ice cold and the shivers begin.

She looks up at him. "You did it again," she says. "You saved me."

"I didn't do anything," he answers, crouching down. "It was all you. You were like Bruce Lee back there. Where'd you learn to do that?"

"I guess I didn't tell you. I've studied a little Tai Kwon Do."

He pulls the blanket tighter around her shaking form then leans in and surprises her with a kiss. "No, you didn't mention that," he says. He starts to move away, but she reaches out and pulls him back to her, never wanting to let him go.

*

For the first time in days Sean prays for the arrival of the authorities, but he doesn't hear or see any boats motoring their way. Julie's head rests on his shoulder as he watches the rear of the barge for any sign of Derrick. There is no motion from back there. After a minute he breaks the silence. "I got your letters," he says.

Her shivers are interrupted by a larger shudder before she says meekly, "And...?"

In the dying light, he looks out across a silver and orange shimmer on the open water. "It's not your fault."

*

What's not my fault?

Before she can vocalize the thought it hits her. The pages she'd added to her old letter. Heather hadn't known what she wrote, but now Julie remembers. She'd come clean. Told Sean what happened, about the rape. And he's still here. Has actually risked his life for her yet again.

She raises her head and he turns to meet her gaze. A different kind of shiver runs through her as she looks into his eyes and the haze of intervening years drops away. This man is not the boy she'd once known; he has turned into so much more. A surge of emotion in her chest threatens to spill out in giddy tears.

And he is lost in her eyes. The idealized memory of her stuck in the back of his mind has evaporated like lake water on a hot day. He is in love with the woman he now holds in his arms. In the end they are one in the same. It's been a backwards fight these last few days, but what appeared to be regression had only been an illusion. They have finally found each other in the present. Together at last.

"You are my first—and only—true love," he says.

She finds herself whispering the words along with him.

Twenty Four

Only a hint of red still tinges the clouds looming overhead like fiery, black sheep. The sun has dropped completely behind the western ridge. Sean leaves Julie at the bow and heads back toward the cabin to restrain Derrick. There is no one else left alive on the boat, she'd told him in a soft whisper. Derrick had managed to take out both Jean and Jason with only three shots.

As Sean approaches the rear of the barge a shadow with a lit torch in one hand emerges from the right cabin door. Obviously, it had been a mistake not to tie Derrick up earlier.

"What are you doing, man?" Sean calls out, trying for a conversational tone.

Derrick cackles. "It's the Fourth of July, Romeo. What would Independence Day be without fireworks?" His other hand rises, clenching a bottle with a rag trailing from its top. Recognition hits as Derrick touches one item to the other and the rag ignites.

"Derrick, don—"

But the Molotov Cocktail is already airborne, sailing through the air straight at him. Sean dives left, behind a rack of fireworks, as the bottle smashes to the deck ten feet away sending up a hissing orange wall of flame.

He pulls himself up and peers over the rack as Derrick heaves another flaming bottle onto the trailing barge. He lights a third and chucks it in that direction as well. A conflagration erupts across the deck thirty feet back as fireworks shells start exploding with pops and whistles, shooting sparks up and out over the water.

"What's wrong with you?" Sean yells. "You're gonna get us all killed."

Concussions, squeals and crackles echo out across the water as more and more fireworks streak up into the darkening sky and out toward the surrounding boats at shallow angles. Most of the shells explode at low elevations, sending multicolored sparks showering down on them.

Derrick lights another bottle and throws it toward the front of the main barge. It flies to Sean's right and he follows it with his eyes. As it reaches the apex of its path Julie screams.

*

She still sits against the wall in the prow of the barge when the first explosion rings out.

He wouldn't, is the first thought through her head as she rises with the blanket draped around her shoulders.

The barges are ablaze and fireworks blast off in every direction. She is at the center of a giant, flaming sparkler. Even from a quarter-mile away Julie can hear people on the surrounding boats screaming. Not the *Ooooo*s and *Ahhh*s normally associated with fireworks. These are genuine cries of terror as the shells shoot straight toward them and explode a story or two off the water.

At the back of the boat, Derrick lights something on fire and heaves it in the air. Julie watches the flaming bottle arc through the encroaching night and understands what the task was that had kept him so focused earlier. *That explains that smell.*

A moment too late she notices the Molotov Cocktail is headed right for her. She screams and turns to run as it smashes to the deck eight feet away and belches flames at her like a sick dragon. The heat and light roar up from behind, climbing over her back and flickering down her arms.

I'm on fire!

She stumbles toward the edge of the barge, realizing belatedly that it's mostly the blanket burning. It had taken the brunt of the splash from the Molotov Cocktail and she sheds it faster than a virgin's wedding dress. She takes a few steps beyond its burning bulk then just stands there, absentmindedly brushing at some flames on her sleeve when someone rudely tackles her from behind.

*

Sean bolts across the deck as the fire from the smashed bottle engulfs Julie and she erupts in flames like a Tiki Torch. He isn't sure whether he screams or just mouths the word: "No!"

She steps away from him, toward the edge of the barge, a mobile bonfire. Before he reaches her she drops the flaming blanket to the deck. Sean hurdles it and takes her down, rolling her body beneath him and patting out her flaming hair with his bare hands.

"What? What?" she keeps saying. "Ow."

Sean puts out the last flame on Julie's smoldering shirt as a shell explodes twenty feet away. Flaming bits of casing rain down on them as he covers her body with his again.

"Sean, get off," Julie says.

He rolls to the deck. "You were on fire."

"I had it under control."

In his head he can still see the slow motion replay of the flames roaring up in her hair. "No," he says, "you didn't." She stares blankly back at him for a moment and he adds, "I think you might be in shock."

"I'm fine." She barely flinches as another huge explosion rocks the barge.

Sean looks at her singed hair, the burns on her arms. Her lower legs looked blackened. She is far from fine, but they have to get off this boat.

"Come on," he says. He rises and pulls her up with him.

Derrick has stopped tossing Molotov Cocktails around for now, but the damage is done. Flames surround them on three sides as the cabin goes up in a smoke-spewing conflagration. Whistling, crackling and pounding fill the night. The thirty minute fireworks display will be over in five and the man responsible is nowhere in sight. Maybe the authorities finally shot him.

Sean finds another length of pipe leaning against the bow wall. He snags it and heads rearward along the edge of the barge with Julie trailing behind. He wants to get his scuba gear back, then they'll get the hell off this burning deathtrap. Sean ducks as a sailing shell nearly takes them out and Julie bumps into him.

"Where are we going?" she asks, her voice far, far away.

"We're getting off this barge."

"Oh."

He leads her along like a mule. As they round the side of the boat a figure materializes out of the wall of flame and approaches from the opposite direction.

"Back off, Derrick. We're getting the hell out of here," Sean yells over the cacophony.

Derrick stops fifteen feet away and raises a gun. "You can't leave before the finale," he yells back.

Sean shades his face with his pipe holding arm and squints into the flaming mess of exploding shells and rockets. "This *is* the finale, man. It's over."

Derrick grins, white teeth gleaming in a soot-blackened face. "It ain't over 'til it's over," he says and motions with his hand for Sean to come to him. "Let's go. You and me. Mano a mano."

A breeze and another close explosion blow flames toward their side of the boat. Sean crouches, pulling Julie down with him this time. A wave of heat and fire scorches the air above as the pipe falls from his grasp and rolls away. Derrick disappears behind the inferno. "We're all gonna die unless we get off this wreck," Sean yells and considers making a run for the side of the boat and the ten foot drop to the water sans scuba gear.

But the blaze blows back the other way and Derrick reappears, gun still pointed at them. "Everybody dies sometime," he says and advances. "It's the way of the world. The circle of life." What unnerves Sean most is that Derrick doesn't sound particularly crazy at the moment. He seems to be in complete control of his faculties.

Behind Sean, Julie says softly, "That's my gun."

Sean realizes retrieving his gear was a pipedream. He turns his head to Julie and whispers, "Get ready to jump," then rises to face Derrick. "You wanna go man to man then put down the damn gun."

Derrick stops ten feet away and laughs. "Certainly. You want me to give it to *Trinity* over there?"

"Just drop it… and drop the damn nicknames, too."

Derrick looks at the gun one last time then gingerly tosses it overboard. A second later Sean charges.

*

Julie sits in a heap on the deck next to Sean, playing with the singed, frayed tails of her shirt. She's hot.

Derrick has her gun. The one with the two bullets. She tells Sean. Sean says something about being ready to jump. A swim sounds like a good idea in this heat. She doesn't understand why they don't go now. The fire is getting kind of close.

Sean stands up. He yells something at Derrick and Derrick throws her gun in the lake. Julie reaches up for Sean's hand. She wants him to sit back down so she can tell him it isn't really her gun. That she would never own a gun. It's important that he knows that.

But Sean takes off. He tackles Derrick and they roll into more billowing flames. Julie tries to rise, but her knees hurt—and her feet. She looks down at them. Why are they so black?

Another explosion rocks the barge, knocking her onto her side. She rolls over once and her head lolls off the edge of the deck. The dark water below beckons her. If she were to lift her feet she could do a somersault—*flip!*—right down into the cool, refreshing lake.

Someone yells. It's Sean. She can't make out the words over the roar of the fire. Then Derrick runs toward her, ducking under flames and a spinning, squealing rocket. Sean is close on his heels.

Derrick has been acting like a complete jerk. She lifts a leg to trip him as he passes by, but he stops, bends down and grabs her, pulling her up into a choke hold. Julie gasps, tries to scream, but the knife is there again. The long, steel blade flashes in front of her eyes before he settles it painfully on her neck.

*

Sean stoops to sprint past an exploding sidewinder as he leaves Julie's side. He hits Derrick in the chest with his shoulder, taking him to the deck and punching him in the side of the head a few times before they separate and come to their knees. Derrick lands a left that makes Sean think the little, rich boy has had some boxing training.

They rise to their feet in unison and dance around for a few seconds, two fighters feeling each other out in the first round of the title fight. Derrick jabs. Sean dodges and makes solid contact with a hard right to the temple. But Derrick recovers too quick and catches Sean in the chin with an uppercut that clacks his teeth together and puts stars in his eyes. He sways and then collapses down on one knee.

Another explosion rocks the boat and knocks Derrick off balance. Sean seizes the opportunity and pushes up with his legs, driving his fist into the other man's jaw with all his strength. Derrick tumbles backwards to the deck and Sean lands three good kicks in his side before he scrambles out of reach, gains his feet and sprints toward Julie.

"You're gonna run just like the first time?" Sean yells after him. "You wuss."

Derrick stops where Julie lies, crouches down and yanks her up into his arms. Then, from behind his back, produces the six-inch-long hunting knife Julie had kicked from his hand earlier. Sean gets within ten feet before Derrick tells him to stop. Julie's eyes are stuck wide, unblinking. Derrick traces her jaw with the tip of the blade then settles it on her neck.

Pure, unadulterated hate boils up inside Sean like hot lava as his jaw and fists clamp down tight. "It's over, Derrick," he growls through set teeth. "Put down the knife."

Derrick's eyes skip frantically, side to side. This is his last ditch effort. He's one move from checkmate still trying to snatch his opponent's queen. "It's not over 'til it's over," he says again, with less conviction this time.

Another explosion—too close for comfort—sends a plume of fire rushing toward them. As the flames wash over, Sean bows down and Derrick shies away from the heat, pushing Julie beneath him as the knife falls away from her throat. Just before the bulk of the inferno hits, off to his right at the base of a flaming fireworks rack, Sean spies his lost weapon.

The conflagration blinds him as he dashes forward, orange flames and searing heat pressing in from all sides. He drags a hand along the deck in the direction he saw the pipe. His fingertips find it and he manages to snag the weapon as he passes. Rising to his full height, he lifts it over his head and prepares to strike, blind. If he misses—if Derrick isn't where he thinks—

Too late.

He brings the two-foot length of steel down in a sweeping arc and the flames recede just as the other end lands in the crook of Derrick's neck with a sound like an aluminum bat swatting a softball.

Derrick's grip on Julie relaxes and the knife flutters overboard like a wounded butterfly.

Sean can't tell if he's knocked Derrick out. His forward momentum is carrying him off the side of the boat and there is nothing he can do to stop it. He grabs for Julie's arm as he stumbles along the last foot of deck.

Still-ringing pipe in one hand, Julie's wrist in the other, Sean tumbles from the barge.

*

The detonation is ear-splitting. The ensuing holocaust rushes across the deck at them like a roiling, orange and black avalanche. The fuel tanks exploding?

Julie can't move. Derrick pushes her to the deck as she watches the cloud of flames engulf Sean. *Noooo*, the voice in her head screams—heard by no one but her. Then Derrick rolls on top of her and she closes her eyes.

The heat hits like an open blast furnace. There's a thud and a clank and Derrick goes limp toppling off of her. She opens her eyes and sees the knife clatter overboard. Then a hand encircles her wrist as a flash of black and silver disappears over the edge of the deck. A moment later, her arm is yanked nearly from its socket for the second time in less than a week.

The force of Sean's weight drags her bare skin across the sandpaper surface of the deck and throws her into the air. Feet flipping up and over her head—cartwheeling, like she'd imagined before—she tumbles through the night air. She lands on top of Sean as they break the water's surface.

The instant cold slaps her from her daze like a bucket of smelling salts to the face. She struggles to the surface, gasps for air, but her lungs refuse it and she gulps and wheezes like an asthmatic as Sean surfaces beside her. He pushes her onto her back, holding a hand beneath her as he treads water.

Had she inhaled superheated air? Burnt her lungs up in one deadly gasp?

Am I dying?

After a few tense moments, her body begins to recover from the shock of the instant temperature change and she sucks in oxygen like an overpowered Shopvac as her lungs remember how to breathe. Sean has shifted her into a lifeguard's grip and is swimming away from the burning barges in a sidestroke with her on her back before she feels she can finally swim on her own.

They stop a moment then and she catches his eyes in the flickering light of the hissing flames. His face is a white oval of determination framed by the diving hood. She wants to hug him, but that would take more energy to recover from in this cold water than she suspects either of them have at this point. She pecks a quick kiss on his cheek instead.

"Thanks for coming home, Sean Connors," she says.

He looks at her a moment longer before closing his eyes and nodding assent.

*

They backstroke away from the Largest Fireworks Display West of the Mississippi watching the remnants spit into the night sky like crippled emergency flares. All has not been lost on the Fourth; the public has definitely been treated to a major extravaganza.

The cold water takes the edge off Julie's burns and cools Sean's hot, partially melted wetsuit. Having his hood up through the whole ordeal had kept his hair from catching fire. Julie hadn't been quite as fortunate, but hair grows back. The rest of her? They'll just have to wait and see.

Like that cold March night so long ago, Julie is shivering uncontrollably when the Coast Guard locates them nearly thirty minutes later. Even in summer, Lake Tahoe's cold water can induce hypothermia in as little as twenty minutes.

In the cabin of the rescue boat, bundled in blankets, Julie and Sean cling together like opposite strips of Velcro. Clearly visible from over a mile away, fifty foot flames still roar up from the fireworks barges. Two floating funeral pyres in the night, spitting sparks to the heavens like lost souls.

Epilogue

Sean walks into the hospital room and a wave of nausea washes over him. For some reason, even though he's been here every day for over a week, it hits him harder this morning. Maybe it's because of what he carries in his pocket.

Julie lies sleeping, tubes and wires running from the bed to various pieces of equipment. The steady scrolling and beeping of the heart rate monitor are the only reassuring sights or sounds other than her relaxed, sleeping face. Sean takes his regular position in the chair next to the bed and leans back. He'll wait for her to wake on her own.

She's scheduled to be released today, July 12th. She'd needed morphine to ease the pain from the second degree burns on her feet and lower legs the first few days, but it had subsided quite a bit since then and the doctors felt she could rest just as well at home now. The burns on her neck and arms were only first degree. The good news was that her leg burns weren't deep enough to require skin grafts. Her doctor said the skin should heal on its own with only minimal scarring.

It was the lake that saved her. The time they'd spent floating in the cold water had sucked a huge amount of residual heat from Julie's skin. Without that natural cooling effect, it could have been much, much worse.

Sean's burns are minimal. Mostly on his hands, but nothing that a little ointment won't cure. The wetsuit had protected him from a lot of the heat, but peeling it off that night had been a bit like getting a hot wax. There are parts of him now shiny smooth that haven't been free of body hair since he hit puberty. The bruise on his chin from Derrick's uppercut is already starting to fade, but it turns out he managed to crack his pelvis with that bear-caused, granite bodyslam.

So far he's avoided explaining to Julie exactly why he's walking with a cane, but one of these days he'll have to come clean.

The authorities still haven't found Derrick's body on the barge or in the water. But that's not uncommon in Lake Tahoe, bodies have a tendency to sink to the bottom and never resurface. The decay that normally brings a body to the surface just doesn't happen in thirty-nine degree water.

The night of the Fourth, Sean had been placed under arrest as he and Julie were transported to the hospital. By the time the next afternoon rolled around, though, he was a free man. Based on Sean and Julie's statements—as well as Derrick's actions—the authorities had managed to piece together a story that implicated no one but Derrick and Jean for the bombing of the South Tahoe Beach Resort. Since then, they'd even found a fingerprint of Derrick's inside a pipe confiscated from Sean's hotel room, which corroborated Julie's story that Derrick had planted the explosives there. While it appeared the cops still wanted to nail Sean and Julie for participation in the bombing, they simply had no proof.

Sean had wanted to celebrate getting off the Most Wanted list, but that was hard to do with Julie lying in a hospital bed whacked out on morphine. Plus, it still looked like Eagle Development would win their fight to develop the Lake's Edge Apartments into timeshares, so she still had losing her home to look forward to. And, if that wasn't bad enough, the South Tahoe Beach Resort sabotage seemed to have merely stoked a fire under the developer to move forward at an accelerated pace.

They'd also found out a little more about Derrick and Jean from a resourceful Tahoe Mountain News reporter's digging. Turned out Derrick had been taking anti-psychotics and mood stabilizers for years to treat Borderline Personality Disorder. They suspected he'd run out of the drugs when he went on the run. Julie even mentioned that she might have seen him shaking a pill bottle that day on the beach. Jean had also been on medication and saw the same psychiatrist as Derrick, so that could have been how they met.

Jake had stopped by for a visit after retrieving the motorcycle from the Safeway parking lot. Apparently the bear that had chased Sean had been turning up more and more around The Estate. It looked like the tree cutting had pushed her into human territory where she would most likely get herself into trouble for dumpster diving and need to be relocated. Jake was doing everything he could to see that didn't happen. He'd even taken it upon himself to clean up the devastated area up on the ridge. Sean had offered to lend a hand once his hip healed.

The first time Sean had seen Julie's mom again she hugged him so tightly she nearly broke another bone. The two of them had run into each other as she was leaving the hospital and Sean was arriving on the Fifth of July. Anne, as she would now like Sean to call her, seemed ecstatic that Sean was back in town. They'd spent a lot of time throughout the week sitting around together in the hospital room or the café, catching up and waiting for news.

Pulling himself back to the present, Sean stretches his neck from side to side and smiles as he looks over at Julie's sleeping face. Relaxed and peaceful, there is still a hint of a grin on her lips. The imp in her peeking out, even in sleep. Pressure wells up in his chest, making it difficult to draw a breath. Is this what it means to love someone so much it hurts? Unable to resist, he reaches out and takes her hand in his. A moment later she stirs and looks at him.

"Good morning," he says and kisses the back of her hand. "How are you doing today?"

Julie takes a deep breath before speaking. "Good," she says, groggy, closing her eyes again. "Tired."

"Yeah, but you get to get out of here today."

"Uh-huh." She stretches her arms over her head and opens her eyes again. "Com'ere and kiss me, you."

Sean has to rise in order to do as he's told. When Julie releases him he remains standing next to the bed. "I rented a place," he says. He clears his throat and looks away out the window before adding, "It's big enough for two… if you want."

Julie bats her eyelashes at him. "Are you asking me to live with you, Sean Connors?"

"Well…?"

She doesn't really need to think about it, she's just teasing him. "When do we move in?" she says.

He leans down and kisses her again.

Coming off the morphine, Julie is finally beginning to feel a bit more like herself. Her memory of the first few days after the Fourth has been lost in a narcotic blur. She remembers only bits and pieces of things. What stands out in her mind the most from the past week is Sean's smiling face. Whatever their differences might be, the two of them are tied together somehow and—whether it's fate, destiny or just hormones—she's finally concluded it's useless to resist.

Memories of what happened on the barge have become jumbled together in her head as well. Someday she'll need Sean to help her sort out how it all went down. Or maybe not. She knows she fought Derrick off—remembers taking him out with that roundhouse kick that she somehow landed perfectly—and maybe that's enough. The rest is just fluff around the two most important facts: she and Sean had survived and she had stopped the same thing from happening to her all over again. In the end, fighting back was the better option than laying back and taking it.

"Guess what else?" Sean says, taking a step back.

"What?"

"I sold my QTC stock."

Julie's jaw drops. "You did? But you said—"

"I know what I said, but it's just money, right?"

"Yeah," she says. "Wow."

Sean had expected her to be happier. Instead she just seems shocked. He'd been thinking about buying some land with the cash—maybe up in the Northern Sierra. He knows she thinks the idea of "owning land" is a farce, but he thinks she might approve of some ideas he has about putting it to use.

He keeps all that to himself for now and hopes he can get her a little more excited about his next surprise. His heartbeat accelerates as he reaches behind his chair and pulls out the bouquet he has stashed there. Her eyes light up at the flowers and Sean slips his other hand into his pocket as he drops down on one knee.

"Julie Thompson," he says, needing another lungful of oxygen before he can continue. "I am so in love with you. You are my friend and my lover and I can only hope you'll agree to be my wife. Will you marry me?"

Sean pulls the ring from his pocket and Julie sits up in bed, a giant smile stretching across her face even as her eyes fill with tears. She opens her mouth to speak as a figure appears in the doorway.

"Oh," Julie's mom says. "Oh, my!"

They both turn and look at her.

"I'll come back," she adds.

"No. Come in, Anne," Sean says, turning back to Julie. "I just asked your daughter a question… and I'm still waiting for an answer."

Her mother's smile has grown almost too big for her face. Julie's eyes flit back and forth between her mother and Sean before finally settling on him.

"Yes," Julie says. "Yes, of course I'll marry you, Sean Connors."

The smile finally catches on Sean's face as he rises, pulls the ring from the box and slides it onto Julie's outstretched finger. "I will always love you," he says. "No matter what."

"Me too," says Julie as the ring sparkles on her hand like an evening star. "No matt—"

Sean cuts her words off with a kiss.

Thank You

I sincerely hope you enjoyed reading this book as much as I enjoyed writing it. If you did, I would greatly appreciate a short review on Amazon or your favorite book website. Reviews are crucial for any author, and even just a line or two can make a huge difference.

Book II of Sean and Julie's adventures in the Anarchy Rising series is in the works. Stay tuned!

About The Author

Paul Healy was born in Illinois, grew up in New Jersey and came of age in Colorado. He spent the prime of his life at Lake Tahoe, began his downhill slide in Florida and is now aging regretfully back in the People's Republic of Boulder. He enjoys mountain biking, skiing, writing and dark-to-middling craft beer. He holds a Bachelor of Arts in English (Creative Writing) from Rutgers University with a minor in Psychology. When he isn't spending time with his family, writing or working his day job he is usually sleeping.

E-mail
paul@inkandanarchy.com

Websites
www.inkandanarchy.com

www.paul-healy.com

Suggested Reading

If you are interested in further reading on any of the ideas Julie and Sean discussed in this story, here are a few books to lead the way:

A Language Older Than Words, The Culture of Make Believe, Endgame (Volumes 1 & 2), The Myth of Human Supremacy (and just about anything else) by Derrick Jensen.

Ishmael, The Story of B and *My Ishmael* by Daniel Quinn.

In the Absence of the Sacred by Jerry Mander.

Desert Solitaire and *The Monkey Wrench Gang* by Edward Abby.

The Natural Alien: Humankind and Environment by Neil Everndon.

Pacifism as Pathology by Ward Churchill (with Mike Ryan).

A People's History of the United States by Howard Zinn.

www.ingramcontent.com/pod-product-compliance
Lightning Source LLC
Chambersburg PA
CBHW031437240626
47154CB00001B/305